DAUGHTERS
OF
SPARTA

DAUGHTERS
OF
SPARTA

A NOVEL

CLAIRE HEYWOOD

DUTTON

DUTTON

An imprint of Penguin Random House LLC
penguinrandomhouse.com

LIBRARY OF CONGRESS CATALOGING-IN-PUBLICATION DATA

Names: Heywood, Claire, author.
Title: Daughters of Sparta: a novel / Claire Heywood.
Description: [New York]: Dutton, [2021]
Identifiers: LCCN 2020047756 (print) | LCCN 2020047757 (ebook) |
ISBN 9780593184370 (trade paperback) | ISBN 9780593184363 (ebook)
Subjects: LCSH: Trojan War—Fiction. | Helen, of Troy, Queen of Sparta—Fiction. |
Clytemnestra, Queen of Mycenae—Fiction. | Mythology, Greek—Fiction.
Classification: LCC PR6108.E99 D38 2021 (print) | LCC PR6108.E99 (ebook) |
DDC 823/.92—dc23
LC record available at https://lccn.loc.gov/2020047756
LC ebook record available at https://lccn.loc.gov/2020047757

Printed in the United States of America
3rd Printing

For there is nothing in this world so cruel and so shameless as a woman when she has
  fallen into such guilt as hers was . . .
. . . her abominable crime has brought disgrace on herself and all women who shall
  come after—even on the good ones.

—Homer, *The Odyssey*

She, the ruin of both Troy and her own fatherland . . .

—Virgil, *The Aeneid*

AUTHOR'S NOTE

The Trojan War has been a perennial subject of Western art and literature for the last three millennia. The story was extraordinarily popular among the Greeks themselves, from Homer through the works of the great tragedians, through pottery and visual culture, and later through to their cultural successors in the Roman Empire. The ancient world largely treated the Trojan War as a historical event that had really taken place, with some even attempting to trace their lineage from its great heroes and thereby claim their share of hereditary glory.

Modern scholarship has taken a more skeptical approach to the war, or at least to the version of it presented in ancient literary and artistic sources. However, there is some archaeological evidence that suggests that a war such as the one described by Homer may have in fact taken place. Ancient Hittite documents refer to a conflict between the kingdom of Ahhiyawa (Achaea, an ancient name for Greece) and the city of Wilusa (Ilios, later known as Troy). Archaeologists also claim to have found the actual site of Troy at Hisarlik in northern Turkey, as well as evidence of its destruction by fire sometime around 1180 BC.

To correspond with this archaeological timeline, *Daughters of Sparta* opens at the end of the thirteenth century BC and is therefore set within the Mycenaean civilization of the Late Bronze Age, so called because of the dominance of Mycenaean culture in Greece at this time. However, my aim in writing this novel was not to argue for the historical reality of the Trojan War. Nor was it an attempt to tell a story that is historically true, but rather to tell one that could be described as historically authentic—that is, a reimagining of the Trojan War myth that was consistent with the material evidence we have for this period of prehistory, as well as being a reworking of and response to the canon of ancient literature that was built upon the myth. *Daughters of Sparta* therefore weaves archaeological reality with mythological tradition, but also imagines a new story to fill the gaps left by each of these frameworks. At its heart the novel is not even a retelling of the war itself, but of the private lives of Helen and Klytemnestra, two characters whom I found to be either inadequately or unfairly treated across the ancient sources. What were these women thinking? What did they feel? What made them act the way they did? If they really had lived, as royal women in Bronze Age Greece, what might their lives have been like? These are the questions I found myself asking, and which I hope I have answered in *Daughters of Sparta*.

If you would like to learn more about this period of Greek civilization, *The Cambridge Companion to the Aegean Bronze Age* (2008) is a good place to start. I would also recommend Bettany Hughes's wonderful book *Helen of Troy* (2013), which was a great source of information and inspiration during my research. And for anyone interested in reading more generally about the experience of women in the ancient world, Sarah B. Pomeroy's *Goddesses, Whores, Wives, and Slaves: Women in Classical Antiquity* (1994) provides an accessible overview and has become something of a go-to guide.

NOTE ON THE NAMES

In the spirit of historical authenticity, I decided to use Greek spellings for both people and places, as opposed to the later Latin spellings with which we may be more familiar. For example, I spell Klytemnestra with a *K*, rather than the more common Clytemnestra, to render it closer to its spelling in the Greek alphabet. I made deliberate exceptions to this rule in a few cases, such as the use of Mycenae rather than the Greek-style Mykene, when the Latin spelling is far more entrenched both academically and in terms of public familiarity. The most extreme case is that of Troy, which would be more authentically referred to as Wilusa or at least Ilios/Ilion, but in which case "historical authenticity" would quite clearly create problems of recognizability.

DAUGHTERS
OF
SPARTA

PROLOGUE

She sat frozen, hands bloody. When she closed her eyes, she could still see it. She squeezed her eyelids tighter, sent her shaking breath into the silence. And still she could see it. White turned red. Eyes dead.

She dipped her trembling hands into the water, tendrils of blood spreading instantly through that once-pure bowl. Now her forearms, now up to her elbows, until the bowl was dark and refilled and dark again. Even once her arms were white, once the dark water had been taken away and the shaking had stopped, in her mind's eye the red remained.

How had it come to this? How did any evil come to be? Was it the work of the gods? A punishment for some other evil? Or did they sit above, impassive, watching as one stone hit another, and another? Blank faces blinking in the dust of the landslide.

PART I

CHAPTER 1

KLYTEMNESTRA

Klytemnestra! Have a care, girl! Your spindle's gone all a-wobble!"
Klytemnestra's eyes snapped into focus at the sound of her
name. In front of her the spindle bobbed, her carefully spun
wool unraveling quickly. She stopped it with her hand.

"Not like you, Nestra," tutted Thekla, turning back to her work.
The crease in her nurse's brow lingered, but at least she had returned
to calling her Nestra. Klytemnestra had never really liked her full
name—it was too big, too cumbersome—but she liked it even less on
a sharp tongue. It was her sister, Helen, who had taken to calling her
Nestra when she was too young to manage the whole thing, and it had
stuck ever since.

Helen was sitting beside her now. They had been working wool
together all afternoon, and Klytemnestra's arm was beginning to ache
from holding up the distaff. Her sister was singing a song to herself as
she watched her spindle twirl on its thread, and though Helen had a
sweet voice, she only knew half the words and kept repeating the same
verse. Klytemnestra wished she would stop.

The women's room was dim, the walls plain, the air thick and still.
As one of the innermost rooms of the palace, it had no windows
through which daylight might spill, nor any fresh breeze to break the

stagnation. It was summer, and the warm air was made warmer still by the many women who filled the room, lamps and torches illuminating their dark heads and their white, working hands.

Klytemnestra's woolen dress clung to the sweat of her back as she looked over her shoulder toward the brightest corner of the room. There stood the looms, three large wooden frames with half-finished cloth stretched across them. Only two were being worked at present, by the most skilled of the household slaves. Admiring and envious, Klytemnestra watched as they led the shuttles back and forth, building their clever patterns thread by thread. It was like watching a mesmerizing dance, or the playing of a complex instrument.

"You know," came Thekla's voice, "we could start you on loom work soon."

"Really?" asked Klytemnestra, pulling her eyes from the dancing hands.

"You're eleven now. In a few years you'll be married, and what kind of wife will you be if you don't know how to weave?"

"I would like that very much," she replied with a grateful nod. Working the loom certainly looked more interesting than spinning.

Helen stopped her singing. "Can I do weaving too?"

Klytemnestra rolled her eyes. Helen always wanted to do what she was doing, even though she was two years younger. She hadn't shown the slightest interest in the loom before now.

"I think you're still a little young, Mistress Helen. You'll get your chance soon enough, though."

Helen made her face into an exaggerated pout and turned emphatically back to her spinning. Klytemnestra knew she would soon forget she was supposed to be sulking, though, and sure enough her face smoothed as her attention became absorbed once more by the motion of her spindle.

The three of them continued working for a little while until Thekla said, "I think that's enough work for one day. Why don't you girls go and find some food?"

Klytemnestra stopped her spinning. "Can't we go and play outside for a little while before supper? It's not dark yet. I can't stand being indoors all day."

"Ooh yes, can we?" piped Helen.

Thekla hesitated. "I suppose so," she sighed. "But you must take a slave with you. So that you're not alone."

"But we'll be with each other!" Klytemnestra protested. "It's no fun when there's someone watching." She gave Thekla a pleading look but the nurse's face was unwavering. "Fine," she said with an indignant huff. "We'll take Agatha." The girl was between her and Helen in age, and a better playmate than any of the sour-faced escorts Thekla might have chosen for them.

The nurse looked unconvinced, but she nodded her assent.

"Agatha! We're going to play outside, come with us," Klytemnestra called across the room before Thekla could change her mind. The slave girl shuffled over to them, head bowed, while Klytemnestra took Helen's hand and headed for the door. The three of them were already halfway down the corridor when Thekla called after them.

"Keep close to the palace! And don't stay out too long or you'll be brown as goatherds! And who will marry you then?"

The three girls left the palace and walked down the hill to the meadow, Klytemnestra leading the way. The grass was high, the dry seeds brushing off on her dress as she strode through it. The sparse trees rustled above their heads and she was glad of the fresh breeze on her arms after so long in the women's room. Once they were far enough away from the palace not to be overlooked, she stopped.

"What shall we play?" she asked the other two.

"I'll be a princess," said Helen, without hesitation. "And Agatha can be my handmaid."

Agatha nodded shyly.

"But you *are* a princess," said Klytemnestra, exasperated. "Don't you want to pretend to be something different? Like a sorceress or a pirate or a monster?"

"Nope. I'm always the princess."

"All right, fine. Then I'll be the king," sighed Klytemnestra. She had learned that it was easier to just let Helen have her way. Otherwise she would start crying.

Helen snorted. "You can't be a king, Nestra. You're a girl!" Helen looked over at Agatha, encouraging her to join in with the joke. Agatha let out a quiet giggle, but clamped her lips shut when Klytemnestra shot her a scornful look. Agatha looked at her feet.

"Fine, then. You can be the princess, Helen. Agatha, you be the handmaid. And I'll be the nurse." She thought for a second. "But I'm a nurse who can make magic potions," she added.

"What are you playing?"

The voice came from behind them. A boy's voice. Klytemnestra spun around to see who had spoken.

The boy was sauntering toward them through the long grass, now only a few paces away. He was a little older than they were—tall, but without his first beard. He had long, dark hair and a smile that made Klytemnestra suddenly shy. She had seen him arrive at the palace with his father a few days ago. Some sort of diplomatic visit, she supposed, or maybe just passing through. People came and went all the time, on their way through the mountains or coming up from the coast. Her father's hearth was always lit, but it was rare to have a guest so young. Usually, the only noble-born boys around were her twin brothers, Kastor and Pollux, but they were too old to play games with her and Helen. And Thekla said it was unseemly for princesses to play with slave boys. Surely they could play with this boy, though? He was a guest.

"He-hello," said Klytemnestra, her tongue suddenly clumsy in her mouth. "We were just about to play a princess game." She cringed at how childish it sounded, and hurriedly added, "It's just silly, really, but Helen wanted to play. We can do something else if you want to join in."

There was that smile again. "No, a princess game is fine."

Klytemnestra was worried he was laughing at them, but at least he wanted to play. "What's your name?" she asked.

"Theseus. My father and I are visiting from Athens."

"Theseus," she repeated. "All right, well, Helen was going to be the princess, and Agatha—she's just our slave—she was going to be her handmaid. And I'm a nurse who can make potions. What do you want to be?"

"I'll be a foreign king. A great warrior."

Klytemnestra smiled, pleased that he seemed to be entering into the spirit. "Well, how about you get shipwrecked on our shore and then I find you and heal you with a potion and . . ."

But Theseus didn't seem to be listening. He had turned away from her and was looking at Helen instead.

"You do indeed look like a princess, my lady," he said, with an exaggerated bow. "You've got the brightest hair I've ever seen." He raised a hand, as if he might touch it. "It's like fire. And your skin's so white—like a real lady. I bet you'll be as beautiful as Hera herself when you're fully bloomed."

Helen giggled, but Klytemnestra was annoyed. People were always commenting on Helen's hair. She didn't see what was so special about it. And her own skin was just as fair as Helen's. Besides, she was nearer "full bloom." Helen's chest was as flat as a boy's.

She tried to bring his attention back to the game. "Anyway, I was thinking you could be shipwrecked—"

Theseus cut in. "How about I've just arrived from a battle, and I've got a wound that needs herbs to heal it. You have to go and fetch the herbs."

"All right." Klytemnestra smiled, glad he had given her an important role. "I'll go and do that."

She walked a little way from the others, toward the river, imagining herself venturing into the mountains on her quest for rare herbs. She could hear Helen ordering Agatha about as she stooped to pick a plant with small white flowers. She went on a little farther until the rush of the river's flow replaced Helen's commands and giggles. She stooped to wash her hands in the clear water, but the wool grease clung to her skin, stubborn as ever. There weren't many interesting plants by the river, but she picked a few wildflowers and grasses nonetheless. She wondered if she'd have to pretend to put a poultice on Theseus's wound. The thought made her nervous, but excited too. She'd never touched a boy before—other than her brothers, and they didn't count.

When she was satisfied she had found enough magic herbs, Klytemnestra gathered the stems in one hand and headed back into the heart of the meadow. But as she drew closer to the place where she had left the others, something felt odd. And then she realized: she could no longer hear Helen's voice. She lengthened her strides.

As she drew nearer she found she could not see Helen either. Nor Theseus. Nor Agatha. She scanned the meadow, squinting in the light of the lowering sun.

She broke into a run. Panic was rising in her throat now. Stupid, stupid! She should never have left Helen. If anything had happened to her it would be her fault. They were supposed to look after each other. What if a wolf had come? Or a boar? They didn't usually dare to come so close to the palace, but it wasn't unheard of. Or what if they had been captured? Taken by slavers or some foreign wanderer seizing the opportunity. Theseus wasn't old enough to fight off full-grown men.

She thought she must be at the place where she had left them now. Still no sign. She kept running. Suddenly her foot caught on something and she tumbled into the grass.

"Ow!" came a small voice.

Klytemnestra sat up and saw what she had tripped on.

"Agatha? What are you doing lying in the grass? Where's Helen?"

The slave girl was holding her stomach where Klytemnestra had kicked her. Wincing, she said, "She's playing with Theseus. He said he was kidnapping her, and he stabbed me—in the game, I mean—and he said I was dead now and I had to lie down and be quiet. I heard them run off, but I don't know where they went. I was being dead."

Klytemnestra's stomach clenched. "You stupid! You can't let Helen be on her own with a *boy!*" She jumped up. "We're going to be in so much trouble," she moaned, almost to herself.

Agatha's eyes had grown wide and fearful. Tears started to shine in them. "I'm sorry, mistress, I'm sorry," she said, her voice cracking. "I was scared of him."

"Sorry's no use," spat Klytemnestra. "We need to find them." She cupped her hands around her mouth. "Helen!" She took another lungful of air. "HELENNN!"

She scanned the meadow, turning until she had come full circle. There was no sign of them, or where they might have gone. She started to run—better to look somewhere than nowhere—but stopped after just a few steps.

"It's no use us running after them. Then we'll be lost too and no one will know what's happened. We need to tell my father."

Tears were running freely down Agatha's cheeks now. "But we'll get in trouble," she whimpered.

"It's too late for that. Come on!" Klytemnestra grabbed her wrist and ran toward the palace, dragging Agatha behind her.

Klytemnestra had been locked in her chamber for what felt like hours, though she could tell from the light that the sun had not yet set, so it couldn't have been very long at all. She wished someone would tell her what was happening. Had Helen been found? Was she all right? She didn't even have Agatha with her to share her anxiety. Her guilt. Father had kept the slave girl with him when he shut her in here. He had been so angry when they'd told him. No, not angry. Afraid, perhaps. She'd never seen her father afraid before. He had sent Kastor and Pollux out on horses, and half the palace guard on foot too, to look for Helen and the boy.

Time passed. Klytemnestra fiddled with her hair, pulling it, tying it in knots. She sat hunched on the edge of her bed, thinking about all the things that might have happened. Even if Helen and Theseus were safe, Helen was still alone with a boy. Klytemnestra knew what boys did to girls. What men did to women. Thekla had explained it all to her when she had asked why the sheep climb on top of one another. And if that happened to Helen . . . well, she'd never get a good marriage. Klytemnestra felt sick. She had let her sister down. She was usually so responsible. Helen was young and sometimes foolish, but Klytemnestra had always been there to keep her safe. She'd been so stupid today, though. Why had she been so desperate for Theseus to like her? He was just a stupid boy. Helen meant more to her than any boy. More than anyone at all.

She started to cry. Silent, angry tears. Angry at Theseus. Angry at stupid, beautiful Helen. Angry at herself.

Then she heard the door bar being lifted. She quickly wiped the tears from her face and stood up. She hoped with all her heart that Helen was about to walk into the room.

But when the door opened it was Agatha who stumbled through, pushed from behind. She let out a pitiful yelp and then the door was closed behind her. Her face was streaked with tears, her eyes red and puffy. She staggered forward a few steps, then stopped, as if she couldn't go farther. She stood frozen, steadying herself against the wall with an outstretched hand.

"Agatha?" Klytemnestra asked warily. She could tell something was wrong. The slave girl had been crying when they told her father about what happened. Irritating, fearful tears that she had no time for. But the fear that had filled her eyes then had been replaced by something more unsettling now. A hollowness. Klytemnestra took a step toward her. And another. It wasn't until she was level with her that she saw it. Illuminated by the flickering lamplight, Agatha's narrow back was striped with gashes. Streaks of nauseating red burst through her shredded white dress, her shredded white skin. She had been beaten, then. This was what she had been so afraid of.

"Oh, Agatha," gasped Klytemnestra. She moved to embrace her but stopped as she saw the girl flinch. "I'm so sorry. I should have told him it was my fault too—"

"He knows it was your fault," Agatha said dully. "That's why he sent me in here. So you'd see."

Klytemnestra looked at her, confused.

"He couldn't beat you," Agatha murmured. "You'd get scars."

All at once, understanding rushed upon Klytemnestra, and she hung her head. Her father was punishing her through Agatha. Her stomach turned at the thought of it. He probably beat her harder just to make his point. She needed to *see* the pain. He wasn't a cruel man, her father, but he could be cold when he needed to be. And his children's safety was very important to him.

She wanted to hold Agatha, to bathe her wounds, but she was afraid of hurting her further.

"Do you know anything about Helen?" she asked quietly.

Agatha shook her head, eyes lowered.

More time passed. Occasionally Agatha would whimper, but apart from that the chamber was silent. The two of them sat on Klytemnestra's bed, waiting. Agatha's blood was dripping onto the bedcovers, sullying them, but Klytemnestra didn't care. She took Agatha's trembling hand in hers.

There was a noise from the corridor. Klytemnestra's eyes darted to the door. *Please let it be good news. Please let her be safe.*

When the door opened, it was her father who stood in its light.

"We found her," he said, but he wasn't smiling. His brow was creased, his face tired. His eyes flicked to Agatha and away again. He looked sad. He stepped to the side, and there was Helen, looking bright-eyed as ever, if a little sheepish. She trotted into the room and their father withdrew, closing the door behind him.

As soon as the door shut, Klytemnestra jumped up and hugged her sister.

"What happened? Where did you go? Are you all right?" She looked Helen up and down, searching for signs of injury.

"I'm fine. Theseus and I were just playing. I don't know why everyone got so scared." She flicked her hair back from off her shoulders. "He kidnapped me and we found a cave downriver and we hid there."

"But . . . did he touch you, Helen?" Klytemnestra asked.

"Touch me? That's what Father wanted to know too. He shook me hard when he asked me. It hurt." She rubbed her upper arm, frowning.

"But did he, Helen? Did he touch you?"

Helen rolled her eyes. "Yes, he touched me. He held my hand when we ran away from Agatha. And then when we were in the cave he stroked my hair, and . . . and he kissed me," she said, with a shy smile. She blushed, but there was something else in her expression too. Klytemnestra thought it looked like pride.

"He kissed you?! And . . . and that was it? Nothing else happened?"

Helen looked more worried now, seeing the concern on her sister's face. "Well, he asked me to sing for him, and I danced too, and then Pollux found us." She started to get upset. "That was all. He was nice. He kept saying how pretty I was. And now Father has sent him away. I bet it'll be ages before there's another boy to play with."

"Truly, Helen? That was all that happened?" Klytemnestra pressed.

Helen nodded.

"Then all is well." She sighed with relief, and allowed herself to smile. "Nothing bad has come of it after all." But as she said it, she remembered Agatha sitting behind her. She wasn't sure Helen had even noticed she was there.

CHAPTER 2

HELEN

It had been a boring day. In fact, it had been a boring month. Ever since Theseus and his father had gone back to Athens, every day had been the same. The same as it always was. Spinning and spinning the wool until it felt as if her eyes were spinning in her head. And today had been even worse because she hadn't had Nestra to keep her company. Her sister was finally being taught to use the loom and so Helen had been stuck with Thekla all day. The nurse kept telling her stories, but she'd heard them all before. They were baby stories. Didn't Thekla realize she was grown up now? She wanted to hear grown-up stories. Real stories. About danger and betrayal and revenge and love. Love most of all. Nestra told her such stories sometimes, but she just made them up in her head.

The afternoon was coming to an end—at least, Helen thought it must be. She'd been in the women's room for hours. Surely the sun would be going down soon.

"Can I stop?" she asked Thekla.

The nurse's brow wrinkled as she considered the modest bundles of spun wool piled in Helen's basket. "Yes, I suppose that's enough for today."

Helen looked over to the corner where her sister sat at a loom. A slave stood over her, giving instruction. Helen opened her mouth.

"Your sister's busy," said Thekla. "Don't go bothering her." The old nurse looked over toward the guard who stood on the other side of the main doorway. Helen's father had taken to posting one there. "You can ask the guard whether he'll watch you outside. You could take Agatha if you wanted."

Helen screwed her face up. Agatha was no fun anymore. She was even quieter now than she had been before and she was always so scared of getting into trouble.

"I don't want to play with Agatha," Helen said, but only quietly. The slave girl was just on the other side of the room, and she didn't want her to hear.

"Well, why don't you go and sit with your parents? They may still be in the Hearth Hall at this hour. I'm sure they'd want to see you."

Helen hesitated. She liked sitting on her father's knee. He would hug her and make her laugh and tell her about all the things going on in the palace. But if her mother was there . . . Helen always felt uncomfortable around her mother. It wasn't that she was cruel to her. She never was. And sometimes she could be very loving. But other times she would be cool and distant. She would pretend she hadn't seen Helen when they passed in the palace, even though Helen had caught her eyes as they flicked away. Sometimes she would leave a room when Helen entered, saying she was tired or that she didn't feel well. A couple of months ago, Helen had found her mother in her usual seat by the hearth, with Nestra sitting beside her. They were spinning wool together, talking and laughing. Helen had wanted so much to join them, but when her mother spotted her she quickly put down her wool and made her excuses. It was like a punch in the stomach. Why couldn't her mother sit with her as she sat with Nestra? It was as if there was something in Helen that repelled her.

Deciding to take the chance over another hour of Thekla's stories, she put down her distaff and headed for the door where the guard stood. Perhaps her father would be in the Hearth Hall after all. As she continued past the guard and down the corridor, he followed automatically. It had been annoying at first, not being allowed to wander the palace alone as she used to, but she had grown used to having a shadow over her shoulder.

She was soon outside the hall, which lay at the very heart of the palace, just off the central courtyard. She stopped under the porch before entering and peered through the partly open door. At the far end of the room her father's throne stood empty. Her heart sank a little. There beside it sat her mother, on her ornately carved chair, the hearth fire burning brightly before her at the center of the room. The only other figure present was one of her mother's handmaids. The two women were sitting in silence, spinning.

Helen didn't want to look stupid in front of the guard by turning around and going back the way she had come. And besides, her mother might be in a good mood today. You could never tell. So she took a deep breath and stepped through the door.

Her mother looked up as Helen walked around the circular hearth toward her. And she *smiled*. Helen let out a sigh of relief and smiled back, quickening her pace.

"Helen, come and sit by the fire with me," her mother said as Helen was drawing near to her. Such a simple request, but it made her heart lift. This was all she wanted. Her mother was so beautiful, so graceful. Helen just wanted to spend time with her, to please her, to be like her.

There were several stools at the edge of the hall. Helen fetched a low one and pulled it up beside her mother. She left a couple of feet between them, though, not wanting to push her luck.

Helen let out another little sigh as her shoulders relaxed and her lips spread into a contented smile. The Hearth Hall was her favorite room in the palace. The fire at its center meant that it was always light and warm, even at night, and in the daytime the sun's rays would spill through the square hole in the ceiling, illuminating the bright frescoes that ran around the walls. Scenes of the hunt, of men feasting, of women in sumptuous skirts, all brought to life in a whirl of blue and yellow and red. Helen liked the animals the best, the lion and the boar and the graceful deer, the way they leaped and twisted, wild and beautiful.

Her mother continued with her spinning, lips silent. She eased the rich purple wool from distaff to spindle, coaxing it down through her long, pale fingers. Helen recalled the touch of those fingers on her skin. The soothing coolness of them, the roughness from years of working the wool. A woman's hands were never still. Even a queen must spin and weave and stitch. But it was the queen who spun the finest wool, who wove the most important cloth. The king's cloth.

"What are you going to make with that?" Helen asked, looking over at her mother shyly.

"A cloak for your father. A king needs a fine cloak when he rides to war."

War? Fear spiked in Helen's chest.

Her mother must have seen it on her face because she said, "Don't worry, child. Your father just needs to help one of his friends. He won't be away for long. And the gods will keep him safe." She gave Helen a reassuring smile, but looked as though she didn't believe her own words.

"When is he going?" Helen asked.

"As soon as he has gathered his men. And as soon as I have finished his cloak," she added with another small smile.

"Then you must stop!" Helen cried in earnest. "Stop spinning. Don't weave his cloak for him, then he can't leave!"

Her mother chuckled quietly. "That is not how it works, Helen. He will still go, cloak or no cloak. But we want him to be warm on his journey, don't we? And for him to look splendid, so everyone will say, 'There goes a great king.'"

Helen nodded, but she was scared. She might be young, but she knew how wars worked. Men went and they didn't come back.

"Now look, Helen, your hair's all a mess," her mother tutted. "Whoever arranged it for you this morning didn't do it tight enough. It's all coming loose on top." She motioned to the handmaid behind her, who jumped to her feet. "We can't have you running about like that. How about you let Melissa redo it for you?"

Helen knew she was trying to change the subject, but nodded obediently. She didn't recognize the handmaid; she must be new at the palace. She was young and plain-looking, with a round face and a kind smile. Helen straightened her back and soon felt the handmaid's fingers working to undo her hair.

"Hello, Mistress Helen," came a chirpy voice from over her shoulder. "So nice to meet you at last. My name's Melissa. You just let me know if I pull too tight."

Helen thought her manner a little overfamiliar for a slave, but she quite liked it. So many of them never spoke at all. They were like ghosts.

Her mother was still spinning her wool to Helen's left. She could just about see the purple-covered spindle as it hovered at the edge of her vision. She kept her head fixed straight ahead, though, so the handmaid could do her work. Despite her fear for her father, Helen was happy. She could feel her mother's presence beside her as they sat in comfortable silence.

Melissa had finished undoing her hair now and began to run a fine-toothed comb through it. The comb made her head tingle as it brushed her scalp.

"Ooh, don't you have such lovely hair, Mistress Helen," she sighed. "I think your mother must have been visited by Zeus himself to birth a child with such fire in her."

There was a sudden movement to Helen's left, then a thwack and a sharp yelp behind her. Helen spun around. Melissa was reeling on the floor, holding her head, fear and confusion in her wide eyes. Helen looked up to see her mother standing over the slave, shaking as she massaged her hand. Her expression was strange. Somewhere between rage and pain.

"Get out." Her mother's voice was low and hoarse. "Both of you. Get out."

Helen was terrified. She'd never seen her mother like this before. She was on her feet and running from the hall before the slave even had time to get up. She never saw Melissa again.

That night, Helen lay awake in bed. She had replayed what had happened in the Hearth Hall over and over in her head, trying to make sense of it. All she could think was that it must have had something to do with her hair. That was what had upset her mother. When Melissa said how lovely her hair was.

Maybe Mother was jealous, thought Helen. It made sense. Queen Leda was famous for her beauty, but her hair was nothing special. It was dark as pitch, like Father's, like her brothers', like Nestra's. Like most of the palace. But Helen's hair . . . it *shone*. Like fire. Like gold. Everybody always said so. It was special, a gift from the gods. Like Melissa had said, just before . . . Yes. It made sense. Her mother was jealous. Maybe Helen could try covering her hair. Maybe then her mother would love her like she loved Nestra and the twins. But why should she have to hide herself? The thought of it made her suddenly angry. Why should she have to barter for her mother's love, when her siblings got it for free? She couldn't help it if she was the most beautiful.

Something else was playing on Helen's mind, too. Her father was going to war. The thought made her stomach feel like it was filled with lead. She wondered whether Nestra knew. *I should tell her,* she thought.

Her sister should know. Besides, she didn't want to think about it alone.

"Nestra?" she called quietly into the darkness. Her sister's bed was only a few feet away. "Nestra, are you awake?"

"Yes," her sister whispered back.

"I found out something today. Something bad." Helen paused. "Father's going to war."

"I know," said Nestra.

"You do?" asked Helen, sitting up.

"They've been making preparations for weeks, haven't you noticed?"

Helen was a little irritated. For once she thought she had known more than her sister.

"Mother's making Father a purple cloak," she offered, though she knew it was hardly prime intelligence. She just wanted to show she knew something Nestra didn't.

"Hmm," was all her sister said in reply. "I asked Thekla and she confirmed it. But she said he shouldn't be away for more than a few months."

"Aren't you worried for him?" Helen asked.

"Of course I am. But he's strong, and clever. He's been to war before. A good king always helps his friends." Her voice sounded like it was wavering slightly, though. She carried on. "Thekla . . . Thekla said that if the war goes well, if the men prove themselves, then he might start looking for suitors. I've already started my bleeding, but she says Father won't want me married straight away. He needs to find the right man, to make sure Sparta is strong."

Helen was silent for a minute. Too many things were changing. Father going to war. Nestra getting married. Everyone was going to leave her. She wished her mother were leaving instead of Father . . . No, that was a horrible thing to think. She loved her mother. And Nestra wouldn't really be leaving. She'd still be here. She was the heiress of

Sparta, so her husband would have to come and live here with her until they became the new king and queen. It was she, Helen, who would have to leave. That was what she really feared, she realized. Once Nestra was married, her own wedding would soon follow. And then she really would be alone.

"Who do you think you'll marry?" Helen asked at last, lying back down.

"Well . . . whoever gives the greatest gifts, I suppose. Or the best warrior. Father will decide who is the man most worthy to rule."

"Yes, but who do you *want* to marry?" pressed Helen. "What do you think your husband will be like? You must have thought about it."

It was a few seconds before Klytemnestra answered. "Someone kind, I hope. And wise. And a good father."

"I hope my husband is handsome," said Helen, imagining what he might look like. Would his eyes be dark, or green like hers? "Tall, and good at running and riding and wrestling. And nice, of course. He has to be nice to me."

"Gods willing, we will both get good husbands. And lots of strong, healthy children," said her sister.

"Yes," Helen agreed. She did *want* to get married. She wanted to become a woman. She wanted to run her own household and be consort to a powerful man. But she didn't want to leave her home.

"I'm scared, Nestra," she said quietly. "I don't want to go and live somewhere else."

"You might not have to," came her sister's voice from the darkness. "Father may get you a husband who'll come and live here with us. Then we can be one big family, and raise our children here together. Wouldn't that be wonderful?"

Helen didn't respond. It was true, her father might do that. But she knew he would have to do whatever was best for Sparta. And so would she.

In the absence of a reply from Helen, her sister continued, "Don't worry about the future, Helen. You never know what will happen. We'll be all right, though. Father will make sure of it. Everything will be fine."

That's easy for you to say, thought Helen as she fell into an uneasy sleep. *You're the heiress.*

CHAPTER 3

KLYTEMNESTRA

THREE YEARS LATER

Father was coming home. He'd sent his herald ahead to announce the army's arrival into Lakonia, and he was due in Sparta this very afternoon. Klytemnestra was feeling like she could finally start to relax. Her father was safe, and uninjured. The campaign had been a success, so the herald said, just like the one before it, and the one before that. And yet every time her father left Klytemnestra's stomach knotted itself like a ball, becoming tighter and tighter as the weeks passed. Every time he left she knew that he might not return. It was a thought she couldn't push from her mind. What would she do without him? What would Sparta do? Her mother had been making sacrifices to the gods all summer, asking for the king's safe return. It seemed the gods had listened, finally.

A huge feast was being prepared in the palace, to welcome the warriors home. The smell of roasting meat had reached the Hearth Hall, where Klytemnestra sat with her mother and sister, waiting. Kastor and Pollux were there too, playing dice at a table in the corner. Father had decided they were too young to join him on campaign, being only eighteen, and had left them to defend the palace instead.

Though Klytemnestra had been worried for her father as the length of the war grew, she had also felt guiltily grateful. The longer he was at war, the longer her marriage would be delayed. It wasn't that she was afraid to marry, but she knew that everything would change once she did. She and Helen would no longer be able to spend all their days together, and her freedom to wander outdoors would be even more restricted than it was now. Her mother barely ever left the palace. And there were other things that came with marriage, too . . . things she was not sure she was ready for. When the time came, though, she would do everything required of her. She was determined to be the best wife there ever was, to win praise for her loyalty, her prudence, her chastity, her obedience, and, gods willing, her many strong children.

There were times she felt frustrated to have been born a girl. She wanted freedom. She wanted authority. She wanted to do something other than work wool all day. To ride and hunt and travel and debate, as she saw her brothers do. To compete and win prizes, to compose songs and not just dance to them, to speak and really be heard. But each time she felt those frustrations rising, she pushed them down. She had to make her peace with that which could not be changed. So she bit her lip, worked hard at her weaving, nodded obediently, and smiled prettily. If the gods had willed that she be a woman, she would be the very best woman she could be.

And that time was fast approaching. She was of marriageable age now and, being the heiress of Sparta, she would not have escaped the notice of Greece's bachelors. She was a valuable prize and there would be many nobles wanting to win her. Soon she would fulfill the purpose she had been preparing for since she was old enough to hold the spindle, the purpose her father and her mother and Thekla had been preparing her for: to secure her house and her father's line, to secure Sparta's future. It was a heavy prospect and yet, despite herself, the thought of it brought a flutter of excitement to her chest.

There was a noise from the far end of the hall. A moving of feet on stone, the deep creaking of the great wooden doors. Klytemnestra gripped her spindle tightly as her father's herald appeared between them. He took a deep breath and addressed the hall.

"Lord Tyndareos, King of Sparta, has arrived."

The feast had been going on for a couple of hours, during which the Hearth Hall had echoed with laughter, song, and tales of valor. The noblest of the warriors were feasting there, along with the king and his family, while the rest of the men and the palace household were getting their fill outside in the courtyard. It was a warm summer evening, and the afterglow of the setting sun still hung in the sky. The meat was finished now, but the wine still flowed. Klytemnestra had even been allowed a cup and sipped it carefully, breathing in the sweet, herbal fragrance. Her sister was sitting beside her, giggling as one of the palace dogs licked meat-fat from her fingers.

Klytemnestra scanned the room, her thoughts still occupied with one subject above all others. *Could one of these men be my future husband?* They were all proven warriors, and wealthy. Perhaps Father would choose a suitor from within Lakonia, one who had impressed him on campaign. She studied each of the faces illuminated by the hearth fire, some lined and weary, some bright and expressive, and wondered whether she was looking upon the face of her future.

Her thoughts were disturbed by a hand on her shoulder. She jumped slightly, and looked up to see her father standing beside her.

"Klytemnestra." He said her name with unusual gravity. "I must speak with you."

Her heart began to race. *This is it*, she thought. She tried not to let her agitation show, rising calmly from her chair and smoothing her skirts before following him from the hall.

He led her out through the revelry of the courtyard and into the quiet of the corridor that led to her own chamber. And there he stopped. There was no one to be seen; everyone was at the feast.

"That should be far enough," her father said. "I just thought we should have a little privacy. I won't keep you from the feast for long." His face looked strange, almost nervous. It wasn't an expression she was used to seeing there.

"What is it, Father?" she asked, as if she had no idea.

"You are betrothed, my daughter."

He has chosen, then. She took a breath, a little disappointed that he had not asked her opinion of the suitors. But perhaps it had been too much to hope for. Her father was wise and prudent; she had to trust that he had chosen the best man.

"To whom?" she asked, trying to keep her voice level. She felt as though he must be able to see her heart thumping through her dress.

"To Agamemnon, King of Mycenae, as he has just become." His voice sounded tight, and he seemed to be avoiding her gaze.

"A king?" she said, confused. "Why would a king want to marry me? He already has a kingdom. Why give up one for another?" There was a bad feeling growing in the pit of her stomach.

"I'm sorry, Nestra," he said very quietly. He was still refusing to look at her.

"Father?" she said, her voice cracking slightly. She was becoming afraid.

"I'm sorry, my child. It was necessary." He looked tired, and sad. He raised his hand to his face, shielding it from her view. "You will marry King Agamemnon and go to Mycenae to be his queen. It has been arranged. As soon as his kingdom is in order he will come for you. I . . . I hope you will be happy."

"But Father . . . I am the heiress. I'm supposed to stay here. To be Queen of Sparta." She tried to take his hand in hers, but he pulled it away. "Why? Why have you done this?" Tears were welling in her eyes.

She could barely talk for the sobs in her throat. "Am I not good enough? I have always . . . I have tried to show you that I am worthy. Please, Father, please. Don't send me away." She sank to her knees and took the hem of his mantle in her fists, sobbing against the pillar of his leg. "Please, Father."

He stood stiffly, but placed a light hand on the top of her head.

"It has been decided," he said. "Your sister . . ." he began, but stopped.

"Helen?" Klytemnestra looked up, suddenly angry. "You've chosen Helen over me? Is that why you're sending me away?" He said nothing. "She's a fool. Just a beautiful fool. And you're a fool if you think she'll be a better queen."

"Enough," snapped her father, and with that she knew she had gone too far. He took his hand off her head and wrenched his mantle from her fingers. "I have told you your duty. Now honor your father and obey."

She looked up at him, speechless, and his eyes finally met hers. They were set hard, and yet she saw an apology in them too. If he was sorry, then why do it? Why punish her when she had only ever strived to be the daughter he wanted her to be—the daughter Sparta needed her to be?

"We all must do things we would rather not." He sighed, his eyes softening a little. "Now, you may calm down and come back to the feast or go to bed. Whatever pleases you."

And with that he walked away from her, back toward the noise of the courtyard. She was left kneeling on the hard floor, her chest heaving with angry sobs. Once she had regained enough control to stand, she made her way to the chamber she and Helen shared.

She lay on her bed, fully clothed, the smoke of the Hearth Hall still in her nose, her father's words ringing in her head. Everything had changed. Her whole life, the life she had imagined for herself, was gone. She would not raise her children in these halls. She would not care for her parents as they grew old. She would have to leave behind everyone she had ever known. And the landscape too, the hills, the river, the trees—the boundary markers of her world. The more she thought about it, the angrier she became. It was a bitter realization to learn that despite all her efforts, despite all the times she had held her tongue, all the limits she had accepted, all the desires she had quashed, she could not even hold on to the future she had submitted to. Not even that was hers.

Tears were running into her ears. She wiped them away with the sleeve of her dress and turned over onto her side. There across the chamber stood Helen's empty bed. She imagined her sister still sat in the Hearth Hall, as carefree as she always was, laughing in her pretty little voice. In that moment she hated Helen for getting to keep the things she would lose. And yet she knew that it wasn't fair to hate her. One of them was always going to have to leave. She had just never imagined it would be her.

Klytemnestra lay there for some time, her sobs coming and going. They ebbed as she calmed herself, telling herself there was no use in tears, but then they would come anew when she thought of leaving her home, of the people she would never see again, of being alone in a foreign land with a husband whose nature she did not know.

Eventually, she was able to master herself. Tears would not help her, but that did not mean there was nothing to be done. She would not give up her birthright so easily. She would go and entreat her mother. She was sure she would disapprove of Father's decision. Her mother had raised Klytemnestra to be queen since she was a small child and had talked about how they would one day raise her own children together, here in the palace. Her mother would support her. She would talk to Father, make him see sense. This was not the end. Betrothals could be undone.

Mother is probably in her chamber right now, she thought. She never stayed late at feasts, often retiring to bed as soon as etiquette allowed. Klytemnestra knew she must go to her now, while she was alone. The sooner the better. Agamemnon might come to collect her at any time.

She got out of bed and left her chamber. She could still hear sounds of revelry from the heart of the palace, but the corridor was quiet. Her parents' chamber was not far from her own. She walked down the corridor a little way before turning into another one. Halfway down it she could see a slither of light on the floor of the otherwise gloomy passage, leaking from beneath the door of her parents' chamber. She was right; her mother was there. Klytemnestra's heart fluttered with hope, and she headed toward the light.

As she drew near, however, she heard voices. Raised voices. One was her mother's, and sounded angry. The other voice belonged to her father.

Klytemnestra stopped. If her parents were arguing this was not the right time to speak to them about her marriage. And if they caught her out here, they'd think she was eavesdropping. She silently turned around and started back the way she had come.

But then she heard her name. They were talking about *her.* She stopped again. She knew she should go back to her chamber, but if their argument concerned her, she had a right to know, didn't she? And if they were arguing about her betrothal . . . The temptation was too strong. She crept back toward the light.

She was at the door now. It was fully closed, but in the darkness she noticed a gap in the solid wood, a small hole where a knot had fallen out, bright with the firelight that spilled through from beyond. She put her eye to it. There her mother sat, on the edge of their marriage bed, her cheeks pink with anger. Father sat beside her, looking weary and concerned at the same time, his hand resting lightly on her mother's thigh. She was looking away from him. It seemed there had been a pause in their disagreement.

"It has to be this way, Leda," said her father, his voice quiet and cautious.

"But it makes no sense," her mother replied, shaking her head. "Why make Helen your heir? She has no real claim, you know she doesn't. And in any case, Klytemnestra is older. It is her birthright." She clasped his hands. "And she has shown more promise. She is clever and temperate and obedient. What has she done to make you spurn her?"

Klytemnestra smiled at her mother's words, warmth spreading through her aching chest. It was just as she had hoped.

"She has done nothing." Her father sighed deeply. "I learned things while I was away. There are . . . rumors, concerning Helen. Such things spread quickly—and widely, it seems."

Her mother's face froze and the flush left her cheeks. "What rumors?"

Klytemnestra pressed closer to the door.

"The boy Theseus, the one who was here a few years ago, the one . . ." Her mother nodded impatiently and he continued. "He has been saying things. Things that are not true. He's been boasting about it to anyone who'll listen, apparently."

Theseus? The name was like a knife of guilt in Klytemnestra's chest. *This is all because of that?* She should never have let Helen out of her sight.

Her mother, on the other hand, seemed to relax. "Well, if that's all—"

"It's not, Leda." Her father took her mother's hands in his. He was looking into her eyes and she . . . she looked scared, as if she knew what was coming. Her bottom lip twitched. "People know, Leda," he said gently. "Or at least they've guessed. They're calling her Helen the Bastard."

Klytemnestra had to clamp a hand over her mouth to stifle her gasp. Of all the things you could call a person . . . She felt suddenly protective. Who were these people who could speak such lies about her sister?

Her mother drew a rattling breath and closed her eyes, tears spilling down her cheeks. Father was squeezing her hands tight. He looked like he might cry too. But as Klytemnestra watched their faces, mirrored in grief, she realized that they were not outraged. Their expressions were almost accepting, as if they had been waiting for this day to come.

"I'm sorry, my love," he said. "I'm sorry we have to talk about this. I would have spared you it if I could." He raised a hand to her mother's face and delicately wiped a tear from it. "But do you see now? Helen will never get a good marriage. Perhaps she won't marry at all. Not when people are doubting her virginity and her parentage both. Not unless we make her a more attractive prospect. If we make her heir to Sparta, they won't care about rumors. They'll fight to marry her."

"But it shouldn't come at a cost to Nestra," her mother croaked. "She doesn't deserve this. She deserves to be happy. My poor daughter—"

"And what about Helen? She's your daughter too."

"What about her?" her mother snapped. Klytemnestra was shocked to see her face twist with contempt. "I wish she'd never . . . I tried . . . I tried to . . . I took herbs." Her mother's eyes were full of pain as she turned her face away from her husband and gazed, unseeing, at the door. "Klytemnestra is my true daughter. *Our* daughter. Born of love."

Klytemnestra began to realize the meaning of her mother's words, and yet it was too much to take in, as if the words themselves were too large, too momentous to squeeze through that little gap in the wood.

Her father looked pained. Lines of sadness were drawn on his face, made deeper by the lamplight. He placed a hand tenderly on her mother's cheek and turned her face back toward him. "You are not a cruel woman, Leda. Think what you are saying. What joy will Helen find in life if she does not marry? If she does not have children?" He lowered his eyes. "I know they hurt you." Her mother gasped back a sob. "I know they did. But it wasn't Helen; she didn't hurt you. It's not her fault."

Her mother was sobbing freely now, body shaking, wrapped in the strong arms of her husband. Eventually she found some composure. When she spoke, though, her voice was barely audible. Klytemnestra had to strain to hear.

"I know. I know it's not Helen's fault. It's my fault. I was careless. But I can't bear to look at her, sometimes. She reminds me of . . . of them, and of what happened, of how I disgraced you. Of how I continue to bring disgrace upon you." Her voice broke again and she shook her head. "I'm so sorry. I ruined everything that day. And now poor Nestra has been robbed of her birthright because of me."

Klytemnestra knew she didn't understand all that was being said, but her mother's pain was clear. She wished she could run in and hug her. Tell her that it was all right, that she didn't blame her.

"Please don't, my love. Please don't say those things." He pressed his forehead to hers, hands cradling her dark head. "It's not true. You know I don't blame you."

Her mother continued, her breathing ragged. "I had hoped that once Helen was married, once she was gone . . . But now I must lose the daughter I love and be haunted forever by the one who remains."

Her father looked up, his head heavy. "I'm sorry. The last thing I wanted to do was to bring you further pain. But I must do what is best—for both of my daughters."

Her mother lifted her eyes to meet his, but Klytemnestra could not read her expression. Eventually she said, "You are a good man, Tyndareos," and let her head fall onto his chest. The fire that had been in her before seemed to have died, leaving a sudden, feeble acceptance behind it. A small, selfish corner of Klytemnestra's heart winced as she saw her mother give in. Her only champion had given up the fight, and yet her mother looked so frail, so broken from her efforts, that she knew she could not blame her. The two of them sat in silence for a minute or so before she straightened up and said, "Tell me more about my daughter's betrothed."

Her father gave a quiet sigh of relief. "He is a worthy match for Nestra. A formidable man, a great leader of men. He has won a wide kingdom, and wealth with it, but that is just the beginning. I believe he will become a great lord of Greece. Greater than myself." Klytemnestra was listening intently, keen to hear all she could about this man who had so impressed her father that he would give her away so easily. She saw her mother scoff, her dark eyes sharp with skepticism. "Truly, my love," he continued, "I have seen it in him. He hungers for power, and has the means to get it. And that is why we must secure our link with his house." Her mother looked as though she was going to interrupt, but Father seemed to anticipate what she was going to say. "He won't take Helen—I have already suggested it. He needs a queen who'll reinforce his legitimacy, not bring it into further question. And he needs heirs now. Helen is not ready. She has not yet started her bleeding, has she?" Her mother reluctantly shook her head. "He is past thirty, waiting until his kingdom was won to marry, but now he needs children to secure his house."

"I cannot argue against you, it seems," said her mother, her tone resigned. "All that you have said is fairly reasoned. I should have expected no less from you." She gave him a small smile, from one corner of her mouth.

"All will be well, you shall see," said her father, returning her mother's half-smile with a full one. "Both your daughters shall be queens. The most praised and envied wives in all Greece. We shall send Klytemnestra to Mycenae with all the ceremony she deserves, and make Helen the most desired bride of her generation."

"By attaching your kingdom to her," said her mother with a sigh.

"Not only that, my love, not only that. But it will certainly help. Men soon forget whispered words when they hear the call of a throne." He grinned, trying to coax another smile from her mother's lips. "We'll turn everything to our advantage, you'll see."

There was a noise from somewhere on Klytemnestra's side of the door. Not close by, but too close to ignore. People were beginning to leave the feast. She had to get back to her chamber. Her parents were still talking, but she couldn't risk being discovered. She stepped carefully away from the door and then walked briskly back to her room. When she got there she quickly tucked herself up in her bed.

Her heart was racing, and not just from fear of getting caught. She had heard so much in the last few minutes, so much that was new and confusing. *Helen the Bastard*, her father had said. Klytemnestra still wasn't sure she understood everything she had heard, and some of it was already slipping from her memory, but she knew what those words meant. Father was not Helen's father. Pulling the covers up to her chin, she wondered if Helen knew. No. Of course she didn't. She would have said something. They shared everything with each other. And surely her parents wouldn't have told her, if it was supposed to be a secret. Helen never could keep her mouth shut. *Should I tell her?* thought Klytemnestra. *If I don't tell her before I leave, she may never know.* But perhaps that was for the best, she thought as she turned onto her other side, trying to get comfortable. Helen loved Father. She was proud to be his daughter. She would be so upset if she knew the truth, and what would be gained?

Something else she had heard was troubling her more than Helen's parentage. People wouldn't marry Helen because of Theseus. It didn't matter that he was lying. He had been *alone* with her. He could claim whatever he liked and people would believe him. The thought of it made her so angry, to think of him bragging about it, laughing as he ruined her sister's future. She could hear it now, that carefree, careless laughter of boys who know the world is theirs to waste.

She threw the covers off herself, suddenly hot with anger, and yet beneath her rage at Theseus there was another feeling, darker and deeper and more difficult to confront. *Guilt.* Helen had only been young; she hadn't known what she was doing. But it had been *her* job to protect her sister. To guard her virginity, her reputation. Helen had only been allowed such freedom because her parents trusted Klytemnestra to be her sister's keeper. And she had let her down. Her sister wouldn't get a good marriage, because of her.

As she lay on her bed she felt her anger at her father, at Helen for stealing her birthright, ebb away. Helen needed it more than she did. And Klytemnestra was paying a due price for her own failure. She could not take back what had happened, she could not punish Theseus for his lies, but she could help to repair the damage they had done. She would not argue with her father anymore. This was the way it must be.

The next day, Klytemnestra was back at work in the women's room. She hadn't gotten much sleep, having lain awake most of the night churning over what she had heard and imagining her new future. She was still preoccupied now, as she worked the loom.

She noticed a fault in the cloth a few lines back. With a sigh she set to work unraveling what she had done—not for the first time this morning. As she did so she felt the slow realization that something had changed. And then it struck her. The usually chatter-filled room had fallen silent. She turned on her stool to see that all the women, bar Helen, had downed their work and bowed their heads. And then she spotted the cause. There, in the doorway, stood her father. She didn't think she had ever seen him in the women's room before. He met her gaze.

"Klytemnestra," he said. "Would you mind speaking with me?"

Would I mind? He was the king, and her father. If he wanted to speak with her she could hardly object. Surprised by his conciliatory tone, she left the loom and walked over to him. He led her a short way down the corridor and addressed her in a soft voice.

"I wanted to see that you were all right, after what we talked about last night. I'm sorry for upsetting you. It must have been quite a shock and I know you are angry with me, but I promise that I have made you a good match. King Agamemnon—"

"It's all right, Father," she interrupted. He blinked in surprise and she forced a smile. "I will do whatever you ask of me. I know you're only trying to do what's best."

He paused, his brow creased in confusion. Then he bent down and wrapped his arms around her.

"You are such a good girl, Nestra," he breathed into her hair. "Your mother and I care for you very much, and hope you will be happy in your marriage." Then he let go of her and straightened up. "I'm glad that we could be reconciled," he said, his tone formal again. And with that he turned and walked away from her.

Klytemnestra let out a slow, shaky sigh. That was it, then. She strode back to the women's room and to her loom. Helen gave her a questioning look as she passed, but Klytemnestra pretended not to see.

CHAPTER 4

KLYTEMNESTRA

It had been three months since Klytemnestra had learned of her betrothal. She had cherished each day since, trying to take in every sight, sound, and smell of the palace that had been the only home she'd ever known, aware that she would soon have to leave it. She sat in the women's room, appreciating the clattering, chattering hum. There would be a women's room at her new palace, no doubt, but it would not be the same. It would have none of the memories this room held. And none of the people. Not Thekla, with her disapproving tuts and the little lines that spread from her eyes when she smiled. Not Agatha, with her shy eyes and gentle heart. And not Helen. She would miss her sister most of all. She could hear her high voice singing on the other side of the room. Right now it sounded like the sweetest thing she had ever heard, and the thought of never hearing it again made her throat tight.

Today was the day she would meet her betrothed. He would arrive in Sparta this evening for the wedding feast, and then tomorrow he would lead her home as his bride. Her sister knew all this, of course, but Klytemnestra didn't think Helen really understood. She seemed to think this wasn't the end, that her sister would come back to visit. But Klytemnestra knew there was little likelihood of that. Married noblewomen did not travel. She would remain in Mycenae for the rest of her life as steward of her husband's household. And perhaps it was easier that way. A clean break and a new life.

As she sat musing there was a polite cough behind her. She turned to see Thekla standing there.

"Mistress Klytemnestra. It's time to prepare you to meet your betrothed." The nurse gave a reassuring smile. "Come with me."

Klytemnestra was prepared in her mother's chamber by the queen's own handmaids. Her mother was there too, directing them as they worked. Klytemnestra thought she caught her mother's eyes shining once or twice, but otherwise she hid her sadness well. She seemed excited as she ordered the slaves about the chamber—calling for ocher, myrrh, oil, amber—and her cheeks were plump with pride. After all, her daughter was becoming a woman.

By the time they had finished, Klytemnestra glistened. Her dark hair had been oiled and curled and the red cloth of her dress had been treated with oil too, giving it a luster as it caught the lamplight. The dress was pinned tighter to her body than usual and the material was thin, making her self-conscious. Necklaces of polished carnelian ringed her throat and thick bangles of gold weighed down her wrists. White makeup had been applied to her face, neck, and arms, and her eyes were edged with black kohl.

One of her mother's handmaids passed her a mirror and she held the polished surface up in front of her face. She looked beautiful. Her mother was looking at her with what seemed to be a genuine smile on her face. Klytemnestra smiled back.

"There is one final thing to do, my daughter, before you are ready," her mother said. She gestured to a handmaid, who came forward cradling a piece of delicate cloth in her hands. As her mother lifted it up, Klytemnestra saw that it was very fine, dyed with saffron and delicately embroidered, with gold threads crisscrossing its surface like a thousand shining stars.

"It is a veil. Made by my own hand," her mother said, looking at it with pride. "You are a bride now, and soon to be a wife and queen. You will need this. First for the wedding and then afterward, to preserve your modesty. And to keep your skin as fair as your mother's," she added with a smile. She stepped toward Klytemnestra and laid the veil over her head. Then, reaching into a small ivory chest, she produced a beautifully wrought golden circlet and laid it on top of the veil, fixing it in place. Her mother stepped back, beaming with pride. Even through the haze of the translucent veil, Klytemnestra thought she could see tears in her mother's eyes.

"There," her mother said. "You are a true bride now. A true woman."

As if on cue the door to the chamber opened and a female servant entered. She glanced at Klytemnestra and addressed the queen.

"Lord Agamemnon arrived not long ago, my lady. He has been bathed and is now waiting with Lord Tyndareos in the Hearth Hall. He asks that the Princess Klytemnestra be brought to him so he may see her before the feast."

Her mother nodded and the servant retreated, closing the door behind her. Klytemnestra's insides started to squirm. She hadn't expected him to arrive for another hour or so. She thought there would be time for her and her mother to sit and talk awhile.

"This is it then, my daughter," said her mother, taking Klytemnestra's hands in hers. She seemed to be resisting the urge to embrace her, not wanting to rub the makeup from her arms or upset her carefully arranged hair and veil. "I am so proud of you." She squeezed her hands and smiled, though there was a twitch at the corners of her mouth, as if something in her was resisting. "You must remember to stand straight. And don't speak unless he asks you something. We will show him that the women of Sparta are the best in Greece."

Klytemnestra forced her shimmering head to nod. Yes, she would be the best bride she could be. Beautiful and obedient. The best wife, the best mother, the best woman. That was the path before her now—it all began here. So much lay beyond her control, but this, *this* was her power. She would make everyone proud.

Her mother let go of her hands and led her from the chamber to the Hearth Hall entrance. With one last encouraging smile her mother nodded to the guard, who opened the heavy wooden door, and side by side they strode into the hall.

As Klytemnestra crossed the threshold her eyes flicked straight to her father's throne—and to the man seated beside him. The room was otherwise empty so the man could be none other than Agamemnon.

He was broad, and powerful-looking. Muscular, but not lean. He rose from his chair as she entered and she saw that he was tall, rising several inches above her father as they stood together. He had dark hair, tied up behind his head, and his beard was black. Her father had said he was over thirty, but Klytemnestra thought he didn't look much younger than Father himself. Even through the mesh of the shimmering veil she could see that his face was hard and weathered, with cuts and creases running across it. He was not unhandsome, though. He had a strong nose and sharp eyes. His expression remained neutral as she approached.

"So this is my bride," he said, his deep voice booming through the empty hall. "Come closer, let me look at you."

She took a few more steps toward him, glancing nervously at her father. She wasn't sure if he could see her expression through the veil, but he smiled and it calmed her. She set her eyes straight ahead, doing her best to look confident and modest at the same time.

Agamemnon stood in front of her for a moment, then began a slow circuit. She could feel his eyes as he moved around her and wished her dress were not so tight, nor so thin. She was glad of the veil now. She thought that even through the white makeup her cheeks must be turning red. And as he came around to examine her flanks, the line of her back, she was glad he could not see her grit her teeth—or perhaps he would like to check them, too? Eventually, he reappeared in front of her.

"Very good. Sparta really is the land of beautiful women," he said, and barked a laugh. "And she is well matured. That is good." He glanced over at her father, who nodded solemnly.

"Did you weave this cloth yourself?" he asked, looking at her dress and veil. With a start she realized he was talking to her.

"Er . . . no, my lord," she replied, a little embarrassed. "But I can weave. I've woven many—"

"Do you dance?" he asked next, cutting her off.

"Yes, my lord. I dance well, so I'm told."

"Good," he boomed, clapping his huge hands together. "You will dance tonight at the feast. I look forward to it."

"Yes, my lord, if you wish it," she said, not sure whether he expected an answer.

"I am glad my daughter pleases you," came her father's voice. "May your marriage bring joy to you both, and lasting union to Sparta and Mycenae."

"Indeed," said Agamemnon. "Mycenae will forever be a faithful ally to Sparta, as she has been our ally in reclaiming the throne of my father. And I am glad to accept your daughter as my wife, so that our two great houses may be joined. You will see that I have brought ample bridal gifts, and will bestow many more upon my wife when we return to Mycenae."

My wife. The words sounded strange, and yet there was a gravity to them that Klytemnestra liked.

"You are most generous, Lord Agamemnon," said her father, inclining his head graciously. "If you are satisfied, shall we begin the wedding feast?"

"By all means!" he replied. "My stomach hungers for meat after our journey."

And with that the guests were summoned, the meat and wine prepared, and the celebrations begun.

Klytemnestra woke up the next morning with Helen's hair in her face. Her sister had wanted to share her bed so they could be close on their last night. She thought Helen was perhaps starting to realize that they might never see each other again, once she left with Agamemnon. As they lay there together, Helen's gentle breaths oddly loud in the silence, Klytemnestra took a moment to cherish the warm comfort of it. She would have quite a different bedmate in a few days' time, once the wedding procession was over and they had arrived in Mycenae as husband and wife. But she didn't want to have to think about that yet. She must take one step at a time, or she feared she would not be able to go forward at all.

She had been glad to leave the feast last night. It had felt like everyone was looking at her and, though it had made her feel special and beautiful at first, it had become unnerving. Even with her face hidden beneath the golden veil, she had felt exposed. The worst part was when her father had called her to dance right in the middle of the hall. She had not been alone—Helen and some other noblegirls had joined the performance—but everyone seemed to be watching her. Agamemnon himself had been only a few feet away, and his eyes had never left her body. She had felt the thin, red cloth of her dress cling to her hips, her waist, her breasts as she moved to the music of the lyre, the rhythm of the drum, and had wanted nothing more than to shrink into the crowd, away from the hungry eyes of the man who would be her husband.

There was a knock at the chamber door and a slave woman entered. Klytemnestra sat up, causing Helen to stir but not to wake.

"Lord Agamemnon wishes to set off as soon as possible, my lady," said the slave. "I am to wash and dress you."

Klytemnestra nodded, relieved to see that the dress the slave was holding was thickly woven. At least she would not feel as self-conscious on her journey as she had last night. She silently thanked the gods that winter was approaching.

Once she was dressed, veiled, and modestly adorned with a necklace of amethysts, she was led to the front of the palace. But before she walked through its huge doors her mother appeared, with Helen in tow.

"Nestra!" cried Helen, running to embrace her. "I was worried you'd already gone!"

"I would never leave without saying good-bye," said Klytemnestra, hugging her sister tightly.

"I wish you didn't have to go at all," Helen complained, looking as if she might cry.

"So do I," she breathed, kissing the top of her sister's shining head. "So do I, Helen, but I must." She pulled away and gave a brave smile so that Helen would not get upset.

"I don't see why, though. You said we could both stay here. You said we'd raise our children together and—"

"I know . . . I know I said that. But the Fates have spun a different future for us. We cannot argue against them. It will all be for the best, you will see," she said, squeezing Helen's soft hands. The words were as much for herself as for her sister.

Helen was silent for a moment, looking into Klytemnestra's eyes.

"I'll miss you," she said quietly.

"I'll miss you too," Klytemnestra replied, fighting to keep her voice steady. They embraced again.

Then once Helen had let go, her light eyes sparkling with tears, the queen stepped forward. Cupping Klytemnestra's cheeks in her hands and looking straight into her eyes, she said, "You are my proudest achievement, and I will always love you." Then she folded her into her arms. It was a desperate, lingering embrace, and Klytemnestra wished it could last forever. Here, pressed against her mother's breast, cradled in her arms, she felt safe. When her mother finally let go she wiped her cheek, adjusted Klytemnestra's circlet, and stepped back. "Now, go to your husband," she said.

And with that the great doors were opened, and sunlight poured into the atrium. With legs shaking, Klytemnestra stepped out toward her future.

CHAPTER 5

KLYTEMNESTRA

I t took a full three days of traveling to reach Mycenae. The winding route through the mountains was slow, and they were hampered by the wagons. Two of them were filled with gifts from her father; one held her dowry of fine cloth and jewelry, and the other carried the guest-gifts bestowed upon Agamemnon: silver cups and bronze cauldrons, sharp spears and sturdy shields. The third wagon was occupied by Klytemnestra herself. It was decked with soft cloths, colored with luxurious purple, but her backside still ached at the end of each day.

She was alone in the wagon, swaying with every bump of the rocky track as her husband rode out ahead. Her brothers had traveled with the procession at first, holding the bridal torches and riding either side of her. At least then she had had someone to talk to, and the company of those she knew. It had made her feel more at ease. But Kastor and Pollux had left them at the edge of Lakonia. They had turned around and ridden back home, giving the sacred torches over into the hands of Agamemnon's heralds, men she did not know. The heralds had introduced themselves, but she had not been listening. All her attention had been on the two figures shrinking into the distance, until they became two dots, and then were gone altogether. In her heart she knew it was the last she would ever see of her family.

She hadn't spoken since Kastor and Pollux had left. No one spoke to her, and it would be improper for her to start a conversation with a man. She had thought the journey might be an opportunity for her to get to know her husband a little, but he had barely even looked at her since leaving Sparta. He seemed content to talk and laugh with his men. What Klytemnestra really wanted was some female company. Before leaving she had shyly asked her husband and her father whether she might take a female slave with her, to tend her needs once they reached Mycenae. She had just wanted a familiar face, any face. But Agamemnon had dismissed the idea, saying he had plenty of slaves at his palace. And so here she was, a girl of barely fifteen, adrift in a sea of men. It would be different once they reached Mycenae, she told herself. There would be women, and girls her own age. People to talk to and laugh with. She would be happy there. She was determined to be happy.

They reached Mycenae the evening of the third day. The first thing Klytemnestra saw were the huge walls of the citadel, which were taller and thicker than any she had seen before. As the wagons drew closer they seemed to grow taller still, rising from the hillside like cliffs of white stone, huge boulders stacked upon one another, so high she feared they would come crashing down on top of them. Her home in Sparta barely had a boundary fence. The bridal torches were still burning as the procession approached, crawling up the slope to the acropolis. They reached the outside of the citadel and entered into a short corridor of stone, the huge walls towering above them on either side. Over the heads of the men and horses, Klytemnestra could see the top of a gateway. The wooden doors were closed, but above the thick stone lintel she could see two fierce lionesses, brought to life from out of the cold stone. Their faces glared out over the procession, illuminated by the flickering torchlight.

Staring up at those stone faces, the frightening gatekeepers of her new home, Klytemnestra nearly jumped out of her skin when a voice suddenly called out beside her.

"Lord Agamemnon, King of Mycenae, has arrived with his bride," announced the herald on her right.

For a moment there was silence. Then she heard sounds of movement from the other side of the gate. Booted footsteps, the thud of wood, the clank of metal. Soon the heavy gates were opened, and her wagon jolted to a start as the procession filed through under the watchful gaze of the lionesses.

Klytemnestra tried to take in all she could as they passed through the citadel, but it was difficult in the darkness and with the veil obscuring her vision. She spotted the shapes of men, stopped in the streets or hovering in their doorways, trying to catch a glimpse of their king's new bride. She was glad of the veil now, as she had been on many occasions during her journey. She did not want people to see how scared she was. A queen was not supposed to be afraid.

It did not take long to reach the palace. Even in the limited light she knew that was what it was—its silhouette loomed larger by far than any other building they had passed. Klytemnestra's wagon rolled to a halt beside a great staircase of stone and as she followed it with her eyes, squinting up at the huge door that stood at its end, she began to shiver. She did not notice her husband standing beside her until he thrust out an expectant arm. She took it gratefully, but even so her legs were not long enough to avoid an inelegant hop to the ground, and she thanked the gods that she managed to keep from falling. Her knees felt as if they could barely hold her weight as her husband led her toward her new home, his gloved hand wrapped around her wrist as she trailed behind him.

They entered through the huge doors to be greeted by a number of slaves and stewards, awaiting the orders of their returned master. Klytemnestra could hear music and smell roasting meat. A female slave bowed before Agamemnon.

"Would you like the girl prepared for the bedding, my lord?" she asked. "We've readied a bath and perfumes and—"

"That will not be necessary," replied Agamemnon. The woman nodded and shuffled backward again.

"Will you be partaking of the feast beforehand, my lord?" asked another slave. "It is already under way. The nobles are in the hall, drinking to the health of you and your bride. They are eager to see their queen."

"No. I will join them later, once the marriage is complete. They may see the Spartan flower once she has been plucked."

Klytemnestra swallowed hard. It would happen soon, then. Perhaps that was for the best. Her nerves were making her feel sick; perhaps she would feel calmer once it was done.

Agamemnon dismissed the slaves and his attendants and carried on through the palace, still leading Klytemnestra behind him. He didn't speak as they marched down corridor after corridor. The palace felt like a labyrinth, far larger than her home in Sparta, but perhaps that was just because it was all unfamiliar, every corridor, every doorway leading to some unknown place. She was beginning to think they were going around in circles when Agamemnon finally stopped outside a large wooden door, ornately carved with vines and stags, and pushed it open. He entered and waved a hand for her to follow.

The room was spacious, with a high ceiling. The lamps had already been lit, but their light was neither warm nor inviting. Somehow it gave the room an eerie glow, like the light cast from a pyre into the night sky. Klytemnestra shivered despite the warmth of her traveling clothes. In the middle of the room stood a huge bed, with thick posts at its corners. It was made up with fine covers, colored with deep purple. Her marriage bed.

Agamemnon had already moved to the bed. He was sitting on its edge, unlacing his boots, while Klytemnestra still hovered near the doorway.

"Close the door, girl," Agamemnon grunted, pulling at the leather strings with impatient fingers. She obliged, struggling a little with the weight of it. Then she turned back to face him, awaiting her next in-struction.

"Come over here." He beckoned. "I'm not going to eat you," he added, barking a laugh. He was not smiling, though.

She stepped toward him, trying to look graceful, but she knew she just looked afraid. She was still wearing the veil and could see the golden cloth quivering as her body trembled involuntarily.

"That's better," he said, as she stopped in front of him. "Now, let me help you out of those sandals."

Still sitting on the bed, he leaned down and carefully slipped her small feet out of their shoes. As he slipped the second sandal off, how-ever, his hands lingered on her foot. Then they moved up to her ankle. He slid his hands slowly up her legs, underneath the floor-length skirt of her dress. Past the knee. Klytemnestra's heart was racing, but she tried to keep still. She mustn't recoil. But it got harder and harder as his hands got higher.

Then he stopped, halfway up her thighs, and removed his hands from under her skirt. He stood up, so that he was right in front of her, mere inches between them. He smelled of sweat and dust and horses. She tilted her head up to look at him, and then in one quick sweep he lifted her veil, and they were looking straight into each other's eyes. She tried to keep her gaze strong and steady. Fearless, but not defiant. He smiled.

"As beautiful as your mother," he said. And then without warning he kissed her, hard, right on the lips. His beard was thick and wiry against her face.

"Did you like that?" he asked. Klytemnestra was surprised by the question. But she had liked it, she realized, in a way. She had never kissed a man before, not even a boy. Now she felt grown-up, and beau-tiful. She gave a shy nod, not sure of her ability to speak. It felt as if there were a stone in her throat.

"Good," he said, and kissed her again, more softly this time. "And before, when I touched you. Did you like that?"

Klytemnestra was less sure of this answer. She hesitated, afraid to give the wrong one.

"Your father tells me you're a clever girl," he continued, not waiting for her to reply. "You must know, then, that marriage is for the creation of children, yes?"

She nodded.

"And do you know how children come to be?" he asked.

She nodded again. She did know, or at least she thought she did.

"Then you know what we must do now," he said, his voice the softest she had heard it since they had met.

She tried to nod again, but it came out as more of a twitch of her head. This was it, then. It was time for her to become a woman.

CHAPTER 6

HELEN

TWO YEARS LATER

Life for Helen had been very lonely since Klytemnestra left Sparta. She had not only lost her sister but her best friend. It had felt like a part of herself had been carried away in that wagon. For months after Nestra had left, Helen had felt lost, with no one to talk to but Thekla and no one to spend time with but herself. At night, her room was too quiet without her sister's gentle breathing. That was when she missed her the most, when she was lying alone in the darkness. How she longed to call her sister's name and hear her reply, and have one of those conversations they used to have, when it was just the two of them, there in the dark. They would talk about important things, sending their hearts out to each other under cover of night, or about nothing much at all, giggling quietly into their pillows until one of them fell asleep.

Her father had noticed her loneliness. After half a year of seeing barely a flicker of a smile on her face, he had presented her with two handmaids. Adraste and Alkippe, two noblegirls captured during the Mycenaean campaign, were of a similar age to Helen, and her father clearly thought they would be able to offer her companionship as well as service. He was right. The three girls had become good friends, as far as is possible when two friends must serve the third.

Adraste and Alkippe were in Helen's chamber now, preparing her for the day. Alkippe was just finishing the complex arrangement of Helen's hair—something she had become adept at—while Adraste riffled through an ivory jewelry box looking for some appropriate adornments for today's outfit. Helen enjoyed this morning ritual. It made her feel grown up to have her own handmaids, and they would chat and giggle together as she was made ready. It wasn't just that, though. There was a kind of magic in it. As each stage was done, each fine item of clothing placed upon her, each piece of gold or shining stone attached to her body, she felt as if she were being transformed, from Helen the girl to Helen the princess. She felt she had grown up a lot in the two years since Nestra had left, and she wished her sister could see her now.

"What do you think about this one, Mistress Helen?" asked Adraste, holding up a necklace of polished amber beads. "It would match your hair so well, but do you think it's too much? Maybe we should save it for a special occasion."

"No, no," said Helen, as Adraste began to lower it back into the box. "I like it, and I don't think it's too much. I *am* the heiress," she said with a grin.

Adraste smiled and nodded, then gently fastened the necklace around Helen's throat. As she did so, Helen heard Alkippe's quiet voice behind her.

"I never really understood that," she muttered as she fixed a flower in Helen's hair. "I mean, why *are* you the heiress?"

In front of her Adraste froze, her eyes wide. Helen opened her mouth to speak, but Alkippe beat her to it, her words tumbling out in high-pitched squeaks. "I'm sorry, my lady, that was so rude of me! I didn't mean . . . only that . . . Well, you have brothers is all I meant.

Isn't it usually the sons that . . . It's just something I'd wondered about, that was all."

"It's all right, Alkippe," said Helen, turning to her with a smile. "I know what you meant. I suppose it would seem strange to you, if they don't do it in Mycenae, but I don't think it's all that unusual . . ." She turned back around, flicking a tress of curled hair over her shoulder. "My sister once told me that it's because Kastor and Pollux are twins. Father was worried they'd fight over the kingdom, so he made it so that neither would be king."

"Lord Tyndareos is a wise man," Adraste nodded, her face thoughtful. "Our kingdom was torn apart by brothers fighting over the throne. It's the reason we're here . . . Not that we're complaining of course, my lady," she added quickly. "We're happy to serve you, and you and your father have been very kind to us."

"Yes, my lady," agreed Alkippe, with a respectful bow of her head.

Helen smiled faintly by way of reply. She sometimes forgot the true situation of her handmaids, the misfortune that had brought them here. Though she knew they were her slaves, she preferred to think of them as her friends. It was easier that way.

Now that she was dressed and adorned, Helen crossed to the corner of her chamber to see to the last phase of her morning ritual. There, on a low table covered with fine cloth, stood a small, painted figure, formed in the shape of a woman with her arms raised. Helen knelt down in front of it and held her hand out toward Adraste. The girl duly passed her a small bottle of perfumed oil, and Helen dabbed a little onto the head of the figurine. There were the rudiments of a face painted onto the clay, large round eyes and a smiling mouth. This is where Helen looked as she said, "Lady Artemis, I offer you this blessing, that you may keep my sister safe." She had spoken these words every morning since Nestra had left. Then, anointing the figurine once more, she added, "And keep her child safe too, that it may live and bring joy to its mother." She had been adding this second request for almost a year now. She knew how fragile the life of a child was. Her own mother had lost two babes to sickness, so Thekla had told her.

Her prayer finished, Helen stood up and left the chamber, her handmaids following dutifully behind her. They went everywhere with her, like a two-headed shadow. It was irritating sometimes, when she just wanted to be alone, but for the most part she liked it. It made her feel like a real royal lady.

Helen walked with measured steps through the corridors, affecting what she hoped was an air of elegance. She was in no hurry to reach the women's room. No longer could she sit and laugh and gossip with her friends, carelessly spinning yarn. Now she was being taught to weave, and she was no good at it. It took too much concentration and she kept making mistakes. Then Thekla would come over to see her progress, and make that *tsk* noise of hers. No matter how grown up she felt, with her handmaids and her jewelry and the breasts finally budding beneath her dress, Thekla could always make her feel like a little girl.

They had reached the Hearth Hall now. They needn't have come this way, but Helen was hoping her mother might be there and that she might be able to sit with her, two royal ladies together. But today, like every other day, she was disappointed. Helen felt as if she had barely seen her mother in two years. Since Nestra had left, she had taken to staying in her chambers most days. She would show her face every now and again when public occasion required it, but when she did she looked gray and lifeless. Helen could barely recall seeing her mother smile, and it was like a worm eating at her heart. It was as if it didn't matter to her that she still had a daughter living here in Sparta. No, Helen knew she was not enough. She was not the *right* daughter. She had hoped that Nestra leaving might bring her and her mother closer together, that there would be more space in her mother's heart, that the shared loss would bind them. But it had made it worse. She felt as if she had lost her mother as well as her sister, and somehow this loss was harder, for the ghost still lingered to haunt her.

She was crossing the courtyard when a voice called after her. Her father's voice. "Helen! Wait, Helen."

She turned to look at him, and smiled. Her father at least was unchanged by Nestra's departure, if a little grayer than he had been two years ago. He always had a smile for her, and she drank it in like divine nectar.

"I need to speak to you," he said, his tone serious but not grave. Helen suspected she knew what this might be about, and she felt a giddy excitement spring up inside her. "Why don't you come and sit with me?" He gestured inside the hall, to his throne beside the hearth.

When they were seated, Helen fidgeting with her hands in anticipation, her father said, "You are to be married, Helen."

She slowly let out the breath she had been holding. This was what she was expecting him to say, and indeed had been expecting for a couple of months. After all, she was as old as Nestra had been when she was married. Now it was her turn.

"I won't have to leave, though, will I?" she blurted out, as the thought struck her. "I'm still the heiress, aren't I? So I'll stay here in Sparta with you?"

"Yes, yes. You'll stay here, don't worry about that," he said. "Whoever you marry shall come here to live with you."

"Whoever?" she asked, slightly puzzled. "So you haven't chosen yet?"

"No, my dear. We will wait to see who is the best match," he said, with the hint of a smile playing on his lips.

Helen's expression was still puzzled, so he continued.

"There is to be a tournament, of sorts. The most eligible bachelors in Greece will all come here to compete for your hand. They'll be arriving within the next few weeks. I've made it known that you are ready for marriage, and now they will flock from all over. All hoping to prove themselves the best man and win you as their prize."

"Competing for *me*?" she asked, incredulous.

"And why should they not?" replied her father with a smile. "You are heiress to a rich kingdom. And they have heard of your great beauty."

Helen blushed. She quite liked the idea of men competing over her. She imagined the feats they would perform, the gifts they would bring, and a broad grin spread across her face.

"There is one thing I should tell you, Helen," her father said, "before it all gets under way."

Her smile waned a little and she nodded for him to continue.

"It's just that, ah . . . the suitors, or at least some of them . . . they believe you to be the daughter of Zeus."

"What?" she giggled. "But that's ridiculous, Father! Why would they think that?"

"Because I have said that it is so," he said with a small sigh. Helen stopped her giggling. "All I ask is that you let them believe it."

She was silent for a moment, looking into her father's eyes. She was surprised and a little confused, but she could not deny that the idea of people thinking she was descended from the gods had a certain appeal.

"Helen?" said her father, a little impatiently. "Will you go along with it?"

"Yes, of course, Father," she answered. "If that's what you want."

He smiled. "Good."

Once her father had left, her handmaids began tittering like sparrows.

"Ooh, how exciting!" cooed Adraste. "You thought it would happen soon!"

"And all those suitors!" chimed Alkippe. "I bet they'll be handsome!"

"Yes," breathed Helen. "Yes, it is exciting, isn't it?"

This is it, she said to herself. *You'll be a real woman soon enough, just like Nestra.* The thought filled her stomach with butterflies, but she told herself they were good butterflies. Womanhood would be exciting and glamorous, and no one would treat her like a silly little girl anymore. This was a good thing, and the tournament would be a spectacle. How she wished Nestra were here to share it with her.

CHAPTER 7

KLYTEMNESTRA

Klytemnestra sat in her chamber, idly spinning wool. Her hand-maid, Eudora, was sitting beside her, but no words passed between them. They were enjoying the silence while Iphigenia slept peacefully in her cradle, and there was an unspoken understanding between them that it should not be broken. Her daughter was almost a year old now, and seemed to grow bigger with each passing day. Klytemnestra loved her more than anything in the world, more than she had ever thought it was possible to love something. If ever she felt lonely or sad or afraid, all she had to do was picture Iphigenia's sweet face, those rosy cheeks, that mass of blond curls, and a smile would come to her lips. There had been times when she had struggled with her new role as wife and queen, especially in the beginning when she was still learning her place, before she knew when to talk and when to keep silent, before modesty had become habit and obedience routine. There were still times when she found it difficult to hold her tongue, when shrinking into the shadow of her husband felt like she was shedding parts of herself, as if one day she might disappear entirely. But then Iphigenia had been born, and the moment she had held her own child in her arms she had known that *this* was it. This was her reward for womanhood.

A dreamy gurgle erupted from the cradle and Klytemnestra felt her chest warm at the sound. The birth of her daughter had helped to bring her and Agamemnon closer together, too. Klytemnestra had pleased her husband by giving him a child so soon. And she felt he respected her more now, treating her like a true woman and wife rather than a child herself. He had been hoping for a son, she knew, but he loved his daughter dearly. Sons would follow, he said.

There was something playing on Klytemnestra's mind as she sat spinning her wool in the cool quiet of the chamber. Her monthly bleed had not come. It had been half a moon since it was due, and every morning she would wake thinking that perhaps it had come, but there would be nothing. She knew what it might mean, of course. It was a blessing, yes, but she could not help but be a little afraid. Her daughter had brought her so much joy and another child would surely bring more, but she knew how lucky she had been for the birth to have gone well, for the child to have been healthy. Perhaps she would not be so lucky a second time. A swollen belly could bring death as well as life. It was the way of the gods.

She hadn't said anything to Agamemnon yet, for fear of disappointing him. She might be mistaken, or it might not last. She would wait until she was sure, or until it started to show.

A noise came from outside the chamber, interrupting Klytemnestra's thoughts. She turned her head just in time to see the door pushed open and her husband appear through it. He did not look at her, but rather headed straight for Iphigenia's cradle. Before Klytemnestra could tell him not to wake her, his hand was reaching in and stroking her hair.

"How's my princess today?" he boomed into the cradle, his loud voice shattering the sacred quiet that had existed a moment ago. Klytemnestra suspected that her husband could not whisper even if he wanted to.

"Shh—we just got her to sleep!" she chastised. A year ago she would not have dared speak to her husband in this way, but motherhood had changed things. Even so, it was too late; Iphigenia was awake now.

Once her father had stopped tickling her and squeezing her cheeks, he came over to where Klytemnestra was sitting.

"You may leave," he said to Eudora, dressing a command as a permission. The handmaid promptly obliged.

Once the door was closed Agamemnon sank his considerable bulk into the chair she had vacated.

"There is to be a tournament for the marriage of your sister," he said in a casual tone.

"Oh," said Klytemnestra, a little taken aback by the sudden delivery of the news. It had been a long time since anyone had talked to her of Helen. "When?" she asked.

"The suitors have already begun to arrive, so I hear. They've never even seen the girl and yet they flock to compete over her." He waved a hand dismissively. "All the noblest young men of Greece, apparently, and some of the not-so-young too," he added with an amused smile. "Your father is a clever man, I'll give him that! To bring this about, over a girl of such, ah . . . questionable reputation."

He hung on the last two words, watching Klytemnestra's face for a reaction, a confirmation of the truth behind the rumors he had heard, perhaps.

Klytemnestra was annoyed to hear him speak of her sister in such a way, but tried to keep her face neutral, innocent even, as if she did not know to what he was referring. She wanted to defend Helen, to tell him Theseus was just a pathetic liar, but she knew she could not dismiss that rumor while ignoring the other . . . And she could not lie to Agamemnon. Not if he asked her straight out what she knew of Helen's parentage. She was afraid to lie to him, afraid he would know, afraid he would get angry. She had not grown so bold that she had stopped fearing her husband. Best to say nothing at all.

Eventually he stopped waiting for a reaction. "I've come to tell you that I've decided to attend the tournament." Klytemnestra broke her vow of neutrality with a look of confusion, but before she could say anything her husband continued, "Not on my own behalf, of course, but upon that of my brother, Menelaos. He's in need of a wife and, thanks to your father, Helen is the most desirable bride of the age. Ha!" He barked so loud that Klytemnestra jumped. "Her beauty is the talk of Greece! Can you believe there are even those who believe her to be a child of Zeus himself? Well, whatever the truth of it"—he shot her a sideways glance once more—"it will be a slight on the honor of our house if some other man wins her. Menelaos must wed Helen."

Klytemnestra sat in silence for a moment, taking in what she had just heard. Helen, the most desirable bride of the age? The talk of Greece? She felt proud and pleased for her sister, but somewhere in the back of her mind there was a twinge of something less pleasant. Resentment, perhaps? Or envy? That this was Helen's fortune and not her own? She brushed that thought aside. She was happy enough, wasn't she? And her husband was a great man, after all. This was a good thing, the very reason she had left Sparta in the first place. Helen would get a fine husband, and Sparta's legacy would be secure.

"I'll be leaving tomorrow morning," came Agamemnon's voice beside her, cutting off her reflections.

"Will you give my love to my father and mother, husband?" she said suddenly, realizing that he would see her family. "And to Helen, if you have the opportunity to speak with her?"

"Yes, if you wish. I'll tell them what a beautiful daughter you've given me, too," he said, smiling in one of those tender moments he granted her sometimes. Then, with one last stroke of Iphigenia's hair, he left the chamber.

Part of Klytemnestra wished she could go to Sparta with her husband. It didn't seem fair that he would get to see her family and she would not. But she pushed that thought down. She must stay and care for Iphigenia. *My family is here now*, she told herself. And when Agamemnon returned, perhaps she would tell him about the new addition growing in her belly.

CHAPTER 8

HELEN

Over twenty suitors had now arrived in Sparta, and each passing day brought at least one more. Helen was not allowed to watch as they arrived, but she would badger her brothers for news—what each wore, if they were handsome, what fine gifts they had brought. As they recounted such details to her, Helen would wonder whether this would be the one, whether this new man would shortly become her husband. There was a kind of romance in the mystery of it. The twins would tell her the men's names too, and who their father was and what kingdom they had journeyed from, but it all meant little to her. It was not a princess's business to know of foreign places, and even less so foreign men. But the other day a man had arrived of whom she *had* heard: Agamemnon, Nestra's husband, attending on behalf of his brother. She had not been expecting him to come and neither, it seemed, had her father. Helen had been with him when Agamemnon's arrival was announced, and an unmistakable look of surprise, perhaps even concern, had crossed his face. For a moment Helen had been excited, thinking that perhaps the Mycenaean king had brought Nestra with him, but her father had quashed any such hope. Nestra was a mother now. Her place was with her child, he had said.

Each evening the suitors would feast and drink in the Hearth Hall, with Father and Kastor and Pollux. But Helen wasn't allowed to attend. Her father was keeping her away from the suitors as much as possible. "A goddess is all the more beautiful for being formed in men's imaginations," he insisted. She *had* thought it strange that so many princes would come to compete over her without any of them ever having seen her, so perhaps there was some truth in what her father said. All the same, she was frustrated at not being able to get a good look at the suitors. After all, it was she who would be marrying one of them.

The closest she got was whenever the suitors were competing, out beyond the bounds of the palace. Every couple of days they would organize a contest among themselves, and Father would take her to watch. They needed to feel as if they were performing for her sake, he said, but she knew that the contests were aimed at impressing her father. She was just the prize. It was he who would decide his son-in-law and successor.

Even when they were watching the contests, she still wasn't allowed to get too close. Father had had a kind of podium erected a little away from the competition ground, on top of which the two of them would sit as they watched the men perform their feats. And Father insisted that she wear a veil, a huge piece of shining cloth draped over the top of her clothes and drawn up over her head. He even made her draw it across her face, "to show them that you are modest," he said. But often she would lower it again when her father looked away, just to let a little fresh air touch her skin. It was stifling under the veil, sitting out in the open under the sun's heat.

Today was a competition day, and she was as hot as ever. She longed to tear off the stupid veil, and her dress too, and go swimming in the river like she had when she was younger. She had to stop herself from giggling aloud at the thought of it. *What a scandal that would cause*, she thought with a grin. Father would not be happy, but she wasn't so sure about the suitors. She saw the way they looked over at her. She knew they were wondering what lay beneath the veil, imagining what their prize might look like once it had been unwrapped. Their looks didn't make her embarrassed, though. She was proud to be the object of so many men's desire. They wanted her, and it felt good. Occasionally, she would even let the veil fall back from her head a little, to reveal a glimpse of her hair. Even at this distance, she knew the suitors must be able to see it, bright as it was, shining in the sunlight. Her hair was her best feature after all, and she saw no sense in keeping it hidden.

There was an archery competition under way. Slaves were throwing apples into the air for the suitors to pierce with their arrows, though it was proving too difficult a task for most. Several had failed at the first attempt, others after two or three. Then there were only three men left. Now two. And then, as the penultimate man missed by a whisker, there was only one remaining. He did not cease, however, but nodded to the slaves to continue, and carried on sending his arrows into the sky, each finding its mark. He looked as if he could carry on forever as he casually drew arrow after arrow from his quiver. Only when the quiver was empty did he stop. Lowering his bow, he turned toward the podium where Helen and her father were seated and gave a respectful nod. Helen saw her father rise from his seat at the edge of her vision, and as he began to clap she followed suit.

"Who is that man, Father?" she asked. "I haven't seen him compete before today."

"Philoktetes, son of Poeas," came her father's reply as he gestured for the waiting attendants to deliver the victor's prize to him: a large bronze cauldron with golden handles. "Some say that bow is the very same that Herakles used to shoot the Stymphalian birds." Helen's eyes widened in awe. "Nonsense, most likely," her father continued, "but he certainly is skilled in its use."

As the slaves were clearing away the apples, Helen asked, "Is that it for today, Father? May we go back to the palace now?"

"No, there will be one more contest, I believe," he replied. "A foot race."

Helen was relieved. At least foot races were over quickly. Then she would be able to retreat to the relative cool of her chamber and take off this stupid, suffocating veil.

The suitors were already lining up to begin the race. Only five were competing, and she recognized three of them from previous contests. There was Odysseus, broad-chested and squat. She thought him rather ugly, but he had done well at the contests so far. Her brothers told her that he hadn't brought any bridal gifts—not a single thing! He was a curious man indeed, and she was quite glad he would not be her husband—how could he hope to be, when he had come empty-handed?

Beside Odysseus stood Ajax. She had heard people call him "Ajax the Great," and she could see why. He was a giant of a man, standing a head above the other runners, and broader than Odysseus. His arms and thighs bulged with thick muscle. Helen was a little afraid of him.

The third man she knew by name was Antilochos. He was like a reed beside the bulk of the other two men, being the youngest and slightest of all the suitors. He was very handsome, though, his fine features matching his boyish frame, and his long hair was a lovely shade of rich chestnut. Of the three men she recognized in this race, Helen knew which one she hoped would win.

She noted that Agamemnon once again stood among the spectators. She had not seen him compete in anything so far. Perhaps it made sense, given that he was only here on behalf of his brother, but she also got the sense that he thought it all beneath him. He had brought the richest gifts and everyone knew it. And he was King of Mycenae, after all; there was no need for him to prove himself.

Taking her eyes away from Agamemnon, Helen realized that the race was just about to begin. Within seconds the adjudicator's yell sounded, and they were off. Odysseus had an early lead, followed by one of the men Helen did not know, then Antilochos. But Ajax's powerful legs were bringing him up fast, past Antilochos, level with the next man. Then a yell and cloud of dust as Ajax fell, and the other man too. And out of the confusion sprinted Antilochos, leaving the fifth man far behind. Odysseus was slowing now, Antilochos drawing level. And then he was past him, his young knees a blur. And it was over. Antilochos had won, just ahead of Odysseus, with the fifth man coming behind them. But Ajax and the other man were still in the dust, and as Helen looked at them she realized they were wrestling. No, not wrestling. Ajax was on top of the other man, his huge hands around his throat. There was a lot of shouting, and it took three men to drag Ajax off the man.

"He tripped me!" Ajax roared. Helen could hear his words despite the distance, so loud was his rage. "I'd have won if not for that Kretan son of a whore!"

Odysseus had come up beside him now, though, and as he spoke to him the huge man seemed to calm a little.

Helen thought it a shame that Antilochos's victory had been overshadowed by Ajax's temper, but he was given his prize nonetheless—a slave woman skilled in weaving, whom she recognized from the women's room—and with that the day's contests were over.

CHAPTER 9

HELEN

It was late in the evening. Today's feast was over and the suitors had gone back to their tents, allowing a stillness to descend over the palace. Helen had been summoned to her parents' chambers, where she was now sitting with her father, mother, and brothers. This was the closest Helen had been to her mother in some time, occupying the seat beside her and breathing in her warm scent. It was nice, all being together like this, but Helen knew they had been gathered for a reason.

"The tournament has been going on for several weeks now, as you are all well aware." Father was looking around at them all, his lined face exaggerated in the lamplight. "Everyone who was due to arrive is here, and all have had ample opportunity to prove themselves. Therefore, I believe the time has come to choose a victor."

A thrill went through Helen; she had been waiting for this moment. Her father rested his chin on his steepled fingers, apparently waiting for one of them to speak. When no one did, he said, "Kastor, tell me who you would choose."

"Well, Father," Kastor began, "I must speak on behalf of Diomedes." *Diomedes*, thought Helen. Yes, she remembered him from the contests. Young, strong, and quite handsome. "He is already a proven warrior, despite his youth," her brother continued, "and his gifts are generous. Pollux and I have hunted with him several times, and we have become good friends. He is as fine a man as any other here and would bring you glory as a son-in-law, I know it."

Before her father could respond, Pollux interjected with his contribution.

"Or if not Diomedes, Father, then surely Ajax of Salamis would be a fine choice." Helen cringed at the mention of Ajax. *No, not him,* she willed, as if her father might hear her thoughts. "His strength is unmatched," her brother continued. "He outstripped all the rest at discus, and you saw him in the wrestling matches—and not only that, but he is a cunning warrior. If we are to protect Sparta, Ajax would be a great man to have with us. True, he may not have brought as many gifts as some, but he has promised to drive together all the sheep and oxen from the coasts near to his kingdom, from Asine all the way to Megara, and present them as a wedding gift."

"Oh, what a ridiculous boast," her mother cut in. "That man is too proud by far, and hotheaded too. I would not trust him to rule our kingdom, nor indeed to be husband to my daughter."

Helen felt a wave of warmth and gratitude toward her mother. She did not want to marry Ajax, but she wasn't sure she would have been brave enough to say so. Her mother still cared for her, despite her distance; she knew that now. Helen looked toward her, hoping to thank her with her eyes, but her mother did not turn her head.

"Which man has won your favor, then, my queen?" Helen's father asked now.

"There are many fine men here, my husband, who would no doubt be good choices; however, I must speak for Antilochos, son of Nestor, above all. He has proven himself a fine young man—fleet of foot and a master of horses—and has brought great gifts to honor our family. Moreover, his father is known to be a man of superior wisdom and is respected throughout Greece. If son follows father, Antilochos will make a fine match."

Helen suppressed a nod of her head. She had to admit that the thought of handsome Antilochos as her husband was an agreeable one.

"Your case is well argued," said her father, his brow creased in contemplation. "But we must not forget that our esteemed friend Agamemnon is here. He is our kin by marriage and our close military ally. It would perhaps be unwise for us to slight his honor by favoring another man over his brother. And he has brought the richest gifts, gold and bronze and horses. No man here disputes that, no man . . ."

Her father looked troubled, torn. It seemed he was trying to convince himself as much as anyone else. Then after a moment he turned his face to Helen and looked at her, properly looked at her, for the first time since they had all sat down.

"Helen, my child, what do you think? Which man would you choose?"

Helen was surprised to be asked. She had assumed she would sit here and listen until a decision was made—was pleased even to be allowed that much. But her own say? She was unprepared for it, and had to think for a moment. She had found many of the suitors handsome and some had certainly impressed in the contests . . . but she hadn't had opportunity to actually speak to any of them. She had dreamed she would have a husband who loved her, and whom she loved in return, like in the stories Nestra used to tell her . . . But she couldn't know about any of that. What difference did it make, whomever she chose? Diomedes or Antilochos or Agamemnon's brother, whom she had never even seen . . . But then she realized. There *was* a difference.

"Father, if I married Agamemnon's brother, that would make me Nestra's sister by marriage. We'd be sisters twice over, wouldn't we?"

"Yes, I suppose you would," replied her father. "But I don't see—"

"And do you think, if we were sisters-in-law, that we might be able to see each other? I mean, when our husbands visited each other, as brothers are sure to do?" Helen was quite excited now, and pleased with herself for seeing the opportunity.

"I'm not sure about that, Helen," said her father hesitantly. "Wives don't often—"

"But it would be more likely than if we weren't sisters-in-law, wouldn't it, Father?"

"I suppose it would, yes, but—"

"Well, in that case I would choose Agamemnon's brother," she said conclusively, with a satisfied smile. The possibility of seeing Nestra again was like a rope she could cling to.

Her father opened his mouth to say something more, but at that moment there was a polite knock on the wooden door of the chamber. The palace steward Nikodemos entered, his head bowed.

"My lord," he began, his voice nervous, "Lord Odysseus, son of Laertes, wishes to speak with you. I told him that you were busy and that it was improper to disturb you in your private chambers—"

"Quite right," said her father curtly. "Send him away, Nikodemos. I will speak with him tomorrow."

"I tried, my lord. But he insisted that it was urgent. He's just outside. He says he is sure you will want to hear what he has to say."

Her father paused, apparently thinking, then sighed. "Very well," he said impatiently. "Send him in when I call."

As Nikodemos bowed and backed out of the chamber, Helen's father turned to her.

"It is not proper for him to see you, Helen. The other suitors will say he has had unfair privilege." He stood up and scanned the room, and having spotted what he was looking for, fetched a large, plain piece of cloth that was hanging over the back of a chair. "Use this as a shawl and cover yourself," he said, passing it to her. "Draw it across your face and keep your head bowed and your mouth silent. Kneel on the floor beside your mother and he will take you for her handmaid."

Helen did as she was asked, though she wasn't very pleased about having to kneel. Once she was covered and settled, her father called to Nikodemos, and Odysseus entered the chamber.

"Lord Tyndareos," he said with a reverent bow. "My lady, honored princes," he continued, nodding to each in turn. His attention skimmed straight over Helen; she was glad her father's idea had worked. "I have come because I know that you must by now have reached the point where you are ready to choose a husband for the princess Helen, and I would like to offer some counsel."

"And what makes you think I need your help in choosing a suitor?" said her father tersely. "I suppose you've come with some clever argument for why I should choose you, despite your failure to bring a single gift, is that it? Yes, I know of your silver tongue, Lord Odysseus, but I'm afraid it will not avail you here."

Helen was worried Lord Odysseus would be affronted, but he simply smiled.

"I have not come to tell you whom you should choose, for I know that decision is already made," said Odysseus. Her father opened his mouth to reply but didn't get the chance, for Odysseus continued, "You will choose Agamemnon's brother, Menelaos. It is the only sensible option in your position. You cannot afford to offend Agamemnon, and another bond between your two families will make you both stronger. Why share wealth and influence with an outsider when you could consolidate it within your joint houses?"

Helen saw that her father had closed his mouth now and was listening to Odysseus, the annoyance on his brow gone.

"It is true that I have brought no courting gifts, and I apologize if this offended you," Odysseus continued, "but I suspected that Menelaos might be one of the suitors, and knew I would have little hope of winning your daughter if that were the case. I simply wanted the chance to see the most beautiful woman in the world with my own eyes." Here Odysseus paused, though only for a heartbeat, and his eyes slid to

Helen, meeting hers through the gap in her shawl. Startled, she quickly looked at the floor, but it was pointless. He knew it was her. He had known all along. She blushed beneath the veil. *The most beautiful woman in the world*, he had called her.

Above her, his voice continued. "Once I heard that Agamemnon was here on his brother's behalf I knew I was right not to have made my suit for Helen in earnest. Instead, I hope I may win another bride with some advice."

"Go on, then," said her father, his voice edged with impatience. "I'll hear what counsel you came to give."

"You are in a difficult position, Lord Tyndareos," Odysseus began. "You know it as well as I. You must choose Menelaos, but you don't want to offend the other suitors, nor make them feel as if the whole tournament were a sham. You must know it will seem that way, when you choose Agamemnon's brother as victor. They will claim it was all arranged, that the two of you conspired to rob them, to make fools of them."

"But it's not true," said her father wearily. "I didn't know that he would—"

"Nonetheless, that is how it will seem," said Odysseus gravely. "Not only will they be angry with you and with Sparta, but there is a danger that one of them may take matters into his own hands, and simply take by force the prize he has been denied. Such is the risk when men's desire has been so skillfully enflamed, and their pride so sorely wounded." Helen could not resist turning her head, looking for reassurance from her father and her mother. Would they really try to steal her? The thought of that brute Ajax carrying her off made her shudder.

"I have seen the danger for myself, but what is there to be done?" asked her father, his voice strained. "I can see no way—"

"There is a way, Lord Tyndareos. A way to guard against any violence or theft," Odysseus replied. Helen saw a slight smile creep into the corners of his mouth as he finally revealed his cunning. "You must make the suitors swear an oath. Before you announce the victor, make them swear to almighty Zeus, scourge of oath-breakers, that they will accept your decision with goodwill, and do no violence against you, nor Helen, nor the victorious suitor. Moreover, make them swear that if any man does take your daughter by force, that they will aid her true husband in retrieving her. They will swear any oath you ask of them, if it is a requirement for being considered as a suitor. But you must strike while the bronze is hot, while the suitors are still so enraptured by the idea of Helen that they have fooled themselves into thinking they have a chance. Do it tomorrow, at dawn. Then hold one final day of contests, to maintain the illusion that the decision has not yet been made, and by dusk you will be free to announce Menelaos as the victor."

His plan laid out, Odysseus smiled with satisfaction. As an afterthought he added, "I would also suggest that you return all the suitors' gifts back to them, once you have made the announcement—to ease the bitterness of defeat. All but Agamemnon's, of course. You'll be deprived of a small fortune, yes, and no doubt the princess will be sad to see the fine clothes and jewelry go"—his eyes flicked to Helen's and away again—"but a war would be dearer by far."

His piece said, Odysseus fell silent. Her father, too, was silent for a while. Helen watched as the lines of his face deepened, his sharp eyes distant as he sat in thought. At length he said, "You are a clever man, Odysseus, son of Laertes, and I judge your counsel to be sound. I will do as you say, for I can find no better solution myself. Let us hope that it goes as smoothly as you predict." He sighed deeply, as if expelling the cares of several weeks with one breath. "I thank you for your advice, but I do not think it was given out of charity. You mentioned before that you hoped to win a bride, but you must know that I have no more daughters."

"Indeed I do know. It was rather your niece that I had in mind. Your brother Ikarios has a daughter who will soon be of age to marry, does he not? She may not come with a kingdom, but I already have one of those. All I require is a dutiful wife and sons to fill my halls."

"Yes, Penelope. A sweet girl," said her father. Helen remembered her cousin from when they had played together as children. Penelope had lived in the palace for a time, but she hadn't seen her for several years. "I will speak with my brother on the matter, as thanks for your service tonight."

"That is all I ask," said Odysseus, with a humble bow. "And now I think I will return to my tent. Good night to you all."

Once Odysseus had left Helen got up from the floor, her knees sore from the hard stone. As she was removing the shawl she heard her mother's voice, quiet but angry. "If you were going to choose Menelaos all along, why did you bother gathering us all here and asking our opinions? Just another sham, to make us feel like we had a say? Is that what it was?"

"No, it wasn't like that, Leda," sighed her father. He sounded tired. "I still thought we might have a choice . . . I wanted to at least talk about it with you. All of you," he said, looking around at each of them. "But Odysseus is right. We must choose Menelaos. And gods willing, his plan will succeed and all will come out well." He turned to Helen. "This is what you wanted anyway, isn't it, my child?" he said with a kind but halfhearted smile. "You said you wanted to be Nestra's sister-in-law, and you will be. I know Menelaos. He is a good man and a fine warrior. He will make you happy, I'm sure."

Helen returned her father's smile, though inside she was a little afraid. It had been all right when they were talking about it before, exciting even, thinking who her husband might be. But now that it was decided it felt so much more real, so much closer. Soon she would be marrying Menelaos, a man she had never seen, let alone met, and whom she knew scarce little about. She felt like an autumn leaf, plucked from its tree by the snatching wind and dropped into the racing river below. All she could do now was to stay afloat as that ceaseless current bore her toward her future.

The next morning, in the mist of the dawn, the suitors were gathered and the oath sworn by all. Odysseus had been right; none objected. And he himself swore along with the rest. Libations were poured, and a spotless white stallion sacrificed. A ram would have done, but Father wanted to make clear the gravity of the vow. Helen knew the horse from the royal stables. It was a magnificent beast, towering over the men as it was led, calm and unsuspecting, to the altar. Helen had to look away as her father slit its throat.

There were contests as Odysseus had suggested, with a chariot race to end the day. And then, when the sun hung low in the sky, her father announced Menelaos, son of Atreus, prince of Mycenae, as the man he had chosen to wed his daughter. And so it was done. Without protest or violence, Helen had finally been won.

CHAPTER 10

HELEN

enelaos arrived in Sparta at dusk, a month after their betrothal had been decided. A great feast was prepared so that Sparta's new heir could meet and drink with Helen's father and brothers, and with the other noblemen of Lakonia. Helen, too, was present at the feast as custom demanded, though she felt more like an elaborate decoration than a guest. Father had insisted she be covered with a veil so thick that she could not see through it—not even the light of the hearth fire. It was such a strange and frustrating experience to hear the feast going on about her, to know that her husband-to-be was so close by, and yet to be unable to see anything. Her father only allowed the veil to be lifted so that Alkippe could give Helen sips of wine and morsels of food, and even then it was not lifted high enough nor long enough for her to get a view of the man to whom she would soon be bound. Though she usually enjoyed the food and music and frivolity of such occasions, it was a relief when after an hour or so she was led back to her chamber, where she could throw off the hateful veil and breathe the unstifled air.

The next day brought a long afternoon of anticipation as she awaited the wedding procession that would take her from her father's palace to her new home a little farther along the river, which had been

built to house her and her new husband until such time as he replaced
her father as King of Sparta. When her handmaids finally came to
prepare her in the early evening, Helen was pleased to see the much
finer veil in Alkippe's hands, like a glimmering net of gold. Now at last
she would be able to look upon her betrothed, she thought with satisfaction. And yet once she was dressed, with the shining veil laid like
filigree over the copper of her hair, and led through the palace to join
the procession outside, her heart sank when she learned that Menelaos
had already taken up his position at the head. She asked her mother
which horse was his, and tried to make out his features in the evening
light, but almost as soon as her eyes had found him her father was taking her hand to lead her to the bridal chariot. She mounted it alone,
the gleaming centerpiece of the whole procession, and though she felt
the eyes of Sparta upon her, as the chariot began to move, she looked
ahead through the crowd and the darkness and the smoke to that
golden helmet glinting in the torchlight.

When they arrived, Helen was told to wait in the marriage chamber. She wasn't alone, of course. Her two handmaids and her old nurse,
Thekla, had accompanied her so that they could perform their duties.
They undressed her from the bridal outfit she had worn on the short
journey from the Old Palace to this new building. The earthy smell of
ocher hung in the still air of the chamber from walls freshly painted
only days before.

The women proceeded to bathe Helen, scrubbing at every inch of
her skin with pieces of coarse cloth until it felt raw and tingling. When
she made a noise of complaint her nurse said, "Hush, we need to wash
the child from you."

Once she was dry they stood her up and set to work on their next
task: massaging scented oil into her skin. It made her smell of flowers
and sage, and gave her white skin a pearly sheen. Finally the women
brought over a small bowl filled with strongly scented rose water. Helen
couldn't see that she needed more perfuming; she already smelled

sweeter than she ever had in her life. But as Thekla dipped a single finger into the fragrant water, she was relieved to see that she was not about to be dowsed. Instead, with delicacy and precision, the nurse dabbed the scent onto the pale pink of Helen's nipples. Helen was a little taken aback, but she did not let it show. She was a woman now, and this was obviously how women were prepared. And when Thekla asked her to lie back on the bed, so that she could put some of the rose water between her legs, Helen obeyed without protest. When she arose, though, there was a sense that something had changed, that parts of her body had been elevated to a level of importance they had never held before.

Her shining skin exposed to the evening air, Helen began to shiver, and was grateful when the women helped her back into the bridal dress. It was simple in style but richly dyed with saffron, with a smell that contributed to the intoxicating cloud of scents that already hung about her. They replaced the fine veil too, but left her hair unbraided, her wrists, throat, and ears unadorned. The time for display had passed; now it was down to her to impress her husband.

Adraste left the room now, no doubt to relay that the preparations had been completed.

Thekla spoke softly in Helen's ear. "Now we are done, your husband will come to you. He will no doubt lie with you as is proper for a husband to lie with his wife. Do not be afraid. I shall be just outside the door. It may hurt when he puts it in you, but you must let him do what he will. Indeed, what he must. It will go better for you if you receive him willingly. Try to please him, Helen. Gods willing, you shall have a blessed life together."

Helen did not understand all that the nurse had said to her, but she gave a stiff nod nonetheless, and returned the woman's kind smile. Thekla shuffled to the corner of the room to wait with Alkippe so that Helen was left standing alone in front of the bed, her eyes fixed on the door. Now that she was here, in her bridal chamber, she realized that she didn't really know what to expect. All her thoughts had been spent picturing what her husband would look like, what she would wear for the procession, what their bridal gifts would be. This part of the wedding had remained a vague blank in her imagination, and it was no clearer now. She wished that she had asked more questions when she had had the chance.

Minutes passed, with no sounds beyond the door, no sound in the room except Helen's shallow breathing and Thekla's restless shuffling. Helen perched herself on the edge of the bed and waited.

A noise. Footsteps in the corridor. Voices. Male voices. Helen quickly rose to her feet and stood as straight as she could, arms by her sides, chin slightly raised. She felt frozen solid as she waited for the door to open. It was only as she heard the bar being lifted that she realized she had been locked in.

The door opened, and in stepped two men. One was fair-haired and of a good height, the other dark and slightly shorter. Helen knew the fair-haired one as her husband from the glimpses she had caught during the procession. He was wearing a fine red tunic and sturdy boots, but had removed the gleaming armor he had been wearing earlier. She couldn't help but be a little disappointed, now that she saw him up close. Even through the haze of the veil she could see that he had a large scar over his right eyebrow, which marred his face with its dark streak. And there was a crookedness to his nose, as if it had been broken more than once. His hair was light in color and not unattractive, but his beard was more mottled and had a dirty look about it. Some of the men at the tournament had been much more handsome.

Helen tried not to be disheartened, though. She had been promised a warrior and a warrior was what she had gotten. Though he was a little rough-looking, he seemed strong and healthy. Her mother had always said that was what was most important, in husbands and sons.

Helen realized she had been holding her breath, and carefully let it go. Menelaos had given her a quick glance when he came in, but was

now muttering something to the dark-haired man. The pair seemed to
agree on something, then faced the room again. Menelaos gave a curt
nod to Thekla and Alkippe, and they scuttled out, the nurse giving
Helen one last look of reassurance before she left.

The dark-haired man closed the door behind them, but stayed in
the room.

"This is Deipyros, my companion," said Menelaos, waving a hand
toward the dark-haired man. His voice was low and gruff. Helen was
expecting him to carry on and explain why the other man was there,
but he didn't.

"I am Menelaos, son of Atreus, your bridegroom. I am come to
conclude the marriage rites."

He spoke as if addressing an audience, though she stood alone. He
was older than Helen by ten years or more, and had a firm, steady bearing, and yet she thought she sensed an uncertainty in his stride as he
crossed the room to stand in front of her.

With no more words he raised his hands and removed the veil from
Helen's head. Their eyes only met for a fleeting moment, however, before he began to slide the saffron dress from her shoulders. His callused fingers felt rough against her skin. She was used to being touched
and handled, dressed, undressed, and bathed by her serving women,
but this was entirely different. These were the hands of a man, and a
strange man at that. She had to stop herself from recoiling.

As the dress fell to the floor Helen felt more exposed than she ever
had in her life. Her heart racing, she maintained her steady gaze, looking straight ahead over Menelaos's shoulder. She could feel his eyes on
her, drinking in the sight of her naked body.

He did not touch her again, however. Rather he took several steps
backward, and continued to regard her. She watched his eyes as they
flicked from her breasts to her hips to her ankles, and came back to rest
on the hair-covered patch beneath her belly.

"Do you bleed?" he asked.

Helen was startled by the sudden question. She realized he meant her monthly blood, so she gave a twitching nod.

Then he turned to his companion. "Her breasts are still buds. Her hips are too narrow. Do you agree, Deipyros?"

The dark-haired man, who was also surveying her from the corner, gave a nod. She felt like a heifer being examined for sacrifice. Her skin was getting pimpled without her dress to keep off the evening chill. She wanted to wrap herself in her arms and turn away from both of them. But she was Helen of Sparta, and a little girl no longer. She fixed her eyes on the wall once again and pursed her lips to stop them from quivering.

"A child too soon would be risky," said the dark-haired man, his eyes still lingering around her hips. "She is still young. I suggest that you wait, but it is your choice, of course."

"You counsel well, Deipyros. I will wait." She couldn't tell whether her husband's face showed disappointment or relief. "But the marriage must still be completed." Menelaos looked at his companion. Deipyros nodded and left the room, closing the door behind him.

Helen knew she had failed in some way. She pressed her lips harder together and blinked to hold back the tears that stung her eyes. Despite all the oils and perfumes, she was not good enough. Not woman enough. But at least he had not left altogether. He was still willing to take her as his wife. She and Nestra would still be doubly bonded, as sisters twice over. She would still be Queen of Sparta, one day.

Menelaos crossed the room once more. Again, he seemed uncertain. Or maybe she was imagining it. Maybe she just didn't want to feel like the only one who didn't know what was going on.

Her husband stopped in front of her. He too smelled of scented oil. She wondered if he had rose water on his nipples, or anywhere else . . . The thought made her blush.

He lifted her chin now so that she had no choice but to look into his eyes. They were dark, and difficult to read. She tried to avoid staring at the scar.

Gently, he took a lock of her hair in his fingers. "Your hair is very . . . fine," he murmured.

She smiled. A genuine smile. Something about her had pleased him, at least.

"Thank you, my lord."

"Yes. I am your lord now, as you are my lady, and so we shall be for as long as we live." He allowed her the smallest smile. Then he hesitated, before leaning forward and kissing her softly on the lips. His mustache tickled her nose and his breath smelled of wine. It wasn't unpleasant, yet she had expected to feel . . . more. She realized he was watching her expression and tried to smile but her face felt stiff. When he spoke again his voice had lost some of its softness.

"Now, we must complete the marriage, if you are to be my true woman-wife." He paused. "That is what you want, isn't it?"

She gave a small nod.

"Then you must lie back on the bed and open your legs."

Her stomach dropped. She remembered her utter nakedness, forgotten momentarily as he touched her hair and kissed her lips. Yet she nodded obediently and did as he had asked.

Menelaos seemed to hesitate. Then, to her surprise, he moved away from her and walked over to the chest beside the bed. He picked up the small pot of olive oil that sat on top of it and poured a generous amount into the palm of his hand. Then he lifted his tunic.

Helen thought she should look away, but her head would not turn. His member was stiff and thick and, as she watched, Menelaos ran his oiled hand over it several times so that it glistened.

Helen had seen men naked before, of course, when they wrestled in the palaestra or ran their races down by the river. She had seen their members, but never like this. And never this close. It frightened her.

The nervous feeling that had been sitting in her stomach all evening flared stronger now. She didn't want Menelaos to come any closer. She wanted to hide under the covers, to call for her nurse. A small whimper escaped her throat.

He was back beside the bed, in front of her, now leaning over her. Her legs were still wide open, despite her overwhelming desire to close them. She felt so exposed. She closed her eyes, as if she could hide behind her eyelids. Then something fleshy was touching the place between her legs. A finger, she thought. No, larger than a finger. And then it was entering her. She gasped at the sudden intrusion. It felt alien, unwelcome. And thick, too thick, burrowing into her body. She wanted it to stop. He was hurting her. She opened her eyes, reached out her small hand toward his chest, trying to push him away. And then it was gone. He slowly straightened up and moved back from her, avoiding her eyes. She snapped her legs shut and rolled onto her side, drawing her knees toward her chest and blinking back tears.

"I'm sorry if I hurt you, my lady," said Menelaos, his voice gruff, but with something that might have been genuine concern running through it. "It is done now. You are a maiden no more, but a woman-wife, in name and in body."

She raised her head a little. "I am?"

But he had already turned away. He stood beside the chest again, wiping the oil from himself with a cloth. His back to her, she allowed herself to uncurl a little.

"I shall not enter you again," he said over his shoulder. "Not until you are fully grown and ready to bear children." His voice sounded strange, but she could not see his expression. Though she was relieved, she once again felt as though she had failed somehow.

When he finally turned to face her he did not smile, but he did not look angry either. He opened his mouth as if to say something more, but closed it again before any words came out. Instead he sat down heavily on the edge of the bed, and stooped to untie his boots.

Beyond his bowed head, over on the chest, Helen saw the cloth he had cleaned himself with. And there on the pale linen, illuminated in the lamplight, she saw the dark streak of blood. *Her blood.* The sight of it made her feel ill. It made her think of her first "woman's blood," as Thekla had called it. This was not the first, nor would it be the last of her blood taken in payment for womanhood.

Suddenly, fear rose again in her chest. The sting of pain that had shocked it back before became something deeper, a hollow haunting that spread through her body. The feeling that she had lost something, that she could never get it back.

Menelaos had stood up again now and was removing the rest of his clothes. She turned her eyes away and spotted the saffron dress, abandoned on the floor. She got up from the bed as lightly as she could, trying not to look desperate as she threw it back over her head, eager to cover her nakedness. As she stood in the middle of the chamber, hugging herself with shaking arms, she realized that Menelaos had gotten under the bedcovers. His face was turned away from her, his breathing quiet.

She hesitated. She should return to the bed, she knew. And yet something held her rooted to the floor. That hollow fear, thumping in her chest.

She could leave. She could go out into the corridor and cling to Thekla's knees, beg her to take her back to the Old Palace, her old room, her and Nestra's, the room of her childhood. She didn't want to sleep here with this strange man.

She listened for any noise beyond the room. Nothing. Perhaps Thekla had gone. Perhaps the dark-haired man was out there. Perhaps she had been locked in again. She felt utterly alone.

As she stood there the restraints she had put upon herself began to crumble. Tears welled in her eyes and spilled down her cheeks. Her voice broke out from her throat in a whine.

There was a sound from the bed. Helen turned to see Menelaos sit up and look at her. He opened his mouth, but seemed unsure what to say, and closed it. When he opened it again, he said, "Put out the lamps before you come to bed," and lay back down.

Helen did as he commanded, still sniffling. When the room was dark she felt her way over to the bed and slid herself in, taking up as little space as she could so as not to risk brushing Menelaos. She lay on her back, silent tears running into her ears. As her husband's breathing slowed and turned to snores, she wondered why she had been so desperate to become a woman. How stupid she had been. Womanhood was strange and painful and humiliating. And there was no going back.

PART II

CHAPTER 11

HELEN

TWO YEARS LATER

All was silent as Helen entered the Hearth Hall, following behind her husband. It was not an empty silence, but live and bristling, full with stopped chatter and stifled coughs. All eyes were on Menelaos as he took his measured strides across the hall, but Helen also noticed them flicking to her, her husband's lesser shadow. No, they weren't looking at *her*. It was her swollen belly that drew their eyes.

Menelaos had reached the hearth and stopped before it. Helen took her place beside him, feeling the heat of the flames on her face as she drew close to them. She wondered if the baby could feel it too. Instinctively her hand moved to her belly, a shield between the fire and the life inside her.

Her husband was handed a large golden chalice, filled with wine. Raising the cup high, for all to see, Menelaos poured its contents into the flames, making them hiss and flicker. That was a good sign; the gods were pleased.

The libation offered, Helen's husband turned his back on the flames and addressed the hall in a loud voice. "The gods accept me as your new king, and demand that you do the same."

Today was the day. Menelaos was finally gaining the kingdom he had been promised more than two years ago when he had won his bride. And Helen was finally becoming a queen. Ever since she had become the heiress, the idea of it had thrilled her. *Helen, Queen of Sparta*, she would announce in her head. She liked the sound of it. But now that the time was here she was a little frightened. It was a big responsibility being the wife of a king, and she already felt the weight of it upon her. The only reason this was even happening was because of her, because of the child she carried. Once the pregnancy had been confirmed, her father had agreed that he would step aside and hand his kingdom on to his successor. It was the reason she had been given such a prominent role in the ceremony, too, placed beside her husband. They needed to put her on show as a proof of fertility, a promise of legacy. She knew that was all she was, really, as she stood here in front of the hearth, silent and actionless. But she felt the pressure of it nonetheless. She was only just seventeen and yet a whole kingdom had put its hopes in her, was dependent on her for its very security. She, Helen, was the vessel of its future.

Her father stepped forward now, taking the crown from his own head. He held it out toward Menelaos, who took it respectfully from his hands. It was a band of finely wrought gold, with long, golden points fixed on top, like rays of sunlight. As her husband settled it onto his own head, his image of royal splendor was complete. He wore an exquisite purple mantle, threaded with gold at the hems and down the front. More gold ringed his neck and hung from his ears and now, with the addition of the crown, it burst from the top of his head too. He shone like the fire in the hearth behind him. Even Helen, accustomed as she was to such finery, had to admit he looked magnificent. She felt a swell of pride as the whole hall looked upon her husband, the king, with reverent admiration.

With the coronation complete, the final preparations for the feast could be carried out. A great number of sheep and goats were sacrificed, as well as two muscular bullocks. The sight and smell of the blood made Helen nauseous, and she didn't like watching as the life was stripped from them one after another. But she knew it would please the gods, as well as the many people who had gathered to see their new king, and both were of great importance today.

Once the gods' share of fat and bones had been burned as an offering, the meat was roasted, and the feast begun.

Helen didn't really feel like eating at the feast. She kept getting pains in her belly and her back was aching. It was nothing to worry about, she knew. Likely just the baby kicking as it often did. But it was uncomfortable all the same, and was spoiling her appetite. She knew the feast was important, and it was nice to be celebrated, even if it was only in the reflected glow from her husband, but really all she wanted right now was to go and lie down in the cool quiet of her chamber.

Helen's mother sat on her right. She, too, was barely eating, but then she never did seem to have much of an appetite. Helen had watched her mother grow thinner and thinner over the past years, since Nestra had left. It was like she was slowly disappearing, shrinking to nothing. Her famous beauty had withered, lost in the hollows of her gray cheeks and the dark patches beneath her lusterless eyes. Helen wished there were something she could do to bring some brightness back to her. But maybe she *had* helped her, in a way, by becoming queen. Helen knew her mother found it hard, going out in front of people, being the focus of attention, letting people see what she had become, but now her mother would be free from public duties. Now she could live out her days in peace and privacy. And perhaps a grandchild would be a new source of joy for her. Helen hoped so, cradling her belly as she thought of hearing her mother laugh again.

"Is something wrong, Helen? Is it the baby?" asked her mother beside her, looking concerned as Helen stroked her belly.

"No, no, everything's fine," she said with a smile. "I was just thinking about what it will be like when the baby is here."

Her mother gave a small nod, and her look of worry ebbed.

"I am proud of you," said her mother quietly. "You know that, don't you?" She glanced into Helen's eyes and down again.

Helen's heart fluttered. "Yes, Mother," was what she said, but she hadn't known, not until that moment. How could she know, when her mother barely spoke to her? When she barely ever saw her? Tentatively, she reached out to her mother's bony hand and gave it a gentle squeeze. She wasn't sure if it was the right thing to do, but she didn't want to lose the moment. She wanted her to know how much her words meant to her, how much *she* meant to her.

Her mother gave a ghost of a smile and patted Helen's hand before drawing hers away.

"I have been praying to Eileithyia that the birth goes well," she said, her face serious again. "There is always a danger with these things, you know."

"I know," Helen replied. "I'm not worried, though," she said, and she wasn't lying. Nestra had already given birth to two children with no problems. Why should hers be any different? There was no sense in worrying about what *might* happen, not until it did. That was what she figured, anyway.

To her left sat Menelaos, in all his splendid regalia. She turned to him now, trying to catch his eye. She was feeling happy and proud, her mood buoyed by her mother's words, and she wanted to share it with her husband somehow. A smile between them would be enough, but he didn't look her way. She began to reach toward his hand with her own, but just then one of the local nobles engaged him in conversation, and the opportunity was lost. Barely a word had passed between them all day; she simply wanted an acknowledgment of their shared fortune.

This afternoon they had become King and Queen of Sparta—didn't it warrant some sort of comment, or at least a tacit exchange?

This frustration was not new to Helen. She had not chosen her husband, not really, nor had she loved him when they were bound to each other, but she had entered into her marriage with an open heart. She wanted love and passion, such as she had heard about in all those stories Nestra had told her when they were little. She wanted a connection. She wanted to share every peak and trough of her life with her husband. But sometimes she felt as though she were married to a stone wall. Menelaos talked little and shared even less. Despite their physical intimacy, Helen felt as if she barely knew her husband. In the absence of words, she could only ever guess what he was feeling, and what he felt about her. He was never cruel, had never raised his voice at her, or his hand, and she knew she should be thankful for that, but she hated being so full of doubt all the time, about whether he was content, whether she pleased him, whether she was good enough. She had never dreamed she would have this problem—she had been the most desired bride in Greece! Men had composed poems about her, competed to praise her, to prove their love to win hers. But Menelaos was different. If he loved her, he did not say it. If he thought her beautiful, he kept it to himself.

But Helen had a new hope now, in the child she carried. Menelaos's feelings were not so unreadable where the baby was concerned. He would stroke her belly with touching tenderness, smiling absent-mindedly as he did so. He had made sure Helen was given every comfort while she was pregnant and showed concern at every twinge. Helen knew he would love this baby, whatever he felt about her, and it was her desperate hope that through this child she and Menelaos would grow closer. After all, not only their blood but their hopes and fears, their joys and worries would be forever united in this new life. Yes, this child would be the beginning of their love, the union of their souls. Helen was sure of it.

Having failed to gain her husband's attention, Helen decided she might have some food after all. She reached over toward some lentil broth, not sure she could stomach the meat, but as she did so the pain in her belly returned, stronger than before. She flinched and knocked over a cup of wine near her elbow. She sensed both Menelaos and her mother turning in her direction, but she was too absorbed by the pain to apologize for the wine.

"Is it your time?" came her mother's worried voice from beside her.

Helen looked up at her, suddenly scared. "I don't know. Is it?"

She felt her husband's hand come to rest gently between her shoulder blades. *Finally*, she thought, feeling the connection she had been looking for all evening. But when he spoke it was not to her but to her mother.

"Is it now?" he asked.

The pain was subsiding. She was about to tell them so, when she felt a wetness down below. Worried she was bleeding, Helen stood up, and as she did so more wetness ran down her legs. Terrified, she lifted her skirt. There was a small puddle on the floor between her feet, but it was not blood.

"It's time," said her mother.

CHAPTER 12

KLYTEMNESTRA

Today, like most other days, Klytemnestra was weaving in her chamber. She had been working on a fine, patterned dress for several days now, and before that it had been a mantle, and before that a tunic. This was how she spent her days, here in this room. Once the children were older, no doubt she would be able to do her work in the Hearth Hall, to watch people come and go and sit beside her husband as he carried out his affairs. Perhaps she would even be able to aid and advise him. But for now her place was here, and she didn't begrudge her confinement. The girls made every day different— sometimes joyful, sometimes trying, but never dull. They were like the sun, painting her world in light and shade, bringing definition to an otherwise gray, formless existence.

Iphigenia was now three years old, her blond curls grown to longer ringlets, and her character blossoming day by day. Her speech was coming on, and she would sing little songs to herself as she played with the wooden dolls her father had had made for her. She had a sweet soul, and was so gentle with her younger sister. Nothing made Klytemnestra happier than seeing the two of them play together, though occasionally a pang of sadness would spring up amid the joy, as she was reminded of times spent with her own sister.

Elektra was only one and a half, but already showing a strong spirit. She had Agamemnon's eyes, and when she set her jaw just so, in a look of unmovable defiance, then more than ever was she her father's daughter.

A pull on Klytemnestra's skirt told her that Elektra was at her feet. Settling herself into a seated position, she began to pull on the loom weights dangling around her head.

"Eudora," Klytemnestra called over her shoulder. "Would you come and move Elektra? She'll spoil my work."

Her handmaid did as she was bid and scooped the child up in her arms, taking her back over to the seat where she sat spinning. Elektra made a protest at first, but soon settled down. Eudora had been invaluable to Klytemnestra these past years, not only as a servant, but as a friend. They were raising her children between the two of them and she knew she could rely on her as an ally in all matters. In fact, if it weren't for Eudora, Klytemnestra would feel very alone in the palace, despite it having been her home for over four years. She was an outsider here, even now.

Her feeling of isolation had grown stronger of late. She feared she was losing her husband, the one person who truly tied her to this place. He still slept in their chamber most nights, but recently it seemed that was all he wanted. Before now they had made love almost every night. He had always seemed to want her, no matter how long the day or how late the hour. And Klytemnestra had looked forward to those times. Not at first, perhaps, when the marriage was new and her husband a stranger, and the experience more daunting than exciting. But she had come to find pleasure in it, and an intimacy that had grown deeper with time. There, alone in the darkness together, Klytemnestra almost felt that she and her husband were equals. She would even sit atop him sometimes, controlling his pleasure with the movement of her hips. She liked that feeling, the power of it. It was a feeling she seldom enjoyed in the daytime, as she performed the head-bowed shuffle of the deferent wife, but there in the darkness, away from the world, she could be different. He could be different.

And then it had stopped. He had only taken her once in the last month, and even then there had been none of the usual tenderness, the playfulness, the teasing, the passion. It had been almost dutiful.

Klytemnestra suspected she knew the cause of her husband's disinterest; he was getting his pleasure elsewhere. A concubine. Eudora said she had seen a new girl around the palace. Young and pretty, and a little dazed-looking. She was not a servant; it was Klytemnestra's business to know the comings and goings of slaves. She was the mistress of the household, after all, even if she did not spend much time outside her chamber.

No, this girl was Agamemnon's new plaything, she was sure of it. Why else would her husband suddenly turn from her? She was not yet twenty, still in her prime. She didn't blame the girl; likely she had little say in the matter. Her husband was King of Mycenae—what girl could refuse him? But that didn't stop her from feeling bitter about it. She knew it was the way of men to take other lovers. She had braced herself for it ever since that lonely journey over the mountains, had told herself that if she could harden her heart it would not matter, that she would still be queen and her children still his heirs. But it had proved more difficult than she had imagined. No amount of bracing could stop that blow, or the hurt it left.

As her hands moved across the loom they became angrier with every shunt of the shuttle. Hadn't her father always been faithful to her mother? As far as she knew, he had. Was it so much to ask for her husband to do the same? Or at least to wait until she was old and used up before casting her aside? A bitter smile twisted her tight lips as she imagined the situation reversed, imagined herself leading some handsome young man to her chamber for all the palace to see. Agamemnon would flay her in the street.

She realized she had stopped her weaving, fingers shaking as she held the shuttle. Was it rage or fear that made her tremble? Her marriage was still in its infancy and yet she felt as if it were already crumbling. If she could not keep Agamemnon in her bed, their intimacy would die; she would lose what little influence she had and be subjected to a life of loneliness, impotence, and irrelevance. The thought of that life stretching out before her made her cold with dread.

But it was not here yet. She had to at least *try* to bring her husband back to her, while he still cared about her enough to listen. She should go to him now, she resolved, while that trembling energy still gave her courage.

Leaving the girls with Eudora, Klytemnestra left her chamber and headed for the Hearth Hall, where she guessed Agamemnon would be at this hour. She hoped her husband wouldn't disapprove of her walking unattended—she was only moving within the palace. On the way she wondered whether she ought to have changed, to have put on something more alluring, if she was hoping to win him back. *No*, she thought. Shallow tricks were not necessary. Her husband was not an animal; he would listen to her words. Reason and duty and, she hoped, his affection for her would win him over, not flesh and finery.

She reached the vestibule of the Hearth Hall with her heart racing. Despite all that had happened between them in the last four years, she still feared Agamemnon a little. But she could already see through the open doors of the hall that he was there, and alone. Now was her chance.

He looked toward her as she entered and sent his booming voice across the hall. "Do you have no ladies with you?"

Klytemnestra flinched inwardly. This was a bad start.

"Eudora was busy with the girls," she said, hoping to soften him with the mention of his children. "It was only a short way."

He looked a little annoyed, but didn't say any more. Instead he beckoned her toward him.

"I've had news from my brother," he said when she was a few feet away.

News from Sparta? The prospect filled her with excitement and worry in equal measure.

"Menelaos has been made king," he said. "Your father still lives," he continued, just as she was opening her mouth to ask, "but Tyndareos has abdicated, passing the throne on to his rightful successor."

"Is there any news of Helen?" she asked. They had been told of her pregnancy months ago, and Klytemnestra had been making dedications to both Eileithyia and Artemis ever since.

"Your sister has given birth to a healthy girl," said Agamemnon, almost with disinterest. "I'm beginning to think the daughters of Tyndareos are incapable of bearing sons," he added with a touch of venom.

Klytemnestra bowed her head a little, as if with shame. She knew Agamemnon was disappointed that she had not yet provided him with a male heir. Though he loved his daughters dearly, he was determined that his kingdom should pass to his son. She wanted to ask whether Menelaos had said anything of how Helen was recovering, but she thought it would be wiser to use the opportunity to broach her intended subject.

"Perhaps I might bear a son, if you lay with me more often," she said quietly, and was immediately afraid that she had been too bold.

"Do I not lie with you enough?" he asked, sounding annoyed. "Only last week—"

"It has been three weeks since we lay together," she said, as quietly as before.

"Are you calling me a liar?" he snapped.

"N-no, my lord," she replied, faltering slightly at the sound of his raised voice. "I only meant that you were mistaken."

He was silent for a moment, but she could feel his irritation. She dared not raise her eyes to meet his. She wished she hadn't started this, but she had come too far to turn back now.

"Forgive me, my husband, but I only wish to be your true wife," she said. Her next words spilled from her mouth before she could properly plan what she was going to say. "And I have heard that you have taken a concubine and I feel that she is coming between us and the closeness we once shared, and causing you to neglect me as your wife. I humbly ask you to—"

"You will ask me to do nothing," growled her husband. Klytemnestra took an involuntary step backward, as if physically forced back by his anger. "It is none of your business with whom I do or do not lie," he continued. "I have every right to take a concubine—several, if I wish it! You should be grateful that I visit your bed at all."

Klytemnestra was standing dead still, eyes on the ground, trying to stop herself from shaking. This had been a mistake, she knew that now. Now her husband hated her, which was surely worse than neglect. Tears began to drop from her eyes onto the paved floor of the hall.

Perhaps Agamemnon saw them, or perhaps his anger had simply cooled, but when he spoke again his tone had lost some of its edge.

"You are a good wife, Klytemnestra. I appreciate the children you have given me and I respect you as my queen, but you have forgotten your place. Do not speak to me of this again."

And with that her husband got up from his throne and left the hall. Perhaps he was going hunting, or perhaps he was going to plow his whore. Klytemnestra didn't want to think about it.

CHAPTER 13

HELEN

Helen opened her eyes. She thought she must be awake, but didn't quite feel as if she were. It felt like she was coming out of a thick fog, but it still hung around her, weighing her down, filling her lungs, clouding her vision, her thoughts, her whole head. She lay still and waited. Slowly, slowly the fog began to lift, and as she lay there she realized she was staring up at some kind of pattern. Blue and yellow lines folding in and out of one another. A ceiling, she realized. *Her* ceiling. She was in her own chamber.

She was aware of her body now. Her throat was sore, her head ached, and her skin was stuck to the covers with sweat. She was sure this was not a dream—it felt too real. But then reality had been a confusing notion of late. She felt as if she had been falling from one dream into another for . . . well, she had no idea how long. It could have been hours, it could have been years. She couldn't remember the last time she had been properly awake.

Yes, she could. She remembered blood and pain. So much pain, for so long. And the blood, more than she had seen in her life. She had not dreamed that; it was there in her mind, there before her eyes when she closed them. A visceral memory.

She remembered thinking she was going to die, right here in this bed. She remembered wishing for it, giving herself up to the gods, feeling herself drift away . . . And yet here she was. Alive, as far as she could tell. If this was Elysion it would be a great disappointment, she thought. And then, despite her utter exhaustion, and the trauma of remembered pain, and perhaps because of the absurd surprise of finding herself to be yet living, Helen laughed.

It came out as a dry wheeze, and turned into a cough. Helen saw movement to her left, and then Alkippe's face appeared above her. Helen thought it was the sweetest face she had ever seen, and smiled weakly.

"Mistress Helen! You're awake!"

Helen tried to reply, but her throat was too dry. Alkippe's face disappeared and when she returned she held a cup of water to Helen's lips. Helen raised her head slightly and gulped the water as if it were nectar, letting what she couldn't swallow run down her neck in cool rivulets.

"Watch you don't choke now, mistress," came Alkippe's timid voice. "You must be thirsty, though, lying here so long. Your mother has been helping you all she could, giving you water when you'd take it, and honey too. But the fever was so bad, we were worried it would claim you."

The cup was empty now and Helen laid her head back down, feeling wearied by this small exertion. She sighed and was silent for a moment, closing her eyes to collect herself. When she felt able, she shifted herself into a seated position.

"What happened, Alkippe? How long have I been here? It all feels so muddy in my head."

"You've been lying here nearly a week now, mistress," replied the handmaid. "It was a bad one. The birth, I mean. I've seen babies born before, mistress—helped my mother when she had my brothers—but yours didn't go how it was supposed to. It was taking too long, hours and hours it went on. Seemed like the baby was never going to come."

"Yes, I remember," said Helen slowly, though what she mostly remembered was the pain. Pain never-ending, so it had seemed. And vague recollections of people hurrying about around her, and the looks on their faces. Fear. Concern. Pity.

"The baby didn't make it," said Helen suddenly, as the realization hit her. It wasn't in the room. She couldn't see it or hear it. It had all been for naught, then. Her eyes stung with tears as that awful thought sank in.

"No, no, mistress! The child lives! Don't cry," said Alkippe, placing a reassuring hand on Helen's forearm. Helen almost flinched at her touch, and it took her a second to realize why. She had been expecting more pain.

"It lives?" Helen asked, struggling to adjust to this new reality.

"Yes, mistress. A little girl, and quite healthy," said Alkippe smiling. "It is a miracle from the gods, for her to have survived such a birth. We must make thank-offerings to Eileithyia."

"Yes, a miracle," Helen repeated vaguely. She did not think she owed anything to Eileithyia, though. She felt as if her body had been torn in two, as if her soul had gone down to Hades and back. And where had Eileithyia been then? Where had any of the gods been, when she was begging for an end to the pain and the blood? She had a daughter, yes, and she knew she should be thankful, but must the price have been so great? Must the gods demand so much of her, and then expect her thanks for the privilege?

"Mistress? Are you all right?" came Alkippe's voice, bringing Helen back to herself.

"Yes, I'm all right. Just tired," she said. Then a thought struck her: if the child was alive, why was it not here with her, where it ought to be?

"Where is my daughter?" she asked, scanning the room as if she might appear upon further inspection.

"She is with the wet nurse," replied Alkippe. "You were so exhausted after the birth, and then the fever came on . . . We had to find someone to feed her, mistress."

"Oh," said Helen. "Yes, I suppose you did."

"But she'll be right back with you, as soon as you're well enough. A child needs its mother," said the handmaid, smiling reassuringly.

Helen managed to summon a small smile in return, though her cheeks felt as if they were made of lead.

"I am so tired, Alkippe," said Helen. "Might I rest now?"

"Yes, of course, mistress," the handmaid replied. "I should go and let people know that you are awake and well. I'll leave you be, but there's a guard at the door should you need anything."

Helen smiled weakly with gratitude. Her friend understood that what she really wanted was to be alone. To not have to think or talk or remember. She might be awake but as for being well . . . her body felt utterly drained, and her head still felt as if there were a haze hanging around it. And there was pain too, lower down. In truth, Helen couldn't tell if it was real or just an imprint of pain remembered, but it hurt all the same.

Alkippe had barely been gone a minute when there was a noise at the door. Helen's eyes snapped open and she saw her husband enter the chamber.

His eyes met hers, but she quickly looked away. Instinctively she drew the covers up around herself. She did not want to see her husband, nor for him to see her, not now. She felt too vulnerable, too exhausted, too ugly. She knew he could not possibly understand what she had been through. No man could. And in that moment, seeing him suddenly here, she realized that a part of her blamed him for her suffering.

He was beside the bed now, and reached out a hand to touch her shoulder. She flinched.

"I am here, wife. The guard heard you talking and came to tell me. I came as soon as I could. I have been worried."

Helen still wasn't looking at her husband. Instead she blinked back the tears that were suddenly in her eyes. She was touched by his concern, knew he was trying to be there for her, but she just couldn't face him right now. It was too soon.

"Are you well? Has the fever passed?"

Helen made an unintelligible noise in response.

Menelaos hesitated for a moment, perhaps sensing that his presence was not as welcome as he had assumed it would be. Then, in a softer voice, he said, "You did well, Helen. I know it was hard on you, but . . . you did well. That's . . . that's what I came to say."

Helen did look at him now. She saw the uncertainty in his face, and something else too. Was it affection? Or if not that, then at least genuine concern. He seemed to be waiting for something, so she forced her mouth into a weak smile.

A faint look of relief passed across her husband's face, and then suddenly his head inclined and he looked as if he were going to lean down and kiss her. Helen looked quickly away and she saw him falter at the edge of her vision. After a brief pause he continued to lean down, and softly kissed the top of her head.

Then he straightened up and, with no more words, he left the chamber.

As soon as he was gone Helen released her tears, letting them roll full and fast down her cheeks. She was annoyed at herself, and at Menelaos. It had finally come, the connection, the tenderness she had been yearning for, and yet she could not appreciate it, not right now. He had been trying to reach out to her, but all she wanted to do was to shrink into herself. She could not bear to enter into a new intimacy right now, not when she felt so broken, and especially not with the man who had been the cause of her trauma.

She would mend, though. In time she would feel better, stronger. She would enjoy the child she had suffered so much for and open her heart once again to her husband. She just hoped this new tenderness of his was still there when she was ready to receive it.

CHAPTER 14

KLYTEMNESTRA

Klytemnestra was in the Hearth Hall today. Agamemnon was listening to petitions and had asked her to attend. No doubt he wanted to put on a show of familial solidarity, of royal health and prosperity, dressing her up in her finest fabrics and jewelry. As she sat there spinning her purple wool—what else, when she was on display?—she didn't know whether to be resentful that she was being used in such a way, or grateful that Agamemnon still thought her important enough to join him. She felt as if her role in his life were shrinking by the day—she wouldn't have been surprised if he had put his concubine in this chair instead of her.

She had a name, Klytemnestra had learned. Leukippe. She had wanted to hate her—somehow that was easier than hating her husband, easier than blaming him for the slow collapse of their marriage—but now that she had seen her she found she could summon no feeling but pity. She had caught glimpses of the girl once or twice around the palace, before abruptly changing course to avoid her. She was pretty, of course, but more than anything she looked like a scared child. Scared and sad and alone. She must be around the age that Helen would be now . . . Klytemnestra would almost feel protective of her, if it weren't for the circumstances.

The current petition—a farmer hoping to gain a concession on his grain contributions—was over before it had begun. She had learned by now that Agamemnon saw leniency as weakness, and yet as she watched the disappointed man shuffle from the hall, his thin face sour, Klytemnestra couldn't help thinking that a man would be better able to provide for his kingdom if he could first feed himself and his family.

The farmer had barely left their sight when the next petitioner entered, announced by the herald as "Kalchas of Argos, son of Thestor, seer and priest of Paion-Apollo."

The man was young, perhaps in his early twenties, but walked with a dignity beyond his years. A priest's ribbon was tied around his head and he held a staff wrapped with more ribbons. He walked around the square hearth and came to a stop in front of Agamemnon.

"A priest, eh?" grunted her husband, shifting casually in his seat. "I suppose you'll be wanting a tax break like all the rest, hmm? For the honor of the gods or some such reason. Ha!"

The man let Agamemnon's words echo around the hall before speaking.

"I do indeed beseech you on behalf of my temple and of the gods, Lord Agamemnon. But it is not on account of our contributions to the palace—we are quite content with our provisions for the greater good." He paused, straightening slightly and seeming to plant his feet more firmly. He swallowed before continuing. "I come rather to ask for the return of a girl who was in service to the gods and in preparation to become a priestess. I am told that you yourself came across her at a festival in the Argolid plain, and brought her back here to your palace. I ask only that you let her return with me to the temple."

Agamemnon was silent, but Klytemnestra could feel a new energy bristle within him. Eventually, he leaned forward and said, "Why should I? Why should I give her back? I did not take her by force, and she makes no objection to staying here. What claim do you have on her that beats the claim of a king?"

There was no doubt now that they were talking about Agamemnon's concubine. Klytemnestra's attention was rapt, though she pretended to be more concerned with her spinning.

"With all respect, Lord Agamemnon," the young man continued, "the claim is not mine but the gods'. Leukippe has been designated as a servant of Artemis. She has been prepared for the life of a priestess from a young age, and remained chaste and unmarried so that her life could be dedicated to the Virgin Huntress. You deprive the goddess of her servant by keeping the girl here."

Agamemnon barked a laugh. "Well, if that's why you've come, I wouldn't worry. I don't think the Virgin will have much use for her now."

Klytemnestra's cheeks burned, both shame and anger adding their fuel to the fire raging within her. How could her husband speak so brazenly, with his wife seated right beside him? Did her feelings, her *pride*, really mean so little to him? Did she?

The priest, meanwhile, looked no better than she felt. There was anger in his eyes, and perhaps a hint of sadness too. His body had taken on a new tension.

"Do you mean to say you have defiled her? A priestess of Artemis?"

"Watch your words," growled Agamemnon. "I will not be accused of impiety. As you say, she was only in preparation for priestesshood. I have committed no crime against the gods."

The priest was speechless. He opened his mouth, but no intelligible sound emerged. Eventually, in a quiet voice, almost to himself, he said, "I have come too late."

"Indeed you have," boomed Agamemnon. "If her chastity was so important, the temple should have sent someone sooner. She's been here over a month, by Zeus! I'd have had to be a eunuch!" He laughed at his own wit, while Klytemnestra's insides squirmed.

"I was away," the young man muttered. "At Thebes. I only returned yesterday . . . the others . . . cowards." He spat the last word, as if the taste of it in his mouth were bitter.

"Well, if that's all—" began Agamemnon.

"Will you not return her anyway?" the man asked, his tone almost pleading now. "She can still serve the temple . . . she belongs in Argos."

"No, I think not," replied Agamemnon, without consideration. "Her place is here now. You should be happy for her. It is a great honor to be chosen by the king."

"An *honor*?" repeated the priest, shaking as he said it. But he seemed to bite his tongue. "Yes, my lord," he said, through barely gritted teeth. "I thank you for your audience."

He bowed deeply and left the hall, his eyes meeting Klytemnestra's briefly before he turned toward the door.

She realized she'd been holding her breath, and let it out as silently as she could. Not able to look her husband in the eye, she focused on the rotation of her spindle and barely heard the last few petitions of the day. Agamemnon carried on in his usual demeanor, as if the priest's request had concerned nothing more than barley crops, but the young man's sad eyes lingered in Klytemnestra's mind. It seemed that she was not the only one suffering on account of her husband's new distraction.

CHAPTER 15

HELEN

Helen felt as though she was slowly getting back to herself. Each day she felt a little stronger. Each day it was a little easier to get out of bed, to talk to people, to do the things she used to do. Each morning her handmaids would come and bathe her, rub her skin with perfumed oil, dress her in soft wool, adorn her with jewelry. It made her feel better—less like a living corpse. She was Helen the Queen once again, not Helen the broken, bleeding girl. And there was a power in that.

Not everything was as it had been, though. She was Helen the Mother now too. She knew it was true, that the baby was real and alive—it was lying over in the corner of her chamber right now—and that her status, her life, had undergone a monumental, irreversible change. People reminded her of it every day. She was a full woman now, they said, as if she had metamorphosed, a new being born out of pain and blood. And yet it did not feel quite real. She did not *feel* like a mother.

She got up and walked over to her daughter's cot. Hermione, Menelaos had named her, while Helen was still in the grips of the fever. As she looked down at that sleeping face, the full lips and the delicate eyelashes, she felt . . . nothing much at all. It was her child, she knew that, and yet it did not feel like a part of her, like her mother had said it would. She had said she would love her child instinctively, but she didn't feel love when she looked at that face. She barely even felt a connection.

She knew she should try to hold the child more but she was scared of doing it wrong, of upsetting her or hurting her. She always seemed to cry when Helen reached down to her.

She couldn't stand the sound of Hermione crying. It made her feel so helpless. Especially when she couldn't do the one thing that she knew would placate her. Helen had tried to feed the child as soon as she had recovered enough strength to hold her, but it had been no good. The milk wouldn't come. She had felt like such a failure when after several attempts they had finally given up and returned the child to her wet nurse. Now every day, numerous times a day, Helen had to endure the humiliation of watching a slave—Agatha, her childhood playmate—perform the duty that should have been hers, and give her child what she herself could not.

Though she heard no words said aloud, Helen could feel the palace talking about her. What kind of a mother could not feed her child? Wet nurses were commonly called upon for babes whose mothers had died, but here she stood, alive and breathing. A flesh-and-blood mother, and yet she was not enough. *Broken. Cursed.* Those were the words she imagined being whispered in the halls as she lay in bed at night.

Just as Helen was standing by the cot, the chamber door opened and Agatha stepped in. The girl was as timid as she had ever been, though she was a full-grown woman now and several inches taller than Helen. Agatha had always been smaller than her and Nestra when they were growing up, despite being between them in age, but she had grown tall and slim like a reed.

Her head was bowed as she entered, her mousy brown hair tied up with a strip of cloth.

"I've come for the feeding, mistress," she said, as if Helen did not know. They went through this little exchange every few hours.

"Hermione is asleep," Helen replied, her tone unintentionally curt. She wasn't in the best of moods and Agatha's arrival had done nothing to raise her spirits.

"Oh," said the girl, lowering her head even further. "Perhaps I should come back when she has awoken."

Agatha turned to leave, but Helen called out to her, trying to make her tone softer but only partly succeeding.

"No, you're here now. You may as well see if she'll take it." She would rather get it over with than be disturbed again in an hour.

"As you wish, mistress," said Agatha, and made her way toward the cot, head still bowed.

It turned out Hermione was ready for the milk after all, and so Helen sat and watched as her daughter pressed her face into a soft, white breast that wasn't her own. Everything about it looked so natural—the way Agatha held the downy head in just the right way, the little sighs of satisfaction that leaked from those milky lips—and yet it gave Helen a queasy feeling in the pit of her stomach.

She noticed Agatha's eyes turn on her, and realized she had been staring. Did the other girl sense her resentment? Her envy? Her feeling of inadequacy? Then a worse thought struck her. Did Agatha *pity* her? The last thing Helen wanted was the pity of a slave.

Desperate for a distraction, she said, "Tell me about your child, Agatha. The one you lost." As soon as the words were out of her mouth she realized it might be cruel to ask about such a thing. But it was said now, so she continued, "They . . . they told me that was why you were chosen to nurse Hermione."

"There isn't much to tell, mistress," said the girl, her eyes lowered. "He wasn't around for all that long before the sickness took him. Just a few months." After a pause she added, "I named him Nikon, though."

Agatha spoke about it so plainly, as if it were just one of those things, but Helen sensed that she grieved for the child. It must be strange for her too, Helen realized, to nurse another's child after losing her own. She wasn't sure whether it would be a comfort or a sadness. Perhaps it was both.

"You loved him? Nikon?" Helen asked quietly.

Agatha replied with a small nod of her head. It was a stupid question, perhaps. Of course a mother loved her child, and mourned when it was taken from her. Perhaps she had been hoping that Agatha would say no, that she hadn't loved the child, that it hadn't lived long enough for love to bloom. If Hermione disappeared right now, what would she, Helen, feel? Anything? Other than relief?

"Who was the child's father?" Helen asked, thinking perhaps she could move the conversation to happier grounds. "Did Father permit you to marry one of the other slaves?"

"No, mistress."

"Ah, a love child, then," said Helen with a knowing grin, secretly glad that Agatha was not as perfect as she seemed.

"No, mistress. I've never been in love," said the slave girl, with a face of innocent seriousness.

"Oh. Well, I only meant . . . who was it, then? The child must have had a father," said Helen, with the hint of a giggle. She was quite curious now.

"One of your father's guests, I suppose," she said, quite casually. "Don't know which one. They come to me sometimes, when they stay at the palace."

"And you let them lie with you?" said Helen incredulously. "Even though you don't love them?"

"It's not a matter of letting, mistress," the slave girl replied, her eyes flicking to Helen's and away again. "I can't exactly refuse them. They're guests."

Helen felt faintly sick.

"And Father knew?" she asked. "And he didn't stop them?"

"Yes, mistress, I reckon he knew well enough," Agatha said quietly. "Reckon he even told them where to find me, sometimes. It'd be inhospitable to deny them, mistress. What's his is theirs . . . it's only proper. So long as they don't damage me . . . and most of them are gentle enough."

Helen was quiet for a moment while Agatha sat watching Hermione feed. She felt foolish, naïve for not seeing the reality around her. And guilty too, for resenting the slave girl. No doubt Agatha envied her as much as Helen envied Agatha. More, most likely. She would make more of an effort to be kind, she decided. Helen's motherly failings were not Agatha's fault. Although knowing that was different than feeling it.

"I think she's finished," said Agatha, moving Hermione away from her breast. Helen looked up and nodded, letting the other girl put her daughter back in the cot.

"You may go now, Agatha," said Helen, attempting to paint a kind, or at least polite, smile on her face.

"Yes, mistress," the girl replied with a bow, and headed toward the door. Before she reached it, however, she stopped. After an uncertain pause, she said, "Begging your pardon, mistress, but I was thinking . . . would it be better if I stayed here in your chamber, so that I can more easily care for the child? I mean, it would be easier for you, mistress. Then you needn't call for me or be gotten up in the night, and I can just feed her whenever she needs it."

Helen didn't reply straightaway, but left the girl standing there looking nervous, probably afraid she had spoken out of turn. She was right, though; it would be easier for her to be near the child. But then another option struck Helen.

"Or how about we move you and the child to a separate chamber?"

Agatha looked confused. "But, mistress . . . surely you don't want to be separated—"

"No, no, I think that way is best. It will be easier for you and for the child," Helen said decisively so as not to invite further comment from the slave girl. She did not mention that it would be easier for *her*, above all. Though she could not admit it, the child made her uncomfortable—that constant presence in the corner of the room. It made her feel like a failure, and reminded her of the ordeal she had gone through to produce it. And what had it brought her? Not joy, nor fulfillment, nor closer communion with her husband—not as yet, anyway. Better to give it into the care of another. And perhaps, in time, she would grow to love her daughter.

"Very well, mistress. If that's what you wish. And if the king agrees," said Agatha, with a hint of doubt still in her voice.

"She is my child and this is my decision," Helen replied, her tone sharper than she had intended. "I am sure the king will agree."

"Yes, mistress," said Agatha, bowing her head. "I'll move in with the child as soon as a room can be prepared."

"Thank you, Agatha," said Helen, softening now that she could see an end to her torment. "And thank you for all you have done for my daughter."

The girl bowed graciously and left the chamber.

CHAPTER 16

KLYTEMNESTRA

I t was a crisp spring day—perfect weather for the climb. Though the afternoon sun shone down on them, dazzlingly bright compared to the dim of the palace, there was a cool breeze to cut through the warmth. Klytemnestra had been glad of it on the hot, hard ascent, and now that they had reached the top of the hill the breeze was stronger still, making her clothes billow around her. She held her skirt down with one hand, afraid it might blow up in one of the stronger gusts. In the other hand she held a bunch of wheat, like all the other women who had made the ascent with her. They had brought them here as offerings to ensure a good harvest. It was one of her most important roles as queen, to lead this ascent several times a year and bring fertility to the land.

She enjoyed these rare trips beyond the citadel, out into the landscape where the gods dwelled. They had not come far at all—Klytemnestra could see the stone sprawl of Mycenae down at the foot of the hill—and yet it was like she was in another world entirely. The rules were not the same here. There was a wildness, a freedom that could not be found inside the palace. For one thing, they did not have to wear veils. This was a women's ritual, so there were no men here to see them—except the male slaves who had helped to carry the offerings up the hill, of course, but they didn't count.

Perhaps the biggest difference of all was the absence of her husband. Up here there was no king, only a queen. Up here she answered to no one but herself and the gods. Up here, she had power.

She felt that power now as she led the ritual, placing her handful of wheat on the large flat stone they used as a natural altar and ushering the other women as they followed her example. Some of the ears blew away, but it didn't matter; she liked to think it was the gods whisking them away to Mount Olympus. She said the words as the libations were poured—oil and wine, and a little honey too—and she herself cut the throat of the suckling pig that had been carried up here by one of the slaves. She let its young blood soak into the dry earth, then took an ear of wheat from the pile and buried it in the red dust.

When she stood up her hands were soiled with blood and dirt, her skirt was dusty, and her knees were sore. But she smiled at a job well done. It felt good to do real work for her kingdom, to be a queen in more than name and finery.

Now that the rites had been completed, they could descend and return to the citadel. But Klytemnestra decided she would rather linger awhile, to enjoy the sun and the breeze and the view. And up here, there was no one to tell her she could not.

And so the women settled themselves on rocks and tufts of grass, and chatted and gossiped and laughed, their voices carried away on the breeze to who knew where. Klytemnestra herself sat a little away from the others. She didn't know any of them very well. Her own ladies, including Eudora, had stayed behind to care for her daughters, and she knew she would make the other women uncomfortable if she tried to join their chatter. Noble though they might be, she was still their queen.

As she sat at the edge of the rocky crown looking out over the Argolid plain, she knew that somewhere out there, far away beyond the distant mountains, lay Sparta. She wondered what Helen was doing right now, if her marriage was happy, if her baby was healthy. She wondered if her mother and father were well, if her brothers had found wives of their own. Suddenly she wished she had wings, that she could fly up in the breeze, soar off over those mountains, and go home to see her family and talk to them and touch them.

As she sat gazing out a shadow fell across her. Without turning her head she knew it was a slave and not one of the other women—the figure was dressed in dull cloth, not fine, bright fabrics.

"Would you care for some refreshment, mistress? I have brought you water and some dates."

The voice wasn't one of the household servants she was used to and yet somehow it *was* familiar . . .

She turned her head and there, looking down at her, was a face she recognized.

"You're the priest," she gasped, a sudden fear prickling her skin. "Why are you dressed as a slave? What are you doing here?"

She looked over her shoulder, wondering whether she should call out. They had brought no guards with them, but there were a couple of slaves not far away.

"Please don't," murmured the man above her. "I only want to talk to you."

Klytemnestra had drawn a breath to shout but now she held it, unsure what to do. The man did not appear to be armed—he had put out his empty hands toward her, as if to stay any action she might take. He looked as worried as she was, and there was a pleading in his eyes.

She let out her breath and relaxed a little, eyeing the man cautiously. His hands still held out, he crouched down beside her, and began to pour a cup of water from the large waterskin he had brought over.

"Please don't be alarmed," he said in a low voice as he poured. "Act normally and they will think I am merely attending you." He held the full cup out for her to take. After a little hesitation, Klytemnestra reached out and took it from him, her fingertips touching his briefly as she did. She drew her hand back quickly.

"I remember you," she said quietly, looking straight ahead of her so as not to look suspicious. "You came to the Hearth Hall last week. About the girl."

"Yes, Leukippe," he said. "My name is Kalchas."

"Why did you come here, pretend to be one of my slaves? You took a great risk. If Agamemnon finds out—"

"Yes, it was a risk," he said, opening a small box of dates at the edge of her vision. "But I had to speak with you. Alone. And I trust you not to tell your husband." He held out the box to her so that she had to turn and look at him. "I can see in your eyes that you have a kind heart."

She took a date and brought it to her lips, but suddenly she felt self-conscious. It was not proper for her to be talking to a strange man without her veil. The rules up here might be different, but the standards of basic decency still applied. She could not cover herself, though—it would arouse suspicion.

She ate the date awkwardly and swallowed as soon as possible, almost choking as it went down.

"What is it that you want from me?" she whispered when her throat was clear.

"I have come on account of Leukippe," Kalchas replied. She could feel his gaze on her, but she continued looking straight ahead.

"Yes, I had assumed that much," she said. "The girl must mean a lot to the temple, for you to risk so much on her account." There was a question in her voice as she said this, but it went unanswered so she continued, "Why have you come to me, Kalchas? You have already petitioned my husband and heard his reply. I don't know what power you think I have but—"

"I came because I believe you are a good woman . . . and because there is something I did not tell the king."

Klytemnestra was silent, waiting for him to continue.

"Leukippe is my sister."

"Your sister?" said Klytemnestra, turning to look at him. She had suspected some personal connection to the girl to risk himself so, but had assumed that he was in love with her.

"Yes. Though sometimes I feel more like her father." He sighed. "Our parents passed when she was young—I have raised her myself, more or less." He paused again and looked directly into Klytemnestra's eyes. "I know that you too have a younger sister—the famous Helen of Sparta. I thought that you might understand . . . that you might help me. I had hoped Leukippe would join the temple so that I could watch over her, but I know that chance is lost now . . . She could still get a marriage, though, a good one to a good man, a happy life. That's all I want for her—surely you can understand?" There was a desperation in his eyes. "That's why I have to get her away. No respectable man will marry another man's castoff, a king's whore. But if we get her out soon, before . . . I can find her a husband in another town, where the gossip hasn't spread. Please. I beg you. Say that you will help me."

Klytemnestra was dumbfounded by the man's torrent of words. His concern was so heartfelt, his distress so sincere. Perhaps she had been too long in Mycenae, but she could not remember seeing a man show such care for the happiness of a girl. And of course she understood—a good life was all she had wanted for her own sister. He couldn't possibly know what she had sacrificed to secure it . . . and yet it felt like he did know. He knew that same love she did, that feeling of responsibility, the need to protect.

"Why didn't you just tell the king that the girl is your sister?" she asked him. "You are her guardian. It is your right to decide where she goes and who—"

"Do you think such rules apply to kings?" he asked simply. "Do you think if I claim my rights, he will just hand her over?"

She didn't have a reply.

"You know your husband. You know I am right," breathed the

priest, more urgently now. "I have heard much about him—I know his sort. If he had known that Leukippe was my sister, he would have known I was acting out of personal concern and not simply as a representative of the temple. He will never put another man's desire above his own, but I thought . . . I thought that he might heed the will of the gods. He may yet."

"I suppose . . . what you say makes sense. And I think perhaps you were right not to tell him," she said with a small sigh. "My husband has a strong will. Once he decides he wants something . . ."

"You must swear that you will not tell your husband that Leukippe is my sister. Please. If you do, I fear I will never get her back."

Klytemnestra hesitated. Could she really keep a truth from her husband? She might even have to lie to him . . . In over four years of marriage, she had never done that. Was she being disloyal, even in talking to this man behind Agamemnon's back? But then Leukippe's face surfaced in her mind. What about her *husband's* loyalty, to his wife? And that poor girl, taken from her home. Who knew what she was suffering? The thought of keeping something from Agamemnon made her anxious, and yet behind that she felt a quiet thrill knocking somewhere in the depths of her chest. The thought that some part of her could exist beyond the bounds of their marriage, that she could have secrets just as he did—there was a strange power in it.

"I promise I will not tell him."

"No, I need you to swear it," whispered Kalchas, looking into her eyes so intensely that she could not look away.

"I . . . I swear it. By the gods," she said seriously.

"Swear by your children. By their lives," he said, grasping the hem of her skirt imploringly.

"My children?" she breathed, leaning away from him. "No, I—"

"If you mean it, why do you hesitate? Please. Then I will know you mean to keep your word."

"I . . . very well," she said, swallowing uncomfortably. "I swear by the gods, by the lives of my children, that I will keep your secret, that I will not tell my husband of your true connection with Leukippe."

"Good," he sighed, relaxing his grasp on her skirt. "Thank you, my lady. I knew I could trust you."

It felt like there was a clod of earth in Klytemnestra's throat. How could she have spoken such words? But then, if she meant to keep her promise, what was the harm? And if the girl could be returned home, if she could have her husband back . . .

"What do you want me to do?" she asked. "How can I return your sister to you?"

"First I want you to speak with your husband. See if you can succeed where I have failed."

"I have already raised the matter with him," she said quietly, pained by the memory of that conversation. "He did not heed me."

Kalchas frowned and seemed to deflate a little.

"I was afraid you might say that," he muttered. "In that case, I have another plan."

Klytemnestra looked at him. The intensity in his eyes was back, and when he spoke his voice was low and serious.

"I want you to help her escape."

CHAPTER 17

KLYTEMNESTRA

t was late. The sun had been set for over an hour and the chamber was lit only by a few flickering lamps. Klytemnestra sat alone, pulling nervously at the skin around her fingernails. Thankfully, the girls were both asleep. All she had to do now was wait for Eudora to return.

She had had doubts about involving her handmaid. If they were discovered, if Agamemnon found out . . . the risk was higher for a slave. But Eudora was the only person she trusted absolutely, and Klytemnestra didn't feel like she could do this alone. Just to have someone to confide in had been a help. And she had only asked her to do this one thing for her. The real task would be down to Klytemnestra herself.

In the quiet of the evening she could make out the distant sound of revelry. Agamemnon was hosting a feast for his military commanders and best soldiers. It had been going on for an hour or so and they had likely eaten by now, but she knew the drinking would continue for at least a couple of hours more—it always did. The feast had been planned for weeks, and it had been Kalchas's idea to use the opportunity. They might not get another for some time.

Klytemnestra was feeling the pressure. She couldn't back out now—the wheels had already been set in motion. But now that it was really happening, now that she was really doing it, acting against her husband, she felt sick. What kind of a wife was she?

A wife who wants her husband back, came a small voice in her head. She knew it was selfish to think of her own happiness when so many others were at stake, and yet the thought that her rebellion tonight might in fact help to mend her marriage was one of the only things keeping her calm. She was doing what was best for them all, wasn't she? And not least for Leukippe. She could well imagine what that poor girl was suffering, away from her family, afraid and alone. She saw a part of herself in the girl, remembering what it had been like when she had first arrived here in the palace, but for her it was different. She had a marriage, and legitimate children. Agamemnon had taken that from Leukippe. He had stolen something that didn't belong to him, and it was up to Klytemnestra to give it back. If she would not help the girl, who would?

And yet she knew that in betraying her husband, she was going against her duty. Her father had always spoken of the importance of duty, how we all had a role in life, how we must do what was expected of us. He talked of duty as if it were something sacred.

Was it sacrilege, what she was planning to do tonight? Was it sacrilege to even think about it? To sit here anticipating it?

But then a different memory surfaced. As she sat in the Hearth Hall with her father, a man had been brought in by the guards, caught trying to steal some grain from the palace store. Father had listened to the man's story—his family was starving, their village had suffered a failed crop. And then her father had let him go. He had ordered that grain subsidies be sent to the village, and that the man be allowed to take what he could carry with him, to feed his family until the supplies arrived.

Klytemnestra had been confused. Hadn't her father always told her that we must do our duty? Hadn't he said that it was a king's duty to uphold the laws? To punish those who broke them?

Her father had smiled. "How can I punish a man for trying to help his family? Perhaps I would have done the same if I were him."

But her little frown of doubt had remained, so he had taken her chin in his hand and spoken in that soft voice he used when he was trying to teach her something.

"Sometimes we must be led by duty, and sometimes by what is right," he had said. "The trick is to know when these things are the same, and when they are not."

A soft tap at the door made her father's smiling face disappear, and she was brought back to the present. A second later Eudora entered, and behind her the pale, frightened face of Leukippe.

Her handmaid's part had gone smoothly then, at least. Klytemnestra had asked her to go and fetch the girl from the chamber where Agamemnon kept her. It would have looked too suspicious if anyone had seen the queen herself calling on the king's concubine.

She ushered in the two women and Eudora closed the door softly behind them. Suddenly Leukippe was on her knees.

"I'm sorry, my lady, I didn't mean you any harm. I know you must hate me, but please . . . please don't hurt me." Tears were running down her terrified face and her arms were raised in supplication.

"Hush, hush!" hissed Klytemnestra. "Someone will hear you!" She turned to Eudora. "You didn't explain?"

"No, mistress. I thought you had better."

Klytemnestra sighed and put a hand on Leukippe's shaking shoulder. "I didn't bring you here to hurt you," she said. "I brought you here to help you."

Leukippe's eyes went from wide fear to narrow confusion.

"Your brother, Kalchas, came to me," Klytemnestra continued, straightening up. "He asked me to get you out of the palace and that is what I'm going to do. He should be waiting outside the citadel gate right now."

"Kalchas?" breathed the girl. "I knew he wouldn't abandon me. I

knew he'd come! I just didn't expect . . ." She looked up at Klytemnestra, shame in her eyes. "I'm sorry for the hurt I must have caused you,
my lady."

Klytemnestra hesitated, looking down into those wide, glistening
eyes. Yes, she had been hurt, but not by this girl. She pushed aside the
feelings of jealousy that had been squirming inside her these last
months, that sickening pang that arose each time she imagined her
husband's hands roving over soft white flesh that wasn't her own.

"None of this is your fault, Leukippe." She spoke softly and tried
to smile, putting out a hand to raise the girl from the floor. "Now,
before we leave this chamber we must change our clothes. No one will
pay attention to us if we look like slaves," she explained, handing a
bundle of plain cloth to Leukippe. "That's the hope, anyway."

The two women took off their fine clothes, Klytemnestra helped by
Eudora as usual, and began to put on their new outfits. Klytemnestra,
thanks to her helper, was ahead of Leukippe, and as Eudora was adjust-
ing her shift she could not help but look over at the younger girl, who
was still uncovered.

She didn't know what she was expecting to see. Some radiant, un-
deniable quality. Some reason why her husband's eye had wandered to
this body over her own. But all she saw was a skinny, shivering girl.
Deep down she knew that the girl's appeal lay in her novelty, the allure
of variety, and yet she could not help making comparisons. Leukippe's
breasts were smaller than hers, and her hips narrower. Though she did
have the advantage of not having borne two children—the skin of her
belly was still smooth and unlined.

And then she saw it. A small swelling in Leukippe's lower belly.
Barely noticeable, unless you knew what you were looking at.

"When was the last time you bled?" Klytemnestra asked, a bitter
taste seeping into her mouth.

Leukippe realized she was looking at her and tried to cover herself
with the cloth she had been in the middle of unfolding.

"N-not since before I came here," said the girl.

Klytemnestra and Eudora shared a worried glance.

"I know it should have come by now, but sometimes it's late—it's happened before. I . . . I thought if I just waited . . ."

She looked scared now. Klytemnestra saw her lip begin to tremble.

"It's all right," she said softly. "Don't worry about that now. Just put your clothes on. We need to go."

Once they were both dressed and their hair undone and wrapped up on their heads with rags, they left the chamber as quietly as possible, Eudora staying behind with the children.

They each carried a basket full of cloth under their arms, so as to look as if they were simply on an errand. With their heads bowed, they set out through the palace.

As Klytemnestra had hoped, they did not come across many people as they scurried through the corridors. It was too late for the actual servants to be bustling around, and those who were still up were likely busy attending the guests at the feast.

They soon reached the front courtyard. *Almost out of the palace*, thought Klytemnestra. But as they broke out into the moonlight a voice called out to them, and a guard emerged from the doorway they were headed for.

"Evening, ladies," said the man, sauntering toward them, his hand resting lazily on the scabbard at his hip. "Bit late for a stroll, isn't it?"

Klytemnestra froze, her heart pounding in her chest. When he was a few paces away from them she tilted her basket toward him, her head still bowed, and muttered something about laundry.

"At this hour? They do work you hard, don't they?" He stopped in front of them and seemed to be looking them up and down. "All right, then," he said eventually. "Mind how you go. You never know who you'll meet out there at this time of night." A low chuckle bubbled from his throat as he stepped aside to let them past. Leukippe went first, and Klytemnestra quickly followed. But as she passed the man she felt his hand touch her lower back, and before she had chance to turn around it had slid lower down.

She spun around, shocked by the intrusion. She scowled, but he just grinned back. She opened her mouth to say *How dare you?* but stopped herself just in time. She was supposed to be a slave—she must act like one. He was a free man, and no doubt used to taking such liberties. And so she closed her mouth and hurried after Leukippe, telling herself she should be thankful it hadn't been worse.

They had reached the main porch now; she could see the moon through the huge front door of the palace. They had made it out. Now just to reach the outer gate and hope they would be let through. Gripping her basket she marched through the doorway, trying to look calm, like she was supposed to be there, and she and Leukippe began to make their way down the Great Stairs to the street below.

Down, down they went. Now five steps from the bottom. Now four. Now three.

"STOP!" came a booming voice behind them. The shock of it startled Klytemnestra so much that she stumbled down an extra step, and only just managed to stay on her feet. She stood motionless, gripping her basket, staring at the floor. She was afraid to turn around, to see the face she knew was there at the top of the stairs.

She could hear Leukippe's terrified breaths beside her, morphing into whines as she began to cry. Then she heard the heavy footfalls begin behind her, growing louder as they fell from step to step. They stopped and she knew he was right behind her. She steeled herself. She was a queen, not a little girl anymore. She should not be afraid. She turned to face him, lifting her chin to show she was not scared. And as her eyes met his—

Thwack.

His hand hit her so hard she fell, dropping the basket as she rolled down the bottom few steps to the paving stones below. She could taste blood, and her face felt like it would burst with the pain.

She had never been struck before. She had seen slaves beaten many times, but had never been on the receiving end of a violent hand herself. Now she knew the pain of it, but what she felt more keenly was the humiliation. She could feel people's eyes on her as she lay on the ground, her hand holding her face. How pathetic she must look. How weak.

Once the initial shock of the pain had subsided, she put her shaking hands out on the ground and pushed herself to her feet, rocking slightly as she straightened up and faced her husband.

His dark eyebrows were like storm clouds over the thunder of his eyes. His thick beard quivered with rage. Leukippe was beside him, silent, her head bowed, Agamemnon's powerful hand around her wrist.

"Did you think I would not know?" he growled, his deep voice charged with anger. "Stupid woman. Even if you had managed to get rid of her, did you think I would not see your hand in this? You jealous bitch."

His words were like another slap in the face. But she told herself they were not meant for her, not really. She could see some of her husband's dinner guests crowded at the top of the stairs, watching everything, and heard more men shuffling behind her—inhabitants of the citadel come to see what was happening. She had defied him, undermined his authority, right here in his own palace, while his men feasted at his table. She knew that he could not let it stand. He had to shame her, to put her back in her place.

Now was not the time for pride. Seeing what she must do, she climbed the couple of steps toward her husband and knelt at his feet.

"I am sorry, my lord," she said, trying her best to make her shaking voice loud enough for all those watching to hear. "I have wronged you and I beg your forgiveness. It will not happen again." Then she kissed his feet, her split lip searing with pain as she did so.

He was silent for a moment, perhaps surprised by her actions and wondering how to respond.

"Get up," he barked eventually, pulling his foot away from her. He marched back up the steps, dragging Leukippe behind him, and Klytemnestra followed, her head bowed conspicuously low, her stinging face set with a grimace of humble penitence.

She hoped she had done enough to stay any further violence, to Leukippe or herself. And as she walked she said a silent prayer that Eudora's part in the scheme had gone unnoted.

One hopeful thought struck her as they reached the palace entrance: Agamemnon had assumed she had been motivated by jealousy, that she was merely attempting to get rid of a rival. He had made no mention of Kalchas or his part in it. The priest had risked more than shame or a beating in plotting against the king, but it seemed that he would be safe from retribution. That was something, at least.

CHAPTER 18

HELEN

It had been a little over two months since Helen had given birth to Hermione. After the initial trauma and gradual recovery, helped by the removal of the child into another chamber, Helen had been preoccupied with a new fear: that Menelaos would want to begin lying with her again. It was not the act she feared—she had grown used to it in the year or so before Hermione was born, and she had healed enough now that she did not think it would hurt—but it was the consequences that terrified her. Sex meant children. And there was nothing she dreaded more than another child inside her. The pain and the blood—she could not do it again. She had escaped death once, but she knew it had been a close thing. She was afraid to test the Fates a second time. Helen loved life, and she had so much of it yet to live. She would not throw it away for the sake of a child, nor for the sake of her husband.

She knew it was wrong to feel this way. Hadn't everyone always told her that bringing a child into the world was the greatest joy a woman could have, that it was the greatest gift she could bring to her kingdom? They spoke about motherhood as if it would make her powerful, but it had only made Helen feel disposable. She wondered if her sister had had this fear with her children. No, she didn't think so. Nestra always did what she was supposed to do, always felt how she was supposed to feel. It was she, Helen, who always seemed to be stepping to the wrong beat.

So far she had managed to avoid any intimate encounters with Menelaos. He had been sleeping elsewhere during her recovery, but over the last couple of weeks he had come and paid a visit to her chamber every other day or so. He would not say why he had come, but would linger uncertainly for a while, perhaps start a shallow conversation. They both knew why he was there, but neither acknowledged it. Sometimes he would even touch her, stroke her arm, or take her hand in his. But she would shift away from him, pretend she did not see his intention. She knew she couldn't hold him off in this way forever— eventually he would lose patience—but for now it kept her safe.

Helen was weaving in her chamber this evening. She still wasn't very good at it, but found she enjoyed it more than she used to. It was meditative in a way, sending the shuttle back and forth, building the cloth layer by layer. Whatever else was going on, she could sit here at her loom and forget the rest of the world existed.

A knock at the chamber door broke that illusion. Helen stopped the shuttle and turned to see who would enter. As the face appeared around the door, a nervous dread crept over her. It was her husband.

Helen remained seated on her stool, not wishing to close the distance between them. Perhaps he would see that she was busy and leave. Or pretend he had just come to ask her some trivial thing, as he sometimes did.

Not today, though. There was a new, purposeful energy in him this evening, as he stepped straight in and closed the door behind him. He walked toward her, a kind of forced firmness in his strides. Then, when he was right in front of her, he put a hand on her shoulder, bent down, and kissed her on the lips.

It was the first time they had kissed since she had had the baby. And despite her nervousness, she enjoyed it. The contact, the affection. It was soft, but firm too, and she found herself craving another. Suddenly she wanted him to hold her in his strong arms, to stroke her hair, to tell her that she was beautiful, that he loved her. More than anything that was what she wanted, all she had ever wanted. And yet it wasn't. Not anymore. Not now that she knew what it could lead to.

He had straightened up now and she sat there gazing up at him, torn between two parts of herself. She should move away from him, put him off. But she was sitting down, with the loom behind her. Where could she go?

"Helen," said Menelaos, before she could act. "Are you . . . well?"

She stood up, feeling trapped all of a sudden. "Yes, I'm fine," she said, moving around him. "Though I am quite tired. I should really go to bed . . ."

She stepped away from him, but he caught her wrist in his hand, his grip gentle but insistent.

"Helen," he said again, turning so that he was in front of her once more. "I had hoped . . . that we might lie together. As husband and wife. Since you are recovered."

He had finally said it. Those unspoken words that had hovered around them for weeks. She tried to pull her arm away but he held on.

"It is too soon," she said in a small voice, not looking into his eyes.

"It has been more than two months," said Menelaos. "I know the birth was hard on you, and I have left you alone. But you are healed now. There is no need to delay any further." He let go of her now slack wrist and took her hand instead. "We need another child, Helen."

She knew she could not be honest with him, could not tell him she did not want another child, that that was the very reason she was resisting him. He would not accept it. A king must have heirs, and a queen must give them to him. Otherwise, she thought bitterly, what was she for? He might allow her to delay another day, another week, another month, but eventually she would have to do her duty. It was futile to try to stop it.

When he kissed her again, she did not pull away. And when he began to slide her dress from her shoulders, she let him.

After it was done, Helen lay awake in bed, unable to sleep. She was
on her back, with her hands on her belly, staring up into the thick
blackness. Menelaos was already snoring.

She could feel his seed inside her, a foreign substance, a poison. She
imagined it seeping into the fertile earth of her womb, becoming in-
grained there, sprouting like a weed. It made her feel sick. She wanted
to flush it out, to reach in with her hand and claw it out. It was her own
death, brewing inside her. She could feel it.

She was beginning to panic. Why had she let him? She had thought
she could go through with it, that she just had to have a little courage.
But she was wrong.

She had to get rid of it. She had to get it out of her. She had to save
herself.

There was no time to lose. She slipped out from under the covers,
careful not to disturb Menelaos, and stepped silently across the room.
She quickly put her dress back on, struggling with the cloth in the
darkness, and then felt her way over to the table near the door. She
thanked the gods as her hands found the jug of water—it was still half
full. She picked it up, along with the lamp beside it, and left the chamber as quietly as she could.

The torches in the corridor were still burning so she lit her lamp
and hurried on to her destination—a guest room down the corridor
that she knew was empty.

Helen went in and closed the door behind her. By the dim light of
the single lamp she had brought with her she scanned the room, sighing
with thankful relief as she spotted what she was looking for. A small
piece of sponge, left beside the bath in the corner of the room. She
could have made do without it, but it felt like a sign, a reassurance that
she was doing the right thing.

She approached the bath and took off her dress. Then, picking up the piece of sponge, she dipped it in the jug of water and put it up between her legs. She reached in as far as she could, twisting it as she went, then withdrew it, washed it in the water, and put it up again. She repeated the process several times, each time feeling more cleansed, as if she were washing dirt from a wound. She carried on, even when she thought it was all gone. She had to be sure. The sponge was beginning to make her sore, but she couldn't take any chances. When she finally stopped, her back ached from bending over and her fingertips were beginning to wrinkle. She squeezed the sponge dry and straightened up.

She stood there, alone in the darkness, naked and shivering. Now that it was done, now that she was no longer occupied with her task, she felt a tide of emotion rise up inside her. She let it take her over for a few minutes, the fear and the loneliness and the guilt, let it wash over in waves, let it leak out in warm tears and quiet sobs.

And then she stoppered it up. Calmed her breathing, wiped her eyes, put on her dress, and went back to her chamber.

CHAPTER 19

HELEN

The next day, Helen was exhausted. After her trip down the corridor she had lain awake the rest of the night, fretting. Had she gotten rid of it all? Had anyone seen her? What would Menelaos do if he found out? What would *she* do the next time he wanted to lie with her?

She sat in her chamber as usual, spinning wool with Adraste. Her handmaid was chatting away in the background, but Helen was too tired to listen. She was watching the spindle twirl at the end of the thread. Its endless rotation had a hypnotic quality, and she found her eyes beginning to close, her head beginning to nod.

"Mistress?" Adraste's worried voice woke her, and she sat up with a start. "You fell asleep, mistress. That's not like you. Are you unwell?"

Helen was embarrassed to have been caught napping, and began busying herself with her wool.

"No, no. I'm fine," she said. "Just a little tired. Go on with what you were saying. Something about your brother . . . or your uncle . . ."

"Begging your pardon, mistress, but you don't look fine. There are dreadful shadows under your eyes. You look like you haven't slept a wink." Adraste was peering at her, concern in her warm brown eyes.

Helen was unsure how to proceed. She could hardly deny it—the proof was in her face. And yet she couldn't tell Adraste the truth, could she? Eventually, she decided to at least tell half the truth.

"The king came to me last night—" she began, but Adraste interrupted.

"Oh, mistress—I didn't realize," she said, a blush coming to her pale cheeks. "Say no more, I understand. I shouldn't have—ah— forgive me for prying, mistress."

Then after a short pause, in which the handmaid pretended to be concerned with her wool, she said, "Oh, that is good, though, isn't it? I'm glad you're well enough to . . . you know. And soon you'll have another beautiful baby, gods willing. I am so very pleased for you, mistress."

Suddenly, quite to her own surprise, there were tears in Helen's eyes, and before she could stop it a sob had erupted from her throat. She turned her head away from Adraste, but there was no hiding it.

"Oh, mistress!" gasped the handmaid, reaching out to touch Helen's knee. "What's wrong? Did I say something I shouldn't have?" She paused, and Helen could feel her worried, intense gaze on her face, searching for an answer she couldn't give.

"I wouldn't worry, mistress," she said at last, squeezing Helen's knee reassuringly. "I'm certain you'll be able to have more children."

But these words were like oil on the flames, and brought forth another shuddering sob from Helen's chest.

Adraste stopped talking now, clearly realizing that she was making things worse. Helen took a few moments to get control of herself, and when she finally looked at her handmaid the girl's eyes were so full of trepidation that she couldn't help but pity her.

"It's all right, Adraste," said Helen, putting her hand on top of the one still resting on her knee. "I'm all right."

"But you're not, mistress," said the handmaid, looking searchingly at Helen's tear-streaked face. "Won't you tell me what's wrong so I can help you? You can trust me, mistress. I promise."

Helen looked into the other girl's eyes, open and earnest. She *did* trust her. And perhaps it would help to share her fears, to tell someone what she was going through. She felt so alone.

Slowly, and with no small amount of hesitation, she revealed what she had done the night before, and why.

When she had finished, both of them were silent, until Helen eventually asked, "Was it wrong, what I did? Do you think I am a bad wife?"

"No, mistress," said Adraste, after a brief pause. "I understand why you don't want another baby just yet. The last one was so hard on you . . . perhaps it is best to wait a while, until you are ready."

Helen nodded in reply, but she knew Adraste had not fully understood her. She was not simply trying to delay pregnancy, but to prevent it entirely. She never intended to have another child, not if she could help it. But she sensed this would be harder for her handmaid to understand, let alone to support. After all, what was a woman worth if she did not bear children? It was a sad life, an unnatural life, and all the more unnatural was the woman who chose it. She could not bear to tell her friend the true extent of her feelings, could not bear to see those warm eyes harden with disgust, to feel her comforting hand slip away in fear, so she said nothing.

"You know, mistress . . ." said Adraste, looking down at her wool. "There are . . . methods. That women use, when they don't want . . ." She glanced furtively at Helen. "I have heard some of them talk about such things. There is a woman, not far away, who they go to . . . She may have something that can help you."

Helen was looking straight at her handmaid now. She tried to keep her expression even, but beneath her dress her heart was hammering. There were *other* women? Others who sought to prevent that terrifying swell? Others who *spoke* about it, as if it were not the greatest sin of their sex to desire barrenness where there should be life? Helen felt strangely relieved. Lighter, to not be alone in her unnaturalness. And yet she felt angry too, that no one had ever spoken of such things to *her*.

"I could find out where she lives," said Adraste. "We could go to her. Together."

Helen squeezed the girl's hand, harder than she had intended.

"Do you mean it, Adraste? You'd go with me?" she breathed. "Even if it meant lying to the king?"

Helen thought she saw a flicker of fear in the handmaid's eyes, but she nodded.

"You are a good friend, Adraste," said Helen, a smile of gratitude and relief coming to her cheeks. "We will go tomorrow."

That evening, pulse racing, Helen told Menelaos of her plans to leave the palace. She said she needed to get out, to see the sun, after her long confinement. And there was a rural shrine not far away, which she wanted to visit. It was said that the gods answered the prayers of those who left offerings there, and she wanted to ask them to give her another child. It was a bold lie, she knew. But she also knew that her husband would not object to such a mission.

He had initially insisted that she take guards with her, as she feared he would, but she had told him that the shrine was for women only, and that she would take her handmaid with her as a travel companion. When he was still not satisfied, she said that she would dress as if she were a common woman, and that two humble women would draw less attention than a queen and her retinue.

Eventually, mercifully, he had conceded. And so that morning Helen and Adraste had set out, plainly dressed, wrapped in the humble, practical veils that were worn by working women. It was liberating in a way, to go out into the world not as Queen Helen, but just as Helen herself, a girl of seventeen out on an adventure with her friend.

There was almost a gaiety in her step as they set out beyond the palace. She felt free, and buoyed up by the hope of securing further freedom when they reached their destination.

It was a long walk, longer than Helen had been used to in recent years, anyway. The soles of her feet were aching when Adraste suddenly stopped.

"I think that's it," she said, pointing to a small building halfway up the hill in front of them.

"Are you sure?" asked Helen, squinting skeptically at the little hut. It looked like little more than a goat shed. She had been expecting something more . . . impressive.

"Yes, I think so," Adraste replied, setting off toward the building, hitching her skirts for the climb. "This is the place they described," she called over her shoulder.

Helen had no choice but to follow her companion. The hut was farther up the hill than she had estimated, and her lungs were burning when they finally came to a stop outside its warped wooden door. The two girls looked at each other.

"Do you want me to knock, mistress?" whispered Adraste, sounding as if she would really rather not.

"I don't know," Helen whispered back. "Now that I'm here . . . Do you think we can trust this woman? What if she tells someone? Or . . . or what if she's some kind of witch? Who knows what she'll do to us?"

"But we've come all this way, mistress, and—"

Suddenly, the door opened. And there before them stood an old woman, small but robust-looking, with skin tanned like leather and a worn cloak wrapped around her shoulders. Her sharp eyes flicked between the two girls.

"I can hear you, y'know," she said. "And I en't a witch."

Helen blushed and smiled apologetically.

"We . . . we heard that you might be able to help us," she said, her voice squeaky with nerves. "Me, I mean. To help me."

The woman looked her up and down. "If y've come for a purgin' I can't help you. I've run right out o' lead and—"

"No, no," said Adraste. "It's not that. She wants something that'll stop it in the first place. Something to stop the seed."

The woman was still eyeing Helen as Adraste spoke, and didn't respond straightaway. Helen worried she was going to turn them away and it made her realize that, witch or not, she wanted this woman's help.

Eventually, the woman said, "You'd better come inside."

The room was as small as it looked from the outside, with the embers of a fire burning in the middle. The woman waved them toward two stools, their seats worn smooth by previous visitors, and shuffled over to a wooden chest in the corner of the room. After a minute or so of rummaging and inspecting, the old woman came and sat down on a third stool, a small jar held in each of her weathered hands.

"Now afore I give you anythin', y'll have to prove y've got the means o' payin' me," said the woman, holding the jars close to her chest. "Though I don't think that'll be a problem with you ladies," she added with a knowing grin.

Helen was suddenly worried, and it must have shown on her face.

"Don't worry, child. Y'd be surprised how many noblewomen I have knockin' at my door. I won't ask yer name as long as you don't ask mine." Then she put the jars in her lap and leaned forward slightly, a wrinkled hand outstretched. "Now what've you got for me?"

Helen looked nervously at Adraste, who nodded, so she put her hand inside her dress and brought out a small cloth bag. She opened it and poured the contents into her own palm: a long string of polished amethyst beads. She had taken them from her dowry box—the clearest stones she could find—and was pleased with her choice. She watched the woman's wrinkled face with anticipation.

Eyes squinting, the old woman reached forward and took the string from her, dangling it in the light from the small window.

"I was hopin' for some wine perhaps, or maybe a new shawl, but this'll do nicely," she said, peering at the smooth stones. "Yes, very nice. Y' can have the full works for this." Then she hid the beads away in the recesses of her clothing.

Suddenly a question bubbled to Helen's lips, and it was out before she could stop it.

"Why do you live here, if you have wealthy women paying you, as you say? Those beads alone are worth . . . well, they're worth a lot. Surely you could afford somewhere less . . . remote."

"You want t' know why I live in this godforsaken hovel, eh? Is that it?" asked the woman with a chuckle. "Well, I used t' live just outside Amyklai—nice place it was. But it was the people what were the problem. Not everyone thinks good o' what I do, y' see. So it's safer t' be out here. And I find the goats make less judgmental neighbors," she added with a toothless grin.

Helen smiled, but she couldn't help pitying the woman a little. What sort of life could she have, out here alone? And yet it seemed the woman always had a smile ready in her cheeks. Alone she might be, but she was also free. Helen felt something strange mingle with her pity. Was it envy?

"Now y've paid, I best be keepin' up my end." The woman's face became more serious. "Your friend says y' want t' stop a baby growin', is that right? And you know there's not one there already, do you?"

Helen nodded.

"How do you know?" the woman asked. "You must have a man visitin' you, or you wouldn't have come t' me. How do you know his seed hasn't already sprouted? If it has, all this'll be for naught."

Helen hesitated. It had been hard enough to speak of such things with Adraste. And yet the woman spoke so matter-of-factly, Helen doubted anything would shock her.

"I recently had a baby," she began in a quiet voice. "So my husband

and I haven't been . . . but then he visited me two nights ago, and he . . . put his seed in me. But I washed it out, so it wouldn't grow. I washed it all out."

"You washed it out?" repeated the woman. "What do you mean?"

"I used a sponge. Put it up there and . . . washed it out," said Helen, but she was feeling more and more uncertain as the woman stared at her.

"Oh, child. That won't work," she said, shaking her head. "No, no. That's not—here, let me show you."

Then she was on her feet and peering around the smoky room. After a moment she picked up a small waterskin and shuffled back to her seat.

"See, child, a woman's womb—you know what that is, don't you? Where the baby grows?—well, a womb is like this waterskin here, 'cept upside down." She turned the skin so that its stopper was pointing to the floor. "This bit here is where the baby grows," she said, pointing to the pouch. "And this bit is what we call the neck," she went on, pointing to the lower section with its stopper. "Now a man's seed is small, y' see, so it can go through the neck and get inside the womb and grow into a baby. But if you try and clean it out, you won't be able t' get past the neck, not with yer hand, and not with a sponge. The hole's too small. What y' need t' do is stop it gettin' through in the first place."

Helen nodded to show that she understood, but her cheeks were burning with embarrassment. She was a woman grown, had already had one baby, and yet she didn't even know this much about her own body. How stupid this woman must think she was. But how was she to have known? Her mother had never spoken to her of such things, nor Thekla, nor Nestra. Perhaps even they did not know. After all, you didn't need to know anything to get a baby inside you. It was stopping it that required learning, it seemed.

"It's all right, child. I'm sure y' did yer best," the woman said with a sympathetic smile. "But y' have to understand these things, so I can help you."

Helen nodded again. But then a frightening thought entered her mind.

"If I didn't clean it out, does that mean it's still in there? Will a baby grow?" Helen felt sick at the thought that all her efforts might have been for nothing, the thought that his seed could be sprouting inside her right now, with her powerless to stop it.

"Maybe. Maybe not," said the woman. "It was only the one time, you said? There's a good chance that nothin'll come of it." She paused, looking thoughtful. "If it does, though, come back t' me and I'll try my best t' help you. I should have the supplies by then."

Helen recalled what the old woman had said when they arrived, something about a "purging." Part of her wanted to ask what it meant, and yet the grim expression on that wrinkled face told her that she was better off not knowing.

The woman adjusted her creases into a reassuring smile and continued. "What we need t' be concerned with now is how we're goin' t' stop it the next time. And that's where these come in," she said, holding up the two jars that had been resting in her lap.

"What are they?" asked Helen, eyeing them with equal parts curiosity and suspicion.

"This one here is full o' cedar resin," said the woman, passing Helen the slightly larger of the two. "Remember that neck I was talkin' about? Well, you need to take some o' this on your fingers and put it up there, *before* he lies with you. That's very important."

Helen took the stopper out of the jar and sniffed inside. The smell was not unpleasant, and she thought it sounded like a simple enough task.

"Yes, I can do that," she said.

"Good," said the woman, "but you'll be wantin' this as well," she said, handing Helen the second jar.

She opened it and sniffed the contents.

"It's honey!" she said, surprised to smell something familiar. "Do I just put it on like the resin?"

"Not quite," said the woman. "Floatin' in that there honey is a clod made out o' . . . various things. After y've put the cedar resin on, take the clod out and put it up there too, as high as it'll go—and make sure t' soak it in the honey again when you're done. It'll stop the seed gettin' into the neck—like this stopper here," she said, pointing to the water-skin that now lay on the floor.

Helen was less certain about this second jar.

"What exactly is in this . . . clod?" she asked.

"Well . . . there's some acacia tips, and some mugwort . . ." the woman replied, not meeting Helen's eye. "And the sheep dung, o' course . . ."

"Sheep dung?!" Helen spluttered, thrusting the jar away from her. "You expect me to put sheep dung . . . up there?"

"I do if y' want t' stop a baby growin'," the woman replied, a sharp edge to her tone. "It's you that came t' me for help, and this is the help I'm offerin'. If you don't want it—"

"No," said Helen. "I'm sorry, it's just . . ."

"You don't have to use both if y' don't want," said the woman, her tone softening slightly. "But it depends how much it matters to you. These remedies are the best I got, but that en't to say they'll work for sure. Yer best chance is to use everythin' y've got, and hope for the best. But if you're willin' to take the risk . . ." she said, putting out a hand as if to take back the honey jar.

"No," said Helen, clutching both jars tightly. "I'll take them."

"Good," said the woman, drawing her hand back. "Just make sure you use 'em like I told you."

Helen nodded.

"Well, if that's all, y'd best be off," said the woman, pushing herself up on her spindly legs. "This valley's no place for young girls once the sun starts t' drop."

They left the hut, the jars safely tucked away in the folds of Helen's clothes. But as she and Adraste were about to head down the hill, the woman took Helen's wrist to stop her.

"I've given you what I can, girl, and gods willing it'll work," she said in a serious voice. "But the best way to be sure o' stoppin' a baby is the one y' already know," she went on, looking at Helen meaningfully. "Every time he lies with you, there's a risk. Just remember that."

CHAPTER 20

KLYTEMNESTRA

I t was the first day of the new moon, and so Klytemnestra was seated in the Hearth Hall, listening to petitions with her husband. She had been taken quite unawares this morning when he had come to her chamber and asked her to join him, but her surprise had been outmeasured by her relief. He hadn't allowed her to attend the last one, it being so soon after her transgression. And though she knew he was still angry with her, knew that he hadn't slept in their bed since the incident, knew that today might be no more than a public show, a demonstration that she had been brought to heel, she nevertheless had hope that this might be the beginning of their reconciliation. He was bringing her back into the fold of his life, and she clung to that thought as if it were a lifeline.

She needed her husband, she had come to realize. Her already small life had become even smaller without his companionship, without his visits to her chamber, without his news of the world beyond Mycenae. And she could tell that the girls missed him. He still visited them, of course, but his manner was stiffer, his attentions more dutiful. For a time they had been a family, and Klytemnestra wanted nothing more than to make them one again.

She had been on her best behavior all morning—keeping her head dipped so as not to look too proud, and holding her veil across her face, even though it was unnecessary, in an attempt to emphasize her modesty. She hadn't dared say a word to her husband, and instead declared her deference to him with her humble silence. She knew this was the best way to be if she was to earn his forgiveness. It was her boldness that had angered him, her independence of will. She must reassure him that he had stamped that fire out, and hide the embers that still glowed within her.

It was midday now, so there was a short break in the petitions while some food and wine was brought into the hall. All the refreshments were set down on a table beside Agamemnon, on the opposite side of his throne from where Klytemnestra sat in her carved wooden chair. Had he ordered that done deliberately, she wondered? Was he punishing her, still?

She was hungry, and parched too, but even now her humility had not brought her so low as to beg. So she resolved to ignore the refreshments, to look straight ahead and keep her hands in her lap until he had finished.

Then she felt something tap her upper arm. She turned to see that it was a cup of wine, held in the thick-fingered hand of her husband. He was offering it to her, she realized, and hurried to take it.

"Thank you," she said in barely more than a whisper, and was surprised at how much this small gesture meant to her. And when he passed her a fig, too, she couldn't help but smile up at him.

He only grunted in reply, but Klytemnestra felt a hopeful warmth spread through her as she nibbled at the sweet flesh of the fig. He still cared for her. She knew that now. And that meant there was still a chance to find happiness and harmony in their shared life. It felt like a dreadful weight was being lifted from her chest as she silently sipped her wine.

Once Agamemnon had finished eating he waved for the rest of the food to be cleared away. Then he called across the hall to his herald, who stood at the entrance.

"Let the next one in, Talthybios," he boomed. "I don't wish to be here all afternoon."

The herald nodded, disappeared for a moment, then came back and announced the next petitioner.

"Kalchas of Argos, son of Thestor, seer and priest of Paion-Apollo."

The warmth that had spread through Klytemnestra before turned into a chill, and she tried not to let her alarm show as the priest strode into the room.

Agamemnon finished pouring a fresh cup of wine and glanced up to see who had entered.

"Ah. Haven't you been here before? You look familiar," he said casually, swilling his wine in its cup.

"Yes, my lord," said Kalchas, looking at Agamemnon very directly. Klytemnestra knew he must have seen her sitting beside the king, but he seemed determined not to glance at her. She was thankful to him. "I came two moons ago, on behalf of my temple. We were concerned about the girl, Leukippe."

He hadn't come last month, then, when she wasn't here. That was wise, Klytemnestra thought. Agamemnon's anger would have been too fresh, and he might have guessed at the priest's involvement in the plot. She tried to calm her shaking hands with another sip of wine.

"Ah, yes," said Agamemnon, sitting up slightly. "Yes, now I remember. Well, I can assure you that she is perfectly well."

"That may be," said Kalchas, looking as if he were suppressing an urge to challenge the king's account. "But I have not come simply to ask after the girl. Rather, I mean to bring her back to the temple."

"Yes, that was what you wanted last time," said Agamemnon, sounding irritated. "Well, my answer is the same as it was then. The girl stays with me. Nothing has changed, so if that's all you've come to ask you had better go back—"

"Begging your pardon, my lord," the priest interrupted, "but something has changed." He took a step forward, his ribboned staff making a dull, foreboding thud on the stone floor of the hall. "I am not only a priest but a seer, my lord. Apollo has blessed me with the gift of foresight, and the ability to divine the sentiments of the gods. And I have come to tell you that this girl will bring you danger. Artemis is angry that one of her devotees was taken from her and defiled. She is angry with you, my lord, and she will punish you. I have seen it. The only way for you to stay her anger is to return the girl. That is why I have come, my lord. To warn you and to save you. Let me take the girl away and you will be safe."

Agamemnon listened in silence to what Kalchas had to say, his great hands gripping the arms of his throne. "Why should I believe you?" he said eventually. "Your powers of divination are not known to me. Why should I take you at your word?" He shifted in his seat. "Perhaps you want the girl for yourself, eh? Is that it? Does the thought of those white breasts keep you up at night, priest?" He gave a low, barking laugh, and Klytemnestra's stomach turned. Then, more soberly, he said, "The girl is mine and I won't listen to your lies."

Klytemnestra could see the anger in Kalchas's eyes. She feared he was going to say or do something foolish, but tried to hide her concern.

"They are not lies, my lord. The goddess is angry and you will suffer for it."

"That sounds like a threat to me," growled Agamemnon, half rising from his chair. "I've heard enough of this. Guards!" he yelled, and within seconds they were in the hall. "Take this man away," he commanded.

"Please, my lord," Kalchas shouted as the guards took him by the arms and half dragged him from the room. "You must listen, my lord! You are in danger! You must give up the g—"

One of the guards punched him in the gut and his words were replaced with a grunt of pain. And before he could gather enough breath to say any more, he was gone.

Klytemnestra's heart was beating quickly in her chest. She felt for

Kalchas. She knew his desperation, had seen it in his fierce eyes as he was dragged from the hall, but he had taken a great risk in coming here. She knew well enough that her husband would snap before he would bend. But then, if she were in his position, if Leukippe were Helen or one of her own daughters, what would she do? She would fight to the end.

She jumped as Agamemnon suddenly addressed her.

"These religious fanatics, eh?" he said, and broke into a throaty chuckle. "Send the next one in, Talthybios!"

CHAPTER 21

HELEN

Three months had passed since Helen had visited the woman in the hills, and three times she had thanked the gods when her blood had come. She had been using the remedies as the woman had instructed, applying them every evening just in case her husband decided to lie with her. At first, she had been worried he would be able to tell, that he would smell it or feel it, but after the first few times her fear had abated. He lay with her as he always had—vigorously, dutifully, and in silence.

Sometimes, remembering the old woman's last words to her, she would tell him that she was tired, or that she felt unwell. Usually he would accept these excuses and let her be, but she sensed that he knew that they were just that: excuses. Helen didn't like it, the lies, the secrets, the cross-purposes. She felt like she and Menelaos were further apart than they had ever been. That wasn't what she had wanted, but neither could she end the deceit, give herself up to fate, and throw her life to the wind. She had to survive.

It was midafternoon and Helen was in her chamber, spinning wool with Adraste and Alkippe. The three of them had been chatting and laughing all day, so much that Helen's cheeks were beginning to ache. She hadn't laughed this much in months. There had been the horror of the birth, and then she had been so anxious about lying with her husband, about the risk of another child. The fear had always been there in her mind. But now she found she was finally beginning to relax. Three months and three bleeds, and no baby. It seemed those precious little jars were doing their job.

There was an unexpected tap at the door.

"Who is it?" called Helen, still half giggling at Adraste's impression of the shy waterboy whom she claimed was in love with Alkippe. Pink-cheeked Alkippe was giggling too, batting at Adraste to make her stop.

The door opened, and Menelaos stepped in.

The laughter died like a flame snuffed out. Helen's handmaids hurried to their feet and bowed their heads.

"I need to speak to my wife alone," said Menelaos.

As her handmaids scurried from the room, Helen started to panic. Why was he sending them out? Did he mean to lie with her? It was too early; she hadn't prepared. He didn't usually come till the evening. Could she make an excuse?

Before she could decide what to do, it was just her and her husband. And he was coming closer.

"I was just about to go and see Hermione," she lied, standing up as if to leave.

"It will only take a moment," said her husband, stepping still closer. "I need to talk to you."

Helen's heart was still racing, but she stayed where she was. "Very well," she said. "If it won't take long."

Menelaos took one of the seats beside Helen, and she sat back down.

"We have been lying together for several months now, and yet you are still not with child," he said in a low voice, fiddling with his signet ring as he avoided her eyes.

Helen's anxiety spiked again. Did he know? Was that why he was here? To confront her? To punish her?

She didn't dare form words for a reply, so she made a small noise of acknowledgment instead.

"I thought it might be time to get some help," he continued. "To hurry things along."

Helen's fear was replaced momentarily by cautious curiosity. "What kind of help?"

Menelaos shifted slightly and cleared his throat. "There is a cave. Not a day's ride from here," he said, his eyes flicking to Helen's then away again. "They say it is sacred to Eileithyia. That if a man and woman make love there, the goddess will give them a child."

Helen almost pitied her husband. He was so desperate for her to become pregnant, and the poor fool had no idea that it was her, not the gods, who was standing in the way of his desire. But then she remembered the pain and the blood, the reality of what his desire would mean for her, and her pity dissolved into fear.

"You want us to go to this cave?" she asked, keeping her voice steady.

"Yes," Menelaos replied. "Tomorrow. It is all arranged."

Helen's fear swelled. It seemed the decision had already been made; she could hardly refuse. And what if it actually worked? What if the cave really was special? What if the power of the goddess was greater than her little jars? Panic was rising in Helen's throat, choking her, suffocating her. But what could she do?

"Very well," she managed at last. "I will go."

The sun was low in the sky by the time they reached the cave the following day. Squinting in the light of those blinding beams, Helen surveyed the gaping mouth in the rock. It was wide and high and the cave itself seemed to go back some way, so that its depths faded into a dark unknown.

A slave appeared by her husband's side, holding a lit torch. Menelaos took the torch in one hand and Helen's slim wrist in the other, and with solemn strides he led her inside.

Helen had applied the cedar resin and honey clod that morning, in the few minutes when she had been left alone. She had been worried that the clod would fall out of place during the jolting ride through the hills, but as far as she could feel it was still where it ought to be. She tried not to part her legs too far as they made their way into the cave, though. Perhaps it was silly, but she didn't want to take any chances. Without her remedies, what chance would she stand against the goddess? As they made their way deeper into the cave Helen imagined those divine eyes watching her, imagined Eileithyia's sweet breath raising the hairs on her neck. It made her shudder. Her own breathing began to quicken, her little gasps loud in the echoing silence of the cave.

Suddenly Menelaos stopped. Helen had been keeping her eyes on the uneven ground as they walked, but now she allowed herself to look up.

From the wavering light of the torch she judged that they were at the back of the cave. The ceiling was lower here, the walls narrower, but it was still spacious. And in front of her, taller than she was, there stood a huge, rounded boulder.

"This is it," said Menelaos in a hushed voice, touching the boulder lightly with his fingertips. "The stone of Eileithyia."

Behind her husband's back, Helen screwed up her face. Was this it? A big rock? It didn't even have a face. But then . . . people said there were places that were special, places where the gods lived, in ordinary trees and rocks and springs. And her husband said there were stories of people who had lain here and been blessed by the goddess. Maybe there was power here after all. Maybe it would actually work. That thought made Helen's heart beat faster, her muscles suddenly tense as if they were telling her to run.

She fought the instinct, though. If she ran, or refused, Menelaos would know her true feelings, would know she was working against him. Perhaps he would find the little jars and destroy them. Where would she be then? Safer to go along with it and hope with all her heart that the stone was just a stone.

Her husband was praying now, pouring a libation and asking for the blessing of the goddess. All the while, Helen chanted a silent counter-prayer in her head. *Let the seed stay out. Let my belly be barren. Let the seed stay out.*

Then the prayer was done, and Menelaos turned to her. She was still wearing the light sun veil she had put on for the ride, and he care-fully lifted it from her head. The gesture reminded Helen of her wed-ding night, the fear and the vulnerability she had felt then. Those feelings were still with her, but they were no longer those of a naïve girl. They were deeper, rooted in experience, watered with her own blood.

His hands were undoing her dress now. No words—of course no words, she was used to that by now. No whispered sweetness. Her husband spoke only when it was necessary to speak. Now was a time for action.

Her dress was around her feet and she shivered in the cold of the cave. The only warmth came from the torch, wedged between two rocks a few feet away.

Menelaos took off his tunic and looked at her. Helen wondered if her husband could see her tremble—from cold, from fear. Did he care which it was? He surveyed her face, his mouth open, his eyes unsure. There was always this moment of slight hesitation, as if he might say something after all, but then his body would win out over his tongue.

He put his hands on her shoulders then moved them down, over her breasts, around her waist. She flinched as they reached the mesh of jagged lines that cut across her belly. Did he notice? It seemed not—his hands were too hungry, grasping at her flesh as if it were his alone. Soon the two of them were on the floor of the cave, his firm brown body pressed against her soft white one. It was hard and uncomfortable, down there on the rough stone, but Menelaos didn't seem to mind. He had come here for one reason, and he was going to see it through. But with every touch, every thrust and stifled gasp, Helen felt as if she were losing a part of herself, a part of the control she had gained, the wall she had built. It filled her with hot terror to think of that fatal seed, to imagine her protections failing under the determined assault of Eileithyia and her husband both. She set her body hard, as if she might become part of that stone floor—imperishable, impermeable. And even when he had finished she lay there stiff, lifeless but for the furious beating of her heart.

They spent the night in the cave—he insisted they must—and although her husband was soon snoring, Helen found it impossible to sleep on the hard rock. She was freezing, despite having put her dress back on. Part of her wanted to move closer to Menelaos, to hold on to him and share his warmth. But another part of her warned against it. What if he woke up? What if he wanted to try again, just to be sure? And there was something else keeping her back, too. She couldn't bring herself to be close with the man who might have just caused her death.

The torch had gone out not long into the night, but now, after hours of utter darkness, a little light was beginning to seep into the cave. Morning had finally come. It was still dim, but Helen was glad to see even a hint of the dawn. She hadn't slept and her whole body ached from lying on the cold stone.

She stood up and stretched, half hoping that her movement would cause Menelaos to stir so that they could leave. It worked, and he sat up.

"Is it morning?" he asked groggily.

"Yes, husband," Helen replied. She was standing a few paces away from him with her arms wrapped around herself, lest he get any ideas.

But to her relief he said, "We have done what was needed. We should leave now."

They had brought no belongings that needed to be gathered, so he simply stood up and began walking toward the light of the day. Helen followed behind him.

But when they were almost out, an idea struck her. She stopped.

"Husband, may I go back to the stone? I want to leave an offering for the goddess. Perhaps if I give her something beautiful she will smile on us." She slipped a gold bracelet from her wrist to show what she intended.

"Yes," he replied, after a short pause. "Yes, you go back. I'll wait for you at the entrance."

She nodded and hurried back into the cave. She was soon back at the stone, and stopped in front of it. In the gloom, the huge boulder loomed over her. It did have a strange power, a kind of ineffable presence. She felt as if she were being watched, as if the stone were waiting to see what she would do.

Helen took the bracelet and threw it to the back of the cave. It landed somewhere in the dark—she didn't care where. Then she stepped up to the stone—and kicked it. As hard as she could without injuring herself. And again with the other foot. Then she spat on it, and watched with satisfaction as her saliva slid down over the immovable rock.

She felt powerful. A little scared, perhaps, but powerful. *Let's see the goddess smile on me now*, she thought defiantly.

Then she hurried back to the entrance, and to her husband. He smiled when he saw her, and she cringed with guilt as his hopeful eyes met hers. But she had no regrets.

CHAPTER 22

KLYTEMNESTRA

Another day, another afternoon at the loom. But as usual, the girls were breaking the monotony. Elektra was much steadier on her feet now, and her favorite game at present was to provoke Iphigenia into chasing her around the chamber. Her older sister was refusing to take the bait today, however, preferring to dress and undress her favorite doll with the miniature tunic and mantle Klytemnestra had made for her. Elektra was beginning to sulk at the lack of attention from her sister and Iphigenia, despite her impressive level of patience toward Elektra, was becoming annoyed.

"Elektra," said Klytemnestra, stopping her work. "Why don't we go out into the courtyard?" Iphigenia could stay here with Eudora, she thought, and there'd be more space for Elektra to wear herself out.

Elektra seemed excited at the prospect of leaving the chamber and came along willingly, holding her mother's hand and swinging on it wildly as they made their way to the courtyard. Klytemnestra wished she could take her outside, to roll in the grass and throw stones in the river as she and Helen had done when they were children, but Agamemnon wouldn't have it. Mycenae lacked the openness of Sparta; to reach the real outdoors you had to leave the citadel, go beyond the outer town. It wasn't safe, her husband insisted.

Over the past few months, since Kalchas's second petition, Agamemnon had softened toward her. Now, when he came to see the girls, he would talk to her as well, ask if there was anything she needed. He had even shared her bed on occasion, and though their previous intimacy was still lacking, it gave Klytemnestra hope. Hope that he still wanted her. Hope that, once he grew bored of Leukippe, he would come back to her. Hope that everything would someday be as it once was. She just had to be patient.

She and Elektra had reached the courtyard now, and as soon as she let go of her daughter's hand she was off running around, pumping her arms in that determined little way of hers. Klytemnestra chased after her playfully, measuring her steps so as not to catch her up too quickly. When she caught her she tickled her ribs so that she squealed, then let her go again. They went on like this for some time, Elektra shrieking and giggling in turn and Klytemnestra laughing so much she had to stop and catch her breath. It was blissful, playing in the sun like this. Klytemnestra almost felt as if she were a child again, and all her other concerns seemed suddenly not to matter as she ran about, her skirts hitched in her hand.

After a while, beyond the squeals and the giggles, Klytemnestra became aware of another sound. At first she thought it was just the daily bustle of the citadel, but then it grew louder and more distinct. A group of people getting closer, and some of them were shouting. Something was happening, and it was coming this way.

Klytemnestra stopped laughing and caught Elektra in earnest this time. "That's enough," she told her, taking her by the wrist and leading her back toward the chamber. Elektra made a protest at first, but followed along when it was clear the game was over.

Klytemnestra was relieved when they reached the chamber door. Whatever was going on, she didn't want to take any chances—not with the children. Best to stay in the chamber and bar the door.

Not long after she had done so, however, there was an urgent knocking and a familiar voice sounded through the wood.

"Lady Klytemnestra? Are you there?"

Though she was glad to hear someone she knew, the urgency in Talthybios's voice scared her.

She unbarred the door and opened it enough to see the grave face behind it.

"It's the king, my lady," said the herald, short of breath as if he had been running. "He's had an accident."

Agamemnon was in a bad way. He was barely conscious, and when he was he groaned with pain. Klytemnestra was not used to seeing her husband so vulnerable, and it shook her with a fear she had not known before.

He had been out hunting with a few of his men when his horse had been startled by a boar. It had come out of nowhere, they said, and rushed straight at them. The king's horse had reared, thrown him to the ground, and landed on top of him. His left leg had been twisted when he fell, it seemed, and crushed under the weight of the horse. Not to mention the cut on the back of his head, and the bruises that were already coming up on his ribs.

She didn't know whether he had asked for her or if she had been summoned simply because she was the queen. With the king incapacitated there was a keen lack of a leader, yet in her panic Klytemnestra felt she was a poor choice to fill the role.

Nevertheless, she had tried to master the situation. She ordered that the king be put in one of the guest chambers and sent slaves to fetch fresh water and linen. She also sent for the royal physician and ordered all non-useful people out of the chamber. It was too chaotic with everyone buzzing like flies around a corpse, but she had another reason, too. She knew her husband would not want the whole palace to see him in this way. He looked so fragile, so mortal, so weak. A king must not be weak.

She mopped his brow with cool water, having already washed and dressed his head wound. It was not as bad as the amount of blood had led her to fear.

The physician seemed most concerned with the king's leg. It didn't look right, lying at a slightly odd angle, and seemed to swell greater by the minute. It was clearly the main source of his pain and he cried out pitifully as the physician pressed and prodded it. Klytemnestra winced at the sound. Even after all they had been through, she cared for her husband. It pained her to see him this way, and she was afraid to think about what might happen if he should die. Would the men of Mycenae choose a new husband for her? Or would they forsake their bond with Sparta and drive her out? And what of her children? Daughters were not a threat to a new king, she told herself, and yet they might become pawns in the struggle for power. She found her chest tightening, and forced herself to take a slow breath. She was letting her thoughts run away with her. Her husband was still living, and he was strong. She had to keep calm, for him and for herself.

When the examination was over, Agamemnon managed to gather himself a little. He finally seemed to register where he was and who was sitting beside him.

". . . nestra . . ." he groaned faintly, looking up at her. His eyes were still full of pain, but at least they were present now.

"Yes, it's me," she said, putting a gentle hand on his shoulder.

"The boar . . . the boar . . ." he murmured.

"Yes, a terrible accident. But you're safe n—"

"No," he said, suddenly moving to grip her hand. "Not an accident." He was looking at her intently now.

Klytemnestra looked back at him, confused.

"What do you mean? Did—did someone do this?" She couldn't believe it, but he looked so serious.

"No . . . not someone," he rasped, pausing while he overcame a wave of pain. "It was the goddess."

Klytemnestra fell silent, not sure how to respond.

"Artemis. She sent the boar," he continued, squeezing her hand. "The priest . . . he was right. We must return the girl. You must . . . get rid of her."

Klytemnestra opened her mouth to respond, but before she could think what to say, he spoke again.

"Get rid of her," he said, and passed out.

She sent a messenger to Argos, and Kalchas arrived the very next day. The king was not fit to receive him and so, as queen, the duty fell upon Klytemnestra.

She was nervous about seeing the priest again. Would he be grateful that he was finally getting his sister back? Or angry that it had taken this long? Leukippe had been at the palace almost six months now. And there was another thing that worried her, more so than anything else: Kalchas didn't know about her condition.

The two women sat waiting in the Hearth Hall, Leukippe on a plain wooden chair that had been brought in specially and Klytemnestra on her usual carved seat. The king's throne stood empty. She had not been sure whether the hall was the appropriate place for such an exchange, but at least it was private. There was a guard at the door, but other than that they would not be overlooked.

Leukippe was tapping her feet nervously. Klytemnestra reached out a hand to hers and squeezed it. The girl smiled back and seemed to settle a little.

It wasn't long before they heard conversation outside the hall, and Kalchas walked in. His eyes found Leukippe immediately and he began striding toward her, a broad, relieved smile on his face. Leukippe gasped with excitement and stood up. As she did, the wings of her mantle fell apart and between them the round swell of her belly appeared.

Klytemnestra saw Kalchas's face change. His cheeks fell and lost their color as his eyes darkened with realization.

But it was only a second before Leukippe was upon him, her arms around his neck and her cheek on his chest.

"Kalchas," she breathed as she let go and looked up at him. "I knew you'd come. I knew you wouldn't leave me."

The priest seemed to snap out of his paralysis and forced a smile.

"Yes, of course I came," he said, and folded her into his arms. But over her head his eyes met Klytemnestra's, and they were full of fear.

She knew what troubling thoughts gripped him, for she too had wrestled with them. Who would marry Leukippe now? What would they do with the child? What future could there be for the two of them?

But Leukippe seemed unaware of her brother's concern.

"Are we going home now? This afternoon?" she asked hopefully.

"Yes," her brother replied, still fighting to overcome his dismay. "Yes, we'll leave as soon as we can, to be back before sunset." His eyes were drawn inevitably back toward her belly and he looked as if he were going to say something more to her, but didn't. Instead he turned stiffly to Klytemnestra.

"Farewell, my lady. I doubt we shall meet again. My regards to the king." And then they were gone.

She noted that he had managed to feign polite reverence to her husband without wishing for his return to health, but she couldn't say that she blamed him. It was her duty to love her husband, but he had wronged that girl and her family, and might very well have ruined Leukippe's life.

When she returned to the chamber where Agamemnon lay, semi-conscious, she took up her seat beside him and poured him a cup of honey water. As she brought it to his lips and watched him drink it down, his heavy brow lined with pain, she found herself thinking that perhaps her husband deserved to suffer a little, for the pain he had caused to others. But she pushed the thought down. That was no way for a wife to think. It was done now. Leukippe was returned, and Kalchas would not be back. She had to focus on returning Agamemnon to his full strength, and perhaps then her own life could resume.

CHAPTER 23

HELEN

Months had passed since the trip to Eileithyia's cave, and yet Helen's belly was still empty. She had been so scared those first few weeks, convinced it had worked, cursing herself for thinking she could resist the power of the goddess. But then the blood had come. And then again the next month. And again and again. Half a year and no baby. With each month Helen had felt more powerful, more invincible. She had taken on a goddess and won.

She couldn't let herself become complacent, of course. She still used her remedies—in fact, she had had to send Adraste into the hills to purchase more—and she would hold Menelaos off whenever she could. She knew she was hurting him, saw in his eyes that he knew she was deliberately pushing him away, but what else could she do? He wanted a child, and she wasn't willing to give him one. There was nothing she could say to him, nothing either of them could do to get past that. It was like an invisible, immovable wall between them.

There had been word from Mycenae that Nestra was expecting another child. It scared Helen, of course, that her sister was facing the same risks that she herself had taken such lengths to avoid, but she was happy for her, too. Nestra had always dreamed of having lots of children; at least one of them might end up with the life they had wished for. Helen, on the other hand, felt trapped. She was caught between life and love—or at least the possibility of it—but as she clung desperately to one she felt the other drift ever further away from her, out beyond her grasping fingertips.

It wasn't just her husband who lay at a distance from her, but her daughter too. Hermione was nearly a year old and yet Helen felt no closer to her than she had when she had given birth to her. Agatha had taken full responsibility for her care, in a separate chamber just as Helen had ordered. And even when Helen went to call on her daughter, it was clear that Hermione preferred the slave girl; she would cry whenever Agatha left the two of them alone. It made Helen feel so terribly guilty that she had not been able to love the child, that she herself had created what felt like this unbridgeable gulf between them. It was as if her daughter knew Helen had not wanted her.

None of this was Agatha's fault, Helen knew that in her honest heart. And yet she resented her. For doing what she could not, for being what she was not, for giving her daughter what she had not. Whenever Hermione smiled at the sight of the slave girl, and grasped toward her with her chubby little arms, Helen knew that really she hated herself. But it was easier to hate Agatha.

She had taken it into her mind that she would go and see Hermione today. It had been several days since her last visit, and she had finally finished the blanket she had been weaving for her. The pattern was a little crude and there were faults in the fabric, but she wanted to give her daughter something, to be with her when she was not. A poor substitute for a mother, she knew, but it was something at least.

When she reached the chamber door she pushed it open without knocking. She entered to find Agatha nursing Hermione, her dress undone to her waist. The girl jumped when she saw Helen.

"G-good afternoon, mistress," she stuttered, trying to pull her dress up with her free hand. "I didn't realize you'd be visiting today."

"I can see my daughter whenever I feel like it, can I not? Or do I need to make an appointment?" Helen's reply had a sharpness she hadn't quite intended.

"Yes, of course, mistress. I mean, no . . . she's finished now anyway," she said, moving Hermione away from her wet, pink nipple so that she could pull her dress up fully.

Helen simply nodded. She knew she had made Agatha self-conscious, but she couldn't help staring. It still fascinated her, in a bitter way, this life-nurturing ritual that she herself had never managed to accomplish.

"I was going to set her down for a while, mistress," said Agatha uncertainly. "She gets sleepy after a feed. But if you'd like I can—"

"No, that's fine," said Helen, still standing on the same spot she'd been on since she had entered. "Carry on, it's all right."

Agatha carried Hermione over to her cot and laid her inside it. As she began arranging her covers Helen remembered what she was holding in her hand.

"I brought a blanket," she said awkwardly, taking a step forward and holding out the piece of cloth.

Agatha turned to look at her.

"The king had one made not long ago, mistress. Didn't he tell you?" But then she seemed to see the disappointment on Helen's face. "No matter," she said, stepping forward to take the blanket from Helen's hand. "I'll use this one instead, mistress. It's very fine," she lied, with a polite smile. Then she went back to the cot and finished tucking Hermione in.

Helen stepped toward the little wooden structure and peered in. Hermione was still awake, but her eyes were drooping heavily. Helen stood there watching her little chest move up and down. She wondered whether she should reach out and touch her. But would it upset her? She wasn't sure, and she could feel Agatha's presence beside her. She always felt as if the other girl was judging her every action.

"I'm a little hungry, Agatha," she said suddenly, turning to the slave girl. "Would you get me something to eat?"

"Of course, mistress," the girl replied.

Helen had to get rid of her, just for a little while. Her natural ease with Hermione only served to highlight Helen's own painful uncertainty, and she couldn't bear it. She needed space if she were to learn to love her child.

The sound of the door closing told her that Agatha was gone. She relaxed a little, but there was still this life before her, sleeping now but still very much real and living and . . . unknowable. What did it think of her, she wondered? Did it love her? No, she didn't think so. How could it? And yet maybe, in time . . .

She stretched out a nervous hand and stroked the soft skin of Hermione's cheek. Her little nose wrinkled and Helen quickly drew her hand away, worried the child would start to cry.

But then her eyes were open, and she was looking up at her. Not upset or angry. Just looking at her.

Helen suddenly felt more confident and she reached out again, this time toward one of the little hands. And then Hermione was holding her finger. Helen wiggled it around in those tiny, gripping fingers, and a little giggle erupted from the cot.

Helen smiled, her nervousness forgotten. With each little burbling giggle she felt she was making some progress, going some way toward forming that elusive connection, the absence of which had lingered around her like a veil of shame for the past year.

But then there was a loud clatter behind them and the spell was broken. Hermione began to cry and Helen spun around to see Agatha in the open doorway, a mess of bread, broth, and broken pottery at her feet.

Anger flared inside Helen. It was as if Agatha had done it deliberately, as if she couldn't let her be happy.

"What do you think you are doing?" she yelled at the slave girl, not sure what else to shout, but feeling a terrible need to do so.

"I'm sorry, mistress," the girl said, getting down on her hands and knees to clean up what she could. "It just tipped and—"

"You clumsy fool!" Helen snapped. "Look what a mess you've made! And you've upset Hermione. I should have you whipped." She took a step toward Agatha, but then a voice from the doorway made her look up.

"What's going on in here?"

Behind Agatha, standing in the corridor, was Menelaos. He looked angry.

"Ah, husband," Helen said, stepping toward him. "Just in time. This idiot has made such a mess, and she's made our daughter cry. She needs to be—"

"That's enough," he snapped, and looked down at Agatha. "Are you all right?" he asked, putting a hand out to help her up.

The slave girl's eyes were still fearful, but she nodded and said, "Yes, my lord. Thank you, my lord." Then she took his hand and pulled herself to her feet.

Helen was still fuming, but her rage was briefly stunned by what she was seeing. What was he doing? He was her husband. Why wasn't he asking her if *she* was all right? How many times had he ever asked her that? But before she could find any words to utter Agatha was speaking instead.

"It's true what she said, my lord. I dropped the tray and it made a noise and—"

"That's hardly an excuse for a whipping, though, is it?" he said, looking at Helen sternly. "Agatha is caring for our daughter, and I expect you to show her a little more kindness."

Agatha's head was lowered, her eyes on the floor. She must feel so smug, Helen thought. It stung her to hear her husband defend a slave over her. Was Menelaos shaming her, for her failure to care for

Hermione? Her cheeks burned with anger, with hurt, with embarrassment, and her tongue felt stuck in her mouth.

After a few moments' silence Menelaos said, "I was planning to
spend some time with Hermione. You may stay if you wish, Helen."

"I was going, anyway," she lied, thinking she couldn't bear to stay
here with Agatha and Menelaos, who made her feel like a naughty
child. So she strode from the room, passing the two of them with her
chin high as she stepped out into the corridor.

And as she did she saw Menelaos put a hand on Agatha's elbow. It
was a small gesture and yet it irked Helen, and she dwelled on it as she
strode back to her chamber. Was he simply ushering her into the
chamber, or was it something more? Was there some tenderness between them, born in those hours her husband spent visiting Hermione?

Like a creeping tide suddenly breaching the harbor wall, Helen realized that she was jealous. She knew that it didn't make sense when she
was actively trying to avoid her husband, when she was deliberately
creating distance between them. And yet the thought that he might
care for another woman left a bitter taste. Despite all that had happened, despite all she had been forced to do, Helen still wanted Menelaos to love her, and only her. And it wasn't until now that the
possibility of losing his affection to someone else had really struck her.

But then again, she thought as she sat at her dressing table that
evening, perhaps she had imagined it. She passed the ivory comb
through her long hair, admiring the shine of it in the lamplight. Her
husband had a decent heart—perhaps he was just defending Agatha as
a loyal servant. Deep down, Helen knew the girl hadn't deserved the
scolding she had given her, and her husband had known that too. He
was just being kind. Yes, it was likely to be nothing more than that.
After all, the thought of it was quite ridiculous. Agatha was very plain-
looking, and she . . . well, she was Helen of Sparta.

CHAPTER 24

HELEN

A few weeks later, Helen was lying in bed. The evening was still young and yet she had already undressed from her day clothes and settled herself under the covers. She knew that Menelaos would likely come to the chamber soon, and she was hoping to avoid any amorous intentions by pretending to be asleep. She had already rebuffed him twice this week, feigning illness or fatigue, and she wasn't sure he would swallow another hollow excuse.

She had run out of cedar resin the week before, but hesitated to send Adraste to fetch more. Her handmaid still believed that the remedies had been a temporary measure and Helen didn't know how much further she could stretch that lie. Of course, Adraste would have to do as she asked in any case, but that was little comfort. What would her friend think of her, a woman—a queen—who refused to do her sacred duty? And worse, what if she told someone? What if Menelaos found out?

She might yet send Adraste, but these fears had delayed her. And now she was stuck, reliant upon only the honey clod and her wits.

So here she lay, her back to the chamber door, hugging the bedcovers tightly. Unable to sleep, she listened for the faintest noise from the corridor. And then she heard it. Bootsteps on stone. He was here.

The chamber door opened and light spilled in from the torch-lit corridor. The bootsteps stopped, as if he had paused in the doorway. Then they resumed, and the bed shifted as he sat down.

Helen's heart was racing, but she tried to keep her breathing slow. The silent seconds stretched on unbearably.

"Helen?" came her husband's gruff voice from behind her. "Are you awake?"

She didn't answer, but lay as still as she could, her eyes shut.

Then his hand was on her shoulder, shaking it gently. "Helen?"

She couldn't ignore him now. She stirred a little, and made a faint sound of waking. She turned her head toward him, but didn't roll over fully.

"What is it, husband?" she asked, with feigned grogginess.

"I . . . err . . ." he replied vaguely. "The sun has only just set. I thought you would still be awake."

"I had a headache so I went to bed early." She let the lie hang in the air, half expecting him to challenge it. But he didn't.

"Very well," he sighed, and into that exhaled breath he managed to pour a sadness and annoyance that made Helen's heart shrink with guilt. In a way, this disappointed surrender was worse than if he had challenged her lie.

Perhaps she should just lie with him, she thought. The honey clod should protect her—she was being overcautious. And she was beginning to miss the intimacy between them, the touch of his skin on hers.

But before she could act on her changed resolve, Menelaos spoke again.

"I'm going to check on Hermione." And within seconds he was gone from the chamber.

Helen lay there for a while, staring into the darkness. The realization loomed that she had pushed it too far, denied him too many times. Her husband resented her. She could feel it, hear it in the hollow way he spoke to her. Was this the price she must pay to preserve her life?

She even began to wonder whether a life so devoid of love was worth preserving.

But perhaps it was not too late, she thought. Perhaps she could still bring him back, and they could share their lives as man and wife should. Perhaps she could still find the love she had always longed for. She could still use her remedies—they had worked so far, hadn't they?—but she would stop pushing Menelaos away. She was bound to him, after all. If she could not find love in his arms, she would not find it at all.

Stirred by this realization, Helen threw off her covers and got out of bed. She put a mantle over her nightdress and silently left the chamber. She would find Menelaos, tell him she was feeling better, bring him back to bed. Despite the risk, she found she was excited. It would be a thrill, she thought, to play the seductress. She couldn't wait to see Menelaos's face. All would be forgiven in her kisses and caresses, she knew it.

Hermione's room was only at the other end of the corridor, and Helen was soon at the door. Though she could hear no voices behind it, she put her hand on the wood to push it open.

But just then she did hear something. Not from Hermione's chamber, but the one just farther along from it. It was a guest chamber, not currently occupied, and yet the door was half-open.

Curious, Helen left Hermione's door and stepped toward the open one. As she approached she heard a gasp—a woman. And a lower voice. A grunt. A murmur. Two breaths mingling in the quiet of the night. Helen thought she knew what she was listening to, but she didn't turn back. Perhaps it was two of the slaves. She should leave them alone, but her curiosity urged her on. And a strange uneasiness too, that she couldn't quite put her finger on.

And then she saw them, and her stomach tightened. There, through the half-open door, were Agatha and her husband.

They didn't see Helen. Menelaos had his back to the door, and

Agatha's eyes were closed. She was naked, perched on a table's edge, and Menelaos had his tunic lifted, his mouth on her neck, his hand on her breast, his hips pressed between her white thighs. The sight of his tensing buttocks made Helen feel sick, and yet she did not look away. He was kissing Agatha's lips now, stroking her cheek, whispering in her ear.

It was this that made Helen look away. She recoiled a few paces and stopped, falling against the corridor wall. Her rattling breaths were so loud she thought they might hear her, but she didn't care. Part of her wanted them to hear.

It wasn't so much the infidelity that hurt her—what else did she expect, when she herself had pushed him away? No, it wasn't that. It was the way he had touched her, kissed her. As if she were all that mattered in the world. He was so tender, so passionate. Why had he never been that way with her? Why had he never shared that part of himself? Even before the baby, before everything, he had not been like that.

And then a dark thought struck her. Was it *her*?

There lay the real source of her hurt, she realized. Despite all her beauty, all her fine clothes and much-lauded charms, her husband did not love her. All the time she had thought it was he who was lacking, he who was unable to feel or to show it when he did. And now she realized that it was she who had been the problem all along. Helen of Sparta, the unlovable beauty.

PART III

CHAPTER 25

KLYTEMNESTRA

SEVEN YEARS LATER

Klytemnestra sat on her carved seat in the Hearth Hall, sewing sequins of gold onto the front of her husband's new mantle. There was a chill wind blowing through the palace today so she had come seeking the warmth of the hearth fire. She smiled as its light caught the gleaming disks, rippling across the work she had already done. It gave her satisfaction to imagine how magnificent Agamemnon would look in his new robe, and to know that the eyes that admired her husband would also be admiring the work of her own hands.

She was starting to feel as if her life were going the way it ought to. The few years after Leukippe had left had been difficult. Klytemnestra had thought the girl's departure would be the end of her trouble, but really it was only the beginning. The hope that had been stirred by her own pregnancy, so soon after reconnecting with her husband, had turned to bitter ash when the baby had finally come. It was blue and still. And the one the year after too, just the same. It was an ill omen to bring forth death where there should be life, but twice in as many years . . . She had been convinced that she and Agamemnon were being punished, that Artemis was still angry about what had happened with

Leukippe. Had her husband's accident not been enough? He had recovered, yes, but not fully. His leg was still twisted and he walked with a permanent limp. But then again, perhaps it was not Artemis who was punishing them. Perhaps they had done something to offend Eileithyia instead, forgotten her in their sacrifices or neglected her shrine. Both goddesses had power over childbirth; it could be either one who was set against them. Klytemnestra had spent many sleepless nights churning over such things, wondering how she might mend them.

To her relieved surprise, Agamemnon had not blamed her for any of it. She had felt as if she were failing him as a wife, and yet he had stayed by her side, had kept telling her that a child would come. If anything, that dark time had brought them closer than they had ever been.

And then a child did come. Chrysothemis, they had named her. Another girl, yes, but after what had happened, Klytemnestra was happy to see a live child come out of her, pink and screaming like it should be. She could have had twelve toes for all she cared; it was a new, warm life to hold in her arms, and that was all she wanted. Even Agamemnon didn't seem to mind that she was a girl. Heir or not, she was a sign that their fortune had changed, that their punishment had ended.

Klytemnestra had still been worried, though. For at least the first couple of years, a part of her had been sure that Chrysothemis would fall ill and be taken from them after all. But she had survived. She was past her fourth birthday now, and Klytemnestra's heart was finally allowing her to trust that she was theirs to keep. Not only that, but she was pregnant again, her belly already swollen and getting larger by the day. Gods willing, it wouldn't be long before she held another child in her arms, and this time she was sure it would be the son Agamemnon had been waiting for. This one felt different from the rest. She couldn't say how exactly, but she knew in her heart that she was carrying a boy.

It had been a long road, and far from easy, but it really did seem that their fortunes had changed. And the Leukippe era, those few months that had caused Klytemnestra so much distress, seemed little more than a distant memory now. If it weren't for Agamemnon's leg, she might have been able to forget it had ever happened.

Klytemnestra looked up from her work. Her eyes were beginning to dazzle from staring at those glittering gold disks, each one sewn with precision. She sat back in her chair, eyes closed, and enjoyed the feeling of the hearth fire warming her skirt. Twelve years into her marriage, she finally felt at home in Mycenae. She was a real queen now, commanding respect throughout the palace. Agamemnon would even ask her advice on occasion. He always invited her to attend public audiences and would have her by his side when receiving guests.

She spent a lot more time beyond the walls of her chamber than she had in those early years. In the afternoons, as today, she would often be found in the Hearth Hall, working on her latest garment or spinning wool with Iphigenia and Elektra. They were like little ladies now, especially Iphigenia. Klytemnestra knew she might not have many more years with them so she savored this time as if it were the last jar of a good vintage. In time they would marry and have children of their own, but not yet. For now they remained here with her, and her little family was whole and happy, and about to get larger.

There was a shout from the courtyard that made Klytemnestra open her eyes. Her husband's unmistakable boom carried easily through the great wooden doors of the hall—indeed, she doubted there was any room in the palace to which it would not carry. He was complaining about something or other, but that was hardly unusual so she closed her eyes once more.

Despite their domestic harmony, Agamemnon had been restless these past months. He could still ride and hunt, despite his leg, and yet even that did not seem to satisfy him when he was in one of his moods. A happy home and a prosperous kingdom seemed to her to be all that a man could wish for, but it was not enough for her husband. She hoped that the arrival of a son might quell whatever was agitating him. Yes, she thought as she rubbed her swollen belly, an opportunity to pass on the lessons of manhood might be just the thing to absorb his nervous energy. But the baby was a good month away yet. For now, her husband would just have to wait.

CHAPTER 26

HELEN

Helen watched as Hermione played in the courtyard, her hair shining in the sunlight. It was darker than her mother's, but still had some of its reddish luster—closer to dark carnelian than dazzling flame, but pretty nonetheless. She had inherited Helen's fair skin too—though she wouldn't keep it for long if Agatha kept letting her play outside. Perhaps she should talk to Agatha about it, tell her to keep Hermione indoors more, but she shrank from the idea. It was strange; she was Hermione's mother and yet she felt she had less authority over her daughter's life than Agatha did. The slave woman— she could hardly call her a girl anymore—was more Hermione's mother than she was, and for the most part Helen let her do as she saw fit. She had decided long ago that it was easier to cede her role than to fight for something she had never really wanted.

She still saw her daughter, of course. Sometimes, like today, she would watch from the shade of the portico as Hermione danced and laughed in the sun; other times, Agatha would bring her to Helen's chamber and a formal exchange would ensue. Helen would ask how her spinning was coming along, or what she had eaten for breakfast, and Hermione would answer politely in her high, soft little voice. Helen rarely touched her daughter—it had been years since she had hugged her or sat her on her knee—but it was better that way. It would feel unnatural, she thought, when such a gulf had grown between them. Better to watch from a distance. Hermione seemed happy with Agatha, anyway. Helen doubted she could compete, so it was easier on her pride not to try.

Agatha had outdone her in another way, too: she had given Menelaos a son. Megapenthes, as his father had named him, was playing in the courtyard as well, curly-haired and pink-cheeked. Agatha was raising the two children together, and Menelaos doted on his bastard son as much as he did his trueborn daughter. Helen did not begrudge Hermione her playmate, nor Menelaos his heir—they had gained something she refused to give and that, she told herself, was to the good—but she could not help feeling a little usurped. Agatha was as meek and unassuming as ever, and Helen was not even sure that she and Menelaos still lay together, but by giving him a son she had raised her station to a level that was dangerously close to Helen's own.

She might still be queen in name, but her role in the palace had felt increasingly undermined over the years, so that now she felt as if she stood on little more than a hollow mound, and that it might one day collapse entirely, plunging her into a twilight of lonely irrelevance. Her mother had met that fate already, her last strut of support having been removed with Father's passing. Perhaps it was inevitable that she, Helen, would sink too.

In a way, Helen's life was simpler now. For one thing, she no longer had to worry about conceiving a child. She and Menelaos still shared a bed, as was proper, but it was rare that he made any move toward intimacy. It seemed the arrival of Megapenthes had made him less determined that she should bear him another child. She supposed she should thank Agatha for that, but sometimes it felt more curse than blessing. What little tenderness she and Menelaos had once had was better than none at all. He was still kind, yes, and respectful, but sometimes, lying awake beside the warm mass of his body, she wished more than anything that he would reach out and touch her.

The sound of brisk boots made Helen realize she had been staring at nothing for some time. She dragged her consciousness away from her marriage bed, from warm hands and soft skin, and back to the sunny courtyard. And there, as if bidden by her straying thoughts, was Menelaos striding toward her. Her heart fluttered hopefully at the sight of him. What did he want to talk to her about, she wondered?

"Helen," he said when he had reached her. "Guests have arrived from across the sea—a royal delegation from Troy. I will be hosting a welcome feast this evening and I would like you to attend."

Helen felt deflated, but forced a dutiful nod. Ah yes, the hollow queen still had some uses, she thought bitterly. After all, what was the point of winning the most beautiful bride in Greece if you didn't show her off to your guests?

Helen sat in the Hearth Hall, on the chair that had once been her mother's, waiting. The wine had been mixed and the food prepared. Her stomach rumbled as she surveyed the feast in front of her, the smell of roasted meat, of coriander and cumin, wafting toward her. She longed to stuff some boar's meat into her mouth, but it would be impolite. They must wait for the guests to enter and present their gifts. Helen wished they would hurry up about it.

To her right sat Kastor and Pollux. Neither had yet married but, as sons of the previous king and brothers of the queen, they enjoyed prominent positions at the Spartan court. Menelaos had every right to send them away if he desired, but he seemed to enjoy their company. And they were both skilled warriors, should the kingdom have need of them.

To the left, on the other side of Menelaos, sat Deipyros, her husband's childhood companion and right-hand man, and to the left of him sat Helen's mother, the dowager queen Leda. Helen was secretly thankful that there was some distance between her and her mother. She still loved her greatly, of course, but it was always so difficult to know what to say to her. Father's death had been hard for them all, but for her mother most of all. Though it had been five years since his burial, she still wore her mourning clothes, the black veil a permanent frame for her specter-pale face. That was a true love, thought Helen, observing her mother with a kind of sad envy. Father had been devoted to her, and she to him, even now. It wasn't proper for a widow to mourn so long, but no one was willing to tell her that. Helen was surprised she had even agreed to attend the feast. Usually she avoided public occasions, but perhaps Menelaos had made a special request.

I should go and talk to her, Helen thought, imagining her mother sitting alone all evening. Her brothers would occupy themselves with drinking and swapping bawdy tales with whomever would listen. Mother's company was too grim for their taste nowadays. No, it would have to be Helen who reached out.

Just then, there was the sound of wood scraping on stone and all thoughts of her mother vanished. Finally, the great doors were opening.

As the wood parted and the slaves stepped aside, there emerged the most extravagantly dressed man Helen had ever seen. His clothes were a chaos of color—rich purples, deep reds, vibrant yellows, all jostling in wonderfully complex patterns. A leopard skin was draped over his shoulders and hung down his back, adding its own sumptuous décor to the mix. His long, dark hair fell in lustrous ringlets down to his shoulders and across his forehead, which was adorned with bands of gold and glittering jewels. Similar ornaments spangled on his ears, at his throat, and on his fingers, so that the overall effect was of a mosaic of light and color, shimmering as it sauntered toward them. The man's companions, following behind, were dressed in a similarly extravagant fashion and yet he was like a beacon among them, a sparkling jewel among polished rocks.

Now that he was close, Helen's attention turned to the man's face. He was very handsome, with fine features and tanned, unblemished skin. He was young, perhaps around Helen's age, and had a lightness about his expression, as if a smile might spring to his lips at any moment. His eyes were a golden hazel and ringed with kohl, so that one could not help but be drawn into them. Truly, Helen did not think she had ever seen a man so beautiful.

To her left, Menelaos rose to his feet, and she followed suit. Then her husband greeted their guests, raising his naturally gruff voice so that all the hall could hear.

"Prince Paris of Troy, Sparta greets you and welcomes you as her guest. May your visit breed friendship between our kingdoms, and may the gods allow us both to prosper from it."

Once the echoes of her husband's final words had faded, the glittering prince made his reply.

"King Menelaos, Troy thanks you for your hospitality, and honors you as a noble host and guest-friend. To mark the friendship between our peoples, I have brought gifts for you and your kingdom."

Here the prince turned around and nodded to his companions. A great chest was brought forward, and the lid raised. One by one the prince lifted items from the box and held them up for the admiration of all present. A fine bronze bridle, two golden mixing bowls, silver-patterned daggers with ivory handles, purple-dyed cloth, a comb inlaid with lapis lazuli . . .

Once all the items had been presented to Menelaos, and received with ceremonious thanks, the prince bent down once more and brought a small, carved ivory box out of the bottom of the chest. Rather than presenting it to the king, however, he turned and held it out toward Helen, managing to bow his head and keep his eyes upon hers at the same time.

"One final gift, for your lovely queen," he said in his strange, smooth accent.

Helen was surprised, and hesitated a moment. Guest-gifts were for kings, not their wives. She glanced at Menelaos, who gave a small nod, so she reached out and lifted the box delicately from the prince's hands. With the attention of the hall suddenly on her, she removed the lid with faintly shaking hands and lifted out the contents for all to see. It was a necklace—three strings of bright, clear amber, and droplets of gold between the beads.

"It is beautiful," she said breathlessly, smiling as it caught the light of the torches.

She glanced up to see the prince smiling too, but his face soon changed to mock disappointment.

"Alas, I thought it would complement the fiery beauty of which I have heard so much, but now I see that it looks pale and dull beside you."

Helen could not help her smile broadening at his flattery, and she felt her cheeks redden beneath her makeup. Was her beauty really known as far away as Troy? In truth, she did not really know how far away Troy was, but his words made her feel as if she were the talk of the entire world. Even after all these years, she still mattered. She was still somebody, to young men in foreign lands if not to anybody here in Sparta. Suddenly, with those few words, Helen felt brighter than she had in a long time.

Now that the gifts had been presented, they were cleared away so that the feast could begin. Helen's mood remained buoyant for the rest of the evening, and though the prince did not speak to her again, she found her eyes meeting his golden ones on several occasions. All thought of talking to her mother was forgotten as she passed the evening in smiling contentment, and watched the glittering prince from across the crowded hall.

CHAPTER 27

HELEN

For the next five days, Paris and his companions were entertained in Menelaos's halls. There was some discussion of politics, but mostly there was drinking and feasting.

Each evening, Helen would attend the Hearth Hall, and each evening she would feel the prince's eyes upon her. She had gone from watcher to watched, it seemed, and although she was shy at first, her eyes darting away when they caught his, she found that she liked the attention. She would choose her best gowns to wear at the feasts, showing as much of herself as she dared, anticipating his gaze upon her exposed skin and feeling a flutter of excitement as she did. It had been so long since she had felt desired, or even noticed, so long since a man had looked at her in that way. Her husband never did, not anymore, and no other man would dare. But Paris was different. He was bold. Even when she caught him staring, he did not look away, but met her eyes and held them. At one point, his eyes locked with hers, he picked up a piece of fig from his plate and put it to his lips, and sucked on its sweet flesh, the red juice making his lips glisten. She had blushed and turned away, glancing furtively around her to check that no one had seen. But even as she started an empty conversation with her neighbor to distract herself, she had smiled inwardly as she felt his gaze still upon her, her skin warming as if those golden eyes were the sun itself.

On the sixth day, as Helen was weaving in her chamber and wondering which dress she might wear that evening, Menelaos came to speak with her.

"I'm going away, Helen," he announced abruptly, stopping a few feet from her stool at the loom. "News has just arrived from Krete. My grandfather Katreus has died and I must go and see to the burial rites."

"Yes, yes, of course you must," she replied, absorbing what he had said. "Will you leave straightaway?"

"Yes, I'm afraid so," he said. "It is ill timing with our guests here, but it cannot be helped. They will understand, I am sure, but that is partly why I wished to speak with you. I must ask you to play host in my stead. Make sure that our guests are well looked after for the rest of their stay, and ensure that suitable parting gifts are given if I should not return in time for their departure. I trust you to represent Sparta and myself in this," he ended solemnly.

Helen nodded stiffly in reply, but a strange, conflicted feeling was growing in her stomach. There was gratitude and no small measure of surprise at her husband's revelation of his trust in her, but something else, too—a kind of nervousness.

"I will do my duty, husband," she said softly. And then, the nervous feeling bubbling up, "When will you return?"

"I shall only be gone a week or so," he replied with a reassuring half smile. "And your brothers will be here."

Feeling as if he were looking for some sort of confirmation, Helen smiled and nodded, pushing down her anxiety. "Yes, I'll be fine. And so will our guests. May the gods keep you safe on your journey."

"Thank you, Helen. Now I must go." And with a final brief nod he turned about and left the chamber.

Once the door was closed, the nervous feeling began to beat stronger in Helen's chest. Menelaos was *leaving*. His presence had felt like a kind of anchor these last few days, while Paris's eyes watched her from across the hall. Yes, the prince was flirting with her, and yes, perhaps she had encouraged him, but having Menelaos seated beside her had made it feel safe, made her feel under control. While she was tethered to her husband, flirtation was just that, and could not be anything more. But now she felt as though she had been cut adrift, and the freedom of it was at once exhilarating and terrifying.

CHAPTER 28

HELEN

Helen sat as head of the feast, Menelaos's empty throne beside her. She had opted for a more reserved outfit than the night before, not wanting to draw more attention than she felt able to handle, nor tempt fate more than was decent. She felt strangely exposed without her husband, and her heart was beating noticeably in her chest as she took her seat and welcomed the guests.

Paris entered, gave a polite nod to his host, and took his seat among his companions. As the feast got under way, as cups were filled and emptied and filled again, Helen waited for those golden eyes to come beaming across the room, to feel them on her skin as she pretended not to notice. But she never felt them, and every time she looked over toward the foreign prince she would find him laughing and drinking with his neighbors. He seemed wholly uninterested in her, barely sparing her a glance all evening. Indeed, he gave far more attention to Helen's brothers than to her.

She was relieved in a way, having been worried as to how his flirtations would escalate with the removal of Menelaos, and yet she found herself feeling a little hurt too. Perhaps she had imagined the prince's interest in her. Or perhaps his eyes had taken their fill. As the evening wore on, she wished she had chosen a more inviting outfit, and picked at her food in deflated silence.

After a couple of hours, Helen decided that her duty as host was fulfilled and left the men to their drinking. She doubted that she would be missed—her brothers were doing a fine job of entertaining their foreign guests without her.

When Helen reached her chamber she was thankful to find it empty. She was in no mood to chat with her handmaids right now, and dressed herself for bed. She knew she ought to be glad that the prince's interest had abated. She need no longer guard herself, or be worried for her reputation. But if this was a good thing, why did she feel so disappointed?

She washed the kohl from her eyes, the lead from her cheeks, the red ocher from her lips, feeling a sting of bitterness as she remembered the nervous anticipation with which it had been applied. What a fool she was. Then she put out the lamps and went to bed.

Helen didn't know what time it was when she was startled awake by a knock at the door. Very late, she imagined, as she had already slept and dreamed awhile since leaving the feast. Surely everyone was in bed by now, so who was this knocking at her door? A slave? But what would they be doing at this hour? Or a messenger, perhaps? Had there been some news of her husband?

Helen sprang from the bed and padded barefoot across the chamber floor. When she reached the door she pulled it open, but only a little, feeling somewhat indecent in her nightdress. And as the light of the corridor spilled through, she was greeted by a pair of golden eyes.

"Prince Paris!" she exclaimed in surprise. The unexpectedness of that face made her tongue seize in her mouth, but when she had found her words she said, "What are you doing here? Is there something you need? I'm sure the slaves will be able to fetch—"

"I want you, actually," he said with a smile. "To speak with you, I mean."

"It is very late," she said, hoping he could not see her blush in the dim light. "I—I am alone and . . . not dressed for company." He simply smiled at her, and she paused. While all these things were true, and she could have used any one of them to send him away, she did not. Instead, she opened the door wider. "Come in, Prince Paris."

"Please, just call me Paris," he said as he stepped past her into the center of the room. "And I hope that you might allow me to call you Helen in return," he continued, turning to face her.

"Yes, if you like," she said shyly. "We are guest-friends, after all." Her heart was thumping at her boldness. It was not right for her to be alone with this strange man, guest-friend or not. She knew she should not have let him in, that she should send him away even now. But another part of her was thrilled by his presence, here in her private space, her marriage chamber, where he ought least of all to be.

Helen turned around to light a lamp and close the chamber door, and when she turned back she was startled to find that he had stepped closer to her so that he was only a couple of feet away. She could smell his perfumed skin, at once earthy and sweet with foreign scents she was not used to.

"Helen," he said suddenly, his silken voice curling around the edges of her name. "Let us not pretend you have no idea why I have come. You must know that I admire you, that I have watched you. You have been haunting my thoughts since I arrived here. I had to speak with you, to confess my heart. Will you allow it?"

Helen stared at him, confused. Had he not ignored her all evening? And now suddenly he was here to confess his heart? It didn't make any sense . . . But then she smelled it, drifting on the air with his perfume.

"You are still full of the wine of the feast," she said, annoyed and strangely disappointed. "You should leave."

She turned to open the door once more, but suddenly his hand was on her wrist.

"No, my lady," he said earnestly, his eyes fixing hers. "I swear that was not what drove me here. I have barely drunk two cups this evening."

"But . . . I saw you," she said, determined not to be swayed by those eyes. "You were drinking with my brothers. I imagine you have only just left them." There was a bitterness in her voice as she said this. To think she might have risked everything for no more than wine-fueled lust.

"You have it wrong, Helen," he said urgently. "I made it seem as if I were drinking as much as they, but that was not the reality. I thought that if I could fill them with wine, I would be better able to visit you tonight . . . unobserved."

Helen was silent, trying to read his eyes for truth. He did not seem drunk, and yet she still felt wary.

He slid his hand from her wrist, and held her white fingers instead.

"I am sorry I ignored you this evening. I did not want to risk suspicion, but now I fear that I have hardened your heart against me. I just needed to see you alone, to speak with you . . . But perhaps you are right. Perhaps I should leave . . ."

He let go of her fingers and made a step toward the door, but this time it was Helen's turn to grasp his wrist.

"No, wait," she said. "Don't leave."

He stopped and turned back to her.

"I believe you," she said slowly. "And . . . I think that you should say what you came to say, now that you are here." She spoke as if he had merely come to make a petition, and yet her heart was thumping at the thought of what he might say.

His golden eyes were searching hers. They seemed so very close now.

"Very well," he said, his voice soft. He moved even closer to her, so that she could smell the sweetness of his breath. "I love you, Helen. That is what I came to say. That I love you with a fire that burns so bright I can no longer see anything or anyone but you. I came to say that your face fills my eyes in the day and my dreams at night. That your beauty makes the sun look dim, that it makes my heart ache, that I would go to the ends of the earth just to be close to it. That the thought of leaving here, of living the rest of my life without you, feels like I am being sent to die, for a death it may as well be if I can never again see your face."

Helen stood silent, unable to speak or move. Paris's outpouring was like a flood after a decade of drought. Right now, it was all she could do not to drown in it.

He took her hands in his, and his touch brought her back to herself. She looked down at those smooth fingers, glittering with their bands of gold, and then back up into his eyes.

"Your husband does not appreciate you for what you are. He cannot, for I have seen the way he is with you. He barely looks at you. If you were my wife, Helen, I would never stop looking at you." He raised a hand to her cheek and laid it there softly. "I would never stop holding you, never stop touching you, never stop—"

And then his lips were on hers, soft and warm. Before she knew what was happening she was kissing him back, her lips eager for that life-giving nectar, like a feast to the starved. She could have stayed there forever, caught in his arms, breathing his heady scent.

It was he who pulled away.

"I'm sorry. That was wrong. I shouldn't have . . . it's just . . . when I am near you it's all I can think of."

"No, we shouldn't have," she said, stepping away and trying to calm her ragged breathing, and yet she wished he would kiss her again.

They stood in silence for several moments, her green eyes held by his golden ones, so close she was sure she could hear his heart beating. Or perhaps it was her own.

"You should go," she said eventually, turning her eyes away. "You shouldn't be here . . . I— You shouldn't have said those things to me."

"Do you wish I had not?"

Helen opened her mouth but could not reply. After a moment she repeated her previous words, though quieter than before. "You should go."

Paris gave a shallow bow and Helen opened the chamber door, glancing both ways down the corridor outside. Sure that the coast was clear, she stepped aside to let him out. But just as Helen was about to close the chamber door behind him, he put his hand against it.

"May I come again?" he whispered.

Helen paused, her eyes searching that beautiful face. Then she gave a brief nod, and closed the door.

CHAPTER 29

HELEN

Paris came to her chamber again the next night, and the next. They sat together in the darkest hours of the night and he would gaze at her, tell her how beautiful she was, sometimes hold her hand or touch her arm. He would tell her stories from his youth, of roaming Mount Ida with his brothers, of racing their horses on the plain or waging mock wars with one another among Troy's winding streets. He would tell her of his travels too, of the places he had seen and the people he had met, in far-off lands of which she knew nothing. He was a year younger than her, she discovered, and yet he had done so much. It made Helen realize how small her life was. She had never even left Lakonia.

She felt she was traveling the world with him when Paris told his stories, and when he said he must return to his chamber, she asked him to stay just a little longer. His words, his gaze . . . they nourished a part of Helen that had shrunk so small with the passing years that she had learned to live without it. But now, with every profession of love, every praise of her beauty, every tender touch of her arm, she felt that shriveled part of her swell. And she could not ignore it any longer. It made her heart throb and her lips hunger for his skin, her skin hunger for his lips. It made her feel alive.

On the fourth night, Helen was sitting on the edge of her bed when the knock came. She was still wearing the fine gown she had chosen for the feast, having insisted to her handmaids that she would undress herself tonight. She didn't like lying to them, but Paris's visits were so precious to her that a little deceit seemed a small price. She could not risk that someone would find out, that Paris would have to leave, that the whole beautiful dream would end.

The knock came a little earlier than usual, and Helen smiled when it did. She went to the door and let the prince in, closing it softly behind him.

"Have my brothers gone to bed already?" she asked.

"No, I left them drinking with my cousin Aineias." He took a step toward her and raised a soft-skinned palm to her cheek. "I had to come. I couldn't wait."

Helen smiled and put her small hand on top of his.

"I'm glad you did. It will give us more time. You can finish telling me about your visit to Hattusa, or about the Queen of Miletos, or the time you saved your sister from drowning—I liked that one." She beamed up at him.

"I had another idea," he said, moving his hand down from her cheek and onto her shoulder. He looked down before turning his eyes back to hers. "Helen, your beauty is like the sun." She smiled and he continued. "But . . . as it is, I feel I have only glimpsed a portion of its splendor, like a beam bursting through a gap in the clouds. I . . . I wondered if you would allow me to see your full beauty. Unveiled."

Those golden eyes looked at her meaningfully, and she blushed as she realized what he meant.

"I'm sorry," he said, stepping back. "I've embarrassed you. I should not have asked. It's only that—"

"No," she said, grasping his hand in hers. "I want you to see me. All of me." She only realized the truth and strength of her feelings as she said it.

Helen lifted his hand, past her thumping heart, to the piece of cloth that lay over her shoulder. He paused, his eyes fixed on hers, and then delicately slid the cloth down over her arm. And then the other side.

Helen took an involuntary breath as she felt the material slip from her breasts, but Paris's eyes did not leave hers. Rather, he lowered his hands, and set them to untying the sash around her waist. Helen could feel herself shaking, but it was not from fear. Her whole body was alive with energy, and as he pulled the fine cloth down over her hips every brush of his hand on her skin sent a warm shiver through her.

The dress was around her feet now and Helen stood transfixed, her rattling breaths the only sound in the room. Paris stepped backward, and his eyes finally left hers, roaming over her white skin, taking in every inch of her. It was strange; she did not feel self-conscious, as when Menelaos looked at her, or even her ladies. Paris's eyes made her feel beautiful, desired, worthy, and she basked in the feeling of it.

"You are more beautiful than I had even imagined," Paris said finally, his golden gaze coming to rest on her eyes once more. "Truly, the goddesses themselves could not overshadow you."

Helen ought to have chastised him for speaking so impiously, but she could not help smiling instead. Paris stepped toward her again and took her hand in his, squeezing it gently.

"Thank you, Helen. I am glad I came tonight. I had to see all of you, before I left."

Helen's heart seized. "You're leaving?"

"Yes. First thing in the morning." He regarded her steadily.

"No, you can't," she said, panic rising in her chest. "You must stay longer. At least until Menelaos returns. You cannot leave yet. I could not bear it." From her happiness a moment ago she now felt on the verge of tears.

"Alas, I must." He turned his body as if already making for the door. "I am needed at home, and it would not be wise for me to be here when your husband returns. I fear he would see what has grown between us."

Helen stood staring at him, her mouth open, her eyes pleading, but she saw from the decision in his eyes that they would have no avail.

Desperate, she drew his hand to her breast, and pressed it there.

"Lie with me, then, before you leave, if you must go. Please," she said, her heart pulsing beneath the warmth of his fingers. "I . . . I cannot bear the thought of things going back to the way they were before you came. Worse than before, now that . . ." She blinked back the tears that threatened to fall. "But perhaps, if I had that memory to cling to . . . perhaps then I could bear it better."

She knew how pathetic she must seem, but she didn't care. Her little piece of happiness was slipping away—she had to grasp it, to keep it for as long as she could, to store some of it away within herself. It was the only way she would survive.

Paris had not spoken and she could not read his expression.

"Say you will," she said, putting her other hand on his cheek. "Say you'll lie with me tonight. Menelaos would never find out. I won't get pregnant, I have ways—"

"Helen," he said softly, moving his hand gently from her breast to her cheek. "I cannot lie with you. It wouldn't be right, to sleep with another man's wife in his own house."

"Nor is it right for you to have seen me like this, to have spoken the things you have spoken to me, but you have done it!"

"To lie with you would cross another line, Helen, and you know it. I will not make you a whore in your own home. You are too good for that."

Helen was angry. Could he not see what he was abandoning her to? What he had awoken within her? It was not fair of him to dangle love when it pleased him and deny it when it did not. Her eyes brimmed with fresh tears.

"Don't cry," he said, lifting her face toward his. She closed her eyes to avoid looking at him, and felt his lips brush her eyelids as he kissed one and then the other.

Even now he made her love him. She winced with the bitterness of it, at her foolishness in not seeing that this end would have to come. She leaned forward and put her head on his chest, wetting his tunic with silent tears.

They stayed like that for some time, Paris's arms wrapped around her, his hands stroking her bare skin. Then, eventually, he spoke.

"What if you came to Troy with me?"

Helen froze. The question sounded so absurd, hanging there in the silence, that she gave a bitter laugh. "As your whore, you mean? I thought I was too good for that?"

"Not as my whore. As my wife."

Helen straightened up, and looked at him.

"Your wife?" The words felt strange on her tongue. She had never even considered the possibility before now. "But . . . I already have a husband," she said.

"Barely," said Paris. "Who is he to lay claim on you? To neglect you as you waste your youth and beauty?" He cupped her face in his warm hands. "I love you, Helen. I could give you a new life, one you deserve, with every comfort you could want. You would no longer be a queen, perhaps, but a princess of Troy is no mean station. And you would have all my sisters and sisters-in-law as your companions. They would welcome you as if you were their sister too. I know you would like that."

She *would* like that, she realized. It had been so long since she had had a sister. He made this new life sound so inviting, so easy, as if she could reach out and take it, if she chose. But she couldn't, could she?

"I . . . you would not want me as your wife, Paris," she said, pulling away from him. "I will not have any more children. I would disappoint you." She knew the weight of those words, and braced herself for his look of confusion, even disgust. But he barely blinked.

"That does not matter to me," he said with a smile, drawing her toward him once more. "I am not the first son. I do not need heirs."

"But don't you want them?" she asked incredulously. Every man wanted sons.

"What I want is you." He leaned forward and parted her lips with his.

Helen was in a whirl. Could she really believe it? That a man might want her for herself alone, and not for the children she could give him? And yet those golden eyes were so sincere, that embrace so comforting. She felt unburdened in his arms, as if the weight of being heir and queen and mother had all drifted away from her. An hour ago she had been Helen of Sparta, the only light on her horizon the thought of another evening with Paris, and the world beyond that an unconsidered blur. But now she found herself faced with the possibility of a new, hopeful, liberated life, the chance to be Helen of somewhere different entirely. It all felt so strange and unstable, as if the world had been pulled from beneath her feet, and the only surety she had to cling onto was that she wanted to be close to Paris, to have him touch her again, kiss her again, to hear him say that he loved her. She didn't think she would ever tire of those words.

"You don't have to speak your answer right away," came that honey voice. "Though we must leave soon or not at all, if we are to avoid being seen." He took her chin gently in his hand. "Think about it, Helen. Think about the life you want, and I will return in an hour to hear your decision."

Then he kissed her again and left the chamber.

CHAPTER 30

HELEN

Helen put her dress back on and sat on the edge of her bed, her head resting on her fist. In less than an hour she would have to decide: did she want to remain Helen of Sparta, or become Helen of Troy? Part of her could still not believe she was even facing this choice. Could she really do it? Could she really just leave, begin again somewhere new? Abandon her home, her family? Was it madness to even think of leaving? Was it madness not to?

There was a knock at the door.

Helen froze. It was too soon for Paris to have returned. But if it was not him, who was it? It was late—no one would have cause to call on her at this hour. Perhaps Paris had changed his mind. Perhaps he had decided the risk was too great. Helen's heart sank at the thought.

A second knock came, more impatient than the first.

Helen rose quickly and trotted to the door. Before opening it, she took a breath, bracing herself for disappointment. But as she pulled the door toward her, it was not Paris's face that appeared.

"Mother!" cried Helen, astonished.

Her mother said nothing but pushed past her into the room, looking about her as she went. From her manner Helen judged that she had been drinking, and the waft of wine that followed her into the room confirmed her suspicion. There were bags under her eyes and her dark hair had come loose.

"What a surprise it is to see you, Mother," Helen said uncertainly, trying to smile. "I wasn't expecting—"

"I know what's been going on, Helen," said her mother suddenly, throwing her a sharp look. "No one pays any mind to poor Queen Leda, no—lost her beauty, lost her daughter, lost her husband . . . But I am yet living, though it's easier for you all to pretend I am not. And I see things . . ." She paused, peering unsteadily at Helen. "I see you . . . *whore.*"

She said the word with such venom that it was like a dagger in Helen's chest. She felt paralyzed, fixed by those hate-filled eyes.

"I knew you would be," her mother continued. "Not like your sister, such a sweet girl . . . But whores are born of whores, and here you are, spreading your legs for any man who gives you a pretty necklace."

No, it wasn't like that. Helen wanted to defend herself but the words stuck in her tightening throat, and her mother continued before she could get them out.

"You needn't worry. I won't tell anyone. It would shame your father in his grave. No, I couldn't heap that shame on him too. Too much, too much . . ." Suddenly she was crying, shaking her head as if fighting something inside it. Helen was bewildered, watching her mother with wide eyes. Part of her was hurt but another part wanted to embrace her, to hold her and keep her from crumbling. But then she seemed to collect herself.

"No, I will not expose your shame." She took a deep breath, and her emaciated chest seemed to shudder with the effort. "What I came to say is that I *see* you, Helen, and what I see makes me sick. You may be my blood, but you are not my daughter. You never have been, not really. And I want nothing to do with you."

She shot one last piercing glare and strode out of the chamber, leaving Helen alone with her mouth still open.

So there it was. Her mother hated her. She had always hated her, in a way. She saw that now, even if she did not understand it. She had never been good enough, never been like Nestra. Helen the whore, Helen the disappointment, Helen the unwanted.

She began to cry, fat tears rolling down her face and neck, squeezed out in painful, soul-racking sobs. For a while all she could do was let the tears fall. It felt as if they had been gathering for years, all her life in fact, rising and rising, waiting for this moment of realization.

But eventually they began to ebb, as if she were coming out of a storm. And as the sky of her mind cleared, another thought slowly surfaced. She did not have to be Helen the unwanted. Not anymore. She could leave with Paris, and become Helen the desired, Helen the loved—she could be Helen of Troy.

What was there left to stay for? Nestra was gone; Father was dead. Her mother hated her and her husband was indifferent. Her brothers would continue to dice and drink whether she was here or not. And Hermione . . . she had once thought that love might grow between them, but it seemed less likely as the years passed. Hermione did not need her. She had never needed her. She had Agatha. Helen doubted whether, in time, her daughter would even remember her face.

She was resolved. Her home had become little more than a familiar shell. No one here would much care if she was gone, so why stay? Faced with a decision between the hollow life she knew and the hopeful one she did not, she had to choose hope.

CHAPTER 31

HELEN

They rode through the night, reaching the southern port of Gythion just as dawn was beginning to break. Helen had not slept, but she didn't feel tired. It was all so exhilarating, slipping away in the middle of the night, riding toward her new life with Paris's chest against her back, his breath on her neck, his arm around her waist. She had been tingling throughout the whole journey and now, as the black ships came into view, a shiver went through her. It was really happening. She was really going to leave.

They dismounted and Helen found herself facing Paris, her hands in his. Her legs felt unsteady after the long ride and she swayed slightly where she stood, smiling up at him. He smiled back.

"I'm glad you came with me, Helen," he said in a low voice, his eyes roving over her face.

"I'm glad too," she breathed.

Then he leaned forward and kissed her, soft and long.

When they parted, Helen glanced over his shoulder and noticed several large chests on the shore, waiting to be loaded onto one of the ships.

"What's in those?" she asked casually, as Paris's men began to haul the first one up the gangplank.

"Just a few trinkets to take back," he said, putting a hand on her cheek to lead her gaze back to him. But she kept watching the men.

"From the palace?" she asked.

He paused before answering. "Yes, from the palace."

"Did my husband gift them to you? I thought he told me—"

"He did not gift them to me, no," said Paris, an edge of annoyance creeping into his voice. Helen turned to him.

"I didn't mean . . . I was just curious," she said, not wanting to ruin the heady excitement of their flight.

"It is right that guests should receive parting gifts. We have only taken what is rightfully ours. And yours too," he added. "A bride must have a dowry. Sparta's wealth is your wealth too, is it not?"

Helen didn't answer, but watched the chests being loaded, a little frown creasing her forehead. It didn't feel right. It was for a host to present gifts, not for guests to take them. Surely Menelaos would not be happy when he returned to find his palace ransacked, along with his wife. She didn't want to cause him more injury than was necessary.

"Helen, look at me," came Paris's voice, and she turned to him. "It is nothing. Just a few trifles. You are the greatest treasure Sparta has to offer. What should I care for gold when I have you?"

She smiled at this. The smoothness was back in his voice, the light in his eyes.

"I wouldn't have taken anything if I had known it would trouble you. I thought you would like some memories of your home, some comforts for your new life. I would take them back if I could, but there is no time now." He looked at her remorsefully, waiting for a response.

"It's all right," she said, with a reassuring smile. "I know you didn't mean any harm. But I don't need treasures. I only need you." She smiled again, and as he smiled back she pushed away her misgivings. He took her by the shoulders and kissed her again.

"Now we must leave," he said. Paris took her by the hand and led her up the gangplank, smiling back at her as she made those fateful steps, so that all she could see was his handsome face, those golden eyes that promised so much drawing her forward. Once on board he took her in his arms, held her and kissed her and stroked her hair so that it felt as if the whole world were melting away and it was just the two of them left, just his strong arms and her beating heart.

Then he let her go, and the world re-formed, and Helen realized that they were moving, that there was already a swathe of water between them and the shore, and growing larger every moment.

Just like that, Greece was behind her, and she had barely noticed. She felt it now, though, felt her old life, her home, her family drifting away, shrinking into the horizon. All she knew and had ever known, good and bad, was riven from her by that swelling band of blue, and it was only now that she truly realized there was no getting back to it.

A strange panic began to pulse in her stomach as she wondered whether she had done the right thing. It had felt so much safer while she still had the option of turning back, but now, with the water all around her . . . She wished she had brought her handmaids with her. What had she been thinking, not to even say good-bye to them? She had been so swept up by it all. Now she would never see them again. And Hermione . . . She wished she had kissed her daughter good-bye, given her one last memory of her. She was sad, too, as she realized she would never see her brothers marry, sad as she thought of the last words her mother had spoken to her. She was even a little sad at the thought of never seeing Menelaos again. He had been good to her, despite everything.

But it was too late for all of that. She had made her decision. Paris was a good man too—and more than that, he loved her, and she loved him. She must love him, mustn't she? To be following him halfway across the world? Something in Paris drew her to him, made her trust him, made her want to be close to him.

She looked to her side, wanting to take his hand and steady herself, but he was not there. She spotted him across the deck, talking with his cousin. Helen turned back to the shrinking coast and gripped the side of the ship instead.

She had done the right thing, she told herself. She had to leave. She was suffocating. No one would miss her. Menelaos least of all. He would understand. It would all come good. Her new life would be a rebirth, a new chance at love.

And as she stood bracing herself against the swaying deck, she prayed to the gods that she was right.

CHAPTER 32

KLYTEMNESTRA

Klytemnestra was sitting in the Hearth Hall, her newborn son gurgling in her arms. She couldn't stop looking at him—and hadn't for the past ten days. He was really here, an heir at last. Their little family was finally complete, and she couldn't be happier. She beamed at the visitors as they brought their gifts and spoke their blessings. This was not just her son but the son of Mycenae, and it seemed half the kingdom had come to celebrate his naming day. A constant stream of reverent faces had been filing in and out of the hall all morning, their gifts ranging from silver rattles to hastily picked wildflowers. All were welcome. Klytemnestra wanted to share her child and her joy with as many as would come.

Orestes, her husband had named him. A good name, she thought. He too had been beaming at the child all morning, proudly announcing him as "My son, Orestes, prince of Mycenae" to all who entered. Just as Klytemnestra had hoped, the birth seemed to have settled her husband. Today it was clear that there was nowhere he would rather be than here with her and their son.

Suddenly, Klytemnestra became aware of a commotion outside the hall. It was understandable, with all the people queueing for a look at the baby, but she wished Talthybios would keep them quiet. She didn't want Orestes getting upset, when he had been so good up until now.

Agamemnon had noticed the disturbance too and was glaring in the direction of the doors. Then suddenly his expression changed, and Klytemnestra turned to see why.

There, parting the queue of people before him as he strode into the hall, was Menelaos.

"Brother!" boomed Agamemnon. "I was not expecting you! Have you come to bless your nephew?" His jovial tone sounded over the noise of the crowd, but his smile waned as he saw his brother's face.

"You must ask everyone to leave," said Menelaos. "I need to speak with you. Alone."

He wore a queer expression that Klytemnestra could not quite read, but his eyes were serious. She instinctively put a hand over her son's head, as if protecting him from an oncoming storm.

Agamemnon nodded to his brother and rose to address the hall.

"I and my son thank you for your blessings, but the audience has now ended. Go back to your homes." He then signaled to Talthybios, who ushered the crowds out.

When the hall was quiet and the doors closed, Menelaos told his brother what had brought him to Mycenae.

"Gone?" boomed Agamemnon. "What do you mean *gone*? Have you lost her?" He exhaled a brief chuckle, but Menelaos was not smiling, and neither was Klytemnestra.

"We had foreign guests staying at the palace, from Troy—"

"Trojans? What possessed you to entertain those bastards? I wouldn't give them a bed if they begged. Let them grovel to their Hittite masters instead, I say." He spat on the ground.

"I thought . . . They came in peace, brother. They wanted to reopen the trade routes, they said. But . . . you're right. I shouldn't have trusted them." Menelaos's expression was bitter. "My men think my wife left with them. I was away—at our grandfather's funeral—and when I returned she was not there. It is not certain . . . how she was taken. But no one heard her shout for help."

Klytemnestra knew what he was implying, but she didn't want to believe it. Helen would not willingly abandon her family. She must have been tricked. Perhaps they had threatened her daughter—she herself would do anything to protect her children.

She feared for Helen. She must be so afraid, taken from her home, raped by a foreign man. But if she had not been raped, if she had left willingly . . . The thought was not much better. *Oh, Helen. What have you done?*

"You were right to come to me," said Agamemnon gravely. "Once the rest of Greece hears . . . what will they say? That we cannot keep our women? That we let our guests dishonor us? No, the House of Atreus will not be mocked. I will not—"

Then a strange look came over his face, as if a thought had struck him. And, quite to Klytemnestra's bafflement, a shadow of a smile curled at the edge of his lips.

"No, we will not be mocked," he repeated slowly. "Brother, this is not a trial the gods have sent us. It is an opportunity."

He was leaning forward in his seat now, a sudden energy animating his features. Menelaos looked confused, and seemed to reflect some of the disbelief that must have shown on Klytemnestra's own face.

"An *opportunity*? Have you misunderstood me, brother?" Menelaos asked tersely. "My wife is gone. Taken. Either by seduction, in which case I am cuckolded and made a fool before all the world. Or she was stolen by force, to be defiled by foreign men, raped and beaten. She may already be dead."

Klytemnestra felt sick, and the rare emotion in Menelaos's voice scared her. She wondered where Helen was right now, and an image of her sister's body rotting at the bottom of the sea forced its way into her mind. She pushed it away. Could Helen have really done this thing? Had she gone willingly? Had she done it for love? She was beginning to hope so.

Agamemnon's booming voice broke her thoughts.

"I understand the situation quite well, brother. Better than you, it seems." Menelaos's brow furrowed in anger, but Agamemnon continued before he could speak. "Do you not see? Your wife, the flower of Greece, has been plucked by foreign guests from your own palace. They have broken the sacred laws of guest-friendship. They have dishonored you. Insulted you. But more than that, brother, they have insulted Greece."

Menelaos was silent for a moment, surveying his brother's face. Then, in a quieter voice, he said, "They emptied my treasury, too. I thought the matter of my wife more pressing, but—"

"Even better," cried Agamemnon, thumping his fist on the arm of his throne. Klytemnestra saw his shadow of a smile strengthen. "Those Eastern rats have stolen from Greece. We must show them that our wives are not theirs to rape, our gold is not theirs to plunder."

"And how do you mean to do that?" asked Menelaos warily.

"By taking back that which was stolen."

Agamemnon's words echoed around the chamber, and it seemed to Klytemnestra as if they had a heaviness to them, a significance that could not be taken back now that it had been breathed into the world.

"You mean to go to war."

And with these words Menelaos gave solidity to the thought that was beginning to form in Klytemnestra's mind.

"Do not be foolish, brother," he continued when Agamemnon said nothing. "We do not have the strength. Troy is a rich and powerful city, with rich and powerful friends. You ought not to underestimate her. Even with the forces of Sparta and Mycenae combined—"

"Sparta and Mycenae? You misunderstand me," said Agamemnon. "It is not us two alone who will wage this war, but all Greece."

"How?" asked Menelaos, perplexed. "How will you convince them? It is not their cause. Why risk themselves for another man's wife?"

"You forget. Helen was not just your bride, brother, but the bride of Greece. Every kingdom from here to Ithaka sent a prince to compete for her. And every one of those men gave an oath that if she was taken from the man who won her, they would aid him to get her back."

A new realization was on Menelaos's face, and Klytemnestra saw in it that what her husband said was true. Fear began to rumble in her belly.

"Greece is ours to command, brother." Agamemnon's voice was live with excitement. "We will remind the suitors of their oaths, tell them how the foreign defilers stole your wife, plundered your wealth. And we will teach those foreign dogs that Greece is not to be trifled with."

Klytemnestra hadn't seen her husband this animated in months, perhaps years. Not even the birth of their son had brought such brightness to his eyes. It scared her. He was a determined man, and once an idea was in him . . . if it was a war he wanted, it was a war he would get. She saw now that he had been waiting for just such an opportunity. A chance to do something great, to grow his power. Mycenae was not enough. His family was not enough. Not even Orestes was enough. In that moment, Klytemnestra realized that her husband would always want more.

Though she feared for her sister, she feared losing her husband too. She couldn't bear for her family to break when it was only just starting to feel whole. And if Agamemnon should die, what would become of her children? What would become of her? But Helen was family too, bonded by blood and the years they had spent together in Sparta. The thought of her alone in a foreign land, at the whim of her captor—or even of her seducer—brought its own terror. In Klytemnestra's head, Helen was still the hopeful, life-loving, naïve little girl she had left behind in Sparta, and now more than ever she wished she could see her again and know that she was safe.

Torn between the family she had left behind and the new one she had nurtured, Klytemnestra gave neither warning nor encouragement to her husband's visions of glory but sat in silence, gently rocking her son as the men made their plans, and the wheels of war began to turn.

CHAPTER 33

KLYTEMNESTRA

Orestes was restless. It was a warm day, so maybe that was it. He had been crying on and off all morning, and had struggled against his swaddling cloth so much that Klytemnestra had finally removed it. She was wandering around the palace with him now, bouncing him in her arms as she went. It seemed to be working and he settled a little, his cries slowly turning to gurgled murmurs.

There was a time when her husband had disapproved of her going about the palace without an escort, but he had grown less concerned with such things in recent years. She hoped it was because he trusted her and not because he no longer cared, but either way it was nice to have the freedom of the palace.

She continued on her way, still bouncing little Orestes in her weary arms, until she reached the main courtyard. Just as she did, she saw a slight man scurry across it from the direction of the Hearth Hall.

She paused for a second, then headed toward the open door he had just passed through. When she was close she peered in, and there on his gilt throne sat her husband.

"Ah, wife," he said, as he looked up and spotted her. "Bring my boy to me. I want him to remember my face when I'm gone."

And there it was: the reminder of what she had been trying so hard not to think about. She knew it was childish, but keeping the thought from her mind made it a little less real, at least for now.

As she reached her husband, she realized he was holding a clay writing tablet, which he put on the floor so that he could take Orestes from her.

"Some news?" she asked, peering down at the clay but knowing it was useless to try to make sense of the strange symbols. It had always seemed a little mystical to her, how men could look at the little lines and see the voice of another man, though he was perhaps miles away.

"The last messenger has just returned," said her husband in a tone of satisfaction. "Lord Odysseus had me waiting weeks. More than a little reluctant, so I'm told. But he's come around in the end, just like all the others. No doubt he's worried about missing out on all the glory!" Agamemnon barked another laugh, his eyes bright. "The whole thing went easier than expected, to tell the truth. Daresay I could have won a lot of them without the oath! Just give them a cause, let them tell themselves they're fighting for Greece, or liberty, or . . . whatever, and they'll jump at the chance for some action."

Klytemnestra smiled weakly, noting that he had said nothing of fighting for Helen; she bit her lip. She had been half hoping that the other princes would refuse the call, but it seemed they were as restless for glory as her husband.

"You will soon be the wife not just of the King of Mycenae, but of the commander of all the Greeks. And our son's kingdom will be greater than any of his ancestors'. I will bring such riches from the Troad."

His eyes sparkled as if already beholding the treasures he would plunder. She tried to force another smile, but the mention of their son was too much.

"What if you do not come back? Mycenae is only ours because it is yours," she said, looking to the little bundle in her husband's thick arms. "Will you leave your children undefended?" She knew it was bold to speak out, but this was what she feared most. With Agamemnon gone, Mycenae would be left vulnerable, with her children the first targets for any ambitious wayfarer hoping to gain himself a kingdom.

Agamemnon's face became serious. "Have faith, wife. The gods would not have given us this opportunity if they did not mean for us to seize it, and for our seizing to come good. You will see."

She nodded, though still unconvinced.

"Mycenae will not be undefended," he went on. "I will leave a garrison of men, and a steward to aid you in ruling."

"Ruling?" she repeated, surprised.

"You are Queen of Mycenae, are you not? Orestes is too young. The people need a figurehead."

She nodded solemnly. "O-of course."

"The steward will take care of most things. I just need you here to remind the people who their king is. Entertain guests and such."

"Oh," she said, realizing she had overtaken his meaning. She was surprised at her disappointment. "Yes, my lord."

"And you must see to the sacrifices, of course. We must have the gods on our side."

"Yes, husband."

"In fact, I've already taken action to that effect, so you can stop your worrying."

She gave him a questioning look.

"A seer. We will need one with us if we are to know the gods' whims. I have already sent for him. The best in the kingdom, so they say, and I don't doubt it."

Suddenly Klytemnestra felt worried.

"Which seer?"

"From Argos. I don't remember the name, but you might know his face. He's been to the palace before, years ago. He was the one who predicted my accident—that's what put me in mind to send for him."

Kalchas.

"Yes, I—I might remember him, if I saw him," she said. Her heart was thumping at the memory of a time she had tried to forget, and of the anger in the priest's eyes the last time she had seen him.

"Are you sure he is the best in the kingdom?" she asked, trying her best to sound unconcerned. "I have heard of many great seers. There is one in Tiryns who—"

"Yes, I'm sure," snapped her husband. "There are many who claim to know the seer's arts, yes, but few have proven themselves, and even fewer to me. He's the one I'll take."

"But husband, do you not remember why he came to Mycenae? It was . . . about that girl. And maybe, with the way things . . . ended, perhaps he might bear you ill will."

"Gods, woman! How you fret! I've said he's the one I'll take and I will. I've already sent to Argos for him."

Even after all these years her husband's bark was enough to cow her. She wanted to say more, to warn him against trusting the priest too freely, but she knew he would not listen to her. He never did. And if Kalchas was already sent for there was little she could do at present.

Agamemnon's flare of irritation seemed to soften as he wiggled his finger at the grasping fists of his son. But then Orestes began to cry.

"Here," said his father, thrusting the child back toward its mother. "Take him back to the chamber, will you? I can't stand it when they cry."

CHAPTER 34

KLYTEMNESTRA

That evening, Klytemnestra was in the Hearth Hall once again, this time seated on her ivory-inlaid chair, her husband enthroned beside her. The children had already been put to bed and Eudora was watching over them. Klytemnestra hadn't wanted to miss the audience. She knew she had to be here when he came. She had to see his face.

Kalchas was standing before her husband, his feet planted on the stone, the hearth flames flickering behind him. He looked older, Klytemnestra thought. A number of years had passed since she had last seen him, of course, but it seemed as if twice as many had passed for him. The youthful cushion of his cheeks was gone, his broad, smooth brow had become lined, and he leaned on his staff as if his body, too, were worn beyond its years.

"You have my gratitude for arriving so promptly, seer." Agamemnon leaned back on his throne, his voice booming effortlessly. "Now that I have my pledges, I wish to make the journey to Aulis as soon as possible. I take it from your presence here that you have agreed to my request?"

"Indeed, my lord," replied the priest, his tone polite but his face unreadable. "I will be honored to serve as seer for the Greeks."

Klytemnestra's heart tightened at the confirmation. She had still hoped that he would say no.

"Good to hear it!" barked Agamemnon with a broad smile. "I haven't forgotten the last time you came to my hall. I knew then that your powers were true. My accident proved you right."

"You mean your punishment, my lord," said Kalchas in his soft tones. "I told you that the goddess would punish you."

"Yes, yes. That's what I meant," replied her husband, waving a huge hand dismissively.

"For taking Leukippe." Kalchas's face was set like stone, his eyes fixed on Agamemnon.

"Ah, yes! That's what it was all about, I remember!" His tone was jovial, as if it had all been a good laugh between them. "How is the little bastard? It must be . . . seven, eight by now?"

Klytemnestra saw the priest's lips tighten almost imperceptibly. "The child didn't survive the birth. Nor the mother."

He spoke levelly, but Klytemnestra could feel the pain behind those still features. She felt it too, sadness at the thought of that poor girl torn from life so young, and of the baby too, her husband's seed. But with the sadness and the pity there rose fear. With those few words the stakes had changed, and she feared that stone face and that calm voice more than ever.

"Ah well, it was the will of the gods," said her husband more soberly, but his tone was quickly excited once more.

"Have you communed with the gods about my campaign? Do they give good fortune? Are they pleased with my sacrifices?"

Klytemnestra was sure Kalchas would not be able to hide his anger any longer, that he would not let Agamemnon move on so easily from the subject of Leukippe, but when he spoke, he could not have been more gracious.

"There is no need to ask them, my lord, for they have this very day sent me an omen. I saw it as I journeyed here from Argos, a dead hare beside the road, its belly full with young. Two birds sat atop it, one black and one white, tearing at the flesh and the treasure inside. Two birds for two brothers, the glorious Atreidai, the one you, my lord, and the other your wronged brother. And the hare, of course, Troy herself."

The image made Klytemnestra feel nauseated, but it seemed to please her husband. "Excellent," he said, rubbing his huge hands together. "Already you have proved your worth, and we have not yet left Mycenae's walls!" He barked a laugh. "Yes, I knew you would be the right choice. It is decided then. We will leave tomorrow, and you shall accompany us."

Kalchas bowed reverently.

"Talthybios will show you to your room and provide you with anything you may need. Sleep well—it may be the last proper bed you see for some time!"

The priest bowed again, and left the chamber in silence.

"Please, husband," whispered Klytemnestra urgently as soon as the doors were shut. "Do not take him with you. Choose another seer. I fear he means you ill."

"Nonsense. Why should he? You heard the omen. He sees my glory, and he will help me to achieve it."

"But the girl—"

"Is that what this is about?" he snapped. "It's a sad business, but nothing that doesn't happen every day to some poor whore. Why should he care? What was she to him? Some temple servant? I should think he thanked the gods he had two less mouths to feed."

Klytemnestra looked at her husband, horrified. Was he really so blind? Sometimes she could convince herself that she loved him, but other times . . . She felt sick, with her husband, with what had happened to Leukippe, with the prospect of war, with her utter powerlessness against it all. She could not tell Agamemnon that Leukippe was Kalchas's sister—she had sworn an oath to the gods on her children's lives that she wouldn't—but even if she could tell him, she wondered whether it would make any difference. It was as if walls had closed around him and wax had stopped his ears, and all he could see was Troy and war and his own shining glory.

"Come," he said, taking her hand and rising from his throne. "I leave in the morning. Let us see if I can put another son in you for when I return."

CHAPTER 35

KLYTEMNESTRA

It had been almost a month since Agamemnon had left, and yet the palace did not feel as changed as Klytemnestra had thought it would. It was a little emptier perhaps, without some of the faces she was used to seeing, and it felt a little larger without Agamemnon's sizable presence there to fill it. But daily life was not much different. She still spent her afternoons teaching the girls to spin and weave, still spent half her nights nursing Orestes. It felt as if her husband were only away on one of his visits and would return any day with new gifts to dazzle the children.

There had been one change, though. Each morning, once the children were washed and settled, she would leave them with Eudora and make her way to one of the modestly sized rooms behind the Hearth Hall. It had long held an air of mystery for Klytemnestra, not least because she had never had cause to go there. It wasn't that it was forbidden to her—not as such—but she knew that her husband would have disapproved. It was not a place to concern ladies, he would have said with a derisive laugh or a scornful wave of the hand. But now, with Agamemnon gone, there was no one to tell her where she ought or ought not to spend her time. And so, the very morning after he had left, this was where she had come.

This morning, as on every morning since that first nerve-filled venture, she tapped on the plain wooden door.

"Good morning, mistress," said the small man who opened it. He shuffled backward and gestured toward a carved chair, finer than the other furniture that filled the room. "I'll just get you a fresh tablet, and we can begin."

This cramped, musty room was where the palace scribes did their work. Here they made records of the goods stored in the palace, of taxes collected from the villages, of sacrifices made to the gods. Here words and numbers were carved in clay, then made solid and stored away in the Archive Room next door. It seemed almost magical to Klytemnestra, and she loved to watch as they scratched busily away as if it were no more difficult than spinning wool.

But what she was really interested in, and what she had primarily come here to learn, was how to understand the symbols that were written. She was the real Queen of Mycenae now, responsible for all that happened both within the palace and outside it. How could she do her duty to her kingdom if she could not read the news brought to her, as a man could? She could not rely on others to report such things. What if they changed the words? What if they left something out? She needed to read it herself.

Eusebios, the head scribe, had been teaching her what the lines meant, the sound they made, how they fit together. She even practiced drawing them too. She was still very slow and would sometimes make mistakes— some of the shapes looked too similar—but she was getting better, day by day. Eusebios had been surprised at how quickly she could learn.

He had been a reluctant teacher at first. He didn't think Agamemnon would approve, and feared punishment upon his return. Letters were not for women to learn, and perhaps queens even less. But she had assured him that she would take the blame, if there was any, and convinced him that Mycenae needed a true queen while its king was absent. And it was true, wasn't it? But as she learned to interpret those mysterious shapes she discovered a whole world that had been hidden from her before. Who knew what her husband, her father, her brothers had read there, how much they had shared with her, and how much they had left silent in the clay? It made her feel powerful, to access that secret world of words without voices.

Perhaps she could share that power with her daughters, she mused as she carefully flattened the surface of the tablet Eusebios had given her. What a gift that would be! And it would be easier for them, to start while they were still young. If they were taught to shape letters like they were taught to spin wool, if they could learn to weave words like they wove their patterns on the loom, in time their hands would do the work all on their own, their thoughts made material almost as soon as they had been conceived.

But not yet. Eusebios had taken a risk in agreeing to teach her, and she did not want to push him too far. Klytemnestra felt that she and the scribe had become friends, almost. It was nice to feel that she had another ally in the palace—other than Eudora and her handmaids. With Agamemnon gone she knew she needed to build her own base of respect and loyalty, if she was to keep Mycenae secure for his return, and for that she needed the support of men.

She had just begun to practice forming the letters with her stylus when there was a knock at the door. She didn't look up from her work but saw Eusebios rise from his stool beside her.

"A message has arrived. From Lord Agamemnon."

Klytemnestra lifted her head at the sound of the steward's voice.

"I was told the queen could be found here," he continued. She thought she heard a trace of disapproval in his voice, but she told herself she had imagined it.

"Yes, Damon," she said, standing up to address the steward. "What news? Does the campaign go well? Was the crossing to Troy a success?" She could see that the seal on the tablet he carried had already been broken, and feared what fortune its words might bring. Surely

Agamemnon would not send a messenger all the way back from the Troad if it was not something serious.

"The fleet has not yet left Greece, my lady," Damon reported. "They wait at Aulis still. Lord Agamemnon has delayed their departure until . . . until the princess Iphigenia is wedded to the lord Achilles, Prince of Phthia. The king asks that she be sent to Aulis at once for the ceremony."

It took Klytemnestra a while to register what the steward had said. Iphigenia, *her* Iphigenia, was to be wed? And not to any man, but Achilles himself? Yes, his fame had reached her ears. A great warrior, so they said, favored by the gods and heir to his father's kingdom. She could not have hoped for a better match, and yet . . . it did not feel so long ago that she had held her in her arms, nursed her at her breast. Her firstborn, so pure and delicate and precious. She had known this day would come, that matches would have to be made, for the sake of the kingdom, but it was too soon. Iphigenia was only eleven—too young by far and not ready to become a woman. She had not even started her bleeding yet. How could she send her away to a lonely life in some other man's palace, far from all who loved her, while her new husband was off fighting a war?

And in that moment, she saw what she must do. She would accompany her daughter to Aulis and negotiate with the men so that Iphigenia might remain at Mycenae for the time being, at least until the war was over. She would not object to the marriage—she was sure Agamemnon must have a good reason for arranging it, to have made the match with Iphigenia still so young—but where was the sense in sending her daughter away when she could not yet be any use as a wife?

Agamemnon would agree, she was sure. All would be well. And it would give her a little more time to cherish her daughter.

"My lady?" came Damon's voice again.

"Yes. We shall send the princess Iphigenia straight away," she replied, already planning her entreaty to her husband in her head. "And I shall be going with her."

CHAPTER 36

KLYTEMNESTRA

They set off the next morning, in a covered wagon to keep off the spots of rain that spattered dully against its canopy. Klytemnestra sat opposite her daughter while a large chest served as a kind of table between them, carrying, among other things, Iphigenia's bridal outfit. Klytemnestra was thankful she had already made her daughter's dress and veil, knowing they would one day be needed, though she regretted that they were not as finished as she would have liked. The dress was missing some of its golden finishings and the veil, though neatly woven, was rather thick. She had been planning to make another, but then everything had happened so quickly . . . She should have packed her own wedding veil, she thought suddenly—the gossamer-fine one her mother had made—but it was too late to go back. They had been on the road for over an hour already.

Orestes would probably be having his second feeding of the day about now, she thought, and a pang of guilt spasmed in her chest. It had pained her to leave him with the wet nurse, her own flesh, so small and precious, but he was safer at the palace than on the road. And right now her daughter needed her more.

She looked over at Iphigenia, who was watching the hills as they crawled by. She had made no complaint about leaving so suddenly, nor any challenge to her father's wishes. She had always idolized him. More than anything she had been pleased that she would be able to see him again before he made the crossing to Troy.

Klytemnestra smiled as she watched her daughter's bright eyes taking in the landscape. It was not often that the girls had opportunity to leave the palace; Elektra had sulked that she was not allowed to come with them. And as she too began to watch the hills Klytemnestra realized that this journey would take her farther from Mycenae than she had been since arriving there twelve years ago. How nervous she had been on that other wagon ride, herself a young bride, knowing and yet not knowing what awaited her at its end. She looked at Iphigenia again, trying to read her. Was she nervous? Was she thinking about the wedding? About what might happen afterward? If she was, she didn't show it. But sometimes it was hard to tell with her. She was always so bright, so sweet—Klytemnestra sometimes worried that she hid away her sadness just to save others from the burden of it.

"They say the lord Achilles is a great man," she ventured, keeping her eyes on the damp landscape. "A great warrior. And faster on his feet than any man alive."

In the corner of her eye she saw Iphigenia turn her head briefly toward her, and then back to the hills.

"Yes, I'm sure he is. A great man, I mean," she said cheerfully. Then, after a brief pause, "I don't think Father would let him marry me if he weren't."

There was the shadow of a question in her small voice, and Klytemnestra swept in to reassure her.

"No, of course he wouldn't. You are a princess of Mycenae. Your father wouldn't just give you away to any man." She smiled across at her daughter, who smiled back.

"Yes, I thought so," she said, almost to herself, and turned her eyes back to the hills.

They sat in silence for a few minutes, bouncing in their seats a little as the wagon made its way over the rocks and ditches that marked the narrow valley road. Eventually Iphigenia spoke again.

"Even if he is a great man—I'm sure he is, if Father has chosen him—but . . . even if he is . . . I'm not sure if I'm ready to be a wife."

Her thin words hung in the air and she kept her eyes on the hills, but as Klytemnestra reached out and took her hand, she turned her neat golden head toward her mother, and for the first time since hearing of her father's request, Klytemnestra saw a little concern in her eyes.

"There's no need to worry," said Klytemnestra with a warm smile. "It's just a little ceremony, to make everything official. You won't have to be his wife yet, not until you're ready. You're too young for all that." She squeezed her daughter's hand. "We'll do the rites and the feast, and you might have to let him kiss you—just a little kiss—but after that you'll be coming back home with me." She smiled again, trying to reassure herself as much as Iphigenia. "You'll see. Your father will listen. And I'll be with you all the time we're there."

Iphigenia exhaled a little and returned her mother's smile.

"I'm glad you're here," was all she said, before turning her eyes back to the hills.

I'm glad I am, too, Klytemnestra said silently to herself, watching her daughter's face, the way the wind rippled her fair hair, the way her eyes darted about the landscape. She didn't want Iphigenia to worry, but her own fears swelled beneath the surface even as she was trying to allay her daughter's. What if she could not convince the men? Was she foolish to think she could even try? Could she really promise her daughter that she would come home again once all this was done? These might be some of the final days the two of them would spend together. Every minute was precious, every second irretrievable. She would savor this journey, and her daughter, as much as she was able.

❧

It felt all too soon when Klytemnestra glanced ahead of them in the early evening of the third day and saw, beyond the next brow, black masts huddled against the gray-blue sky like tall, leafless trees. She swallowed at the sight of them, nerves rising in her throat, and touched Iphigenia's arm lightly.

"We're here."

The soldiers' camp was large and sprawling, with temporary buildings and firepits and trodden mud paths that looked like they had been in use for some time. The smells of leather and horses and things less pleasant were a little overwhelming after the fresh air of the hills, and as the men started to take note of their passing, Klytemnestra was doubly glad of her thick veil. Drawing it across her face, and feeling guilty that she had not given Iphigenia her own veil before entering the camp, she tried to ignore the lewd comments that rose around them, the shameless stares and the nudging whispers.

She supposed they must look a little odd, two women entering a soldiers' camp with no male company but their driver and a small rear guard. Perhaps word had not yet spread of the wedding—perhaps Agamemnon was keeping it quiet to stop other men from demanding a similar privilege to Achilles. Yes, that would be sensible. She did not think she could bear to give away another daughter. Not yet, anyway.

Even if she could understand their curiosity, Klytemnestra regretted that she had not sent one of the men ahead so that Agamemnon could meet them outside the camp and escort them through. She doubted even the boldest of the men would have dared show such disrespect if her husband had been with them.

Just then she heard a familiar sound, more bark than voice, and was surprised by how glad she was to hear it. Up ahead, the inimitable boom of her husband rose above the general din, and soon she caught sight of the dark head to which it belonged.

"Look," she said to Iphigenia, pointing over the girl's shoulder as she squeezed her hand. "We're here at last."

Iphigenia flicked her blond head around and Klytemnestra could see her cheeks lift as she beamed.

"Father!" she cried excitedly. And somehow, above the shouts and brays and clatters of the camp, he heard her and turned his head.

He did not return his daughter's smile, but turned seriously to Talthybios who was hovering, as so often, beside his elbow. Klytemnestra saw her husband's lips mutter a command, and the herald scurried off, likely to make preparations for their stay. But even once Talthybios had gone, Agamemnon did not return his eyes to their wagon.

It was only as they drew to a stop beside him that her husband acknowledged their arrival.

"I did not ask you to come," he said, his hard gray eyes on Klytemnestra. "You should not have come."

Klytemnestra opened her mouth uselessly. She didn't know what to say. It was not the welcome she had expected after their long journey, and she felt a little bruised by it.

"Father!" cried Iphigenia for a second time, as she hopped from the wagon and threw her arms around him. "I'm so happy to see you, Father!" she chirped, burying her golden head into his broad midriff.

He stood stiffly, like a tree resisting the caress of the wind, and though he half raised a hand as if to pat his daughter's head, it hung in the air as he hesitated. Instead, he put both hands on her narrow shoulders and pried her gently away from him, forcing a half smile as she looked up.

"I'm glad you have arrived safely," was all he said before turning back to Klytemnestra, who had by now descended from the wagon.

"You should not have come," he said again. There was a deep crease in his brow. "The camp is no place for a woman. You undermine me by being here. And what of our son? You have abandoned him—what will the men think? To see my wife here while my son is left at home. You dishonor me."

The last words bit like teeth, and Klytemnestra was sure he had said them just to hurt her. Why was he acting this way? If the camp was no place for a woman, why had he called for Iphigenia? Had he really expected her to send their daughter alone? She had tried to do right, by him and by her children, but under that stony glare she was beginning to doubt herself.

"I know you did not ask me to come, but neither did you forbid it. I thought—"

"Enough." His voice was uncharacteristically quiet, which somehow made it more menacing. "You will leave tomorrow morning. The hour is too late now."

"But I will miss the rites!" she pleaded. "Might I not stay for the wedding, now that I have come all this way? Our daughter does not even have a maid to dress her!"

Iphigenia was looking between her parents, her young eyes pleading her mother's case.

"No. It is not possible. You cannot be here. I am sorry."

His concession of an apology disarmed her, and she was silent for a moment, staring up into those gray eyes, trying to read something there, some hope that he would change his mind. But she found none.

"Very well," she said stiffly, not able to meet her daughter's gaze, and the disappointment, or worse, that she might see there. She had promised her, *promised* her she would be there with her. "I will leave tomorrow morning," she conceded, "but first I must speak with you concerning the arrangements for after the wedding. Please, husband. I hoped that—"

"Yes, yes. Very well. I will speak with you before you leave in the morning. I have things I must attend to now."

She would have preferred to speak with him sooner, to reassure both herself and Iphigenia, but fearing to lose what little ground she had gained she simply said, "Thank you, husband."

He nodded. "A tent has been prepared for Iphigenia. You may both sleep there. Talthybios will show you the way—here he comes." And before his herald had even reached them, he was gone.

As they stood in the mud, watching those broad shoulders disappear down one of many well-trodden paths, Klytemnestra weathered her hurt in silence, with her hand wrapped tightly around that of her daughter. She had thought that Agamemnon would be pleased to see her. It had been a whole month since they had parted, and the gods knew how many more it would be until they saw each other again. Perhaps they never would. Maybe she had been wrong to come, but she was here now, and yet he did not even want her to share his tent.

You're being silly, she said to herself. *Like a little girl.* She wasn't a girl anymore, or even just a woman. She was a queen, and she had to remember that. She was married to a king, and not just any king, but the commander of all Greece. At the moment that duty came before being a husband, or even a father.

CHAPTER 37

KLYTEMNESTRA

Klytemnestra struggled to get to sleep that night. The men of the camp stayed up long after the sun had set, drinking and dicing around their fires, their voices carrying through the thick canvas of the tent. It was not they who kept her awake, however. Her brain buzzed with uncertainties. What if she could not convince Agamemnon? Could she really leave Iphigenia to get married alone, to be sent away to some foreign kingdom? Could she refuse to leave? Defy her husband? That would not be wise, but poor Iphigenia . . .

She could hear her daughter's slow, shallow breaths at the other end of the tent. At least one of them was able to sleep, though Klytemnestra did not know how she could. Perhaps she had faith in her father, that he would not send her to waste her youth in lonely redundance. Or trust that her mother would not let it happen. Klytemnestra wished she could have the same faith.

She must have fallen asleep eventually, for when Klytemnestra next opened her eyes the voices of the camp had fallen silent and the faint light of its fires had vanished.

But wait. No, there was a light still. Just one, quite close by her side of the tent. And getting closer.

She barely had chance to raise her head from her pillow before the tent door was suddenly raised, and the moving light shone through.

"Husband?" she whispered. No, the figure behind the lamp was too short. But if it was not Agamemnon . . .

The light moved toward her. She opened her mouth to call for help, but as she did the figure lifted its hood and a familiar face emerged.

"*Alkimos?*" she whispered in amazement. "Is that really you?" She thought perhaps she might still be dreaming. Here before her was a man she had not seen since childhood. A slave of her father's, who used to make her giggle by pulling funny faces when her mother wasn't looking. He was older now, of course, but he still looked strong and healthy. The sight of him made her feel suddenly homesick.

"What are you doing here?" she hissed, keeping her voice low so as not to wake Iphigenia. "In the camp, I mean?"

"I am here attending the king, my lady," he whispered back.

But Father is dead was her first thought, before realizing that he meant Menelaos. It had been a silly question—she was still only half awake.

"Yes, yes, of course you are," she replied, looking up at that dark, lamp-lit face. "It's so good to see you," she said, and meant it.

"I am glad to see you once again too, my lady. But I have come on a matter of great urgency."

His face held none of the playful smiles she remembered. Instead it was grim, his body agitated. Klytemnestra straightened herself, suddenly wide awake.

"You and your daughter must leave," he whispered. "Before sunrise. Leave your things, take a horse and get as far as you can before he knows you are gone. You still remember how to ride?"

Klytemnestra nodded vaguely, perplexed by what he was saying. "Before who knows we are gone?"

"Lord Agamemnon," he whispered, looking over his shoulder as if speaking her husband's name might summon him.

"But . . . I don't understand."

"There's no time, my lady. You'll find a horse outside the tent. The guards shouldn't bother you but—"

"No," she said, more certainly this time. "I will not take my daughter into the wilderness in the middle of the night without knowing why!"

Alkimos looked at her, then briefly over to the bed where Iphigenia lay. Her daughter was still sleeping soundly.

"It isn't safe. For her," he murmured, his eyes flicking to Iphigenia once again. "Your husband means her harm."

"What harm? Do you mean the marriage? Is Achilles a cruel man?"

"No, no, my lady. You don't understand. There is no marriage."

She was even more confused now.

"What do you mean, no marriage? Why else would he have brought her here? It doesn't make any sense—"

"It was a lie— All a lie— I . . ." He paused. "May the gods forgive us all, my lady. He brought her here to kill her."

Klytemnestra had heard people speak of blood running cold, but never before had she understood what they meant.

"No," she uttered. "You're lying. He wouldn't—he couldn't."

"It is true, my lady. I had hoped to spare you this, but you wouldn't listen, and I couldn't—You have to leave. Now."

But his words just sounded like rushing water in Klytemnestra's ears.

"But *why*?" she asked. "Why would he . . . he loves her. I don't—"

"There was a prophecy. The winds have been ill for so long . . . Lord Agamemnon asked his seer why the gods were preventing our crossing—"

"His seer?" asked Klytemnestra suddenly.

"Yes, my lady. The seer told him that he had killed a hind sacred to

Artemis, that he had angered the goddess. He said the princess was the sacrifice the gods demanded. That the ships can't sail until—"

But Klytemnestra was no longer listening. She had sprung from her bed and hurried over to where Iphigenia lay.

"Hmm?" What is it, Mother?" her daughter said groggily as Klytemnestra shook her shoulder. Then, seeing her mother's face, "What's wrong?"

"Nothing," she lied. "You're safe. Everything is fine. But I need you to get dressed. Put on your traveling clothes."

Iphigenia looked at her questioningly, and then her eyes widened as she spotted the man behind her. "Who's that?"

"A friend," she whispered. "He'll stay with you until I return. Don't worry—he won't look."

"But—where are you going?"

"Not far. I'll be back soon. Now do as I say, there's a good girl." She leaned down to kiss her daughter's forehead, and could not resist a quick embrace.

"I love you very much," she whispered, trying desperately to keep the fear from her voice.

Then, straightening up, she turned to Alkimos. "Which way to the seer's tent?"

CHAPTER 38

KLYTEMNESTRA

Klytemnestra's bedclothes dragged in the mud as she marched through the camp. There was no time to change—she had not even put on sandals in her hurry. Stones jabbed at the soles of her feet but she barely noticed. All she saw was the tent ahead of her, its holy ribbons fluttering in the moonlight, just as Alkimos had described.

Anger was swilling in her mouth. How could he? How *could* he? Iphigenia . . . *her* Iphigenia . . . She had to speak with him. Even if they fled her daughter would not be safe. She had to set it right.

The tent was just a few paces away now. She was gripping the lamp so tightly that her hand was shaking. *How could he?*

She flung the tent door open and stepped inside. She glanced around the room, and in the lamplight made out a bed, a blanket, and the sleeper beneath it. He was alone.

"Gods curse you, Kalchas!" she growled, pulling the blanket back. "Gods curse you! How could you? My Iphigenia . . . what harm did she ever do you?"

She had been determined not to cry, but already the tears were welling. It was a strain to keep her voice from cracking.

Kalchas sat up in his bed, looking calmly up at her.

"Lady Klytemnestra," he said evenly, as if it were perfectly ordinary that she should have come to him like this in the middle of the night. "Is there something I can do for you?"

His calmness infuriated her.

"You know very well why I am here, Kalchas," she spat. "You know what you have done. My Iphigenia . . . *why?* I tried to help you! You and Leukippe . . . I . . . I betrayed my husband for you, I—"

"The gods demand what they demand, my lady. I only read the signs—"

"Don't you dare lie to me," she hissed. "I am not so blind as my husband!" She stopped to gather herself, realizing she had raised her voice. "You must take it back, Kalchas. You have to tell him it's not true. Gods know why you would say such a thing in the first place."

"You know why." His eyes were on her, steady and hard like rock.

"So you would avenge one innocent life by taking another?"

"I . . ." He paused, his eyes wavering a little. He gave the smallest sigh. "In truth, I did not think he would go through with it. I thought, if I . . . if the gods demanded the unimaginable, that he would be forced to give up. That his campaign would be ruined, his reputation with it. I thought he would be humiliated, and go home."

"But . . . surely the men would not expect him to sacrifice his own child? He could have just said no. They would not have blamed him."

"Would they not?" Kalchas looked up at her again. "These men, who have sacrificed so much of their own to fight for him? To fight for Greece? They have left their kingdoms vulnerable, their sons without fathers, their fathers without sons. Many of them will likely give their lives. And yet he, their leader, their summoner to arms, not willing to sacrifice one child? And a daughter, not even an heir? He would have been shamed."

Klytemnestra's mouth hung open, but she didn't know what to say.

"I thought he would take the shame," Kalchas continued. "That would have been enough, to see him fall from so high. I could have moved on. But I . . . underestimated him. His pride, his vanity. His ambition. He has made Troy his goal. It is as if a fever has infected his mind." His tone was of disgust. "All he sees is Troy, and his fist around it. He will stop at nothing, I see that now."

"But it isn't true!" said Klytemnestra desperately. "He doesn't need to make the sacrifice at all! The gods do not demand it, only you! You can tell him that you lied, or that you were mistaken, or that the gods have sent a new augury! The winds will come, and the ships will sail and—and I will still have my daughter." Her final word was almost a sob.

"I'm afraid I cannot," said Kalchas, his tone even once again.

Klytemnestra looked at him sharply. "But you must! You're the only one who can stop this madness!" She paused, her eyes frantically searching his. "You are a good man, Kalchas, or you were once. You loved your sister, you know what it is to lose someone you love. I know how much it hurt you . . . How much *he* hurt you, and I am sorry for it. But killing Iphigenia will not bring Leukippe back!"

She knelt on the floor and pleaded, grasped his bedcovers and poured her breaking heart out through the tears that rolled down her cheeks. But his eyes stared dully back at her, like stone once more.

"I am sorry," he said quietly. "Do not think it gives me pleasure. No, indeed, I—I hardly feel anything anymore." He made a hollow sound, like a laugh without the breath to carry it. "Your husband is an evil man, and he must suffer. I have that opportunity now and I will not lose it, no matter the cost. I cannot do as you ask. I will not give him that escape."

Klytemnestra was paralyzed. What more could she say? What more could she do? She stared at him, looking for something, anything, some way to make him change his mind, some opening in the rock face. But those hard eyes stared back at her and she knew there was nothing. She was just wasting time.

She rose to her feet and turned to leave, but halfway to the door the priest's voice made her stop.

"You can hate me, if that makes it easier. I know you do. But it is your husband who has led us down this path, and keeps us here." She shook her head and took another step, but stopped again as he continued. "You may try to convince him—by all means, try. Tell him to turn around and go home. You may succeed where his brother has failed. Perhaps you have that influence." She looked over her shoulder at him. "But remember the oath you made to me. You vowed by the lives of your children that you would not tell your husband of my relation to Leukippe. Do not risk the children you have for the chance to save one already lost."

"I know what I vowed," she growled bitterly back at him. And, turning before another tear could fall, she hurried from the tent.

CHAPTER 39

KLYTEMNESTRA

Klytemnestra marched back through the camp, her chest heaving with short, strangled breaths. Panic had set in now. Their only option was to run. She had wasted so much time already. She had to get back to her daughter. They had to leave.

Her mud-soaked skirts dragged at her shaking legs. She gathered the wool in her hands and widened her strides. Almost there now. She could see their tent. Just a few more strides.

She whipped the tent door aside and hurried in. "I'm back, my darling. Are you r—"

But it was not her daughter who stood before her.

"Husband," she choked, taking a step backward. "I—I did not expect you so late." She peered around him. "Where is Iphigenia?"

"I have sent our daughter to sleep in my tent. I thought she might be safer there."

He knew. She could tell from his tone, the dark look in his eye. Someone must have seen her.

She could not see Alkimos. Had he been here when Agamemnon had come? He must have been. Or maybe he slipped away . . .

Then she saw it. What she had taken for a pile of cloth, near Iphigenia's bed. Except it was moving. And whimpering.

Guilt stabbed her gut. She should have just left when he had told her to. If she had . . . Oh, poor Alkimos. And Iphigenia . . .

"You can't do this," she said quietly. "Please, husband. She is our daughter."

"The ships must sail."

"Why? Why must they? When the price is so high? We could just go home. It is not too late." She was trying to appeal to his eyes, to his heart, but he would not look at her. She touched his sleeve. "Husband—"

"You understand nothing," he snapped, pulling his arm away. "How can a woman know what it is to be a man? What a man must do? What a man must be? You speak of what you do not know."

"I know what it is to be a mother. To bear a child—*your* child. To birth her. To nurse her at my breast. To be terrified that the summer sickness will take her, to dread the winter chill. To raise her to be good and kind and strong. To cherish her each day. I know that."

He made a dismissive sound. "You blame me for this when it is your sister's doing. You hate me for her wrong. We sail to bring her back, or had you forgotten? Would you have me abandon her to the foreigners? A whore bitch to some Eastern dog?"

His words stung, and made her pause. Amid all her fear for Iphigenia, she had almost forgotten about Helen.

"My sister would never have wanted . . ." she murmured. Then, louder, "Our daughter does not need to die. The winds will come!"

"Foolish woman. The slave said he had told you of the prophecy. Do you doubt the gods?"

"Only their messenger," she replied, looking steadily into his eyes. "The seer cannot be trusted. He—"

"You are grasping at the wind," her husband barked. "You have had it against my seer since before the campaign began. I do not know what he has done to offend you but—"

"It is what *you* have done," she snapped back at him. "Do you not remember? The girl and the child and . . . How can you be so *blind*?"

There was a crack of skin on skin as his hand met her face. She reeled, cradling her searing cheek.

"You forget yourself." His voice rumbled like a storm above her. "It is not the place of a queen to question a king's judgment. You are lucky I do not beat you for the way you dishonored me tonight." She glanced at the pile of cloth that was Alkimos, no longer moving. "But I pitied you, for what must be done. Do not test my patience."

Slowly, cheek still throbbing, she straightened herself up and looked him in the eye once again.

"Kalchas is lying," she croaked, willing him with her eyes to see that she was right, to see what she knew.

"I believe him," said her husband gruffly. "He has been right before. It would be foolish not to heed him." Her eyes became more desperate, blurring as tears brimmed at their edges. "And even if I do not believe him," he continued, "the men do. They have heard the prophecy. They know what it is I must do, and what it means if I do not. I have promised them glory. Their blood runs hot for it . . . You must realize that if I do not do this thing, they may do it instead. And perhaps they would not stop with Iphigenia. We would lose everything and gain nothing."

"You mean you. *You* would gain nothing." She was surprised by the contempt in her voice. She was shaking now, with anger, with pain. But it made her bold. She braced herself for another strike, but none came. Agamemnon just looked at her with those gray eyes, as if for him the discussion were already over. Her heart was beating in her throat, her legs trembling beneath her. He was trying to scare her, to make her give in. But she would not be cowed. This was her daughter's life. Her Iphigenia. A part of her knew she should be silent, but she had come so far already. She could not let him leave, knowing what it would mean if he did. She had to fight.

"Is it because she is only a girl that you are so willing to throw her life away? If I ever harmed Orestes you would never forgive me."

"What did you say?" He stepped toward her and seemed to grow taller, his shoulders bristling. "Don't you dare threaten my son."

She stepped back. "I—I didn't. I wouldn't. I only meant that—"

"I'm doing this for him, don't you see?" There was a terrifying energy in his body, a queer light in his eyes. "All of this! To show him that his father is a great man, as my father was. So that he can be proud to be called the son of Agamemnon. To give him a legacy!"

"And what about Iphigenia's legacy?" she shot back, anger overtaking fear once more. "What marriage will she make? What children will she bear? What will her legacy be?"

He looked at her evenly. "Her legacy will be Greece's glory. Her blood the blood that launched a hundred ships. The savior of Greece, they will call her—what greater legacy could she hope for?"

His eyes sparkled with the grandeur of it, as if he were convinced by his own words. It made Klytemnestra feel sick and she stepped back from him, against the wall of the tent, her tongue paralyzed in her mouth. In that moment she realized she would not convince him. That dreadful look on his face . . . He was so enamored by the glory of it all—of the campaign, of Troy, of his own great legacy—that he couldn't see the terrible reality, the beautiful, flesh-and-blood daughter whom he talked so easily of destroying. Dazzled by the dream of conquest, he was blind to all else.

He might try to blame Helen, or the gods, or the army; he might try to claim he was doing it for the sake of his family, for the sake of Greece even, but he knew and she knew that he could stop it all if he wanted to. He alone had chosen this path.

"Iphigenia will remain in my tent tonight, and you will return to Mycenae at dawn."

His voice sounded muffled in her ears, as if he were far away, but she realized what he had said—and what it meant.

"No," she croaked. "I won't leave." *I won't make it easy for you*, she said to herself. "If you must kill our daughter, you will do so with me there." She glared at him, her eyes hard, daring him to challenge her.

"Very well," he said. "Though I warn you not to interfere."

She forced her head to nod.

"Let me be with her in the morning," she said suddenly. "Let me . . . prepare her. As if for her wedding." When he looked skeptical, she continued. "It will be what she expects. I think it best if she does not know," she continued, her voice shaking. "Please, husband. Let her last hours be happy ones."

"Very well," he agreed. "I will have you watched, though."

She nodded stiffly once again. It was as much of a concession as she could hope for.

He turned to leave but stopped as his eyes stuck upon the crumpled pile of cloth. Klytemnestra followed his gaze, watching for some small shift in the fabric to show her that Alkimos was still breathing. All was still.

"I will send Talthybios to get rid of that," Agamemnon said curtly. "Then I suggest you get some sleep." And with a disapproving look at her soiled skirts, he was gone.

Klytemnestra was shaking. She staggered toward her travel chest and collapsed onto it, her head falling into her hands.

She had failed. There was nothing more she could do. Her daughter was out of her reach, and tomorrow she would leave it forever. Terrible, terrified gasps heaved at her chest. Nausea rose in her throat.

What was there left? There must be something. Some way she had overlooked. Could they get away tomorrow? Steal a horse and . . . But as soon as she thought of it she knew it was hopeless. Agamemnon would keep a tight rein now. Their chance for flight was gone. And where would they run to?

She sobbed, bitter tears dripping onto her skirt. Wet and sorrowful and utterly useless. She was so weak, so powerless . . .

A thought struck her.

The gods. Why had she not thought of it? She must ask for their help. Beg for it. No, she needn't pray to them all. She knew who would aid her.

She stood up, wiped her tears hastily on her sleeve, and heaved at the lid of her travel chest. So many fine clothes, so many trinkets—what use were they now? She pushed them aside, plunged her arms through the soft fabrics until . . .

There. She had found it. Carefully, she raised it from the chest, unwound the gold-threaded shawl she had wrapped it in.

"My lady," she sighed, cradling the small wooden figure in her hands.

It was no larger than her forearm, and the paint had lost its luster— it was worn away entirely on the face and breasts where countless fingers before hers had rubbed. The statue had been kept at Mycenae for generations—no one could tell her exactly how old it was. Some said it had fallen from the sky, sent by the gods. Whatever its history, it was a long one. And that gave it power.

Klytemnestra closed the chest and set the statue down gently upon its lid, a lamp beside it. She knelt down and looked at the bare wood of the face—the small bump where a nose was suggested, the carved line of the mouth. She had brought the Lady Hera with her to grant her power in the negotiations with the men, and now she needed that power more than ever.

"Lady Hera," she croaked, and cleared her throat. "You are a wife and a mother, as I am, so I know that you know a mother's love. Save my daughter, O Hera of the white arms, and I will sacrifice one hundred rams at Mycenae. Stop her blood from spilling, and I will spill theirs for you. Do not let a father kill his daughter, against what is right, as your father tried to kill you. I am weak, but you are strong. By the mothers' blood that bonds us, by all that is right, protect my daughter Iphigenia."

Her words stopped and the tent was silent again, as if they had never been spoken. The wooden face stared blankly.

She had spoken from the heart, had offered sacrifice, had done all she should, and yet . . . and yet it was not enough. This was not a prayer for harvest, a petition for a safe journey. This was her daughter's *life*. And it was being taken away from her, against all laws of decency, of sanctity, of justice. And by the man who should be her greatest protector. It wasn't right. It wasn't *right*.

Before she knew it she was speaking again, the words spilling like water over a cliff.

"Lady Hera. I vow to you now, by my own life, by all that I hold dear, if my husband does this terrible thing, if—if Agamemnon kills our daughter—I vow that I will kill him in return." She stopped, her lips faltering briefly at what they had spoken. "Do not make me a husband-killer, O Lady Hera," she went on. "As you love your children, and as I love mine, make my husband see what is right, and stop this madness."

CHAPTER 40

KLYTEMNESTRA

I t is morning, my lady."

The voice of Talthybios came through the canvas, telling her what she already knew. She had watched the tent lighten over the last hour, listened to the servants feeding the horses nearby, as her stomach grew heavier and heavier.

"I am awake, Talthybios," she called back, the words cracking in her dry throat. "You may enter."

The flap of the door was pulled back. She made herself sit up.

And started.

There by the herald's side was her daughter. She didn't know whether to cry with love or sorrow at the sight of that fresh face, but stopped herself short of either.

"Lord Agamemnon thought it best if the princess was readied in your tent, mistress, since you have the travel chest."

"So early?" she asked. "The sun has barely risen." Could Agamemnon not have given their daughter a few more hours in its light?

Talthybios simply nodded.

"He bid me attend you," he added stiffly. "If you require any assistance you need only ask."

He spoke as if he were their servant, but she knew he was really their guard.

"Thank you, Talthybios," she said nonetheless, before turning to her daughter. "Now come, Iphigenia." It was hard to smile, but she managed it. "We must make you a bride."

Iphigenia asked about the night before, of course, but Klytemnestra swept it aside.

"I thought we might have to leave, but I was wrong," she lied, helping her daughter out of her bedclothes. "I'm sorry for waking you, my darling. Did you sleep well in your father's tent?"

Was it wrong to keep the truth from her? She might be the only soul in the whole camp who didn't know why she was really here. And yet . . . yes, it was better that way. Why terrify her? She was smiling, content—a little nervous, perhaps, but still bright. Klytemnestra could not bear to take that from her. Not when it was all she had left.

And perhaps she need never know. In the depths of her heart, Klytemnestra still thought that her husband would change his mind. It was that hope that kept her hands from shaking as she brushed her daughter's golden hair and lifted her cheeks every time Iphigenia turned her head. The thought of that sweet life being snuffed out, like a lamp only just lit . . . and that terrible vow she had made last night, suffocating in the grip of desperation . . . It was too much for a living heart to bear.

No. He would not go through with it. She convinced herself more and more as she dressed Iphigenia in the fine bridal clothes. Perhaps he could bear the idea of it, even bring himself to the brink, but when the moment came, when his loving daughter stood before him, he would not be able to do it.

"Are you all right, Mother?"

She realized she had been straightening her daughter's sleeve for several minutes.

"Yes, dear." She forced a smile. "I was just thinking how beautiful you will look for your husband."

"Have you seen him?" she asked eagerly. "The lord Achilles. Is he handsome?"

"I have not," she replied, trying to mimic her daughter's light tone. "But it is said he is the most handsome of all the Greeks."

Iphigenia repaid her false grin with a genuine one. "I hope he thinks me pretty," she sighed.

Klytemnestra took hold of her daughter's shoulders. "He will think you beautiful," she said. "Or he is a fool."

Iphigenia giggled, her cheeks turning pink. "Maybe once you've finished getting me ready."

Klytemnestra smiled and nodded, but as she combed Iphigenia's already pristine hair once more, a lump grew in her throat. She wished she would never be ready, that she could comb her hair until dusk, and go home tomorrow without today ever happening.

"I have spoken with your father," she said as she was winding the hair on top of her daughter's head. "And he has agreed that you may return home after the wedding feast. So you needn't worry about that."

She didn't know what made her say it, but it seemed to make Iphigenia's shoulders relax a little, so she was glad she did.

"I'm glad I'll get to tell Elektra all about it," she chirped. "And we have to bring her back a present. I promised I would."

She chattered on for a while about what Elektra might like—maybe a sea pebble from the beach, or a shell if she could find one—and whether she ought to find something for Chrysothemis and Orestes too. Klytemnestra let the sweet song of her daughter's voice wash over her as she plaited the final strands of honey-colored hair. And as she fixed the braid into position and drew her hand away it felt as if the last warmth of summer had faded.

She tried to tell her daughter how pretty she looked, but the words stuck in her throat. Instead she turned away from her and lifted the saffron wedding veil from the travel chest. As she felt the weight of it in her hands, she was glad of its thickness. Better that Iphigenia could not see through it.

She turned and looked at her daughter—really looked at her. She knew that this might be the last chance she would get, and didn't want to forget anything, not a single freckle.

"What are you waiting for, Mother? I want to see how it feels."

Klytemnestra smiled apologetically, and Iphigenia smiled back.

Then, hands trembling, she lifted the thick piece of cloth and laid it over her daughter's head, fixing it in place with a golden diadem.

"It's so dark!" Iphigenia exclaimed, waving her arms in front of her. "I can't see a thing!" She giggled as she turned her head this way and that. "It seems a shame to cover up my hair, doesn't it? When you've done it so prettily."

"Yes, I suppose it does," said Klytemnestra quietly, finally allowing the smile to fall from her cheeks now that Iphigenia could not see. "But the veil is a very important part of the wedding. You mustn't take it off, or even lift it. Do you promise me?" Klytemnestra grasped her daughter's narrow shoulders. "That is for your husband, after the sacrifice." She almost choked on the last word.

"Yes, I know, Mother." Then she gave a small sigh. "I wish I could see how I looked."

"You look . . . like a princess of Mycenae," said Klytemnestra, her eyes stinging with tears. "I am so very proud of you."

"Are you all right, Mother?" Iphigenia must have been able to hear the tears in her fragile voice.

She clasped her daughter's hand. "It is an emotional day when one's daughter is given away in marriage."

"But I'll be coming home afterward. Don't be sad, Mother," came the little voice from under the veil.

Klytemnestra had to stop the sob that rose in her throat. Not able to reply, she nodded pointlessly.

❧

It was still early when Talthybios led them from the tent. The sun was low and there was a remnant of pink hanging in the clouds. Klytemnestra clasped her daughter's hand tightly, guiding her small, blind steps.

"The wedding sacrifice is to be performed in the meadow outside the camp," the herald informed them, as he marched ahead. Men and horses cleared a path in front of them, while grim faces watched from either side.

As they made their slow way, Klytemnestra kept expecting her husband to appear, for him to tell them to turn back, that there would be no sacrifice after all. She scanned the camp for his dark head, but as the tents thinned and they began climbing the slope toward the meadow, he was nowhere to be seen.

Klytemnestra's legs shook beneath her as they approached the brow of the hill.

"Nearly there," she said to her daughter, hoping she would take the quaver in her voice for shortness of breath.

Agamemnon will stop it. The goddess will save her. Agamemnon will stop it. The goddess will save her. She began chanting the words inside her head. Surely the Lady Hera had heard her prayer. She would do something. Her husband would see sense. He would stop all this. She knew it. As soon as he saw—

And there he was. His broad shoulders emerged over the brow. And beside him a priest—not Kalchas, the coward—and nearby . . .

An altar.

Klytemnestra's stomach dropped and she stumbled as if dragged with it.

"Are you all right, Mother?" asked Iphigenia, touching her arm blindly. "What is it? Are we there?"

"Yes, dear. Almost. Just a few more steps." She fought to keep the terror from her voice, but when Iphigenia next spoke Klytemnestra could tell she sensed something was wrong.

"Why is it so quiet, Mother? Where is the wedding song?"

Klytemnestra didn't have the strength to answer, but kept leading her on, all the while battling the urge to turn and run.

Agamemnon will stop it. The goddess will save her. There is no sense in running. Agamemnon will stop it.

Her husband stepped toward them. "You are here, my daughter," he said, his voice thinner than usual. Dark shadows lurked beneath his eyes.

A little sigh of relief came from beneath the veil. "Father."

"Come. It is time."

He took one of her pale hands in his and gave Klytemnestra a sharp look, indicating that she should let go of the one she clung to.

She hesitated, tightening her grip, but he grabbed her wrist and squeezed so tightly that she winced. Her daughter's hand fell from hers.

He led Iphigenia toward the altar where the priest now stood and left her there, returning to stand beside Klytemnestra. He grasped her wrist in his huge hand once more.

He will stop it. The goddess will save her. The voice in her head was more urgent now.

"Father?" called Iphigenia. "Mother? What's happening?"

"I'm here," Klytemnestra called back. "Don't be afraid." Her heart was pounding.

Agamemnon will stop it. The goddess will save her.

The priest had taken up a knife from beside the altar.

Klytemnestra turned to her husband, a silent plea ready in her tear-filled eyes. But he had turned his face away.

Coward. He could not even bear to watch. He would leave his daughter to suffer alone. But her mother would not abandon her.

She turned back.

The goddess will save her. Something will happen. She won't die. She cannot die.

Her daughter was crying.

The priest raised the knife—*Agamemnon will stop it, the goddess will save her*—and lifted Iphigenia's veil a little, enough to expose her throat.

It was happening. Her father would not stop it. The goddess would not save her.

Klytemnestra lurched forward, but Agamemnon held her wrist.

"No!" she cried.

The knife swept across Iphigenia's neck.

CHAPTER 41

KLYTEMNESTRA

Klytemnestra screamed.

She wrenched herself free from Agamemnon's grip and rushed forward, reaching her daughter as she fell.

"No no no no no no no . . ." she breathed.

It was as if a horse had kicked her in the chest. So much blood. White skin streaming red. She pulled the veil off but her daughter's staring eyes were lightless.

She put her shaking hand to the blood, not quite believing it was real. Pressed her hand to the wound as if she could bring her back. But she knew Iphigenia was already gone. She clutched her daughter to her chest, rocking her as she wailed.

"I'm sorry, I'm sorry," she whispered between sobs. "I failed you. I'm sorry."

She looked behind her for her husband, but he was still turned away.

"You will not take her!"

Klytemnestra swiped wildly at the priest and his attendants with one arm, the other still clutching Iphigenia's limp body.

"The rites must be performed, my lady," said the priest, taking a step backward.

"I will not see my daughter burned like an ox!" she yelled, tears rolling unfelt down her numb cheeks. "You tell my husband that. She will be buried in Mycenae, where she belongs."

She glared up at the men surrounding her, daring them to defy her.

"Very well, my lady," said the priest after a moment. "We will tell him." They shuffled off, heads bowed.

She was still kneeling on the grass, in the spot where it had happened. She was covered in her daughter's blood—her hands, her arms, her chest. The air was foul with it. From something so pure the stench of evil flowed, and now released, could not be contained.

The horror of it swirled inside Klytemnestra, like a savage beast trapped in a cage. She screamed and sobbed and wailed and cursed but the beast remained, clawing at her heart. She clawed back, raking her cold cheeks with her nails till beads of her own dark blood dropped to mingle with her daughter's. She barely felt it.

Agamemnon must have agreed to forgo the burning, for when the servants returned it was with a wagon and shroud.

Even then she clung to her daughter, not yet ready to let her go. Patiently, cautiously, the servants pried the body from her, and finally she let them wash the blood from it and wrap it in the scented cloth. She knew she should be the one to do these things, but it was as if her feet were rooted to the earth, her arms too heavy to lift from her sides. So she watched in bewildered silence as the daughter whose sweet voice she had heard not an hour ago, whose warm hand she had held, was lifted onto the back of the wagon, a corpse.

Klytemnestra followed the wagon back through the camp, her feet shuffling one after the other without her bidding. She barely saw the faces that turned to stare, barely heard the gasps and muttered prayers as they saw the blood. She almost walked into the wagon when it eventually stopped.

"My lady," came a voice beside her. She turned and, after a second or two, registered that it was Talthybios's face she saw.

"You should change your clothes, my lady," he said in a low voice. His calmness of earlier was fractured now, his face pale. It wasn't until he lifted the door flap that she realized they were outside her tent. "Quickly. Inside, now. There we are, my lady."

She stumbled through the gap in the canvas and the flap closed behind her. She looked ahead of her, and there it was. Iphigenia's bed.

It was like a veil had been pulled off, and the wind of reality whipped the numb haze from around her.

Her daughter was dead. And she had let it happen.

She should have saved her, instead of leading her to her death like a fool. She was wrong to rely on the goddess. *She* should have done something. And now . . . now it was too late. And it was all her fault.

No. It wasn't.

It was Agamemnon. Agamemnon who had given the order. Agamemnon who had made it happen. Agamemnon whose ambition was so great he could sacrifice his own child—their child—to get what he wanted. And that was it, wasn't it? Her whole life, since she had moved to Mycenae, had been directed by what *he* wanted. The wife he wanted her to be, the children he wanted her to have. All she had ever wanted was a family, and she had earned it, hadn't she? With her dutifulness, her obedience, her suffocating meekness. All those hours of spinning wool and bowing her head, of shutting her mouth and opening her legs. And still he could not let her keep this one thing for herself. The injustice of it raged inside her, for herself, for her daughter, for those blank staring eyes that had once held the light of her world.

And then she remembered her vow.

I will kill him in return. That was what she had whispered in the dark night. Her stiff lips mouthed the words, remembering the shape of them. And didn't he deserve it? Their daughter lay cold in a shroud. And for what? A good wind? A chance at glory?

Her cheeks were hot now, her heart pumping. The longer she stared at that empty bed, the harder it pumped. And the more determined she became.

She didn't change her clothes. If she lingered she might lose her resolve. Instead she turned straight around and left the tent.

Her husband's tent was not far—she could see its top from where she stood. She set off with long strides, ignoring the stares and the whispers.

As she neared the tent she realized she didn't know what she was going to do when she got there.

Kill him, said the beast still clawing inside her.

How? came her own meeker voice. But there was no time. She was there.

No guard. It was as if the Lady Hera were willing her on. Her hand trembled as she pulled the door aside.

Agamemnon sat at the other end of the tent, his broad back to the door. He didn't seem to hear her enter. She paused inside the door.

Could she really do it? She raised her hands before her, still smeared with her daughter's lifeblood. Were they the hands of a murderer?

She could do it for Iphigenia.

Stepping silently, she glanced about the tent.

There. On the table between her and her husband—a dagger. Its golden handle glinted encouragingly, as if placed there by Lady Hera herself.

She picked it up and carried on toward her husband's broad, exposed back.

Almost there. Her legs stiffened but she carried on. She raised the dagger. He was so close she could hear his breath, smell his sweat.

She hesitated, dagger hanging in the air. It was as if something were holding it there.

She had to do it. She had made a vow.

She raised the dagger higher and—

"My lord."

Klytemnestra snapped her arm down by her side and turned toward the doorway, where the voice had come from. She managed to push the small blade up into her sleeve just as Talthybios entered.

"My lor— Lady Klytemnestra," he said with surprise. "Your clothes— I thought you were going to change?"

"Yes, I—"

"What are you doing here?" came her husband's voice from behind her.

But as she turned to him his look of confusion turned to concern— or perhaps it was revulsion.

"Your face . . ." he said. "Talthybios, I thought I told you to see to my wife? Why is she still covered in blood? Has she been walking through the camp like this? And those cuts . . ."

"Y-yes, my lord. I mean, I tried—"

"Have a servant come here to attend her. I won't have her wandering the camp. And make sure they bring fresh clothes."

"Yes, my lord. Right away."

Talthybios hurried out, leaving the two of them alone once again. Klytemnestra was still stunned by what had happened—by what had almost happened. She looked up at her husband dumbly.

"Iphigenia will be buried in Mycenae, as you asked," said Agamemnon gruffly. He seemed unable to look her full in the face. "May it bring you comfort. I . . . It is a terrible thing that you have suffered today. I suggest you return home as soon as possible."

Even now he could not apologize, could not take responsibility for what he had done. She stood glaring up at him, her hand shaking as it still held the dagger's hilt. Just a few more seconds. That was all she had needed. Those few seconds of hesitation. If she hadn't been such a coward.

"I will have your wagon prepared," he said. "I will not see you again before you leave. The seer spoke true—the winds have begun to change already. I must make arrangements for our departure." He headed toward the door.

"Husband," she murmured, and he paused, looking back. But no more words would come. She squeezed the dagger hilt.

"Farewell, wife," he said. "Until I return."

And then he was gone, and her opportunity with him.

PART IV

CHAPTER 42

HELEN

TWO YEARS LATER

Back and forth. Back and forth. Helen sent the shuttle between the threads. After all these years there was a comforting familiarity in the loom. The rhythm of the shuttle, the smell of the wool, the rooted solidity of the wooden frame. If she closed her eyes, she could almost imagine she was back in Sparta.

On the other side of the chamber Paris sat arranging his hair, combing sweetly scented oil through each ringlet and assessing his progress with a silver mirror. Every now and then the polished metal would catch the light from the window and flash at Helen through the threads of her loom.

Troy was at war, but for the most part life went on as usual. Since its arrival two years ago, the Greek force had spent much of its time pillaging the surrounding settlements, growing fat and rich from Troy's extensive hinterland. Paris had told her they had even raided some of the islands off the coast. He called them cowards.

"Troy's walls cannot be breached," he had assured her. "Your Greeks know this, and they fear our men. Let them kill farmers. They will never take Troy."

The city certainly seemed well defended. The citadel, where the royal palaces were, sat atop a rocky acropolis, with walls so high and so wide that Helen thought they must have been built by giants. And down on the plain, like the flesh around an olive stone, lay the lower city, itself bounded by another wall, and beyond that a great ditch. What few skirmishes there had been—all within the first few months of the Greeks' arrival—had taken place beyond the city, on the plain between Troy's boundary walls and the beach where the Greek ships had landed. If it weren't for the food restrictions, it would be difficult to tell there was a war going on at all.

The Greeks claimed they were here to take her back, but for now they seemed more interested in plundering the Troad for all it held. Helen sometimes wondered which theft had grieved her husband more: hers, or that of Sparta's royal treasure.

But why should she care? She had a new life now, and a new husband. Paris was handsome and rich and . . . She had everything she needed here in Troy.

Helen continued with her weaving. Back and forth, back and forth. As she worked she began to hum, a familiar tune that came without thinking, a tune from her childhood, one she used to sing while she and Nestra spun their wool in the women's room . . .

The notes stopped in her throat, as a horrible feeling spread through her chest. *Oh, Nestra.*

Word had reached Troy of what Agamemnon had done to bring his army to their shore. *Poor Nestra.* Thinking of her sister always used to bring Helen comfort, but now it brought only guilt. She had never meant for anything like that to happen, not to Nestra, not to anyone. She hadn't really meant for any of this to happen. It just had.

"Why do you look so miserable?" Paris had turned to face her, his hair satisfactorily arranged. "You look much prettier when you smile."

Helen wiped the tear that had been about to fall and forced her cheeks upward.

"That's better," Paris said, and rose from his stool. "I'm going down to the armory. My sword needs a new scabbard—this one is so dull."

"Can I come with you?" asked Helen, rising quickly from her seat. She didn't like being in the chamber alone.

Paris laughed. "Do you fear a harpy will come to snatch you while I am gone?" He threw his leopard skin around his shoulders. "The armory is no place for a woman. Go and sit in the hall with the others if you want some company."

Helen hesitated.

"Come," said Paris, stepping toward the door. "I have to go that way anyway. I will escort you."

Helen nodded, not wanting to admit that the women's hall scared her as much as the prospect of being left alone.

Paris walked with her the short way to the hall as he had promised, striding between the fine buildings that crowded the middle terrace as Helen trotted just behind him. When she arrived, one of the doors to the hall was ajar and she could hear voices coming from inside. She turned to bid Paris farewell, but he was already disappearing through the gate to the lower terrace. She took a breath and slid herself through the gap between the large wooden doors.

Silence rippled across the hall as she entered. Helen avoided meeting any of the gazes she felt upon her and shuffled, head bowed, toward the nearest unoccupied corner. Gradually, the general hum resumed, though Helen still sensed the occasional disapproving head turn her way, and whenever she heard women speaking in the local tongue she was sure they were talking about her. She listened out for her name among the blur of foreign sounds, but they spoke too quickly.

Helen cursed herself for not bringing her spindle to the hall; it would certainly have helped to make her look less awkward. She felt such a fool, sitting there in her lonely corner, staring at her sandals. She should just leave. An empty chamber was better than this. It was just her silly fear that made her feel vulnerable. No one would even dare enter the chamber, not while Paris wasn't there.

Helen was just about to stand up when a blue skirt shuffled into her eyeline. She looked up to find a young girl staring back at her.

"Hello," said the girl, smiling brightly. She was fair-haired and slight, with bony elbows and friendly eyes. "My name's Kassandra. Can I sit with you?"

Helen was a little taken aback by the girl's sudden apparition, but managed a reply. "Y-yes, I suppose. Sit down—if you wish."

The girl beamed and pulled up a nearby stool. She sat with her hands in her lap, fiddling with the material of her skirt.

"I'm Helen."

"I know," said the girl. "You're married to my brother."

"Ah. So you're one of King Priam's daughters," Helen replied, almost to herself. There were so many women at Troy—the king's wives, the king's daughters, the king's sons' wives—she got confused about who everyone was.

"Your hair is ever so lovely," said Kassandra, pronouncing each word carefully. She spoke Greek perfectly, though it was not her mother tongue. "My brother Polites teases me about my hair," she continued, glancing from Helen's eyes to her own lap. "He says the gods forgot to dye it. But I told him that's stupid. The gods don't dye people's hair."

Helen giggled, surprised by how at ease she suddenly felt.

"Well, I think your hair is very pretty," she said, smiling cautiously.

"Why are you sitting over here on your own, instead of with the other ladies?" Kassandra asked quietly. "Don't you like them?"

"It's not so much . . ." said Helen, glancing over to the other women. "They . . . it's just that I don't really fit in with them."

"Oh," said Kassandra, nodding her blond head sagely. "I don't fit in with the other girls either. They talk such nonsense. And they never really understand when I try to . . . Some of them call me names."

Helen didn't reply, but sat watching the girl's face as she stared down at her knees.

Eventually, Kassandra looked up. "Do you mind if I stay over here with you for a while?"

Helen nodded. "If you like," she said casually, and silently thanked the gods that one person in the women's hall wasn't treating her as if she had plague.

CHAPTER 43

KLYTEMNESTRA

Ah, Theophilos. Has a bull been chosen for tomorrow's sacrifice?" Klytemnestra asked as she spotted her head priest crossing the courtyard toward her. "The last one had a bad temperament. We cannot have another incident like last time."

The priest bowed a greeting. "Yes, my lady. This one is sure to please the Lady Hera. A fine beast."

"Good," she replied, without slowing her pace. "Thank you, Theophilos," she called after him, as the elderly priest shuffled on toward the royal shrine.

As she turned her head back around she saw Damon, the steward, waiting at the doorway in front of her.

"Lady Klytemnestra," he said graciously, walking alongside her as she strode through the cool palace interior. "Have you thought what we should say to Argos? Only you told me I wasn't to send our reply until—"

"Yes, Damon. Thank you for reminding me. Tell them we appreciate that the harvest was not as good as last year, but that they are better off than most. Tell them that the kingdom needs their contribution," she said briskly. Then, pausing her pace, she turned aside and added,

"But make sure you flatter them a little. You know what the Argives are like."

"Yes, my lady," Damon replied with a curt nod, and turned down a side corridor, while Klytemnestra continued on her route to the main entrance.

Behind her trotted Ianthe, a young handmaid she had taken on soon after returning to Mycenae. She had thought the girl could help Eudora with the children, while she herself was suffering through the worst of her grief. But that was before she had decided to send Orestes away.

She had to do it, she knew that. As the male heir he was a target for those who might wish to take Mycenae in her husband's absence. And yet it had been so painful, so soon after that other loss. Whenever she began to regret her choice and to think of her son growing up without knowing his mother's face, she told herself that in her life she must make many hard decisions, as a mother and as a queen, and she could not let her heart rule her head. So now her beautiful son was growing up in Phokis, at the palace of King Strophios and his wife, Anaxibia, Agamemnon's sister. It was farther than she would have liked, but at least he was with family. He would be safe there, and that was most important.

As Klytemnestra stepped out of the palace and began to descend the Great Stairs, she took a deep lungful of morning air. Mycenae felt more and more like her true home. She had the respect of the palace, the love of the people—the artisans of the citadel smiled and bowed as she passed by—but despite all the people that surrounded her, she found that loneliness still had a way of creeping past them.

The loss of her mother had affected her more than she would have thought it could. The news of Queen Leda's death had reached Mycenae a little over a year earlier and it still pained her, like an open wound on her heart. She couldn't help thinking that if she had been there . . . She must have been so alone after Father had died. And then with

Helen gone . . . Her mother had dismissed all her ladies by that time and was hardly seen around the palace, so people said. It was two days before they found her. The thought of her bloated body hanging there, unmourned, unmissed, haunted Klytemnestra's dreams.

People said that she did it out of shame—because of Helen. Perhaps they were right, perhaps the scandal had tipped her mother over the edge, but she had always been fragile. Even as a child Klytemnestra had seen her mother's sadness. It had hung around her like a cloud. But then there would be these breaks and the cloud would lift awhile, and her mother would shine through—her *real* mother, with all her warmth and her humor and . . .

She hadn't seen her mother since the day she had left Sparta, and yet she felt her absence all the same. It was as if there were one less anchor tying her to the world, as when her father had passed. So many people had left her; she felt as if there wasn't enough of her to patch the holes they had left behind.

Her children were her anchors now, and they renewed her every day. Elektra was already a young lady and Chrysothemis was hurrying to catch up with her older sister. It gave Klytemnestra comfort to watch them grow, to see them play and laugh together. But there was a sadness too, when she thought of the sister who should be there with them. She had not told the girls the full truth of what had happened—how could she? Whenever they asked about it, they must have seen how it upset her, and eventually they had stopped asking. Now Iphigenia's name was barely spoken at all, as if she had never even existed.

That was why Klytemnestra had to make her daily journey beyond the citadel walls. Someone had to remember. She had to keep her daughter alive, if only in her own head.

She had passed through the gate now and was almost at the tomb— she could see it ahead of her, rising from the ground like a giant beehive. She came to a stop before the monumental stone doorway. It was sealed, of course, until such time as the tomb was reopened for the next burial. She made a silent prayer that it would not be for another of her children and set about making her offering to those she had already laid to rest.

She gestured to Ianthe, who brought forth the wineskin and silver goblet. Klytemnestra filled the cup to its brim and, pouring the dark liquid onto the dusty earth, made her prayer.

"For my daughter, Iphigenia. May the Thirsty Ones bless and protect her soul in the place beneath the earth."

Then she refilled the cup and poured out its contents once more.

"For my two babes, who never saw the sun with living eyes. May the Thirsty Ones look kindly upon them."

The two infants she had lost at birth lay inside the tomb with their sister, wrapped lovingly in gold leaf. Though they had never known each other in life, Klytemnestra gained a little comfort from the thought that her children were together in death. One day she too would be laid to rest in the stillness of the tomb, and she hoped that their souls might find one another in the hereafter.

She stood for a moment, remembering the children she had lost. She called Iphigenia's face from her memory, though it was blurred and shifting and grew less distinct with every day that passed. Instead she remembered her kindness, her laughter—yes, those were less easy to forget. But so was her fear on that morning, the tears in her voice as she cried out for her mother—

No. Some memories were too painful. The dead felt no fear, she told herself.

Before leaving the tomb she laid out some honey cakes on the ground—Iphigenia's favorite. Then, straightening up, she headed back the way she had come, with Ianthe following behind her.

As Klytemnestra approached the Lion Gate, she looked up at those two fierce beasts that had so terrified her on that night when she had first arrived here in Mycenae. A strange feeling rose in her chest—half amusement, half sadness—to think of her fear then. A childish fear—for what had that girl known of true terror? Now she had grown used to those stony stares, and she felt a kind of security as she walked beneath them, to be guarded by those ferocious lionesses. She was one of them now, she thought, as she made her way through the smoky streets of the citadel. She had to be, for the sake of her children, for the sake of her kingdom. A protector, a provider, a leader. A Lioness of Mycenae.

She was not far from the Great Stairs when Damon appeared in front of her, a little out of breath.

"My lady, I was just coming to find you," he said, with a quick bow. "A man has arrived at the palace, seeking hospitality. He claims he is of noble blood. Will we receive him or would you like me to send him away?"

"Are we barbarians, Damon?" she asked, though she smiled when she saw the seriousness of his expression. "Of course we will give him hospitality. Gods know guests are few in times of war. I daresay we could do with a new face."

"Very well, my lady," Damon nodded with grave sincerity. "I will show him to a chamber."

He turned to stride away but Klytemnestra called him back.

"Wait, Damon. I will accompany you to the palace," she said, starting up the sloped street. "I would like to see this visitor with my own eyes."

CHAPTER 44

HELEN

Helen sat staring into the flames of the hearth, cradling her wine cup in her slender fingers. She had only been inside the Trojan Hearth Hall on a few occasions since her arrival to the city. It was a place for important men, for the royal family, for sacred ritual and matters of state. It was the jewel at the peak of the citadel, the ordered heart of the city—not to be upset by foreign wives who brought war and death behind them.

But today every nobleman and noble woman in the citadel had been admitted to its sacred space—or at least to the courtyard outside, for those not royal enough for a place in the crowded hall. Helen sat inside, beside her husband. All the other princes had their wives in attendance, so she supposed they could not exclude her.

At the head of the feast, beside King Priam on his painted throne, sat Paris's elder brother Hektor, heir of Troy. He was broad and tanned, with a black beard and steady eyes. Beside him sat his wife, Andromache, with black hair to match her husband's and large almond eyes. And in her arms, a squirming bundle of cloth. The feast was in celebration of the birth of Hektor's son, heir to Troy after his father. Even with the supply routes threatened and the food stores preciously guarded, an occasion such as this demanded a little indulgence. They had named the boy Astyanax, "Lord of the City." It was a big name for such a small thing—but then, Helen mused, we are all born to our fates.

Paris sat on Helen's right, though he had barely spoken a word to her all evening. He did not mean to ignore her, she was sure, though she wished he would realize how alone she was without him. At present, he was deep in conversation with his cousin Aineias, who sat on the other side of him.

"Hattusa will send its forces soon, and all this will be over," she overheard her husband say in a casual tone, as he swilled his wine. "You worry too much, cousin!"

"But they have troubles of their own," Aineias replied as she strained her ears to listen over the din of the hall. "Just last week they sent word that the Assyrians had . . ." But Helen couldn't hear any more as a raucous song started up somewhere on her left.

Feeling as if her mouth would soon seal shut with not talking, Helen turned and put a hand on Paris's forearm. He didn't respond, so she gave it a light squeeze and raised her thin voice through the din.

"Do you like my dress, husband? I just finished it this week."

"Hmm?" was his response, turning half toward her. "Yes, it's very nice," he said, without looking at it, and turned back to his cousin, taking a swig of wine on the way.

Helen let out an inaudible sigh and poked around at the lentils on her plate. She thought of when she and Paris had first met, when she had felt as if she were all he desired in the whole world, how he would talk to her all night in those smooth tones of his, and kiss her as if her skin were the air itself. He still desired her—at least, he still lay with her—but their life together wasn't quite as she had imagined it.

As she raised a few of the spiced lentils to her lips her gaze slid to Hektor and Andromache, illuminated by the glow of the hearth as if they were made of gold. Hektor was encouraging his son to grasp his finger, tickling the baby's palm and laughing softly as the tiny fingers closed around his own. Andromache was beaming down on them both, radiant in her motherhood. It made Helen a little sad to look upon the scene, and to think of the child she herself had borne, how different it all had been. But she was glad too. She rarely saw Lord Hektor smile, and it suited him. He was usually so serious, though she didn't blame him. In fact, she admired him greatly. The defense of Troy fell upon his shoulders and he bore his duty solemnly. He was little older than Paris and herself, and yet he was so noble, so stately . . . He would make a great king one day, Helen knew.

She was still staring at the happy couple, unable to draw her eyes away. The way they looked at their child, the way they looked at each other . . . Hektor raised a gentle hand to his wife's cheek and it was like only they existed. Watching them brought a strange ache to Helen's heart, but it was like a bruise she couldn't help pressing.

Her absorption was broken by a sudden jolt from her left. Deiphobos, another of Paris's brothers, had leaned toward her, knocking her arm with his cup-filled hand.

"Apologies, my lady," he slurred, spilling wine over her plate. Then he turned his head and looked intently at her face, his eyes a little glazed. "By the gods, you *are* beautiful." He spoke as if seeing her for the first time, though they had met on many occasions. "I don't blame my brother for bringing you here," he carried on, as his eyes gravitated downward.

Suddenly there was an arm behind her back, a hand on her waist. Helen looked to her right, but Paris was occupied talking with his cousin. Deiphobos pulled her toward him. "Perhaps I should have stolen you myself."

Helen shifted away from him.

"Husband," she said, a little shakily, and the hand retracted. "May I bestow a favor on your nephew?" she asked quickly.

"Hmm? Yes, whatever you like," he replied, before returning to his conversation.

Helen rose from her seat and began to make her way across the hall. She had barely taken five steps when there it was again, the pregnant hush that followed her wherever she went. Songs stopped, cups were lowered, and all eyes seemed to fall upon her. She began to regret leaving her seat.

She carried on, though, putting one self-conscious foot before the other, until finally she was standing before the royal couple.

"I . . . I wanted to offer my congratulations," she said nervously. "And my blessing for the child. Here," she said, taking the golden hoops from her ears—some of the only jewelry she had brought with her from Sparta. "A gift for the lord Astyanax."

Helen held out the offering in her trembling hand, but Andromache turned her face aside, pulling her son close as if she thought Helen might infect him.

Helen was about to draw her hand away when Hektor spoke.

"Thank you, Helen," he said, taking the earrings from her. "You are most kind."

She smiled weakly and nodded in reply, gratitude swelling within her. As she walked away the noise of the hall began to resume, but through the hum Helen thought she heard the admonishing tone of Andromache behind her. She turned her head just in time to read Hektor's lips as he leaned toward his wife and said, "Hush now, it's not her fault. She's just a foolish girl."

Those words echoed in Helen's head for the rest of the evening.

CHAPTER 45

KLYTEMNESTRA

Klytemnestra sat alone in the Hearth Hall, sipping unwatered
wine. She had needed something to settle her nerves before going to bed, and so she had come to the hall to drink and to
think and to be alone.

The previous day a rumor had reached Mycenae that King Agamemnon had been slain in a skirmish at Troy.

"We will pay no heed to rumor," Klytemnestra told her staff, and
yet inwardly her heart had risen with a strange hope. Could it be true?
Was her husband really dead? She saw his still body laid out on the
Trojan plain, and it was as if a boulder had been lifted from her chest.
Relief, cold and hot at once, had spread through her. Would she really
not have to face him?

But then today, just an hour ago, a messenger had arrived from the
Troad, requesting fresh supplies and affirming that the king was indeed
alive and well. And Klytemnestra's infant hope had died almost as soon
as it had been born.

As the war lengthened, the question inside her grew. *What would she
do when her husband returned?* She had made a vow to the goddess, and she
had meant it. She had held the dagger in her hand. Blood for blood.

And yet . . . she had been half-mad with grief, hadn't she? Could she still do it, when the time came?

But the alternative . . . How could she face him? How could she look upon him each day, serve him as his wife, share his bed? She visited Iphigenia's tomb every day, and would continue to do so for the rest of her life. She had failed her in life; she would not abandon her in death. But how could she mourn the daughter she had lost while playing wife to the man who had ordered her death? Who had weighed her gentle life against his own hard ambition? The man whose very name made her heart clench? It was an insult to Iphigenia's memory. It was unthinkable. It was unbearable. It was . . . it was—

Suddenly there was a crack. The thin stem of the wine cup had snapped in her hand, spilling wine over her skirt. It was only then that she realized how tightly she had been gripping it.

She sighed, watching vacantly as the dark wine soaked into her fine clothes. *It may never come to that*, she said to herself. This time the rumor had been wrong, but it hadn't been the first, and would not be the last. As wicked and cowardly as it made her feel, the best she could do was to hope that one day the news of her husband's death would be true. That he would die far away on that foreign shore, and the terrible choice would be taken from her.

She was about to stand and leave the hall when one of the heavy doors creaked open, and Damon's face appeared.

"My lady," he called across the hall. "Our guest requests to share your hearth. Should I admit him?"

Klytemnestra was about to say no, but changed her mind. The guest had been here two nights already and she had not yet entertained him. What would people say of Mycenaean hospitality? And besides, his company would be a welcome distraction.

"Yes, yes," she called to Damon. "Tell him he is welcome to share my hearth. And have the slaves bring more wine. And some fruit, if you would."

"Of course, my lady," Damon replied, and his head disappeared once more.

Moments later, another appeared in its place, and then a whole man, stepping humbly into the light of the hearth fire.

"You have my thanks, my lady," he said with a bow. "For granting me the pleasure of your company. I know you must be busy."

"It is only proper," she said with a smile, gesturing him toward the seat beside her. "You are our guest, after all."

The man was taller than average, but otherwise unremarkable in appearance. His skin was weathered, though he still had a youthful energy, a kind of robust vigor, as you saw in farmers and the like—lean but strong. He was younger than her husband but older than herself, she estimated. And the eyes that stared out from his tanned face held a kind light.

When he had first arrived at the palace he had worn a thin traveler's cloak and tough, simply made boots. If it were not for his refined manner of speaking and the dignified confidence with which he carried his wiry frame, she would have doubted that he was of noble blood at all. Now, seated beside her in a fine tunic, with hair washed and skin perfumed with cardamom, he was like a new man.

Damon had followed the man in and was sitting near the doors. Even though she was the ruling Queen of Mycenae, it would be improper for her to be alone with a male guest—especially after what had happened with her sister. Still, she could not help but be a little insulted that the steward did not trust her.

"I hope your stay has been comfortable so far," she said, pouring a cup of wine for her guest. "Have you been well attended?"

"Oh yes, my lady, very well," he replied, taking the cup from her. "Though I am glad to finally meet my host—properly, I mean."

"Yes, I must apologize for not entertaining you sooner. Indeed, I have forgotten your name, so much time has passed since our first brief meeting."

"You can be forgiven, my lady, for I don't believe I gave it." He gave a gracious smile, his eyes watching hers. "Aigisthos is what my noble father named me."

"Aigisthos," she repeated, rolling the sound of it around on her tongue. "Quite unusual, is it not? And yet I feel I may have heard it before."

"Of course you need not remind me of your name," said Aigisthos, cradling his wine cup. "Your noble reputation is known even by those who live as far away as I, Queen Klytemnestra."

She smiled. "And where exactly is it that you live, Lord Aigisthos?"

"Oh, here and there," he said with a playful smile. "But my family has ancient ties with Mycenae. Such an interesting place, is it not? Such a rich history."

Klytemnestra nodded politely. "Yes, I suppose it is. Though I confess I do not know much of its history, not having been born here myself."

"Mmm," Aigisthos replied, popping a grape into his mouth. "No, I suppose not." He picked another from the stem and rolled it in his fingers before turning his eyes back to her. "Did your husband ever tell you the story of how he came to be King of Mycenae?" he asked.

"Well, yes, I know that my father helped him to overthrow the previous king—that's how I came to marry Lord Agamemnon, you see—but . . . now that I think of it, that is all I know. My husband . . . well, he isn't really one for stories." She smiled weakly, trying to hide her unease at the mention of Agamemnon.

"Perhaps you will allow me to tell the rest," said Aigisthos, leaning toward her slightly. "It is quite the tale, if you would like to hear it." He smiled, but there was no humor in his eyes.

Though Klytemnestra was not keen to hear tales of her husband, she was curious. What kind of queen did not know the history of her own kingdom?

"Go on," she said, picking up her wine cup. "I'm listening."

Aigisthos shifted his weight a little, cleared his throat, and began.

"Well, as with so many stories, it all began with two brothers. One was named Thyestes, and the other, the younger, was named Atreus." Klytemnestra opened her mouth to interject but was beaten to it.

"Yes, you may well know that name, for Atreus was your noble husband's father. Well, the two brothers were sons of the great king Pelops, but were exiled from their native kingdom when, in their desire for the throne, they plotted to murder their half brother. Deprived of their kingdom, the brothers wandered all Greece until finally they found welcome at the hearth of Mycenae. For King Eurystheus, who ruled this land all those years ago, had fathered no sons, and feared for the security of his kingdom.

"The brothers spent their youth happily in Mycenae for two summers, and might have continued to do so if it had not been for the caprice of the Fates. For before King Eurytheus could choose which of the two was to be his heir, he died.

"Thyestes and Atreus, good friends and brothers as they were, ruled the kingdom together for a time. But, though Thyestes had more claim as the elder brother and had proven himself a fine ruler, Atreus was the more ambitious. He feared the people would favor his brother over him and began to hold audiences without Thyestes, and to take measures to diminish his brother's power.

"And perhaps Atreus would have been content with his larger share of the throne. But one of his spies, whom he had appointed to watch his brother for fear that he would be usurped, revealed to Atreus that they had seen his own wife, Aerope, visiting Thyestes's chambers on several occasions—alone.

"Burning with jealousy, Atreus confronted his wife and, fearing her husband's rage, she told him everything. She begged him not to harm Thyestes—for she truly loved him—and to send him away instead. But Atreus had other plans.

"He invited Thyestes to feast with him, playing the loving brother as he plied him with wine and delicious stewed meat. It was only once his brother's belly was full that Atreus revealed the evil he had done. Asking Thyestes if he had enjoyed his meal, he had a platter brought into the hall—this very hall where we sit now—and on it were the heads and hands of Thyestes's young sons. And he knew then what his brother had done, and what he himself had unknowingly done."

Klytemnestra felt sick. She gripped the arm of her throne to steady herself, but then drew her hand back. Was this the very throne where that monstrous man had once sat?

"How can men do such things?" she asked hoarsely. "And to their own kin?" Her stomach turned with a remembered horror that she tried to push away. "I—I'm not sure I want to hear the rest of the story."

"But you must, my lady," urged Aigisthos. "Now that we have begun. It is a tale full of evil, yes, and violence and loss. But such is life, is it not?" He looked into her eyes.

She looked back. Did he know of her own loss? "Such is life, yes," she said, trying to keep her voice steady. "But I do not revel in hearing of it."

Aigisthos nodded apologetically. "I have saddened you, my lady. But please, let me finish the story. The rest is not so evil."

Klytemnestra paused, eyeing her guest warily. "Very well," she said. "Go on."

Aigisthos settled back into his seat.

"For the crime of consuming human flesh, Thyestes was exiled—not just from Mycenae, but from all civil society. He could enter no sanctuaries, take part in no rites. He wandered for many months, turned away at every door, until a goatherd and his family took pity on him. They gave him work and a home, such as their humble dwelling was. And in time Thyestes took to his new life and even fathered another son, with the daughter of the kind goatherd.

"Thyestes had made peace with the fate that had been threaded for him, and so his son grew up knowing nothing of his royal blood, nor the life he might have had. But when the boy reached manhood and began to ask more questions than his father had answers, Thyestes knew he must tell his son the truth of his history. And when he heard what his father had once been, and what his cruel uncle had done, the boy was incensed—for his father and for the brothers he had never known, and for himself, robbed of his own fortune.

"That night, while his father slept, the boy ran away. He journeyed to Mycenae and found King Atreus, his uncle, exposed on the shore, performing a sacrifice. The boy took his opportunity and killed Atreus right there on the sand, though he himself was still barely a man. And Mycenae, suffering under years of misrule, welcomed back Thyestes and his son as their kings.

"Now Thyestes, being a kinder man than his brother, let the sons of Atreus live, and merely exiled them from his kingdom. But this—as I'm sure you can foresee—was his mistake. For five years after the death of Atreus, his sons—your noble husband, Agamemnon, and his brother, Menelaos—were able to gather enough allies to return to Mycenae and take it for themselves. This part you know, of course, for your father was the greatest of those allies. Even now it seems Lord Agamemnon has a gift for summoning armies." He gave a sad, lopsided smile. "They killed Thyestes, and would have killed their father's murderer too, had the palace servants not helped him to flee.

"And so there it is," sighed Aigisthos. "The history of Mycenae, such as I am able to give it."

"You give it well," Klytemnestra said graciously, though there was an uneasy feeling in the pit of her stomach. "Indeed, I am impressed by how much you know."

"Oh, it is common knowledge, for those who seek it."

"And what of Thyestes's son—the one who escaped. Is his fate known?" She gave Aigisthos a long look, holding his gaze in her own.

"By some," he said slowly. "And by you, I think."

Klytemnestra's unease turned in her stomach.

"Damon, summon the guards," she called across the hall, keeping both eyes on Aigisthos. Did he have a blade? She could not see one.

"Damon!" She had not heard him move. She turned her head and saw him sitting just where he had been before, looking at her levelly. "Damon?"

And from those dark eyes it struck her, like an arrow shot across the eerie quiet of the hall. She had been betrayed.

CHAPTER 46

KLYTEMNESTRA

Klytemnestra went to scream, but a hand clamped on her mouth.

"Please, my lady," said Aigisthos, his eyes inches from hers. "I have not come to bring you harm." He must have read the true fear in her eyes, for he quickly added, "Your children are safe. No one will hurt them. I just need you to listen to what I have to say. Will you do that?"

She searched his eyes for truth, desperate. But she did not know this man. Her children could already be dead. They might have blades at their throats at this very moment. She looked over toward Damon, her eyes blazing at the man she had thought her ally.

"He is telling the truth, my lady," the steward said, wringing his hands. "I'm sorry . . . I—your children are safe, I promise you."

She looked back at Aigisthos, his salty palm still pressed against her teeth. She glared at him, daring him to be lying. But his eyes looked earnest. They were almost afraid.

Slowly, warily, she nodded.

The hand withdrew, and she did not scream. But her eyes stayed on those of Aigisthos, shadowing them, watching for danger.

"It is as you have deduced," he said. "I am Aigisthos, son of Thyestes. Murderer of Atreus and cousin to your husband. But I have not come to avenge my father, nor to steal back his throne. I have come to make you an offer."

Klytemnestra choked a disbelieving laugh. "Is that so? And this little ambush"—she threw a sharp look at Damon—"this was designed to make me more receptive, was it?" She drew in a shaky breath. "No, I—I think you should leave now. Both of you. Before I call for my guards."

She stuck her chin out a little, jaw fixed hard, hoping he would not see the fear behind her glaring eyes.

Suddenly Damon's voice chimed out from across the hall. "I advise you to hear him out, my lady."

Klytemnestra's jaw tightened still further. She had trusted the steward, even thought him her friend. She did not turn to look at him.

"My lady—"

"Why should I?" she shot at Aigisthos. "You have taken advantage of my hospitality, slithered your way into *my* home, where my children—" She broke off, feeling her throat tightening. "You are lord of nowhere, king of no one. What could you possibly have to offer me?"

"Security," said Aigisthos evenly. "For you and your children. For Mycenae too. That is what I offer."

"I've heard quite enough," Klytemnestra snapped, beginning to rise. "How you think you could—"

"By becoming your consort."

She stopped, her mouth open in astonishment.

"Before you say anything, I would expect nothing from you. You may treat it as . . . a kind of trade deal, I suppose. I would gain my rightful home, and you would have my protection."

"Lord Aigisthos," she began. "I do not need a consort. I have a husband. And I am doing very well at ruling without him."

"Yes, Damon has told me. Everything is going well for now. But you are vulnerable. Your authority derives from your husband. The men follow you because they fear him. And while he lives, perhaps your enemies will keep their distance as well. But if Agamemnon should die, what then? Mycenae will be taken from you. Either from within or from without. Your children will be killed outright. And perhaps you will be too, or else kept as a trophy, a slave in your own home, to be bid and bedded and beaten as your new master sees fit."

Klytemnestra's mouth hung open, but silent.

"You know that what I say is true," Aigisthos continued, his voice quiet. "You fear it yourself."

And she did. She had lain awake with these thoughts on many nights. No matter how well she ruled, no matter how much respect she gained, she was only queen because Agamemnon was king. Without a man, a woman was nothing. Those smiling faces that served her now would scorn a woman who dared to rule alone. It was a bitter truth, and yet she could not deny it. And Aigisthos did not even know her full turmoil—that even if Agamemnon returned home safe, she might still kill him herself. She did not fear the act so much as the danger she would bring upon her surviving children, in avenging the one she had lost.

"If your husband dies in this war, you and your children will fall with him," Aigisthos said gravely. "You stand upon a knife edge. I am offering you another way. Ally yourself with me, and I will vow this very night, with sacred oaths and sacrifices, that I will never harm you or your children, that I will do all I can to protect you. I still have supporters in Mycenae and its hinterland, people who were loyal to my father before his exile, people outraged by what Atreus did, people who served me and my father before we were deposed. Damon is one of them. His father served my father, helped run his affairs. He was killed for it, when your husband took Mycenae. Damon had to pretend he was a kitchen boy to save his own life. And he saved mine too—helped me escape the palace. He is loyal to me, yes, but he is no less loyal to you because of it."

She glanced over at Damon, who was looking at his feet.

Aigisthos continued. "My lady, if I reclaim the throne of Mycenae, few here would stand in my way. Indeed, Damon assures me that many would welcome my return. There is much resentment toward your husband for his unnecessary and expensive war. But you, my lady, you are popular with the people. If the two of us united, we could lead this kingdom with strength and a fair hand. And I vow that your children will be as my children. Your daughters will grow up in safety and happiness. And your son, Orestes, will still have his birthright, should he return to Mycenae to claim it."

He stopped speaking and there was silence as he awaited Klytemnestra's response.

"You . . . are asking me to betray my husband," she said eventually, though it was more a statement of fact than a protest. What sort of wife would she be, to hand her husband's throne to another man? But then, what sort of wife hoped that her husband would be killed, or contemplated that she might be the one to kill him?

"Agamemnon has taken from us both," Aigisthos said softly. "I have seen you at your daughter's tomb. I have heard the story of how she came to be there. You owe him nothing."

Klytemnestra straightened in her chair, trying to keep her expression even. What did this man know about Iphigenia? He had not known her, had not heard her sweet voice, had never held her soft hand in his. Would he sink so low as to use her memory for his own aims? And yet when she studied his eyes she found nothing but sympathy there. And as he looked back at her she felt that he understood something of the pain she tried to hide.

"But . . . it is not possible," she sighed. "You speak as if there will be no bloodshed, but . . . I cannot believe it. My husband will want news of his kingdom. When he hears that he has been deposed, he will come back to reclaim his throne. There will be civil war. I cannot bring that on my kingdom."

"He will not hear of it," said Aigisthos confidently. "Not if we control what news he receives. You send regular supplies to the Troad, yes? Then we send a report with each ship—give him the news before he asks for it. Damon tells me you have the loyalty of the scribes. They will write what you ask. And we send our own men to deliver it—men we trust."

"And if he sends his own messenger?"

"We send one of ours back. He is far away, and must rely on what you send him. Tell him that all is well, and he will believe it—for it is what he wants to hear. In the two years since this war began, how often has Agamemnon returned to his kingdom? Not once. His concern is with Troy, not Mycenae. He takes his sovereignty here for granted, while his hand grasps for more elsewhere. His back is turned to us."

"But it is not as simple as that," Klytemnestra protested. "What about outsiders? The other kingdoms? They will know the truth. They may send word to Agamemnon."

"I will avoid foreign audiences. You will remain the figurehead of Mycenae, at least until Agamemnon is no longer a threat. But foreign guests are few in any case. How many have you entertained since your husband left? They are all either fighting in the fields of Troy or trying to hold their own kingdoms together." He paused, leaning closer. "Trust me, my lady. I know I have given you little cause so far, but for the sake of yourself and your children, you must see that this is your best course. The longer you wait, the greater the chance that your husband will die in the field. He may be dead already. And as soon as that news reaches Greece, the wolves will descend. And then you will wish that you had a lion to deter them, a friend to defend you. That is what I offer."

His piece said, Aigisthos leaned back in his chair, watching her face closely. He knew her situation, understood it as well as she did. All he had had to do was get in to see her, to pluck her as if she were a ripe piece of fruit.

"Well, I see you have figured it all out," she said sharply. "But there are things you don't know, things that . . . you don't know me at all. And I do not know you."

"No," Aigisthos replied, leaning forward once more, his hands clasped together. "No, I don't dream that I know you, my lady. Though I hope that we will get to know one another, in time. Damon tells me that you are a remarkable woman—kind and brave and intelligent." He glanced over at the steward and she followed his gaze. Damon's eyes flicked up toward hers briefly, and then back down at his feet. She felt her cheeks warming.

"But above all else," Aigisthos went on, "I know that you are a mother, and that a mother would do anything to protect her children. I am giving you that chance."

Klytemnestra was silent, looking at Aigisthos critically. Could she trust this man? Did she trust her husband any more? Could she really trust anyone except herself? And yet he was right. She was vulnerable. Even a lioness could not rule alone.

"I will need time to consider your proposal, Lord Aigisthos," she said, adopting a stately tone. "In the meantime, you will remain here in the palace—under guard."

"If you wish it to be so," Aigisthos replied with a humble nod.

"I do," she said, folding her hands across her lap. And yet it was all pretense. She had already made her decision.

Aigisthos was right; she would do whatever it took to protect her children, to secure their future. She just had to summon the courage to trust him, and to pray that the gods would not strike her down for becoming that worst manifestation of womanhood: a traitorous wife.

CHAPTER 47

HELEN

SEVEN YEARS LATER

As Helen sat weaving in her chamber she could hear the clash of bronze through the window. The fighting was close to the city today—usually she would have to strain to hear it, if she could at all. The sound didn't frighten her as it used to, though. There would be battles most days now, outside the city walls, out on the plain, or away down by the Greek camp on the beach. The Greeks had exhausted the hinterland's plunder a year or so ago, and the Trojans had grown tired of being shut up inside their walls—not to mention all the trade wealth they were losing as the war dragged on. And so all there was to do now was to fight, man to man, prince to prince, until one side won out.

Since the Greeks had turned their attention to the city, it had become harder and harder to get supplies through. The nobles in the citadel complained about the lack of wine and spices, the meat rations, and the ban on feasts, but Helen knew that it was the people in the lower town who truly suffered. Kassandra would go out with her mother to tend the sick and raise morale—when the fighting was away from the walls—and she had told Helen that the people were living on the bitter vetch they usually kept for their animals.

This war had taken from rich and poor alike. Each day the women of the citadel would wait by the West Gate for their husbands and sons to return from the fighting. Helen used to wait with them, even when Paris was safe in his chamber. She would watch each day as the sun lowered and the crowd dwindled, each woman crying out with relief as her man appeared through the gates. Even those who had been injured, who were carried through by their comrades, bleeding or unconscious, were a welcome sight to those waiting eyes. But at the end of every day there would always be some women left waiting. And every day more women would have cause to hate her.

She didn't go to the West Gate anymore. She didn't go to the women's hall either. She couldn't face the glares and the curses, but neither did she blame the women. She knew the war was her fault, that so many men's lives were on her hands, and other lives too—her mother's, and Iphigenia's. If she could take it all back, she would. But as it was, all she could do was to endure her punishment—their hatred and her own terrible guilt.

Paris was sitting across the chamber from her, polishing his greaves as the sound of battle continued to drift through the window.

"Are you not needed on the plain?" she asked innocently. "The battle has been going on for some time, and yet you are here."

He did not look up.

"Women know nothing of warfare," he said, dipping his cloth in fresh oil. "If you did, you would know that it is important for some of the men to remain fresh, so that they might relieve their weary brothers."

Helen went on weaving her thread.

"It sounds like they need relieving now," she said quietly.

He didn't reply, but his face was sour as he turned his attention to his helmet, which already shone brightly.

As she watched her husband, with his carefully curled hair and his unsoiled tunic, the bile of resentment sat in her stomach. To think that she had caused so much strife and horror for his sake. She had had such hopes for her new life, for the love and happiness she would find in Troy, but the reality had turned out to be quite different. It had been intoxicating at first, but she had quickly learned that her new husband was like a wine jar—beautifully decorated and so inviting, but once the wine was drunk all she had been left with was an empty pot. But then that was all she had ever been to him, wasn't it? Slowly, slowly, over the long years she had spent in this lonely citadel, she had let go of the lie she had let herself believe, and had come to realize the truth. That she, Helen, the flower of Greece, the jewel of Sparta, was just another ornament to adorn his chamber.

And yet, aside from Kassandra's friendship, Paris was all she had to cling to at Troy. She could resent him, hate him even, but she could not forsake him. And he knew that.

Just as she turned her eyes away from her husband, there was a noise from the door of the chamber.

"Paris!" Hektor's voice rang through the marble-floored chamber.

He strode into view from behind the curtain screen, his brown skin shining with sweat, his breastplate spattered with blood. Helen was afraid he had been hurt, but she could see no injuries.

"Paris," he growled, his brow set hard, his voice a little hoarse from running. "I thought I could not see you on the field! What are you doing, hiding here? You coward. The men fight for you and you are not with them!"

Paris stood up, shining helmet in hand.

"I was about to join the fighting, brother," he said, keeping his chin raised as he met Hektor's fierce gaze. "Come, Helen. I asked you to help me with my armor."

Helen's mouth fell open, but it was pointless to argue. She rose from her stool and dutifully made her way to him, her lips tight.

Hektor's eyes were still glaring, but he too decided not to waste words.

"Go straight to the gate when you are ready," he said, already turning to leave. "I will meet you on the field."

And as quickly as he had arrived he was gone again, hurrying back to join his comrades.

Helen was silent as she tied the straps of Paris's armor, pulling the leather a little tighter than she needed to. Once she had finished she straightened up so that they stood facing each other, her eyes fixed on the leopard paws tied at his throat. As he leaned toward her she turned her face away, before realizing that he had only been reaching for his shield. Then he left for the gate, without a word passing between them.

The battle continued to rage beyond the city while Helen remained in her chamber. She was not alone for long, though—Kassandra came to sit with her soon after Paris had left. She seemed to have a knack for knowing when Helen needed her company.

Kassandra was a young woman now, and Helen's best—and only—friend. It had been strange to watch her grow, knowing that her own daughter was of a similar age. She sometimes thought of Hermione, across the sea, spinning wool in Sparta's halls. Did she ever think of her mother? Did she even remember her?

Helen had found it much easier to be a friend to Kassandra. The two of them would often sit together, spinning and talking, though only when Paris was elsewhere. He did not like the chatter of women. Helen was surprised that Queen Hekabe had let her and Kassandra become so close. She knew the queen disliked her, or at least distrusted her—after all, she was Helen the Whore. But then Kassandra did not have many friends among the other women, so perhaps her mother was happy for her not to be alone.

Kassandra was humming to herself, as she often did. There never seemed to be a tune behind it, just sounds strung together, but Helen found it oddly comforting.

"Do you think animals ever marry, Helen?" she asked suddenly, without looking up from her spindle. "It's a queer thought, isn't it?"

Helen smiled and nodded. She was used to Kassandra asking such questions, and not knowing what to say in response. She had found it was best to simply let her talk it out with herself.

"I suppose people do it because other people do. They think they ought to," Kassandra mused, unhooking the finished thread from her spindle. "It's funny how much of life works like that."

Helen nodded again. They sat in silence for a while before her friend spoke again.

"Father says I'm to be married."

She said it so simply that it took Helen a moment to respond.

"Really? When? To whom?"

"His name is Othryoneus," she said quietly, as if it were a secret. "He arrived at the city a fortnight ago, from Kabesos. He . . . is not a rich man, but has promised my father that he and his men will drive the Greeks from our shores in return for my hand. He is out there fighting right now." Her young brow was creased with concern.

"Have you met him?" Helen asked.

"Oh, yes. He asked to meet with me, when he first arrived. He wanted to ask whether I would consider marrying him."

"To ask *you*?" Helen asked, surprised. "Well, that *is* unusual. Surely he knew it would be your father's decision."

"Well, yes, but he said that he only wanted me if I wanted him."

"And what did you say?"

"Well, we talked for a while. He confessed that he was not as wealthy as other suitors might be, that he could not offer a bride price worthy of my birth, but that he would do all he could to make me happy. And . . . I believed him. I liked him. So I said that if he could convince my father, I would marry him."

Kassandra's cheeks were pink, but there seemed to be a genuine excitement beneath her shyness. Helen wondered how long she had been waiting to tell her.

"So when will you wed?"

"Father told him that he couldn't have me until he had fulfilled his promise and the Greeks were gone. But we can still see each other in the meantime—when Mother is there, and there are no battles to fight. He says I am like no woman he has met before." Her face spread into a bashful grin, and Helen could not help smiling in return. She was glad to see her friend so happy.

"I hope the war will end soon," she said, leaning over to clasp Kassandra's hand.

They continued their spinning for an hour or so, comfortable in their silence as in their chatter. But Kassandra never could abide sitting for too long.

"I'm going to go down to the gates," she announced, putting down her distaff. "I want to hear what news there is."

Helen nodded, but did not rise with her. "I'll stay here," she said. "Paris wouldn't want me to dirty my skirts." She gave a weak smile.

Kassandra nodded back. They both knew the real reason Helen didn't want to go to the gates, but she was grateful not to have to admit it. The thought of those hateful stares made her wince.

Alone once again, Helen returned to her loom. Tracking the threads was a greater distraction than spinning. It gave her brain less space to think, less time to reflect.

She wasn't sure how much time passed, but she slowly became aware that the noise outside had quietened a little, so perhaps the battle was finally drawing to a close. *How many women will be left waiting today?* she wondered, but quickly pushed the thought from her mind. *Focus on the threads*, she told herself.

Suddenly she heard running footsteps, light but urgent, and seconds later Kassandra reappeared.

"Helen," she gasped. "Come quickly. It's Paris." She stopped to take a breath. "He's going to fight Menelaos."

CHAPTER 48

HELEN

"Come on! They're just waiting for the rams." Kassandra began to pull Helen toward the chamber door by her wrist. "We can watch from the walls."

Helen stumbled after her, still trying to make sense of what Kassandra had said. *Paris was going to fight Menelaos? Why now? After all these years?* A couple of hours ago he had not wanted to enter the fighting at all.

As if she had heard Helen's thoughts, Kassandra called back to her over her shoulder.

"Menelaos challenged him—that's what I heard. And I suppose he couldn't refuse. He'd be called a coward—or worse."

They were at the steps that led up to the battlements now. Kassandra held her skirts in one hand as she took them two at a time. Helen followed, her legs growing more unsteady with every step.

Once at the top they looked out over the wall. There outside the city, little more than an arrow's flight from where they stood, the two armies were amassed, face-to-face, with a clear avenue running between them. And in that avenue were the figures of four men.

Even at this distance she knew three of them instantly. There was Paris, his leopard skin draped around his shoulders, his golden helmet glinting in the sun. Its plume of horsehair swayed and flicked as his boots scuffed the dusty earth. Behind him stood Priam, his father, the white-haired King of Troy. And there, opposite them, the figure that made her heart skip: Menelaos. He was older, of course, but his build was little changed. Still the warrior, his thick arms strapped with leather, his chest covered with a battered corselet. His straw-colored hair fell beneath a boar tusk helmet, which left his face exposed—a face she knew had been so close all these years, and yet she had not seen it since leaving Sparta. Her chest grew strangely tight at the sight of it.

Beside Menelaos stood another, broader man who was leaning on a thick staff of wood. She realized that it must be Agamemnon, though his face was turned from her. He was saying something to his brother, but Menelaos's eyes seemed fixed ahead of him, to the spot where Paris stood.

If he looks up at the wall, will he see me? she thought suddenly. *Will he know me?* Would his chest clench as hers had? Or would he feel something else? Hatred? Anger? Disgust? She ducked her head a little, pulling the veil tighter to cover her flaming hair.

"Do not be afraid for Paris," came Kassandra's voice from beside her. "My brother has a way of avoiding harm." She turned and smiled at Helen. "The Greeks will have to breach the walls of Troy before a drop of his blood falls."

She knew her friend was trying to reassure her, but Helen was barely listening. She was still watching Menelaos. The tiny figure of her husband was pacing impatiently down on the plain, so distant as to barely feel real, and yet so real that it was as if he were right here in front of her, as if she could smell his sweat and hear his heartbeat.

Her own heart beat in her throat as she watched him, and she thought of those years they had spent together, and of her home in Sparta. It was another life, and yet seeing him there, so close, so palpable, she felt as though she could reach out and take it all back.

"They've brought the rams!" Kassandra announced, leaning over the battlement to see as a chariot carried two thick-fleeced rams, one white, one black, out of the city gates. A path was cleared through the Trojan ranks, and the chariot came to a stop beside King Priam.

"What are they for? A sacrifice?" The rams were being unloaded from the chariot now.

"They've made an oath," Kassandra replied, not taking her eyes from the scene on the plain. "The sacrifice is to seal it. My father doesn't trust the Greeks' honor."

"What oath?" Helen asked, as King Priam cut the throat of the black ram.

Kassandra finally turned to look at her.

"They fight for you, Helen! I assumed . . . I thought you knew," she breathed, the wind half-whipping her words away. "Whoever wins shall have you as his wife, and all the Spartan treasure too. And the war will be at an end."

Helen gripped the battlement, her heart suddenly beating faster. Would this really all be over? She watched unseeing as the white ram's blood spilled on the plain. Behind it her former husband gripped his spear, his muscles wound tight, ready to spring. Meanwhile, Paris was speaking into his father's ear, his expression angry, urgent. But King Priam shook his head and turned from his son to climb onto the chariot that had brought the rams. As it drove back to the city, Agamemnon too stepped away from his brother and into the Greek ranks.

There were just two figures left in the barren avenue now, with the spilled ram's blood a dark threshold between them. And as Helen watched them pace, spears in hand, she found herself hoping that Menelaos would win.

Paris was the first to throw his spear, dashing forward to hurl it and then quickly running back again. It flew straight but missed Menelaos as he darted aside, light on his feet despite his size. And he didn't stop moving, but sprinted toward Paris, spear arm raised. He let loose and kept running, and when the spear stuck in Paris's shield Menelaos drew his sword, pressing forward all the while. Paris backed away as if repelled, farther back and farther, until the Trojan crowd was at his back—solid, unyielding. At last he drew his sword, just as Menelaos reached him. The bronze sang as the two blades clashed, the sound reaching Helen up on the battlements. *Menelaos will win*, came a voice in her head. *He is the fiercer.*

But then his sword broke—shattered into pieces, as if struck by Zeus. Menelaos stepped back, but he was not done. He launched a new assault, swinging his shield like a beast enraged. Paris hesitated, visibly unsettled by Menelaos in his whirling fury, unsure where to strike. He took his moment, thrust out his sword arm, but the swinging shield blasted it aside, and the sword flew from his hand, falling uselessly several feet away.

Paris leaped toward it, but Menelaos was too fast. He surged forward and gripped Paris by the horsehair of his helmet, wrenching him off his feet. Menelaos began to drag him, his hands and feet scrabbling in the dust.

This is it. Helen felt sick and relieved at once. Paris's hands moved to his throat, clawing at the strap under his chin, and Helen realized he was choking. That wasn't right. Didn't Menelaos realize? Despite everything, it pulled at her heart to see Paris so desperate. This was not a man's death.

And then suddenly the helmet was yanked away in Menelaos's hand—the strap must have broken. And Paris was on his feet, was running before Menelaos could realize what had happened. He turned in pursuit, but it was too late. Paris was at the Trojan ranks. And then he was in them. Helen's pity turned to disgust as she lost sight of him among the hundreds of heads. *The coward.*

Menelaos stood alone in the open arena, chest heaving. He yelled something Helen did not hear and hurled the empty helmet at the Trojan crowd. He shouted again, his arms raised, but the words were drowned out by the clamor that was growing on both sides, as the men realized what had happened.

When it was clear that Paris would not reemerge, Menelaos turned to his own men, then back to the Trojans. Helen watched as Hektor appeared from the crowd and began to talk with Menelaos. But he had barely reached him when Agamemnon came out from among the Greek ranks and joined the two men in the middle. Even at this distance Helen could see that Menelaos was angry. He paced back and forth, shield still gripped in his hand. It seemed Hektor was trying to appease him, but it was Agamemnon who was speaking back, arms crossed over his broad chest.

What was happening? Helen's heart was beating hard as she leaned over the battlement. She wished she could hear their words. Had Menelaos won? Was she going home? But as she saw Agamemnon shake his head and walk back to the Greeks with Menelaos following, Helen thought she knew the answer, and was surprised by how far her heart sank.

Hektor stood for a moment, watching the backs of the two brothers, before returning to the Trojan ranks. Shortly afterward the two armies began to part ways—the Greeks back to the beach, and the Trojans through the Skaian Gate into the lower city. Today's fighting was over, but the war was not.

She and Kassandra stood silent on the wall. Kassandra leaned over to watch the Trojans flow through the gate, but Helen's gaze stretched farther, trying to follow the figure of Menelaos as it disappeared into the thinning mass of the Greeks. With a pain she would not have thought possible only hours ago, she wondered if she would ever see it again.

When her Greek countrymen were no more than black specks, Helen announced that she was returning to her chamber. For once, she felt as if she could not bear Kassandra's company. She felt shaken. Divided. As if pulled in two directions. A moment ago she had thought she was going home, but now she found herself stuck, still, behind these walls, among the Trojans but not one of them.

She was self-conscious—even more so than usual—as she headed back through the citadel to her chambers. She wrapped her veil tightly once more, cursing the bright hair that had once made her so proud, and kept her eyes on the cobbles as she pushed through the crowds. Everywhere she heard voices discussing the duel.

—*What happened?*—

—*How did Paris escape?*—

—*Is he keeping the Greek whore?*—

It was a relief when she finally reached the quiet of the chamber. But as she stepped past the curtain screen she saw that she was not alone.

"Oh, it's you," said Paris dully. He lay reclining on a cushioned couch, his armor removed. "I thought it might be Hektor, come to tell me what a coward I am." He scoffed, and reached for a grape from the bowl beside him.

"You *are* a coward," Helen said, her arms stiff by her sides. "Now the war will continue because of you. More people will die."

"Watch your tongue," Paris snapped. But as he stood up, his face softened. He stepped toward her and laid his hands on her waist. "Lips so beautiful should not make ugly words." But as he leaned to kiss her she turned her face away.

"You would deny me?" he asked, half playfully, but with an edge to his voice. "After I just fought for you?"

"You fought because you had no choice," she said quietly, but clearly. "And even then you could not see it through."

"You ungrateful bitch," he said, his handsome face twisted in anger. He pushed her away from him and turned to pour himself a cup of wine. "You know, all these years my brothers, my father, my mother, they have all begged me to give you up. Send her back, they said, and perhaps the Greeks will leave. And every time, do you know what I said?"

Helen was silent.

"I said no." He looked straight into her eyes. "And I have paid my friends generous gifts to say no, too. Each time the matter is discussed. Gods, do you know how much loving you has cost me?"

Cost *him?* she thought bitterly, taking a step away from him. And what had it cost her? What had it cost Greece? Or Troy?

He moved toward her. "And your husband, when he came. I said no to him too. Even when he said I could keep the treasures I stole. I said no. And I will keep saying no. Because you are *my* woman. I won you and I took you. The most beautiful woman in the world is mine, and no other man shall have you while I live."

He took another swig, as Helen stood unmoving. There was a time when those words would have disturbed her, but it was long since passed. Now they only confirmed what she already knew: that she had only ever been his prize, like that poor beautiful creature he wore about his shoulders. No, it was not those words that caught her attention.

"When did Menelaos come?" she demanded, a strange heat rising in her chest. "You never told me that."

But it was as if she had not spoken. Paris took another long drink, a little of the red wine escaping to run down his neck. He wiped his mouth lazily, and Helen wondered how she had ever thought him beautiful.

"Now, since I have paid so dearly for you," he said, letting his empty cup clatter on the floor, and stepping yet closer. "Since I have fought for you and faced death for you"—he placed a hand on her shoulder, and drew back her veil with the other—"will you not comfort me now, as my wife?"

For you. For you. The words itched in her ears, and she felt her teeth clench. What had he ever done for anyone but himself?

He pulled her toward him, and pressed his lips against hers, his wine-breath filling her nostrils. But this time she did not turn away. She did not speak as he untied her sash, did not flinch as his hateful hand grasped her breast. What point was there in resisting? He was right; she was his woman. Her life had never been her own. She had been foolish to think it could be. Let him have her. Let him use her. It made no difference.

CHAPTER 49

KLYTEMNESTRA

Klytemnestra was a little late to Iphigenia's tomb this morning, though she performed the rites with her usual care. It was the quietest part of her day, out here beyond the citadel walls, just her and Ianthe and the wind.

Once the prayers were said and the wine poured, it was back to the palace and another busy day. Damon had requested a meeting about the grain stores, then she had an audience with the new head priest of Argos, and then she had promised Chrysothemis that she would help her with her writing. Perhaps Elektra would join them—Klytemnestra hoped she would. She saw so little of her these days.

She had just reached the top of the palace steps when she heard Eudora's voice.

"Yes, there she is. I told you she would be back soon."

Klytemnestra grinned as Aletes wriggled free from Eudora's hand and ran toward her. He was getting fast on his feet now—it was fortunate that Eudora had Ianthe to help her.

As Aletes reached her Klytemnestra scooped him up in her arms. He was getting heavy too.

"Did you miss me?" she asked, nuzzling his nose with hers. Aletes giggled. "Has he been good?" she asked Eudora, lowering him to the ground. "Do you mind watching him for a while longer? I still have some business to attend to. Ianthe will help you."

"Of course, my lady." Eudora smiled, the gaps in her teeth showing. "We'll find something fun for the prince to do, won't we?" She grinned down at Aletes, whose little hand was back in hers. "I left Chrysothemis with her sister," she said, turning back to Klytemnestra. "I hope that's all right, my lady."

"Oh yes," she replied, bending down to kiss Aletes good-bye. "They're young ladies now. I'll go by their chamber once my business is finished. Thank you, Eudora."

The older woman nodded, and led Aletes away through the palace.

Her audience with the priest concluded, the heavy doors of the Hearth Hall were closed and she sat alone in the square chamber. The sun was still high, its light streaming in through the hole above the hearth fire, illuminating the bright paints that daubed the walls. Men of red and women of white processed around the hall, leading their horses, carrying their baskets, striding through a world of blue and yellow. She leaned back on her seat, admiring the elegant figures who surrounded her. How long had they been marching? On and on around the hearth. How long had these walls stood? How long had the fire burned? Longer than she had lived, and her mother before her, and her mother before that. There was a strange comfort in it, in the grounded permanence of these walls.

She took a deep breath, the smoke of the eternal flames filling her nostrils. This fire would continue to burn after she had gone, and who would remember her then? Once her children too were gone, and their children after them. What voices would sound here in the echoing hall? Would the name of Klytemnestra ever be spoken across the crackling hearth? What would those faceless tongues say? How wise she was? How just? How dutiful?

Her fingers gripped the arms of her throne, palms sweaty as she stared at the flames. Her face grew hot in their light and she leaned back, forcing her fingers to loosen. She closed her eyes as if the voices might drift to her on the hearth smoke. What was she hoping to hear?

The bark of a palace dog brought her attention back to the present. She remembered her promise to Chrysothemis and pushed herself up from the gilded chair. Leaving the hall and crossing the courtyard, she had just started down the corridor to her daughters' chamber when a hand touched her arm. She turned, and smiled.

"I didn't expect you back unt—"

But Aigisthos stopped her with a kiss. His lips were warm on hers, his hand pressed against the small of her back.

"Good morning to you, too," she said breathlessly, leaning back a little to see his face. "Did you catch anything?"

"A couple of hares," he shrugged. "The boar eluded us. We decided we'd be better going back out tomorrow, once the horses are rested." His cheeks were red from riding hard.

"Yes, you're probably right." She smiled, glad to see him so full of energy. "Chrysothemis will be pleased with the hares in any case— she's been wanting a new collar for her winter cloak."

He beamed. "And she shall have it!"

Klytemnestra laughed. "That girl has you wrapped around her finger. I think you'd give her the sun if she asked for it."

"I'd certainly try my best." He grinned and kissed her again. "And for you, my queen, the moon and the stars!"

"That's a fine offer, but I think we'll leave them where they are. I don't need anything but what I already have." She smiled, her hand on his shoulder.

"Well, we're not done quite yet," he said, resting his hand on her belly.

"Don't," she said, pushing it gently away. "It's only a feeling . . . I don't want you to be disappointed."

"You could never disappoint me," he said, moving the hand to her cheek instead. He smiled, and she smiled back.

They stood there for a moment, their breath mingling.

"I should bathe," said Aigisthos eventually, stepping back from her.

"Not in our chamber," said Klytemnestra. "I'll be helping Chryso-themis with her writing. Come and meet us when you're done though—you can show her the hares."

He grinned. "I won't be long." Then he hurried off toward the guest chambers.

Klytemnestra smiled as she watched him go, and once he had turned the corner she herself turned and continued down the corridor to the girls' chamber. With an acknowledging nod to the guard outside, she knocked and opened the door.

"Good morning, girls," she said brightly. Her daughters were spin-ning wool.

"Good morning, Mother," Chrysothemis replied with a smile. Elek-tra did not look up from her spindle.

"Do you still want me to help you with your letters?" she asked her younger daughter. "I have the tablets ready in my chamber."

Chrysothemis nodded enthusiastically, abandoning her spindle and crossing the room toward the door.

"Would you like to join us, Elektra? There's a tablet for you too. Or you could bring your spinning."

Elektra finally looked up. "Will *he* be there?"

Klytemnestra paused. "Yes."

"Then I will not."

Klytemnestra bit her lip. She didn't like her daughter being so dis-respectful, but she feared that reprimanding her would only serve to push her further away.

"If you will not join us then you will have to spend your afternoon with Eudora and your brother."

"He's not my brother," Elektra said flatly, watching her spindle once more.

Klytemnestra bit her lip again.

"I cannot leave you on your own," she said.

"I am nineteen, mother," Elektra replied, not bothering to hide the impatience in her voice. "I have the guard."

Klytemnestra opened her mouth to argue, but thought better of it. Her daughter was right. She was a woman now, even if she was not married. It was just that Klytemnestra feared she was shutting herself off.

"If you change your mind, have the guard escort you to my chamber."

Elektra didn't respond.

"Come on," she said to Chrysothemis, trying to rekindle her brightness. "Lord Aigisthos has a surprise for you."

Her daughter's eyes lit up, and Klytemnestra smiled, but the happiness she had felt just minutes ago had faded.

CHAPTER 50

KLYTEMNESTRA

Klytemnestra lay in bed, a lamp still burning on the table beside her. Aigisthos had wanted to tell Aletes a story before he went to sleep, and she was waiting for him to return. He wouldn't be long, she knew—Aletes's eyes always started to droop before the story was halfway told.

Klytemnestra's new life still felt odd sometimes. Most days she would go along living it, too busy to do anything else. But then she would catch herself, and it was as though she were living another's person's life. It felt fragile, as if a strong wind might blow it away, or as if one day she might go to sleep and awake to find that it had all disappeared. But most of the time these fears lay silent, and she just enjoyed living it.

It was strange to think back to that first evening, when Aigisthos had revealed himself to her. If a seer had come to her that night and told her what was to come, she didn't think she would have believed it. For more than a year, nearly two, her relationship with Aigisthos had remained strictly formal. To begin with, she had not even let him meet her daughters, and would merely join him for dinner each evening before they each retired to their own separate chambers.

But in time, despite her caution, she began to find herself enjoying his company. He was warm and intelligent. He made her laugh—truly laugh, as she had not done in so long—and, perhaps most of all, he had made her feel less alone. He had been a friend and a partner to her, and still was, giving her counsel when she asked for it, encouragement when she needed it. He helped her to rule without ever trying to rule her.

And he had been so good with the girls. Chrysothemis had adored him instantly, for his jokes and his gifts. And though Elektra had been much less trusting, he had never stopped trying to win her approval.

Her present marriage—for that was what it was, in her eyes at least—was so different from the first. She had found a new happiness with Aigisthos, a new security she hadn't thought possible. It was only from being with him, learning to trust him, that she had realized how much her former life had been dictated by fear. Fear that she would say or do the wrong thing, fear that she would anger Agamemnon, fear that he would hurt her, or worse, her children. She still had fears, of course, but now they came from without. They did not prowl her home, brood in her bed. It was as if she could finally uncurl and be her full self.

She heard familiar footsteps in the corridor outside and the chamber door opened. Aigisthos's face appeared, smiling.

"I didn't even get to the centaurs' feast today," he said, closing the door softly behind him. "Eudora must have worn him out." He untied his boots and slid into bed beside her. "I checked on the girls, too— they're fine. Well, as fine as Elektra ever is."

He leaned over and kissed her cheek. She did not turn her head.

"What's wrong?" he asked. "Are you still thinking about the grain stores? I think Damon is more cautious than he needs to be—"

"No, it's not that," she said, turning to look at him. "It's just . . . I'm worried about Elektra. She's so unhappy." Aigisthos's face was sympathetic. "She barely speaks to me. I understood at first, why she was wary, but I hoped that in time . . ."

"I am not her father. I do not expect her to love me," he said.

"But she hates you. And she resents me for loving you, for betraying her father. She still loves him. It's different for Chrysothemis—she barely remembers him. But Elektra . . . I fear she will never accept it."

Aigisthos didn't say anything, but reached out for her hand and squeezed it.

"Perhaps I should find her a husband," Klytemnestra continued. "Let her begin her own life, in her own palace. If she can find her own happiness, perhaps she will forgive me mine. Gods know she is old enough—even Chrysothemis is in her bloom now. They have grown so quickly, it makes me feel old."

She looked at Aigisthos, wanting him to tell her what she should do.

"You are not old," he said with a smile, stroking her cheek. "And yes, any other girl Elektra's age would likely be married by now, but she is not any girl. Do you really think she will be ruled by a man?" He raised a playful eyebrow. "A husband is not the answer. And I know you do not want to send her away."

"No," she said softly. "I wish I never had to send either of them away. I just want them to be happy."

"I know," said Aigisthos, and kissed her forehead. "Give her time. Perhaps things will change if Agamemnon . . ." But he fell quiet.

She knew what he was going to say. *If Agamemnon dies.* They had both been waiting for that day, and year after year it had not come. Nine years her husband had been at war. She had never expected it to go on for this long, and perhaps neither had he. But one day it had to end, and then what would happen?

"He may still be killed," she said quietly.

Aigisthos nodded, but he was deep in thought.

"Aigisthos?"

"What if he is not?" he said in a low voice. "He has survived this long. I said that I would keep you safe."

"And you have."

"But if Agamemnon returns . . . there will be civil war. You know it as much as I. And every life lost will be blood on my hands." He looked away from her. The usual humor of his cheeks had fled.

They were both silent for a while.

"I once vowed that I would kill him myself."

It was strange to say the words. They sounded ridiculous as they came out of her mouth, so much that a mirthless laugh broke from her throat. It felt like a lifetime ago, and she had never spoken of it to anyone, not even to Aigisthos.

He looked up at her, his eyes questioning.

"The night before Iphigenia was killed. I vowed to Lady Hera that if Agamemnon killed my daughter, I would kill him in turn. And I almost did it, I had the knife in my hand. I—"

Aigisthos's face wore a strange expression. Was it horror? Disgust? Did he think less of her, now that she had told him her darkest secret? She wished she had kept silent.

"You should do it," he said suddenly. "If he survives, if he returns to Mycenae. You should kill him."

His eyes were earnest. He was gripping her hand, but she felt afraid.

"I was only . . . I can't."

"I will help you. We can do it together. Think of all the lives we could save. Civil war would tear this kingdom apart. Better to kill him alone. Let him think all is well, let him come to the palace, let him believe he is safe. And then . . . you know you could do it—you're the only one who could."

She was silent, looking into his fervent eyes, still afraid.

"He deserves to die," Aigisthos continued, his cheeks flushed again. "For what he did to Iphigenia. The gods will not blame you. He has committed the greater crime."

"One crime does not forgive another," she argued. "I would be condemned by gods and men! I have already abandoned my sacred duty as his wife, but to desecrate it so completely . . . I would be known as the evilest woman who ever lived."

Her breath rattled unsteadily. Somehow, the prospect was so much more terrible than it had been all those years ago. Then she had felt as if Agamemnon had taken everything from her. She hadn't cared what would happen afterward, what people would say, what her life would be. She hadn't cared if she lived or died. But now . . . now she was happy. There was so much more at stake, and the thought of losing it terrified her. Then another thought came to her.

"What about my children? I cannot put that upon them—the knowledge that their father was slain by their mother. It would destroy Elektra. She would never forgive me."

"And what about *our* child?" Aigisthos shot back, his eyes as fearful as hers. "If Agamemnon returns, you will have no choice but to send Aletes away, to pretend he never existed—or Agamemnon will certainly kill him. You know this."

As she looked into his eyes, she realized he was right—it was not only their lives at stake. She could not bear to lose another child. Anything was better than that. And yet the thought of Aletes brought another innocent face to her mind. Her beautiful Orestes, still a babe when she last laid eyes upon him and yet he must be almost ten now. In killing Agamemnon she would likely lose Orestes forever—why would Anaxibia return him to her brother's murderer? But at least he would be safe. Wasn't that why she had sent him away? He would still have a home and a family and a future, but Aletes . . . she could not condemn her sweet boy to the life of an exile.

She and Aigisthos looked at each other, their eyes shining, their expressions intense. Klytemnestra wished that such a terrible decision were not hers to make, that her new life could go on as if the old had never existed. But deep in her heart she knew the truth, had known it all these years. She had made her decision the day she agreed to Aigisthos's proposal.

"I will do it," she said, her voice barely more than a whisper. She felt Aigisthos squeeze her hand.

"We will do it."

CHAPTER 51

HELEN

They were in Kassandra's chamber this morning. It was smaller than Paris's, but comfortable and brightly decorated. Kassandra was a skilled weaver and would hang her finished cloths on the walls. The patterns were full of animals and flowers and all the beauty of nature—gentle and vibrant at once, like Kassandra herself. Helen liked to study them as she sat spinning.

The sounds of battle clattered in the distance, farther from the city today. Many of Kassandra's brothers were down on the plain and, though she tried to maintain her usual lightness, Helen could tell that her friend was afraid for them. She kept glancing at the window, as if news of the battle might be borne in on the breeze.

"Do you think I should go down to the gates?" she asked suddenly, her foot tapping nervously on the rug-covered floor. "There might be some news. Or maybe I could do something to help."

She looked at Helen, seeking direction.

"Go down to the gates if you like. I can stay here."

But Kassandra hesitated. "I don't know. My mother may want me to help her with the libations . . ." She looked to the door and away again. "She says Apollo favors the young. If she calls for me and I am not here . . . no, I should stay."

She nodded her fair head decisively, and yet her brow remained furrowed. They were both quiet for a moment.

"What of Othryoneus?" Helen asked brightly, hoping to turn her friend's mind to happier things. "Does he still visit you? Perhaps it will not be long until you are wed."

As Kassandra's worried face broke into a girlish grin, Helen knew it had worked.

"Yes, he still visits. Sometimes Mother lets him hold my hand." Her smile broadened. "But mostly we talk. He is such a great-hearted man. And he knows so many things. You know, he told me that—"

She was cut off by a hammering on the door.

Kassandra sprang to her feet and was there in a moment, pulling it open to reveal the pallid face of her twin brother, Helenos.

"Brother!" she cried as he stumbled over the threshold. His left hand was a mass of blood-soaked wool, hanging limply at his side.

"My hand," he mumbled. Beads of sweat dripped down his brow. He looked as if he were about to faint.

Kassandra led him quickly to the chair she had just left, and he fell into it.

"What happened?" she asked, scurrying to fetch a jug of water from the table.

"My hand," her brother groaned again, his face tight with pain. "The spear went right through it. I . . . Agenor bound it up. It's ruined, Kass." His voice cracked, and he looked up at her, his young face filled with so much fear. "You've got to help me."

"I'll help you, don't worry. Hush now."

She crossed over to her bed and took up the woolen veil that lay there, dipping its end in the water jug and wiping her brother's brow.

"It'll be all right. You're with me now. I'll look after you."

Helen had been so absorbed by Helenos's entrance that she hadn't noticed the other figure who stood in the doorway. As Deiphobos stepped forward into the room, Helen turned and saw him. His right arm was red with blood.

"Kassandra," Helen said, directing her friend's eyes to him.

"Deiphobos! You as well?" Still soothing Helenos, she gestured for her elder brother to sit on the bed. "Helen, would you help him?"

Helen nodded and crossed the room, though reluctantly. Deiphobos made her uncomfortable—the way he looked at her whenever they crossed paths. She would feel his eyes on her, even as she walked away. But he needed her help. And so did Kassandra.

"What should I do?" she asked, sitting down beside her brother-in-law. The blood was coming from a long gash on his upper arm. His face was set hard, but she could tell he was in pain.

"Try cleaning off some of the blood," Kassandra replied, as she began to unwrap the wool from her twin's hand. But she stopped when he cried out with fresh pain.

"I need to get some supplies," said Kassandra, getting up off her knees. "We need honey and herbs for the wounds. And fresh wool for the binding. Will you wait here with them until I get back?" She hurried toward the door without waiting for a reply. "I'll bring some strong wine for the pain, too," she called back to her brothers as she disappeared down the corridor.

How was it that Kassandra always knew exactly what to do? Helen sat on the bed, feeling useless, as the smell of blood filled the small room—she could taste it on her tongue. Helenos sat on his chair, whimpering incoherently. Better not to touch him, she thought. Kassandra had told her to clean Deiphobos's arm, but she was afraid to touch it. Her hand hung in midair, clutching the wet cloth. What if she hurt him?

"Just do it," Deiphobos said, watching her. "Go on."

She looked at him, sucked in a breath, and put the cloth to his skin. The older blood had already begun to dry, so she had to rub a little to get it off. She saw Deiphobos grit his teeth as her cloth went near the gash, but he said nothing. It was only when most of the arm was clean that he spoke again.

"How does it feel?" he asked quietly. "To see men bleed for you?"

His question caught her off guard. Her lips fell open but no words would come to them. *They do not bleed for me* was what she wanted to say. But was it true? They fought for the *idea* of her, but did that really make any difference to the men lying dead in the sand? To the widows waiting at the gate? Her numb lips were saved from forming a reply as Kassandra trotted back into the chamber, her arms full with various jars and bundles. She passed Helen a wineskin.

"Give some to Deiphobos while I make the poultice. You'd better save most of it for Helenos, though," she said, looking at her twin with concern. "He'll need it."

It was some time before both wounds were cleaned and dressed. Kassandra did most of the work, but Helen helped where she could—bringing fresh water, pouring more wine, holding poor Helenos's good hand through the worst of the pain. His left hand was so mangled that it made Helen feel ill to look at it. Despite Kassandra's efforts, she doubted he would regain the use of it. For now, the best they could do was to give him more wine and let him rest.

He lay propped up on his sister's bed, quieter now but still pale. Deiphobos, whose wound was shallow by comparison, had taken a chair next to Helen and Kassandra, his arm tightly wrapped with wool.

"The fighting was thick today," he said, taking a swig of wine. "Many more than us two were wounded. Some killed, too."

"And the Greeks?" asked Helen. "Were many of them killed?"

"If it's that Spartan husband you're worried about, you needn't bother," spat Deiphobos. "He was in fine form. Probably hoping he would run into our dear brother Paris again."

"It was him who hit me," came a thin voice from the bed. "The fair-haired one. Sent his spear right through my—" He winced at the memory. "Split my bow in two as well. He was wild, he was. Think I cut down one of his companions. Must have been what set him on me."

"Who?" asked Helen. "Who did you kill?"

"I don't know. His charioteer maybe. He was short, with black hair."

Deipyros? The description sounded right. She felt a pang of pity for Menelaos. They had been companions since they were boys.

"I wouldn't waste any tears on one poor Greek," Deiphobos said to her abruptly. "Men are dying every day. And they'll keep on dying. It seems the gods have willed this war to go on until every one of us has been sent to Hades."

"I don't think that's true," came Kassandra's soft voice. "The war is at its height now. I think it will come to an end before the next winter."

Deiphobos laughed bitterly.

"You do, do you? And what would you know about it, sister? You have not fought on the plain. You have not witnessed the spirit of the Greeks. They will fight until their last breath."

"I did not say they would give up," Kassandra replied, but she said no more about it. The four of them sat quietly for a short while before she spoke again. "Who else was injured in the fighting?" she asked. "Was Hektor still unharmed when you came back to the city? And Paris?"

Helen realized that she had not asked for news of her own husband.

"Yes, they were both still among the ranks," Deiphobos replied. "I think I saw Aineias too."

"And Othryoneus?" Kassandra asked. "Did you see him, too?"

"I did not," he said slowly. "But he may have moved down the bea—"

"No."

The sound came from the bed, and they turned to see Helenos push himself upright.

"Kassandra, I'm so sorry. I was going to tell you."

"Tell me what? Was he injured?"

Helenos shook his head heavily. "He went down in the fighting. I saw it."

"But are you sure?" Kassandra asked, her voice rising. "He may have only been wounded."

Her brother shook his head again. "He's dead, Kassandra. He took a Greek spear to the gut. It went straight through his corselet."

Kassandra's head fell a little, as if nodding. Even Helen knew that such a wound could not be survived. Kassandra's lips hung open, but soundless. She sat staring straight ahead, and Helen saw her eyes begin to glisten. Helen's heart was like a stone as she watched her friend's grief spread silently through her.

And as Kassandra eventually turned her head and looked into Helen's eyes, her stone heart sank into her stomach. There on her friend's face was the look she had seen a hundred times before. The look that followed her through the citadel and haunted her at its gates. It was sorrow and pain and loss. But more than that, it was blame.

CHAPTER 52

HELEN

Helen sat in the corner of the women's hall, alone. It was the first time she had been to the hall in months, and she would have continued to avoid it given the choice. But she had nowhere else to go. She and Paris had argued, and he had sent her from his chamber. She should not have riled him, she knew that, but it was so difficult to remain meek when all her unhappiness was his doing. Why should his life go untroubled and hers be torn in tatters?

In the past she would have retreated to Kassandra's chamber, but that door was not as welcoming as it once had been. She still saw Kassandra sometimes—in passing, or if she came to Paris's chamber on some errand—but their closeness had been fractured by Othryoneus's death, and had split wider in the weeks that followed. Now, whenever their paths crossed, her friend would smile politely and they would exchange a few words, but their stilted encounters would leave Helen with a heavier heart than if she had not seen her at all.

Part of her was angry. What cause did Kassandra have to blame her? If not for the war, Othryoneus might never have come to Troy—they would never have been betrothed if he had not had the opportunity of winning her hand with his spear. It was not fair, Helen told herself, that his death be added to all those that already weighed upon her. It was not fair that her one friend now could not bear her company.

And yet she suspected that Kassandra knew this. If she truly blamed Helen, she would hate her, revile her, rage at her. The truth was that Helen, whether guilty or not, trailed death behind her. She was like a cloud of pestilence, harming all she touched, spreading grief and misery and decay. She didn't blame her friend for running.

Kassandra was in the women's hall this afternoon, sitting in the center mixing poultices with some of the other noblegirls. The hall had become a place to tend the wounded, and a row of straw mattresses had been laid out along one side. All but a few of them were in use.

On one mattress, not far from where Helen was sitting, lay Prince Hektor, attended by his wife, Andromache. He had been brought to the hall the day before, so she had gathered. He had no bleeding wounds, unlike the other men who lay in the hall, but had been hit in the chest by a great stone, hurled into the melee by one of the Greeks. He lay without a tunic, his skin a swell of red and purple beneath the black hair of his chest. He kept telling his wife not to fuss over him, and yet Helen could tell he was in pain. He would wince whenever he had to sit up to take water, and she had seen him cough up clots of blood. She was worried for him and couldn't help looking over to his bed whenever Andromache's head was turned away from her.

The fighting had been hard since the early morning. Even from the hall they could hear the clash of arms, the screeching whinnies of the horses, the bellowing war cries. The Greeks had pressed right up to the city walls and had been sending men to the hall all day, bleeding and broken. It was as if some new spirit had entered them, a new rage, a thirst for blood—or perhaps simply for an end to the war.

Hektor had grown more and more frustrated as the day wore on, as more and more of his brothers and comrades filled the mattresses beside him. Many more, no doubt, lay dead on the field. And yet he could do nothing about it. He could not defend them, nor avenge them, stuck as he was inside the citadel walls.

Helen had witnessed several attempts by Hektor to leave his bed. But each time Andromache would chide him.

"Do not be foolish!" she would say. "If you die, Troy will be lost! And what then of your son? What of me? You cannot protect anyone if you are dead."

Her tone was severe, but Helen could see genuine fear on her face. She had dark circles beneath her eyes from tending her husband all night. It was clear that what she dreaded most was losing him.

In the midafternoon, a slave woman entered the hall and went straight to where Hektor lay.

"Lady Andromache," she said with a bobbing bow. "The lord Astyanax wants you, my lady. He's in such a terrible temper."

"Well, can't you calm him?" she said irritably. "I must care for my husband."

"Yes, my lady, I've tried that. Only, he says he wants you. He's got himself into such a state."

"Well, why don't you bring—no. I don't want him in here," she said, looking about at the bleeding men. "Very well, I shall come."

She got up from the cushion she had been kneeling on, then leaned down to kiss her husband's hand.

"I won't be gone long," she said, her expression torn. She clung to her husband's hand, and seemed unwilling to let it go. "He's probably just scared. You know how he gets."

"Go," said Hektor. "I'm sure he needs you more than I do. I'll be here when you get back." He smiled up at her reassuringly, and let go of her hand.

Andromache hurried from the hall, with the slave woman following at her heels.

She had been gone a short while when a voice called Helen's attention from her spinning.

"Helen."

She glanced around to see Hektor looking toward her.

"Would you mind sharing your water?" She saw that his cup stood empty, and gave a shy nod. She picked up the jug from the table beside her and stepped toward his mattress. Helen was surprised that he had asked her of all the women in the hall, but she supposed she had been close by, and the others were more occupied than she. When she reached his bed, she knelt on the cushion Andromache had been using and began to fill Hektor's cup. Her hands shook a little as she tipped the jug, which only made her more self-conscious. She so admired Hektor, and while part of her was pleased that he had asked for her help, she felt nervous under his scrutiny.

Suddenly, as she poured and the silence stretched between them, Helen felt she had to say something, while she had this chance.

"I am sorry, you know," she murmured. "For everything that has happened." Her eyes flicked to his and away again. "I never realized what coming here would mean and . . . I know that you think me a fool. But I didn't mean for anyone to die because of me."

She could feel his eyes on her as she stared down at her knees, her small words sinking into the silence.

"If I think you are a fool, it is for loving my brother," he said.

She looked up cautiously.

"I have thought of trying to leave him. Leave the city," she whispered. "Even now I could give myself up to the Greeks. I thought maybe—"

"It would make no difference," Hektor sighed. "Not now. Maybe not even in the beginning. This war is about more than you, Helen."

She didn't know whether he meant to alleviate her guilt or chastise her self-importance. But he didn't look angry. Just sad. Whatever his meaning, she felt something shift inside her, as if a heavy weight had been lifted a little.

As she put the jug down on the stone floor, a shadow fell over her. She looked up to see the scowling face of Andromache.

No words were needed. Helen left the jug and hurried to her feet. Without meeting Andromache's eyes again, she scurried back to her chair in the corner and took up her distaff.

When she dared to look up, she saw that Andromache had resumed her place on the cushion and was holding her husband's cheek in her delicate hand. They were speaking in low tones that Helen could not hear.

It was late in the afternoon when the messenger arrived. A young man, healthy and fit, yet his face was gray as he entered the hall.

"Lady Laothoe."

Somehow his fractured voice carried through the hall, and a hush fell.

"Lady Laothoe," he said again, as she stepped out from a cluster of finely dressed women. She was the youngest of King Priam's wives—younger than Helen—with large, pale eyes.

"I bring news that your two sons have been killed, my lady." He bowed his head. "Their bodies are being borne to the citadel."

"M-my sons?" she asked, her fair face confused. "No, you must be mistaken. They weren't . . . they weren't in the fighting. The king said they were too young. It can't be them." Her voice sounded far away, and her large eyes shone.

"It is them, my lady. Lord Polydoros was running spears down to the men, and Lord Lykaon was helping to bear back the injured. Both were cut down by the one they call Achilles. There were many who saw."

Without warning, a terrible cry broke from Laothoe's mouth. The women near her rushed to stop her from falling as painful sobs began to rack her body.

"I need to see them," Helen heard her mumble. "They can't be alone. I need to be with them."

It made Helen's chest tight to watch her, to hear the pain in her voice. She had seen the two boys running around the citadel over the years. The youngest of Paris's brothers, they had been small children when the war began. Now it had claimed them both, before their first beards had grown.

Once she was steady enough to walk, Laothoe was led from the hall with some of her companions, taken to tend the corpses of her only children. It made Helen feel angry and guilty at once. How many more lives would the gods demand in payment for her folly? She squeezed her distaff until the wood cracked. But then another sound turned her head.

"No! Hektor, please!"

Andromache was clinging to her husband's forearm as he stood beside his mattress.

"What kind of a man kills little boys?" he thundered, raising his voice to the hall. "I will give the Greeks a real man to contend with."

His bruised chest heaved with rage as he began to strap his corselet about it.

"Please, Hektor," Andromache begged again, her eyes wide with a desperate fear. "Please. Don't go out there."

Suddenly another voice sounded through the hall.

"She is right, brother," said Kassandra, her words soft but clear. "You would be right to fear Achilles. He has killed many men today. His violence is at its highest swell. You should wait until it ebbs."

But it was as if Hektor could not hear her. He bent to put on his greaves—his face creasing in pain as he did. Andromache wept as she stood helplessly beside him.

"Today's fighting is already over, brother," Kassandra continued, stepping toward him. "Save your strength for another day."

Hektor put his helmet over his head, as if to block out her words.

"Please," Andromache begged a final time, pressing her hands to his face. "Please, husband."

He stopped and looked down at her, stroking her wet cheek with his hand. "I fight for you, and for Troy."

And with that Hektor strode from the hall, Andromache hurrying behind him.

The hall was silent for some time, as if Hektor had taken the very air with him. Helen sat motionless, her distaff abandoned on her lap. She had heard terrible things about Achilles. They said he was the most deadly of all the Greeks. The fastest on his feet, the strongest with a spear. Hektor was the greatest of the Trojans, but he was wounded. Fear grew in Helen's stomach, grabbing at her insides and twisting them like rope.

As she sat, she began to feel a familiar sensation—that of eyes boring into her, of anger and sorrow hurled at her as if they were sharpened spears. She glanced up from her lap to see hate-filled faces, despairing and afraid faces, pointed at her. She imagined that every face in the room was turned to her, though she didn't dare look up long enough to know. She wanted to find Kassandra's face among them. To find one pair of friendly eyes. But she was afraid of what she might see there instead.

So she ran. She left her wool and hurried from the hall, head bowed. She would go back to her chamber. Paris would have forgiven her by now. He had to. She couldn't stand to be so alone.

She made her way through the citadel, avoiding the gaze of those she passed, veil drawn across her face. It was as she was crossing the courtyard to Paris's chamber that she heard it. A terrible scream that made her stop dead.

And as she stood and listened, it turned into a wail. Like a wounded animal, a wild and formless sound. Pure emotion pouring from a throat. And then it spread and began to sound from other directions. And soon it was as if the whole city were wailing, one body with a thousand voices.

Helen's heart was clenching painfully as she turned back the way she had come. Then up, up, climbing the stairs to the battlements. She could barely breathe as she stumbled forward to clasp the wall, looking over it to the plain below.

It took her a moment to realize what she was seeing. There outside the city, in plain view from both its walls, a chariot drove back and forth. And behind it, ankles bound with rope, there dragged a body. The flesh was torn, black blood mixed with dust, and the head bounced against the stony ground.

Helen knew it was Hektor. Just as she knew it was Achilles who drove the chariot. The city was mourning the death of its prince, the loss of its protector.

A sudden sickening sob rose in her throat and she looked away. She could not bear to look upon that body, so disgraced and lightless. It made her feel nauseous. It made her chest feel as if it were being crushed.

She leaned against the wall to steady herself, taking in stabbing lungfuls of air. And there below, on the outer wall above the Skaian Gate, only a stone's throw from where she herself stood, Helen saw the figure of Andromache. Her black hair streamed wild in the wind, whipping about her as she screamed and sobbed, clawing at her breast, at the white skin of her bare arms. Helen realized that this had been the poor creature to utter that first piercing death knell, and she watched as Andromache's grief poured out of her in an unending stream. Beside her stood the dark figure of Queen Hekabe, quite still beside the storm of Andromache, though Helen could see her aged shoulders shake as she watched the ravaged corpse of her firstborn dragged before her.

All around Helen the city continued to wail, the sound growing louder as the news spread. Her tears fell silently, streaming down her cheeks as she stood alone with her grief.

Hektor, the Lord of Troy, was dead.

CHAPTER 53

HELEN

SEVERAL MONTHS LATER

Helen awoke suddenly, surfacing from a deep dream that was forgotten as soon as she left it. The chamber was dark. Paris lay beside her, unstirred. So what had woken her?

She turned over to burrow back into the warm bedding. And then she heard it. A shout. And then another. And a woman's scream.

"Paris."

She shook his shoulder, an ear still turned to the open window.

"Paris. Wake up."

He grunted, and she shook harder.

"Do you hear that? Something's happening."

"Hear what? I don't hear—"

But then there was a crash of wood, distant but not so distant. And more shouts.

Paris was sitting up now.

"It may be nothing," he said. "A brawl in the lower town." And yet even in the darkness Helen could see that he looked afraid.

He stood up from the bed and began to put on his tunic. Helen groped around for the dress she had discarded that evening and hastily threw it over herself, fixing the shoulder pins with fumbling hands.

When they were both dressed and sandaled they left the chamber, stepping into the moonlit courtyard. There was more shouting now, or perhaps they could hear it better. Helen thought she heard the clang of metal too.

"Cousin!" Suddenly Paris hurried forward, spotting Aineias across the courtyard. "What is happening?"

"I don't know," Aineias replied, looking as fresh from sleep as they were. "I heard the shouts and—"

"I'm going to the wall," said Paris, putting a hand on his cousin's shoulder.

Aineias nodded, looking about the empty courtyard. "I should wake the others."

Paris did not tell Helen to follow him, but she did. Her sandals slapped the stones behind his, her skirt held up with one hand while the other clutched an oil lamp. The moon was full enough not to need it, but she was glad of its light nonetheless.

They were at the bottom tier of the citadel now. The sounds had grown louder than ever. Paris headed straight for the stairs up to the battlements, and Helen followed. When they finally reached the top and looked over the wall, her breath caught in her throat.

The lower town was under attack. The Skaian Gates hung open, a stream of Greek warriors pouring through them. The streets below were already filled with their round shields. She watched as brave townsmen were cut down, as others fled their homes in terror, children clutched in their arms. And all the while the shields pressed closer to the citadel.

"How did they get through?" Helen asked the darkness, bewildered by what she was seeing. Still foggy with sleep, she squinted down at the dark gate. It looked splintered, as if rent open by the claws of some huge beast. There between the battered doors she thought she could see the outline of some great, looming structure, but what scared her more were the endless shields that continued to stream either side of it. "We have to warn—"

There was a choking sound by her left ear. She turned.

Paris stood beside her, as before. But as she raised her lamp she saw it. A black arrow, shot through his throat. Blood bubbled from his mouth, his eyes wide with shock. There was a terrible gurgling sound and he fell, choking and spluttering, clawing the ground, holding his throat. Helen watched, transfixed, as his body writhed and jerked. And then it went still.

It was as if she were still in her bed. As if this were the dream and not the waking. She stood, dazed, looking down at Paris's body. The blood began to pool around his head, soaking into the soft ringlets of his hair. His white eyes stared up at nothing. Death had hung around Helen for so long, and yet she had never been this close to it.

"Helen!"

She dragged her eyes from Paris, unsure how long she had been staring at him. It took her a moment to recognize the figure of Polites, one of Paris's younger brothers, striding toward her. He stopped suddenly as he spotted his brother's body.

"Helen," he said shakily. "What are you doing up here?" He reached over and knocked the lamp from her hand, so that the oil spilled and the flame was snuffed. "Do you want an arrow too?"

She looked at him blankly, her lips numb.

"Go to the Hearth Hall," he said, gripping her forearm. His touch made her focus a little. "Some of the women should already be there. You must shut yourselves in until we've driven the Greeks from the lower town. Do you understand?"

She gave a small nod, and he seemed satisfied. Without waiting for her to move he rushed off down the stairs.

It took a moment for Helen to recall the use of her legs, but once she had made that first step, and the next, she kept going. Even as she reached the stairs to descend from the wall, she did not look back.

She stumbled through the citadel, shoulders brushing and bumping her as she went. There were men rushing past in the direction of the gate, spears and shields in hand, and women overtaking her, jostling past as she climbed the tiers to the Hearth Hall. She barely noticed them. As her feet carried her through the panicked streets, there was only one face she was looking for.

She had reached the top terrace now. The palace courtyard opened before her, with the Great Altar standing stoically at its center. The ancient laurel tree that sheltered it was shivering in the night breeze. Helen watched it as she passed, tuning her ears to the rustling leaves. The shouts of the lower town were so distant now that she could almost block them out.

When she finally reached the Hearth Hall one of its great doors stood ajar—she had just seen another woman hurry in, dragging a crying child behind her. Helen slid herself through the gap.

The hall was bright compared to outside—the eternal hearth flame burning as ever. It took Helen a moment for her eyes to adjust, and to take in the frightened faces that stared at her as she entered. Some she recognized, some she did not. But there was still no sign of the face she had been looking for.

"Have any of you seen Kassandra?" she asked the room at large.

There was silence as sandals shuffled and faces turned away from her. But then one young woman stepped forward.

"I think she was among those heading to the Sanctuary of Athena," the woman said quietly. "They have gone to supplicate the goddess. Queen Hekabe was with them."

Helen gave a silent nod of thanks. In the absence of any other replies, she had to assume that the woman was right, and she turned to leave. If Kassandra was at the sanctuary, that was where she would go.

But just as she stepped toward the door, a new group of women entered. And at their center was Andromache.

Helen shrank back into the corner of the room. Andromache wore her black mourning veil—so long it trailed on the floor. By her side, his little hand clasped in hers, stood Astyanax, the heir of Troy. His resemblance to his father was striking.

Helen wanted to leave—now more than ever—but the hall had only one door, and she feared passing Andromache. As she stood in her shadowy corner, the black veil turned her way and those dark eyes met hers before moving on.

She couldn't leave now. Andromache would think it was because of her. Because she felt guilty, because she was afraid—and she was. What if Andromache challenged her? What if they all did? What if they thought she was running to the Greeks? No, she had missed her opportunity to leave quietly. Hopefully, Kassandra would come to the Hearth Hall once the prayers had been said. Helen just wanted to know that her friend was safe.

For now, though, she remained rooted in her corner, avoiding the eyes of the other women as they waited together in silence and listened to the distant rumble of battle.

CHAPTER 54

HELEN

The sounds were getting closer. The shouts and the crashes. There were horns blowing now, too. And inside the Hearth Hall the nervous chatter grew.

—*What was happening?*—

—*Were they inside the citadel?*—

—*Would they reach the palace?*—

Helen tried to ignore them. She tried to ignore the sounds outside too, but they pounded in her head—every cry, every scream. Was some poor Trojan dying? Or a Greek? Was Menelaos out there somewhere? Was Kassandra safe? And the slaves—there hadn't been room for all the slave women in the Hearth Hall, never mind the men. Was it their cries she was hearing? Each one pierced her like a knife.

Paris had said that the walls could not be breached, that the Greeks would never step foot in Troy. But Paris was dead. It had happened so suddenly that Helen had to remind herself it was true. She closed her eyes and saw his lightless face once more, frozen in surprise as if he had not quite believed in his own mortality. What did she feel, to know that he was gone? Grief? Release? Fear? She had come to Troy for him. Had left her home and family, crossed seas and risked all that she had for the love he promised. And now? Now she was alone, no longer a

Greek and yet never a Trojan. She looked at the fearful faces that surrounded her. Not one friend among them. She began to cry—for herself, for her foolishness, and for Paris too. For the Paris she had fallen
in love with, for the beautiful dream she had chased. Now finally dead
and gone.

Helen's eyes snapped open at the sound of the great doors being
unbarred. Had Kassandra come from the temple? But as she watched
the wood drawn cautiously back, it was the disheveled form of Queen
Hekabe that emerged.

Her veil was torn, her face gray, and blood trickled down her aged
cheek from a cut above her eyebrow. She swayed on her feet as if she
might fall, but when Andromache stepped forward to support her, the
queen waved her away.

"They have breached the citadel. They have taken the sanctuary,"
she said, struggling for breath. "All is lost."

There was silence while the words settled on the air. And then the
panic began. Some women screamed, others cried, others shouted in
anger.

But through it all, Helen pushed her way to the door.

"What about Kassandra?" she asked the queen, clasping her sleeve
to get her attention.

Hekabe turned, her face hollow.

"Spoiled," she croaked, her mouth stiff. The room had gone quiet
again, seeing Helen move from her corner. There was an unspeakable
pain in Hekabe's eyes as she looked down at Helen. "Right there in the
sanctuary." She closed her eyes and sucked her teeth, as if there were
poison in her mouth. "To have no fear of the gods . . . a beast, not a man."

Helen's face spread in horror as she realized what the queen was
saying. A quiet cry came from her throat.

"I tried to bring her," the queen continued, her voice distant. "I
tried to take her away from there. But she would not stand. She would
not move. I——" She swallowed painfully. "I had to leave her."

Helen was weeping freely now, tears streaming down her cheeks. Hekabe turned away from her and sank onto a stool, her eyes staring blankly at the hearth flames.

Suddenly another figure stood before Helen.

"Why do you weep?" asked the hard voice of Andromache.

Helen looked up at her, confused.

"Why weep for Kassandra, when every woman in Troy will meet the same fate before the night is out?"

Her words rang through the hall, the truth of them rippling across the pale faces illuminated in the hearth light.

"You must know that, Helen." Andromache spat out her name as if it were dirt. "You must know what your coming here has cost us. What it *will* cost us. Or are you really that stupid?"

Andromache stepped toward her, and Helen shrank back.

"I . . . I . . ."

"Why couldn't you have just stayed in Greece? What was so terrible that you had to leave? That you had to come here and ruin all our lives?" The anger spewed from Andromache like venom. "Your life was easy. Do you know how old I was when I was taken from my home? When I came here, to Troy, with no one? I made a life for myself. I had a home and a husband and . . ." Her voice was ragged. "But now . . . now you have taken all that away."

Andromache stood, her black veil shaking, and Helen stared up into those dark, terrible eyes. It could have been her own sister speaking those words.

The tears continued to spill down her cheeks, for Kassandra, for Nestra, for Andromache and for Hektor, for all that had happened, for all the misery she had caused. She could barely breathe. She had to get out of the hall. She had to get away from those eyes.

She pushed her way to the door and out into the courtyard. The cold night air almost choked her as she sucked it into her lungs. She stood, chest heaving, not knowing where she should go. The courtyard was empty, but she could hear men fighting to the west. For a moment she thought of running to the sanctuary, to Kassandra, but fear held her back. That way would take her through the fighting. So she turned and ran down the east steps instead—toward her chamber.

By the time Helen reached her chamber she was shaking. The cold had leached through her dress and her heart was racing. She shut the door behind her and lit a few of the torches that hung on the wall. The light and the warmth made her feel better—as if they might somehow keep danger away.

She sat on the edge of the bed, trying to slow her breathing. Tears still brimmed in her eyes, but she blinked them back. Her thoughts were full of Kassandra, picturing her alone on the sanctuary floor. Was she still there? Would she survive the night? Women were usually spared when a city was sacked—kept as slaves or sold—but there were fates worse than death. Helen whispered a prayer to Artemis, for Kassandra and for herself, but her heart wasn't in it. What good had the gods ever done? They didn't care about the lives of mortals. If they did, they would never have let her leave Sparta.

Fresh tears welled, and she sobbed pathetically, self-hatred and regret gnawing at her insides until she felt as if she would throw up.

She was so consumed that she did not hear the chamber door open. Nor the boots on the stone. Not until they were only a few paces away.

"Deiphobos," she said, startled. "You scared me." She stood up and hastily wiped the tears from her cheeks.

He didn't say anything but took another step toward her. There was a strange light in his eyes.

"Are you injured? Have the Greeks been pushed back? Did you see Kassandra?"

But he didn't answer. He had stopped, and was regarding her.

"Deiphobos?"

"So much ruin," he said slowly. "Over so common a thing."

Fear had begun to stir in Helen's belly now. She went to step backward, but the bed was behind her.

"Is the world not full of women?" Deiphobos asked, his dark eyes flashing. "And yet my brother had to have you." He stepped forward, narrowing the gap between them. "Why? What makes you so special, Helen? What makes you worth a kingdom?" He came closer and took her chin in his hand, tilting her head a little to regard it. "It seems unjust, does it not? That Paris was the only one to know the answer, the only one to benefit from you, when we have all paid your bride price."

And before Helen could react his hand had moved to the back of her neck, and his tongue was pushing its way into her mouth.

She tried to pull back, but he held her head, his fingers buried in her hair. She bit his tongue and he recoiled for a second, long enough for her to twist out of his grip.

"Bitch," he spat, and she cried out.

"You think anyone will help you?" he sneered. "Do you think anyone will want to?" He stepped toward her again. "You're nothing more than a whore."

Helen's heart was pounding. She stepped back toward the wall, her eyes never leaving Deiphobos. And as he strode forward she reached and grabbed a torch from behind her.

"Stay away!" she said shakily, sweeping the torch in an arc before her. "Paris will come back. He'll—"

"Paris is dead."

He knew, then. Flawed as Paris was—vain and selfish and cowardly as he had turned out to be—he had been her shield all these years at Troy. Now she had no one.

Her eyes darted to the door. She could make a run for it. Take her chances in the citadel. But Deiphobos was fit and fast. He would catch her.

Suddenly he leaped forward, seizing one wrist and then the other. He twisted and she dropped the torch. She cried out again, spitting and snarling, wrenching to be free as they grappled in the middle of the room. He was too strong. He pushed her against a table edge, both wrists held in one of his giant hands, high above her head. He thrust the other into the top of her dress, the shoulder pin snapping as he wrenched the material aside. Hard fingers dug into her breast. She turned her face away, determined not to meet his eye. There on the floor the dropped torch still burned, and the woolen rug with it. As Deiphobos's hand moved to her skirt she squeezed her eyes shut. She wanted to block it out—the violence and the fire and the pain. She would pretend it wasn't happening. She would pretend—

And then Deiphobos's grip seemed to slacken. She opened her eyes and there were his, staring back at her in confusion. As he stared she watched a trickle of blood spill from the edge of his mouth.

Her eyes moved down and she saw it—something sharp and bloody sticking out from his tunic.

Deiphobos let go of her, his hands moving to touch the blood spreading from his navel. There was a sound of metal through flesh and he fell heavily, knees cracking on the stone. And as he did, she saw the man who stood behind him.

Menelaos.

She cried out in surprise, an animal relief that broke from her throat before she could think what his being here meant. He looked at her, and she looked back. Neither moved. Neither spoke. His sword was still raised, his arm tense, his eyes afire.

Would he kill her? Was that why he had come? So that he could be the one to do it? Would he plunge that sword into her exposed, hateful breast? Did she not deserve it?

Their two chests heaved in the stillness.

At the edge of Helen's vision, she saw flames rising. The burning rug had set fire to one of the wall hangings.

"The fire," she said hoarsely. "We should put it out."

Menelaos's eyes did not move. "Let Troy burn. I am done with it."

"And me?" Helen took a shaking step toward him, moving around Deiphobos without her eyes leaving Menelaos. "Are you done with me?"

Another step. Menelaos's eyes were still intense, his sword arm fixed. She reached out a hand and rested it on top of the blade, her eyes looking up into his. They stood like that for a moment, before the sword slowly lowered.

Around them, the room had begun to fill with smoke. Menelaos coughed.

"We should go," he said.

And, taking Helen by the hand, they left the chamber together.

CHAPTER 55

HELEN

When Helen awoke the next morning, it took her a moment to remember where she was. Instead of a ceiling, there was canvas. And on the bed beside her . . . there was no one. The straw was springy and unslept on, the animal skins cold. Menelaos had not come back, then. He had driven her to his tent in silence after they had left the city, but once she had stepped down from the chariot and he had indicated which tent was his, he had driven right back out of the camp again—back toward Troy. She knew he must have returned to help his men, but part of her also wondered if he had gone back to be away from her, to delay the words that would eventually have to pass between them.

The camp had not been loud last night, but now it was a different sort of quiet. Helen could hear boots trudging and horses breathing. She heard campfires crackle and greetings exchanged. But none of it told her anything. She had to see.

She was still wearing her dress from last night. She slipped on her sandals and picked up an animal fur from the bed to wrap around her shoulders, as if it might make her invisible. Then she stepped toward the tent door and pulled back the heavy canvas.

She needn't have worried about being seen; no one was looking her way. Each man was occupied by his own business. Nearby someone was cooking blood sausages for breakfast—Helen could smell them as they spat their fat into the flames. Outside the next tent, a man was dressing a wound on his leg while another cleaned blood from his armor. But Helen's attention was taken by another man, carrying great armfuls of golden cups and plates, which he added to an already enormous pile at the center of the camp. It glittered in the morning sun, swelling from the earth like a great burial mound of gold and silver and ivory.

It was then that she saw it. There on the horizon, rising behind the pile of plunder, was a great column of smoke. Troy was still burning.

Helen gasped at the sight of it. She had seen the flames last night, reaching up from the citadel like grasping hands as the chariot had carried her away across the plain. But even then she had thought the fire would be quenched; Troy was too great to burn. But as she glimpsed the tips of its black silhouette over the tent tops, she knew that the city was gone.

It was a shock to see it, to think of the grand terraces burned black, the serene temples stripped bare, and yet Helen realized she did not mourn those lonely halls that had been her home for so many years. Her own dream of Troy had faded long ago. But it was the people that haunted her. The lives lost in the long war, names she knew and names she didn't, faces she had seen and those she imagined. She thought of Iphigenia, killed before the war was even begun. Of Hektor, his proud body defiled, just as his beloved city was now. And all the new dead, those lost in the fighting last night. Was their blood on her hands too? Could she take the weight of them upon her shoulders? It was too much for one person to bear. Her chest grew tight, her eyes stinging as she watched the black smoke of Troy stream toward the heavens. But then she remembered what Hektor had said to her that afternoon in the hall before he had gone to his death. The war had not been fought for her. Not really. She knew it was easier to believe that than to face the terrible alternative, and yet it also seemed the more likely truth. What did men ever sacrifice for the sake of a woman?

The women, Helen thought suddenly, remembering that hall of terrified faces. *Had they made it out?* But as her eyes returned to the camp, she found her answer.

Among the men and the tents and the horses, women were being pushed and dragged, hands bound, hair streaming. Helen recognized many of them from the citadel, though their fine clothes were torn and dirtied. The longer she looked the more of them she spotted—tied to posts outside their captors' tents, kneeling in the mud. Some were crying. Others were silent, their eyes empty. Helen wondered if it would have been better for them to have perished in the fire.

Helen spotted one woman digging her heels as she was led through the center of the camp, and realized with a jolt that it was Andromache. Her black veil was gone, her dark hair a tangled mass, her right eye horribly swollen. There were clear tracks through the sooty grime of her face where tears had fallen.

As Helen stared, Andromache's wild head turned and the good eye fixed on her.

"Bitch!" she screamed, pulling on her bonds to get closer. "Whore!"

Helen shrank back into the doorway, but it was too late. Andromache was shrieking like a wild animal, wrenching her wrists against the rope that tethered her.

"They threw my boy from the walls! Do you hear me, bitch? May the gods curse you! May you never—"

Her words were cut off as the young prince leading her sent a sharp elbow into her face. She dropped to her knees, blood dripping, and gasped as the prince wrenched her forward.

As she began to raise herself, shaking, from the mud, Helen turned her face away. She stepped farther back into the tent, not wanting to see any more. But just as she was about to turn her back on the camp, another figure caught her eye. Slumped by a door post, fair hair hanging from a lolling head, thin wrists bound to the wood. The longer she looked, the surer she was.

Helen quickly poured a cup of water from the jug inside the tent, and hurried across the muddy thoroughfare.

"Kassandra," she whispered, crouching down. "Kassandra. It's me, Helen."

There was no response from the hanging head. She reached a tentative hand to the bare shoulder.

"Here. I brought you some water. You should drink."

Finally the head stirred. As it lifted, the fair hair fell aside to reveal a face.

Helen gasped. It was her friend, yes, but that sweet face was so changed. The young cheeks were hollow, the pink lips pale and cracked. There were grazes and bruises but . . . it was her eyes that disturbed Helen the most. Gone was the brightness she had once looked forward to seeing more than anything else.

"Please. You must drink." She held the cup to Kassandra's lips, her voice strained with rising tears.

Only then did Kassandra seem to see her.

"Helen," she said, a flicker of that old light returning. Her lips split into a strange smile, but it only made Helen more afraid.

"I'm so sorry," she breathed. "For everything." Helen wanted to throw her arms around her friend, to hold her, to shake the life back into her, but she was afraid that she might shatter.

"I'll help you," she said. "I'll speak to Menelaos. You can come back to Sparta and—"

"I am claimed," said Kassandra, looking at something Helen could not see. "Lord Agamemnon said he wanted me, and so I am his."

Fat tears rolled down Helen's cheeks. "Well, perhaps . . . perhaps he will change his mind. I'll talk to Menelaos and . . . I can't just let you—"

"It's all right." Kassandra turned her head so that she was looking straight at her. "It's not your fault, Helen. It is the way of the world. The gods' will." She paused, her eyes losing focus for a moment before returning to stare at the cup of water Helen still held. "I do not think I will suffer for long. I feel it, even now. Death awaits me in Mycenae."

"No," said Helen, taking her friend's cheek in her hand. "You must not say that. Lord Agamemnon is my sister's husband, and she is kind. She will treat you well."

Kassandra looked up at her. "I wonder whether she will be the same sister you once knew."

Helen opened her mouth, but Kassandra's gaze slid away from her once more.

"Lord Agamemnon's homecoming may not be as he expects," she said vaguely, as if she spoke of things distant from herself. She fell silent, her gaze elsewhere, and as Helen watched her friend's vacant face—lips curled somewhere between a smile and a grimace—she knew that something in her had broken. It was as if she were slipping away from the world, or had simply ceased to care what happened in it.

Helen let her hand fall from Kassandra's cheek and set the cup of water down in the dirt. She didn't know what to do. She didn't know how to make things right, or if she ever could.

She slowly stood up and stepped back, away from the slumped body that had been her friend.

And as she moved away, eyes still stuck to that face, she felt a firm hand grip her shoulder.

"Helen."

She turned to see Menelaos standing behind her.

"It's time to go."

He led her unresisting down to the sand. None of the other ships had been readied yet—there was still plunder to divide, slaves to allocate—

but Menelaos seemed impatient to set sail. Helen could not even see any gold on board.

"Will you not miss the victory sacrifices?" she asked quietly, as they stood on the deck, waiting for the anchors to be taken up.

"It is my brother's victory," was his gruff reply. "Let him celebrate it. I have spent enough of my life on these shores, and spilled enough blood into their sand."

They were standing side by side, looking out over the open water. Helen's insides squirmed as the silence spread between them. The guilt she felt for the war was one thing, but this was quite another. She had convinced herself, all those years ago, that leaving with Paris had been the best thing for them all. That Menelaos didn't care enough to miss her. That he had all he needed, and all that she was willing to give him. But to see him now, to see how he had aged, his tanned face lined with weariness and loss, she knew that she had hurt him. "I'm sorry," she said, though the sound barely came out. She thought she felt Menelaos shift a little.

The silence spread again, a little thinner than before.

"Will I be your wife again?" she asked to the sea. "When we return to Sparta?"

The waves lapped the side of the ship.

"Is that what you want?" asked Menelaos eventually.

The question surprised her, and she realized she had yet not asked it herself. Ever since she had seen Menelaos from the battlements a strange feeling had grown within her. A longing for home, for family, for her old life—or parts of it. But could she really go back? Could she be Helen of Sparta again? And Menelaos—was that what she wanted? To be his wife once more?

"I was not a very good one," was all she could think to say.

There came a noise from beside her, almost like a laugh. And yet there was no humor in it.

"Perhaps we were deserving of one another," said Menelaos quietly.

Again, Helen was taken aback. She had expected rage, blame, curses—had been dreading them since Menelaos had appeared in her chamber in Troy. A part of her wanted to hear it, to feel the lashes on her tainted soul. She had been prepared for it. She had been ready. But this?

"It does not excuse what you have done," he continued levelly. "And I do not—cannot—forgive you. Not yet. But I know that I played some part in your unhappiness. In driving you away."

Helen swallowed the sudden emotion that rose in her throat. It surprised her to hear him admit his part, and to feel how much it meant to her, to have even a little of her guilt lifted. "You were good to me, in your way," she whispered. "You did not deserve . . . I was just so lonely. He saw that and he . . ." She could not bear to say Paris's name aloud. Not to him.

"A wife should not be lonely in her own home," he said stiffly, still facing out to sea. The waves continued to lap, slapping the wood beneath them. After a moment he spoke again. "I never knew how to be with you," he said, his voice so low it was almost carried off by the wind. "All of Greece had wanted you for its wife. You were mine, but I had not won you."

He had never spoken like this before. Helen listened to every word, not wanting to interrupt.

"I thought that a child would change things. But it just made everything worse." He sighed into the wind. "You seemed to despise me."

"No," she said, reaching to lay her hand over his. "I never despised you. Nor Hermione." She swallowed. It was the first time she had said her daughter's name aloud in many years. "I was just so afraid. I didn't want another child and I pushed you away. But I still cared for you. Even then. Especially then."

It felt like a confession, to finally speak that unnatural, unwomanly truth out loud to him after all this time. She turned to look at him, and saw his brow furrow. But he did not look angry, only thoughtful, and a little sad. They were both quiet, watching the waves.

"I cared for you, too," he said at last.

The words were so simple, so few, and yet they struck Helen like a gust of wind.

"I am not a man of words," he said gruffly. "It is not always easy for a man to make his feelings known."

"What about Agatha?"

The words were out before Helen could stop them. And for the first time Menelaos turned toward her.

"I saw you once. With her," she said, the memory rising, blurred and sharp at once. "I saw the way you touched her. The way you kissed her."

Menelaos stood looking at her, his face weary.

"That was . . . different," he sighed. "Simpler. She was a slave and I was a king. She could not reject or despise me, but neither could there be real love."

He turned his face away again, gripping the ship's rail in his callused hands. He spoke so plainly, without apology, as if his infidelity were nothing. And what pained Helen was knowing that it was true. No one condemned him for it. No blood had been shed for his unfaithfulness. No widows cursed his name.

Helen's own shaking hands gripped the rail as he went on. "Agatha gave me the son I needed, and I was grateful. But a man's feelings for his wife are different." He drew in a slow breath. "They go deep, like old roots. Twisted and confusing—difficult to separate from himself. Difficult to dig out."

Helen stood looking at him. Was he saying that he had loved her? That a part of him loved her still? He had returned to staring out at the waves, but she did not push him to say more. She felt that they had said more to one another in the last few minutes than in all the years of their marriage.

Something had changed between them. An almost imperceptible shift, born somewhere in the words they had spoken. The silence that stretched between them now was of a different texture, full with their consciousness, and the invisible wall that had once stood there felt as though it had been eroded, at least in part. Helen took a deep breath and sent it out over the glittering sea. Her fears felt smaller now. After all that had happened, after all she had done and said, Menelaos did not despise her. He had listened, *really* listened, and so had she. She knew that the home she was returning to would not be the same one she had left. And Hermione—that other guilty wound on her heart— would barely remember her. Maybe she could begin again. She would try her best to be a mother to her, or at least a friend. Her daughter would be about Kassandra's age. Yes, she could do that, she told herself. She could go home, she could try again, she could make things right. Not as Helen of Sparta perhaps—that name felt too heavy now, that crown too tight. No, maybe this time, finally, she could just be Helen.

As the ship began to move and clear water filled the space between them and the shore, Helen and Menelaos stood side by side, watching the horizon.

CHAPTER 56

KLYTEMNESTRA

I t had been six days since the rumor had reached Mycenae. Troy burned. The Greeks victorious. At first Klytemnestra had not believed it. So many stories had reached her halls over the past ten years, and there had proven a lot more chaff than wheat. But for the last few days a rumbling nervousness had been growing in her gut. Could it be that this story was true?

The rumors had brought no word of Helen—the very cause for which the Greeks had claimed to fight. If Troy truly had been taken, she had to believe that her sister was alive. That she was on a ship bound for Sparta, or already there in those painted halls. She had to believe that the war had been for something, that all those lives—Iphigenia's included—had bought something other than gold and glory.

She knew it should bring her relief to think of her sister safe and well at Sparta, but in allowing herself to entertain that truth she had to confront another, more fearful possibility—that Agamemnon was at this very moment making his way back to Mycenae.

She had made preparations, just in case. There were men posted from here to the coast, each with a beacon stacked high and instructions to set them alight should Agamemnon's ships be spotted. If her husband did return, Klytemnestra would know about it. Since the preparations had been made, she had taken to strolling the citadel walls several times a day. Aigisthos walked with her this afternoon, so she was trying to keep her pace measured, her glance casual. It was not working.

"I wish you would stop worrying," said Aigisthos, squeezing her hand.

She looked at him, feigning ignorance.

"I can see you scanning the hills," he said. "You are many wonderful things, my wife, but you are not as subtle as you believe." He gave a teasing grin, but she found it hard to pay back.

"I'm just anxious," she said quietly, her eyes returning to the hilltops. "It feels as if something is approaching. Something terrible."

"Well, if the war is truly over, then your noble husband may be on his way right now."

"I didn't mean—"

"I know what you meant," he said, his voice becoming sober. He squeezed her hand again. "But if he does come, we will be ready for him. There's nothing to fear."

She wished she could believe him.

"Promise you'll help me," she said, turning to face him. "When the time comes. Promise you'll be there."

He stopped walking and put his hands on her shoulders.

"Of course I will."

She allowed a ghostly smile to curl the edges of her lips. It felt as if they had been made of lead these past few days.

"Whatever comes, we'll face it—" But Aigisthos's lips stopped moving, his eyes caught by something over her shoulder. Klytemnestra turned.

A beacon was burning.

Klytemnestra's heart began to race, her skin suddenly hot as if the fire had been set in her own flesh.

He's here.

Aigisthos stood frozen beside her.

"Find Eudora," she said. "Have her shut the children inside their chambers." She turned to him, steadying herself in those familiar eyes. "You know the plan."

And with no more words they hurried down from the wall to make their preparations.

Klytemnestra stood at the top of the Great Stairs, heart thumping. She felt the sweat bead on her brow and wiped it away. Her mouth tasted of blood.

Could she really do this? Standing there in that tent, ten years ago, dagger in hand, she had been ready. She had been willing to take his life. But now? So much time had passed. The anger she had felt then, the tearing pain, the burning grief, they were as old scars now. Deep and sad and quiet. An ache where there had been agony. They still woke her in the night, still twisted in her gut each morning as she made the journey out to her daughter's tomb. But she wondered whether her husband carried wounds of his own. What trials he must have faced in the long war. What pains, what losses. He too must have grieved for Iphigenia, for the evil he had done. What remorse must have weighed upon him all these years. Perhaps the man returning to their shore would not be the one who had left it.

Was there still time? Could she still go inside and tell Aigisthos that she had changed her mind? He could flee before Agamemnon reached the citadel. She could keep Aletes at the palace—pass him off as a bastard of one of her serving women. She could see him every day, and keep him safe. And Aigisthos . . . at least he would be alive.

She had been fooling herself that she could make a new life. Her life had been chosen for her all those years ago. By her father, by her birth, by her sex. Who was she to rail against fortune? To turn her back on duty?

She had been a good wife. Wasn't that what she had always strived to be? And she could be one again. All this had been a madness. A beautiful insanity. But even now she could make it right. She could be loyal to her husband for the rest of her days. Even if she hated him, she could do it. She would still have her children.

As she stood, heels sprung, ready to turn back and yet unable to move, she heard it. The clang of metal, the heavy scraping of wood on stone. The colossal gates of the citadel were opening.

Too late. Too late. Legs shaking, she began to descend. With each step she imagined him drawing closer. Through the Lion Gate. Up the ramp. Could she hear the wheels of his chariot? The breath of his horse? She pictured him gray-faced, war-beaten.

And then she saw him. And he looked . . . the same as he always had. Tall and strong atop his chariot. Chest out, cheeks ruddy. He held up a royal hand to greet the men and women whom he passed, and he was . . . smiling.

And beside him—

Klytemnestra's heart stopped for a moment as she saw the blond head. But it was not her daughter. The frail creature behind her husband, clinging to the chariot's edge and swaying as it rumbled over the stones, was unknown to her. Even from this distance it was clear the girl was terrified. She looked younger than Elektra, her eyes wide and wild. And as the chariot drew closer Klytemnestra spotted the bonds around her raw wrists.

Suddenly her fear was gone, forced aside by a swell of anger. Her husband had not changed. He would never change. He would continue to ruin lives, to take what he wanted, to waste and spend and abuse. She fought to keep her face smooth as she descended the last few steps, her fists clenched as they held her skirt.

"Lord Agamemnon," she called, as the chariot and its entourage drew up. "Husband." She was surprised at how steady her voice sounded. "Welcome home."

"It is good to see my own walls once more," he said, dismounting from the chariot. As he stepped toward her she saw that his limp persisted, yet he held himself proudly despite it. He looked up the empty steps behind her. "Is this it? No crowds to greet and honor their victorious lord?" There was a crack in his smile. "Where are my children?"

"They are inside, husband. All safe and well." She forced a smile. "I thought you would be weary after your journey. I have prepared some refreshments for you. And the slaves are drawing you a bath as we speak."

Agamemnon paused to consider, but after a moment gave a satisfied smile.

"Yes. Plenty of time for celebrations later. And the gold has not yet been brought from the boats . . . Yes, better to wait." He glanced back at the chariot. "I'll need two baths drawn. One for the girl."

The girl in the chariot flinched at his mention of her.

"Of course, husband," said Klytemnestra, as graciously as she could manage. "I'll have one of the guest chambers—"

"No. The girl stays with me. Have another bath brought to my chamber. Side by side."

He looked down at her, as if daring her to object.

"Yes, husband. I will have it done just as you say." She bowed her head serenely, though inside it her thoughts were racing. She hadn't expected this. Would it ruin their plan? No. It would make no difference. She mustn't lose her nerve.

She led the way up the steps, with Agamemnon and the girl following. The rest of the king's companions stayed below to stable the horses—so that was a relief, at least. The fewer people in the palace, the better. She could deal with them later. She would make them see. Or if not . . . she couldn't think about that now.

They were at the entrance. As they passed into the atrium, Klytemnestra called to the slaves who were waiting, in a voice louder than was needed.

"The king requires two baths drawn. Have one of the guest baths carried to his chamber. As quick as you can."

She hoped that Aigisthos was close enough to hear. What else could she do? While she was sure the girl would pose no threat, she was a factor they had not anticipated.

"The water has already been heated," she said, turning back to Agamemnon. "It will not be long."

As soon as she had finished speaking a slave appeared at her elbow, a large jug of wine and two cups in his arms.

"Your refreshment, husband," she said, passing a full cup to Agamemnon.

"This has not been mixed," he said, eyeing the dark liquid with a frown.

"This is a time for celebration, not moderation," she said with convincing joviality. As he nodded and began to drain his cup, she hoped her relief did not show. The wine would do little, but she would take every advantage available to her.

She filled the second cup and offered it to the girl.

"Here," she said gently. "You must be thirsty."

But the girl simply stared at her, as glassy-eyed as she ever had been.

"It will make you feel better," said Klytemnestra, holding the cup closer, but the girl did not move.

"You'll get nothing out of that one," grunted Agamemnon, taking his lips from his cup momentarily. "Hasn't said a word all the way from Troy."

Klytemnestra looked at the girl—at the tear trails on her cheeks and the fading bruise around her eye. She wished she would take a little wine, for her own sake.

As Agamemnon emptied the last of his cup, a slave appeared in the entrance hall.

"The baths are drawn, my la—I mean, my lord." He looked uncertain as his eyes passed between the two of them.

"Thank you, Nikias," she nodded, and the boy hurried away again.

Klytemnestra's mouth was suddenly dry as she walked with Agamemnon down the corridor, the girl trailing behind them.

The chamber was dark and humid, the steam from the two baths rising in the lamplight.

Klytemnestra insisted on attending Agamemnon herself, and he made no quarrel. Wasting no time, he threw off his tunic and lowered his aging bulk into the hot water.

"Come, girl," he said, seeing that his Trojan prize still stood by the door. "The other is for you. Take off your dress."

The girl did not move.

"Would you like me to help you?" Klytemnestra asked, but the girl shrank away from her outstretched hand.

Her wild eyes flickered between Agamemnon and the steaming water, and she seemed to reach a decision, or at least an acceptance. With bony hands she pulled the once-fine cloth up over her body.

Klytemnestra had to stifle a gasp. The girl's pale flesh was covered in bruises. Some old and yellow. Others fresh and dark. They speckled her arms, her waist, the inside of her thighs.

Klytemnestra's stomach turned. The poor girl. And how many others like her? Carried off to Greek palaces, with the gold and the bronze and the ivory. At least this one's suffering would be over soon. She could protect her, let her live in the palace, where no one would ever hurt her again.

She turned away, realizing that she had been staring. She let the girl lower herself into the empty bath as she turned her attention to Agamemnon. It took a stomach of stone to put her hands on that chest, to scrub that skin, to wash the dirt from that hair. It was a wonder her hands shook as little as they did. And all the while she felt the knife's hilt press against her hip, hidden among the folds of her dress.

Where are you? What was taking Aigisthos so long? It felt as if she had been here for an age.

And then the door creaked.

She let out a silent sigh. And yet her heart was beating faster than ever. He was here now. The time had come.

"Some fresh water, my lady," he said in a gruff voice. He wore a hood, but it was not needed. Agamemnon did not even turn his head.

With her left hand still nestled in his hair, her right went to her hip. Aigisthos knelt beside her, but she didn't turn. She saw his arms rise and raised her hand too.

One breath. Another.

And then she pulled. Agamemnon's head came back and her knife went down. Across the neck and into the chest. And again and again. His blood spurted and the water splashed, his great body writhing like a sea beast. But his arms were pinned. His strength poured out of him into the churning water, spilling over onto the marble floor.

The smell was sickening, but Klytemnestra was like a woman possessed. Like a priestess at the sacrifice. As the knife cut through that detested flesh it was as if she were shearing off pieces of herself. The calluses, the scars, the layers of stinking rot—the heavy casing that had sat upon her all these years, bloated, hardened, suffocating. It all fell away in the plunging of the knife.

As her arm tired and slowed, she saw that Agamemnon's strength was spent. His face stared up from the black bath, his arms limp, no longer held in Aigisthos's grip.

She turned her head, looking for those eyes, for strength, for relief.

He had moved away, was knelt beside the other bath, something glinting in his hand.

"No!" she cried, but it was already done.

The girl choked but made no fight, the lifeblood pouring from her throat unstemmed. Klytemnestra's knees scrabbled across the wet floor, but there was nothing to do but stare at the white throat and the red blood and the fair hair stained black, and to scream and scream.

CHAPTER 57

KLYTEMNESTRA

It was a strange day for a funeral. Or perhaps it only felt that way to Klytemnestra. The sky was too clear, the breeze too pleasant. There was a voice in her head, kneading at the edge of her consciousness, telling her that it should be harder, that she should feel more. But all she felt was relief.

The emotion had already come and gone, last night in that bloody chamber. Like a great wave, it had smashed and crashed and broken her, like wood against the rocks. Now all that remained was the calm.

She and Aigisthos walked at the back of the procession, Aletes with them. Elektra was leading at the head, her guttural song ringing out above the other mourners. Klytemnestra knew it would be inappropriate for her to lead the song, to walk beside the body of her husband. And yet she knew she must be here, to show her respect, to do her duty.

"He left my father's body for the dogs to tear," muttered Aigisthos beside her as the cortege passed through the Lion Gate. "You do him more honor than he ever gave."

"He was a king," was all she said in reply.

As they reached the bottom of the slope, Klytemnestra's stride stiffened. To the left of the road, among the older grave monuments, was a

mound of fresh earth. She clenched Aigisthos's hand as she dragged her
eyes away.

He had been so sorry. Had held her as she screamed, rocked her as
she shook.

"But you asked for two baths." His confused voice drifted back to her. *"I
thought that meant . . ."*

He was only trying to help her. That was what she told herself.
How could he know? But to do it so easily . . .

"She was his whore."

No. She was a girl. Just another girl swept along by the world. With
parents and a home and her own spirit, once. And that had hurt more
than anything. That punching realization that even her sweet, loving
Aigisthos, even he did not understand.

But she had forgiven him. How could she not? This new world was
too terrifying to face alone. And how could she hold him to shame,
after what she had done? They must each bear their own burden.

The procession came to a stop, swelling around the royal tomb as
the doorway was unsealed. Klytemnestra could see her daughters now.
Chrysothemis's young head was bowed, solemn and thoughtful. But
Elektra . . . her eyes were fierce, blazing in their grief, tears running into
her mouth as it poured out its wailing song. As Klytemnestra watched,
chest heavy, their eyes met, and the song grew louder, angrier, the notes
breaking from Elektra's throat like curses. For the first time that morning, tears stung in Klytemnestra's eyes.

She knew that her daughter might never forgive her. She felt it in her
knotted heart. But what should she have done? What else *could* she have
done? She loved her children above all else, but each was like a rope
tethered to her breast, pulling in its own direction. She could not let
Iphigenia's death go unavenged, but had justice for one daughter lost
her another? Would she have lost a son—sweet, blameless Aletes—if
she had not done it? Would she lose a son still, if Orestes was not released back to her?

Her heart was racing, her head suddenly light. She grasped Aigisthos's arm to stop her knees from buckling and drew in a few steadying breaths.

She had always tried to do what was best, hadn't she?

Yes, she told herself. She had tried.

With silent lips she made a prayer to the gods. That she had made the right choice. That the future would be easier. That her children would be safe. Lastly, she prayed that her new life would be a blessed and happy one, as far as any life can be.

ACKNOWLEDGMENTS

There are many people whom I would like to thank for the part they have played in making this book possible.

Firstly, I would like to thank my very first readers for their feedback and encouragement: Dr. Kathryn van de Wiel, Steph McCallum, and especially Ilona Taylor-Conway for being my first fan and convincing me that what I had written was worth reading.

I would like to thank my agent, Sara Keane, for believing in my manuscript, for inducting me into the world of publishing, and for her ongoing support and advice. I would of course like to thank the team at Hodder for making this book a reality, especially my fantastic editor Thorne Ryan for her insight, encouragement, and hard work in making *Daughters of Sparta* the best it can be. I would also like to thank Stephanie Kelly for championing my book across the pond at Dutton, and for her valuable editorial contributions.

Lastly, thank you to my family and friends for all their support. It can feel like a bit of a lonely leap into the unknown to start writing your first novel, so thank you to everyone who has taken an interest and cheered me along. Thank you to my parents, Juliette and Martin Heywood, for their love and support, for fostering my creativity and my love of books, and for providing a roof over my head while I was writing much of the first draft. And finally, special thanks to my partner, Andrew, for his endless encouragement, patience, and good humor; for keeping my spirits up during the rough patches; for celebrating the little victories with me; and for supporting me to pursue my dream. I couldn't wish for a better partner to share the journey.

ABOUT THE AUTHOR

Claire Heywood is a scholar of the ancient world, with a bachelor's degree in Classical Civilization and a master's degree in Ancient Visual and Material Culture from the University of Warwick. *Daughters of Sparta* is her first novel.